Lexie Winston has been an astronaut, rock star, princess and time traveller. In her dreams. But none of the dreams have lived up to what becoming an author has been like. She gets to live in a world of pure imagination, and her heroines get to do the things she's always wished she could.

When not writing books, Lexie is a mother of two gorgeous teenagers and the wife to a patient and understanding man. They live in Western Australia and are lorded over by a black toy poodle. She loves camping, reading and if her iPad was stolen, her world would explode. (It has the kindle app on.)

And check out my website at lexiewinston.com

Also by Lexie Winston

The Collectors Division

(Reverse Harem Series)

Guardian

Guardian's Blood

Guardian Ascending

Arbor Vitae Coven

(Paranormal Romance Series)

Candy Conniptions

Dreamy Delights

Fangtastic Fireworks

Neighpalm Industries Collective

(Adult Bully Reverse Harem)

Abandoned Girl

Broken Girl

Tormented Girl

Cherished Girl

Seductive Sins Collection

(Reverse Harem Series)

Glorious Gluttony

Gangs, Guns, and Glory

Galaxy Circus

(Sci-Fi Reverse Harem Series)

Apprentice

BROKEN GIRL

LEXIE WINSTON

First published by Neighpalm Publishing in 2020

Broken Girl: Neighpalm Industries Collective

Mobi format: 978-0-6487933-4-2
Print: 978-0-6487933-5-9

Cover design by Infinity Cover Designs
Edited by Inked Imagination

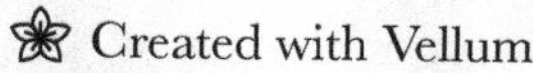

To Michelle.

Thank you for making my words so pretty. I couldn't do this without you

Chapter One

Harlow

I'd had all of forty-eight hours to wallow in my shame and misery before Chuck called me to say the horses would be delivered the following day. I'd been lying on the couch at Shane and Alex's place, stuffing my face with junk food and generally feeling sorry for myself, when the call came through.

"Is everything okay, Harlow? You're sounding a little down." Chuck's words were a kick in the ass, and my heart-beat sped up as I ran a frustrated hand through my hair. "Has something happened?"

If he hadn't heard about the incident, I certainly didn't want to be the one to tell him. He and Brad had been friends for years, and I didn't want him thinking badly of him for something that was out of his control.

"Yeah, I'm okay. Life out here is certainly different than

being at home, but I'm really enjoying getting to know Brad. Nana and Poppy are awesome as usual."

"And Brad's kids?" he prompted, sounding more suspicious now. I guess he'd caught that I hadn't said anything about them. Chuck always did have a way of reading between my lines. I didn't want to lie, but I didn't want him fighting my battles for me, and I knew if he or Melinda found out how bad it was, they would either be convincing me to come home or booking the next flight out, guns blazing.

Blowing out a deep breath, I answered, "Look, it's fine. I knew it wasn't going to be easy. I'll be okay."

"You don't sound so sure." His voice held a note of worry, and I bit my lip with guilt. On one hand, I wanted to tell him everything and beg to come home, but on the other hand, I refused to let them chase me away. "Do I need to speak to Brad?"

"NO!" I snapped before switching to pleading. "No, please don't. It's not his fault, and he did *offer to step in, but if I can't hold my own against them, they'll never respect me."*

"Do you want me to have the horses moved? I can easily find somewhere else to board them until the director is ready for them."

"NO!" I snapped again, instantly regretting it as a wave of guilt flooded my body. "Sorry, no. Really, it couldn't have come at a better time. I'm feeling incredibly homesick, and having them here is going to go a long way toward making me feel better."

"Well, okay then. As long as you're sure. I sent a surprise along as well, so I'm sure that will help." There was

still a hint of worry, but it had softened. We chatted a little more about the training needs, and he assured me he'd sent my safety gear before we hung up.

A moment after I set down my phone, an arm around my shoulder had me startling. I'd forgotten Alex had been asleep on the other end of the couch. Shane had had to go to work, leaving the two of us to veg out for the day. It was a long ago scheduled shoot for Neighpalm Energy Drink, Kai's branch of the company, and though he had offered to cancel, I told him not to bother. Kai had been the least horrible out of all the siblings, and I still had hopes of possibly winning one or two of them over to the idea of me being a part of their lives, even if only in the friend capacity.

As for the others, Alex and I had spent the last two days plotting the revenge they definitely deserved. Fuck taking the high road. Mind you, my friends margarita and mojito may have had a lot to do with that. If I was being honest, Ben and Jerry may have also played a part or two in planning out nefarious deeds. That was, until we both passed out from too many drinks and copious amounts of junk food.

"Are you sure you want to do this? You don't ever have to go back to that place again. You don't owe any of them anything," Alex said gently, pulling me against his side where I rested my head on his shoulder with a sigh.

"No, I don't want *to, but I'm going to. I promised Chuck, and they've done so much for me. I don't want to let him down," I told him.*

"Do you want me to come with you for support?" I sat up and shook my head, my eyes wide. Just the offer had my skin prickling with emotional goosebumps. With Max so far

away, it was nice to know that someone else had got my back. Max would always be my sister, but Alex filled a void I'd never known I had, like a platonic soulmate. Despite the experiences we shared together, it was always in the back of my mind that Max might only be friends with me because of proximity. That she wouldn't have been had our parents not brought us together.

"No, I need to do this on my own. I also need to go and talk to Dad, Nana, and Poppy. They've been blowing up my phone since it happened, and apart from sending a group message to tell them where I am, I haven't spoken to any of them." Again, the guilt swamps me, but I just wasn't ready to face anyone or even have a phone conversation. But I felt stronger after wallowing in my misery for a few days.

He raised his eyebrows in surprise. "Why not?"

"I didn't want to say anything I might regret. Once I got over the humiliation, all I felt was anger, and I didn't want to take it out on the wrong person," I explained to him, standing up. Looking around the living room, I realized we'd done quite a bit of damage during my pity party. Empty cups and take-out containers were everywhere. Empty chip packs, even what looked like bright orange cheeto dust, crushed into the carpet.

"God, look at this place! I'm so sorry," I blurted out, but he waved his hand.

"Please, it's the last thing you need to worry about."

Completely ignoring him, I started to pick up containers, taking them over to the garbage can in the kitchen before going back for empty cups and glasses. I loaded the stack into the dishwasher, cringing at the smell of long-dried tequila. Definitely better when it's fresh and covering up your feelings.

"Fine. I'm going to let it go for now, but you're right. You need to speak to the people who love you. They must be worried sick, even if they understand where you're coming from."

"Yeah, well, I'm not going to apologize for my anger. As much as they tried to fix things, that picture is out there now. Everyone knows the internet lives forever, not to mention the tabloids will print whatever they want regardless of Brad giving them the real story. No, that wasn't juicy enough for them, so they ignored it and went with the original speculation. All that crap is out there, and quite frankly, I could lose out on job offers because of it." I was practically shouting at him now, doing exactly what I had wanted to avoid in the first place.

"Whoa, babe." He put his hands up and walked over, pulling me in close and holding my shaking, angry body tight. "I know, I know, I wasn't attacking you. I just know how I'd feel if you disappeared and wouldn't speak to me."

My shaking slowly got under control, his reassurance helping, and he placed a kiss on my head before stepping away. "Come on, let's finish cleaning up, and then you need to have a shower. We're going to go out and get some food. Some fresh air will do you good. I'll call Shane and tell him where to meet us."

And he was right. The fresh air and food did do me good, and I felt better when nobody gave me a second look. Maybe it wasn't as big a deal as I thought it was, and the people that mattered, like the zoos I'd applied to, hadn't seen it.

The clattering of horse hooves as the truck pulls to a stop brings me back to the present. As the truck driver jumps out and greets the Summers' stable manager, Josh, I thank fuck that no one else seems to be around at the moment. I'd expected to be bombarded by Dad and the grandparents the minute Alex dropped me off at the stables, but apart from Josh, the place is deserted.

The creaking of the hinges as the driver lowers the side door is loud as I focus on the job in front of me. Dust and the smell of horses and manure hit my nose, and the snorting of impatient horses is music to my ears. I'm already feeling a lightness, this sense that my world has tilted a tiny bit back onto its axis now that this little piece of home is so close to me.

I watch as the driver opens the first gate and leads Delilah down the ramp. He passes her off to Josh, the stable manager leading her out to one of the yards we've put aside for them. The pretty white mare snorts and prances, her ears pricked and nostrils flaring as she takes in all the new surroundings and the other horses in the nearby yards who have all put their heads up to check out the newcomers. Smiling for the first time in days, I turn back to the truck and walk up the ramp to take the next one off his hands. Hercules nickers when he sees me and stomps his feet, his excitement making me smile. I rub his silky nose and blow a breath into his nostrils in greeting. "Hey, buddy."

He bumps his head against my chest as I attach the lead to his halter. Sliding back the latch, I open the sideways gate and walk the big bay warmblood down the ramp. He, too, has his ears pricked in interest and head high, but he calmly walks to join Delilah in the paddock. And that's as long as the peace lasts. As soon as I let him go, the two of them rear and turn, racing off to the other end of the yard before skidding to a stop at the fence line. Both throw in a couple of happy bucks before racing back again.

Typical 'I've been cooped up in a box for too long' behavior. It's a pain in the ass though, because now we have to get two more into the paddock while they're going crazy.

Shaking my head with a smile, I turn around to find Josh bringing out an 'on his toes' Zeus, who's snorting and carrying on, but the experienced stable manager is able to get the warmblood into the paddock with the other two crazies without too much hassle. So that just leaves me with my favorite, and he doesn't disappoint. I can hear him whinnying his impatience as I climb the ramp one more time. The snorting and stamping telling me that Samson wants out, and he wants it *now*. The driver heads to get him, but I wave him back.

"'I'll do it," I tell him, ignoring his relieved expression as I enter the truck. The minute our eyes meet, he stops his racket. He still snorts, but all of the stamping and head tossing ceases as he waits, body quivering for me to remove him from his cage.

Samson, being a stallion, will be in a different yard from the others. One that has electrified fences around him. He's a good boy, but mares in season are his weakness, like all horny males. *Sounds sort of familiar. My* mind goes back to both Oliver and Jaxon and the interactions I had with both of them. Those stolen moments obviously meant more to me than them. Wish I was like those mares who couldn't care less who mounted her.

Moving quickly but calmly, I hook him on the lead line and open his gate, talking quietly to him the whole time. His ears twitch back and forth to the sound of my voice, and I bring him down the ramp and out into the open, watching him closely. The minute his hooves hit solid ground, he screams his annoyance, and up on his hind legs he goes. Stepping back to avoid his front hooves, I let the lead line slide through my hands so that I avoid rope burn while still having a hold of him.

Gasps from behind tell me I'm no longer alone, but I can't look, my focus on the black Friesian in front of me.

"Get down here, you great lump," I call out, rolling my eyes at his theatrics. Had I known there were people present, I might have been a little more on the ball. This damn horse loves to perform for an audience. I give a couple of tugs on his lead, and he drops calmly to his hooves, letting me guide him in the direction of his special yard. The raging stallion from before is gone, a docile lamb now casually trotting next to me.

I get him into the yard and turn to face our audience as he calmly walks off to graze on the green grass. The other three have settled and are doing the same thing, giving me an opportunity to study who's here, a moment that I'm not entirely sure I want. When I glance back at the stables, Dad and my grandparents are waiting for me. Nana has a look of worry on her face, mouth downturned just enough to be noticeable, but Dad and Poppy have proud smiles.

Before I can join them, the sound of hooves clattering down the ramp draws my attention back to the truck. *Shit, did one of the other horses get loose?* But when my eyes find the driver, he's leading in each hand a sight that makes me burst into tears.

Jenny and Devil Spawn are both pulling him, hurrying to get to me. Sobbing, I take the leads from his hands and throw my arms around my donkey, but a nip to my ass has me quickly dropping down into a crouch to throw my arms around that mini too.

"Mr. Boston said that they're to stay here with you until you're ready to return home. He also said that you would be transporting the others to the movie set."

His words surprise me; he usually has a trucking company deliver them where they need to go, but I can't say I mind the extra time with my babies. "Oh, um, he didn't say anything about that to me."

"Oh, that was me, Harlow, sorry." My dad approaches us quickly, an apologetic look on his face that I'm sure is about much more than surprise arrangements for the horses. "I told Chuck we'd use our truck to take them to the set. It's one of our movies anyway. He said you had your truck license, so it wouldn't be a problem."

"Oh, no, that's fine," I tell him, shaking off my surprise. The driver nods his head and closes up before leaving in a cloud of dust, not caring what happens next now that his job is over.

"Who do we have here?" My dad's voice is curious, and as I turn around, I see him reaching out to pat DS.

"No!" I shout, but DS seems to be on her best behavior because she not only allows Dad to pat her, she nuzzles her little head against him.

"That's Devil Spawn, and trust me, she is *not* normally this friendly," I warn him as they continue to bond. He takes her line from me, and I let him lead her to the stables. Dad's confidence assures me he can handle anything she throws at him, though it looks like that is going to be nothing today. *Suck up.*

"Let's see if we can find you an apple or a sugar cube," he coos to her, and she prances next to him in that way that only minis can. Fickle fucking creatures that they are.

Jenny nudges me with her head, and I grab one

of her big ears, giving it a rub as Nana and Poppy approach me, cautious smiles on their faces.

"Jenny's looking really good, Hally," Poppy says as he gives her a pat. Nana runs her hand across her soft face as she studies me, her kind gaze feeling much heavier than it should.

"How are you doing, sweetie?" Her words are gentle, and the sympathy I see in her eyes is like a cold dash of water as all that has happened comes back to me. The horses had been a perfect distraction, but I guess I can't avoid talking to them anymore.

Before I can say anything, Josh approaches us. "Shall I take her? I can find somewhere for her to go."

"Are you sure? I know you weren't expecting to end up with a donkey and a mini," I reply, worried about what he'll say, but he just grins.

"Actually, I did know about them. Mr. Boston asked Mr. Summers if it was alright that he sent them, and of course he said yes. It's not like we don't have the room. How much trouble can a donkey and a mini be?" With those naive words, my eyes widen just a tiny bit, and the better part of my nature pokes at me to correct his assumption.

"Ah, the donkey not much, but the mini... you should watch her like a hawk. She's crafty and clever, and quite frankly, she has more escape tricks than Houdini," I warn him, but he just laughs, taking Jenny off my hands.

She trots off with him, and I'm left standing there awkwardly with Nana and Poppy. It's awful. Never have I ever felt like this around these people, and I'm just not sure what to say. I feel like I'm a teenager again, forced to attend social outings with the Bostons where I know everyone is judging me behind the forced smiles and tight eyes. Not that *they* would judge me, just that same awkward feeling.

Nana puts her hand on my arm, and my eyes meet hers. "Come inside. We'll have a cup of tea and talk about this."

I look up at the house and shake my head. "I'm sorry, Nana, but I really don't want to go in there at the moment."

"Don't worry. None of them are here," my dad growls from behind me, and I jump in surprise as he comes back from the stables minus a mini. "Come on, we've got a lot to talk about, and I hope you give us a chance to make it up to you." His eyes practically beg me to listen, so I take a deep breath and nod my head. Knowing that none of the siblings are here makes a big difference. I'm not entirely *happy* to go inside, but I'm a lot more comfortable and don't feel like starting an argument that will lead to hurting their feelings.

Dad and Poppy lead the way, and Nana tucks my arm under hers as the two of us walk a little slower behind them. "Samson looked magnificent when he reared up like that, but weren't you scared?" I appreciate the small talk to break the uncomfortable silence, and I squeeze her hand in thanks.

“I can't deny my heart doesn't race every time a horse does that, but he was just showing off for you. He’s a ham,” I explain, a fond smile growing. “He’s actually my favorite. I've always wanted a Friesian. Maybe one day when I settle down I’ll look into getting myself one, but for now I’m happy being able to ride him on occasion.”

We reach the back deck where there’s a brunch spread laid out on the table we ate at the night of the bet, and my heart skips a beat at the thought of Oliver. Out of all of them, I think his betrayal hurt the most. He was the one I’d spent the most time with, and I’d thought we were getting along. Shit, the way he had me up against the wall at his studio made me think we were more than getting along. For him to not at least warn me makes me so disappointed. The others, well, I guess I should have expected something like that, especially from Jacinta, but I thought both Oliver and Kai were warming up to me.

“Come on, let's have some cakes and a coffee.” Nana gives me a kiss on the cheek before sitting down, and I join her at the table with Poppy and Dad and wait for what’s going to be one of the more uncomfortable conversations of my life.

Chapter Two

Harlow

The silence is heavy as Nana pours coffee into mugs for us all, offering sugar and milk to me. Once we all have one sitting in front of us and she's plied us with cake, Brad refuses to let the silence continue.

"Harlow, I don't know how I can apologize for the other night. I'm at a loss right now because I never expected my supposedly adult children to be capable of such pettiness." I go to say something, barely getting my mouth open before he holds his hand up, stopping me. "Please let me finish. I'm under no illusion that it was one of them who made that billboard happen, and I've seen to it that Jacinta has been put on a leave of absence because I know for sure that all final promotions get run by her. Whether it was her idea or she'd been put up to it by one of the others doesn't matter. She could have stopped it, and she didn't."

My heart races at his words, unable to believe he did that. What are the chances she's going to be gunning for me even harder now? A lot higher than I'd like, that's for damn sure.

Nana pats my hand in reassurance, likely seeing the panic in my eyes. "Don't you worry about Jacinta. She's going to be too worried about keeping her company to mess with you anymore." Her words are cold, and frankly, scary. I don't doubt that Jacinta is in for a world of trouble; I know how ruthless this woman before me can be when she feels it's warranted.

Poppy takes over, his voice less fiery than Nana's. "I know we have no right to ask this, and if you turn us down, none of us will hold it against you, but would you please find it in your heart to stay?" Gah, the guilt just continues to pile on. On one hand, I believe my reaction is warranted, but on the other, I just want to give these wonderful people what they want.

"We know that having the horses here is the only reason you're still around," Brad says gently, and my eyes widen just a bit. Nana and Poppy have known me long enough to have a general idea for how I might deal with uncomfortable situations, but I'm surprised Brad already has me figured out.

"I rang Alex when you wouldn't talk to me, and he said to give you time, but to not be surprised if after they were gone, so were you. Don't be mad at him, please. He was only looking out for you," Nana assures me, and I nod for them to continue, putting any reaction to Alex's meddling on pause.

"We'd like you to stay and get to know us, and I still want you to get to know the kids." My stomach rolls with Brad's statement. *Yeah, because that went* so *well last time.*

I take a measured breath, hoping to at least start my answer with a calm tone. "How can you ask that of me? You might not know the extent of the abuse I suffered at my mother's hands, but to ask me to continue to suffer abuse at the hands of your children is downright awful." *Yeah, that zen didn't last long.* I'm angry now, not bothering to hide it, and he drops his eyes, looking ashamed.

"What about this? Instead of having anything to do with my kids, I assign you someone else to show you all our businesses?" There's something desperate in his eyes, and while I understand Poppy asking me to stay for his, Nana, and Dad's sakes, I really don't understand this insistence for me to give the "kids" another chance or get involved in Neighpalm Industries.

It's my turn to hold my hand up and stop him. "Why, Dad? Why is it so important to you that I learn about them? I don't want anything to do with them, and I definitely don't want your money or anything like that. I just wanted to get to know *you.*"

His eyes fill with unshed tears, and he reaches over and grabs my hand, squeezing it tight.

"Thank you for saying that. You don't know how much it means to me to hear you say that. But Neighpalm Industries is your legacy now, and you're now going to be subject to scrutiny by the press and our competitors," he explains. "I need you to be informed so that if you're asked a question, you can respond accordingly. I don't want the press to eat you alive, and there's a good chance they will if you come across as ignorant. I've had decades to protect my other kids and grow them into knowing the businesses, but with you, I've missed out on so much time. I just want to keep you as safe as I can, and the spotlight is a dangerous place to be." I take a moment to consider his words, unfortunately finding them pretty reasonable, and when I look at Nana and Poppy, they're nodding their heads in agreement.

"Okay, I can see how that could be important, but are people really going to care about me?" I ask, not able to believe that they will. Sure, I've stood out throughout my life; the foster kid of a family as rich as Max's was always a topic of conversation no matter how many years had gone by. But in the midst of all this- modeling shoots, movies, energy drinks, and more- does little old me really cause such a splash?

"Honey, the other children get stalked on a regular basis by the media and groupies. I don't mean to make *any* kind of excuse for my grandkids, but those experiences are part of the reason they're so damn prickly," Nana explains to me.

"Prickly?" Brad snorts, not in amusement. "More like wrapped in razor wire. Like I said, I can't apologize enough for my children's behavior."

"Nor should you have to," Poppy bellows all of a sudden. "Please don't hold this over Brad's head," he begs of me. "Those children are adults and as such made their own decisions. Just believe us when we say we don't support them, and if you don't wish to ever have anything to do with them again, we will *not* force it." His gaze moves to Dad and Nana like he's giving them a warning not to push me.

His fierce frown has me believing every word he says, and I start to feel a little better about the situation. It seems to me that the Summers siblings have fucked up big time, but I have every doubt that they're all of a sudden going to start being nice to me. They're spoiled enough to believe that the consequences for their actions won't have a huge impact on their lives, but I have a feeling they're in for a rude awakening.

"Let's just give me a few days to deal with the horses. They'll rest today, and then I'll work with them every day until they're needed on set. As long as Maxine is finished with the movie she's working on by then, she'll take over with the horses. If not, I'll have to stay and manage them for the director until either they finish with them or Maxine wraps up her job," I explain. They all nod in understanding, Dad and Nana taking the advice to go with my lead and not try to push me.

"After that, I'll see how I feel. Is that okay with you? There are still some things I haven't done here yet, so there's a good chance I'll stay for at least a little while after the horses are sent back. Shane and Alex are going to do some more sightseeing with me and take me down to SeaWorld in San Diego as well. I'm really interested in seeing how they're trying to make things better for their killer whales. Even though they should be in much larger tanks or released back into the wild, at least they're no longer doing the daily shows with them," I ramble slightly, and even worse, I'm completely aware that I'm rambling. The word vomit is a nervous habit that I thought I'd broken years ago, but I guess stressful situations can bring it back.

They smile, and Brad lets out a sigh of relief. "Thank you."

"But I think I should stay with Alex and Shane," I tell them, forcing the words out before I lose the opportunity, and the smiles turn into frowns, so I quickly explain. "Although their behavior was atrocious, they're still your kids, and I don't want them being kicked out of their home for me. That's just going to cause more resentment, which, I think we can all agree, is the last thing we need."

"But it's quite a drive from Shane and Alex's every day to get here," Nana reminds me, "and that's not fair to either of them if they have to drive you."

"Stay here, please. The others are on their way home now, and their tails better be firmly between their legs if they want to be permitted to stay. They'll have a lot of groveling to do before I allow that to happen. You don't ever have to speak to them or even look at them, but please move back in," Brad pleads again, but I shake my head.

"As much as I dislike your children at the moment and appreciate what you're trying to do for me, please don't put a rift in your relationship for my sake. I know what it's like to feel tossed aside for someone new and shiny. My mother had a new boyfriend every other week that she tried to force me to like, and that was never going to happen. You can't force them to like me, and making them feel like you're choosing me over them will destroy any chances of us ever getting along. They need to do it on their own, or it's never going to work." I glance around the table at them, making myself look each person in the eye even though this conversation is far from comfortable.

"Let it be. It will either happen or it won't, and we need to work that out on our own, but I promise you that it won't affect the relationship the four of us have. If it needs to be a long distance one and I return home, it still won't change things. The three of you are my family just as much as Max and her parents, and I won't cut you off and spite myself because of the others' feelings." They go to argue one last time, Nana's eyes filled with something a little desperate, and something inside me starts to waver. It might not make sense because I am the majorly wronged party, but it feels like I *am* already putting a crack in our relationship if I can't withstand Brad's other kids for the sake of spending more time with Nana, Poppy, and Dad.

Taking a deep breath, I make up my mind. It's not what I want to do, and I have a strong feeling I may live to regret this decision, but I can do this one thing for them. *Plus,* I reason with myself, *it'll be a lot easier to pay them back if you're living in the same house.*

I reach out for Dad's hand and give it a squeeze. "Look, I'll stay here. Will that make you guys happy?" All three respond with nods around the table, a fragile hope lighting up their eyes. "But I will not be making any roads into forgiveness for a while. I may even hold a grudge, a *big* fucking grudge." I reach for my cup and take a sip of my coffee while I gather my thoughts, debating just how direct I should be. "As much as your press conference was supposed to right their wrongs, it actually did nothing but cause more speculation, and those gossipy rags had a field day. I'm hoping that it didn't get as far as the East Coast and that I may still be able to get a job out there if everything fails here. Chuck didn't seem to have a clue, so it looks like your PR team was successful in stopping it from spreading further."

My dad's tension eases slightly, especially with those final words. I think he's probably dreading having his best friend find out what his children have done to me. Especially since Chuck was the one to support me through so much of my mother's crap. Chuck had a knack of making me feel better every single time my mom brought me down, which was basically every time I had to visit her. The minute I got back to the Bostons', he would have something planned to distract me from my misery and negative feelings. Even if it was just something as simple as a board game or a movie night. Brad's got some big shoes to fill as far as being a dad to me.

They all nod again, their understanding warring with their anger. "I may be petty enough to not want to be in the same room as them again, but you have to promise to let us all be. We're big kids, and we'll sort this out in a way that will suit us all. *Promise me.*"

I can tell by the looks on their faces that they really don't like the sounds of this, but these are my conditions. I've been fighting my own battles for a long time, and a couple of spoiled rich brats are not going to break me. Now that I've had my pity party, I'm ready to move on to the next phase. And I may even execute those plans for revenge because I don't know how this is going to affect my chances of getting an internship.

"Okay, sweetheart," Nana agrees. "We'll stay out of it, but if it gets too much or they take it too far, I want to know about it." A wicked glint fills her eyes, and she gives me a quick wink. "And if you need any help with some payback, I can be quite creative myself."

Poppy scoffs, "You can be downright evil. Maybe leave your Nana out of this, Harlow. We wouldn't want the others thinking that she was playing favorites."

"Oh, but I am at the moment, and I have no problem letting the others know that. They'll not only have to work their asses off to get back into Harlow's good graces, they're going to have to kiss my ass too." Nana crosses her arms in defiance, and Dad and Poppy chuckle.

"Between the two of you, I feel a little sorry for my children, but I won't interfere." Dad chuckles, but his smile and eyes show how pleased he is that I'm staying. He gets up, heading inside through the glass doors to a nearby buffet cabinet. Pulling open one of the drawers, he grabs something out before coming back to the table and tossing it at me. Squeaking in surprise, I reach out my hands and catch them right in time, a set of keys now clasped in my hand.

"What's this for?" I ask, dangling them on one finger.

"Keys to one of the cars in the garage. I figure you need to be able to get around and won't want to rely on one of us or Alex and Shane to drive you everywhere. It's also a means to escape if you need to. I'd offer to get you a driver, but I've gotten the impression that you'd prefer to be a bit more independent than that, and I want you to feel like you have control of when you can come and go."

I look at the emblem of the keys, a niggle of discomfort wiggling into my stomach along with a slightly petty sense of satisfaction. "But isn't this...?"

"Yep, that's Oliver's Aston Martin. I saw your face when he left the house the other day, how thrilled you looked to be riding in it. I figure it's the least he can do for being involved in the incident. Do what you want with it. There's a card for gas in the glove compartment; I've written down the pin for it on a piece of paper."

A wicked grin crosses my face, ideas already running through my mind. "You know, normally, I would say no to this, but I really do like that car. I need to head back to Shane and Alex's to grab my stuff and speak to them, thank them for everything."

I get up from the table and go around, placing a kiss on everyone's cheek. When I get to my dad, he stands up and pulls me in for a big hug, whispering in my ear, "Thank you for this. I know it's a big ask of you, but I appreciate it so much."

Pulling away, I nod. "I'm sure everything will

work out in the long run." *Hopefully he believes that more than I believe myself.*

Waving goodbye, I walk out to the garage, flipping the keys around in my hands while going over my plans for revenge in my head.

When I reach the garage, the scent of car polish and engine oil hits my nostrils. A very different smell to the hay and horse manure I'm used to, but it still causes a wave of goosebumps to cover my skin. The thrill of getting to drive a car like that is akin to being on the back of a rearing stallion. Just a different kind of horsepower.

Jumping into the Vanquish, the goosebumps intensify because it smells just like Oliver. That sharp citrusy scent that he wears. I remember breathing it in when he had me pinned against the wall, and with the memory, my anger intensifies. I'd thought about sticking shrimp in the hubcaps of this car, but having Brad hand me the keys is even better.

Hitting the switch on the visor for the garage, I slide the key into the slot and press the button, revving the engine as I wait impatiently for the door to rise. As soon as it's high enough for it to clear the car, I'm putting my foot on the accelerator, tearing out of the garage like the hounds of hell are on my trail and whooping with joy. Navigating around the front of the property, as soon as I clear the cobblestone turning circle, my foot goes down again, kicking up gravel.

I push the car faster and faster down the driveway, the trees green blurs as they go past, but as I get to the entrance, a large black limo pulls into the drive, taking up both lanes and causing me to have to brake more than I'd planned. Slowing down as it passes, I cackle with glee.

Through the open window I can see Oliver shouting furiously while his other siblings are frozen, looking kind of stunned. I wink and blow Oliver a kiss before practically drifting the car out of the drive and onto the road. Today, I have no interest in trying to see the abandoned house next door, but it's next on my list of things to do while I'm here. If I have to be at that house to enact my revenge, I'm going to be spending my time how I want to. And exploring that house is one of my main priorities.

But for now, I need to brainstorm a little more with Alex and then return to wreak havoc on the Summers siblings.

A wicked grin crosses my face as I contemplate all the ways I'm going to get my payback. Did they really think that something like their billboard was going to get me to run away? Sure, I was humiliated, and yes, it possibly made my job prospects zero, but all they did was paint a target on their own backs. I have put up with enough shit over the years from so many people that it was only a matter of time until I snapped. Unfortunately for them, they finally pushed me to my very limit. *Payback's a bitch, and so am I.*

The Summers siblings are not going to know what hit them. I bet they've never had anyone fight back before. I bet everyone that's ever challenged them has tucked tail and run in the face of that kind of humiliation, but they have no clue what they're up against. They have no clue about the shit I've been through and the humiliation I suffered from the kids at school. Maxine doesn't even know it all because I wasn't willing to tell her, knowing she would have wanted to fight my battles for me. I didn't cave then, and I'm certainly not going to cave now.

Good-looking assholes are a dime a dozen back home. And bitchy princesses? Please, like I don't know how to handle them. Nope, the Summers siblings are going to wish they had never tried to chase me off.

Chapter Three

Jacinta

When the limo pulls into the driveway, the silence in the car is heavy. Nobody has had much to say since we received our summons to the estate. Dad hadn't even bothered to call us; we got a group text message from Cecelia requesting our appearance for lunch.

But as we start the long trek up the driveway, Oliver's shout breaks the tense silence, grabbing our attention. He rips his sunglasses off his face like he can't believe what he's seeing and slams his finger down on the window control next to him. As the tinted glass goes down, we can all see his Aston Martin screaming toward us.

"What the fuck? Someone stole my fucking car!" he shouts, but it slows down as it reaches us, the window lowering.

It's like we're all suddenly going in slow motion as we pass one another. Harlow's wicked grin appears, followed by a wink, and she blows a kiss to Oliver before time speeds up again.

Huh, if I wasn't determined to hate the bitch, I'd be impressed. Taking Oli's car is certainly one way to figuratively kick him in the nuts. Maybe I should feel bad for the guy. I mean, he barely did anything except keep his silence, but the possessive part of me that doesn't want to share her brothers or put her family at risk is loving any little wedge that gets driven between them and my new "sister." Could I have given her a chance when Dad first told us about her? No. Absolutely not. The world has a very harsh way of correcting my mistakes, and others have paid a very dear price for my inability to make wise decisions about who to trust.

The limo is silent again, but this time it's a stunned silence, until Kai starts to chuckle.

"Well, it looks like Dad's not going to forgive anyone so easily this time." He's slouched back, looking far too unconcerned, but then again, Kai's always loved his freedom and adrenaline rushes more than he's ever loved *things*. Unless Dad plans to lock him in the house until he gives Harlow a fair chance, there's really not much that he can take from my most carefree brother. Plus, it's not like Dad would even have to fight that hard to win him over. I love Kai the same as all my other brothers, but he doesn't have that bite to him that some of the rest of us do. I know my strongest ally won't be found in him.

My gaze moves from him to Holden and Thomas who both have frowns on their faces, likely trying to figure out what Dad might have in store for them. Neither of them has been particularly vocal about the new arrival, both sitting back and allowing the rest of us to do what we've wanted. From them, my eyes find my two brothers who have actively been helping me try to get rid of the interloping bitch. Both Jaxon and Declan look as furious as Oliver, like giving Oliver's car to her has offended them as much as it's upset him, and I smile to myself. *At least I still have three on my side.*

Harlow's reaction to the spectacular billboard's unveiling was delicious, and I thought that we'd seen the last of her, but the subsequent fallout was more than I had anticipated. After Dad kicked us out, we'd had a family meeting, and Kai was the first to attack me.

"You can leave me out of it. I like the girl. She has a backbone, and who are we to say she doesn't get a chance? In the past, it's been women or men trying to get at us to get a piece of the pie, but she's not doing that. She's here to get to know Dad, and she deserves that chance, just as much if not more than we did when he adopted us."

"Bullshit, like she wouldn't take the money if she was offered it," Declan grumbled from his place on the sofa.

"But she was *offered it, and you saw how offended she seemed when Dad tried to give her one of the company credit*

cards. She was horrified." Thomas' quiet words had me rolling my eyes. The softie was so easily fooled, never learning his lesson even though both he and almost the company had been a victim of that naivete in the past.

"Jesus, it's lucky you guys have me, or you would have all been conned by the first woman to welcome your cocks into their warm pussy. It was an act. What better way to make it seem like she isn't here for the money?" I explained to them all, but Holden shook his head.

"I don't know about that. She did seem genuinely surprised." He shrugged, his eyes flashing with annoyance. "I'd like to get to know her a bit better so that I can make my own judgment." I couldn't stop myself from bristling at the combination of his words and that look on his face. Generally, Holden and I were on the same page when it came to protecting our family, so it was a bit of a surprise to know he was changing his tune. Granted, he hadn't helped much with the billboard, but sitting back and letting me keep us safe made my life much easier than him going out there and giving the bitch a chance!

"Hey, you didn't say anything when I first told you about this plan."

"Yeah, but you were all family first, rah, rah, rah, and I didn't want to let you down. But to be honest, I hate how angry Dad is at us, and I don't want to upset him or Nana and Poppy anymore. You remember how grateful I was when Dad took us in." His eyes go to Oliver, our brother pretending not to hear him. Which was pretty much the norm between those two. One would reach out, albeit tiny glances or steps toward having some kind of connection, and the

other would shy away. "I just don't want to rock the boat anymore."

"Arrghh!" The scream easily filled the limo despite how spacious it was. "Well, I'm not giving up, and I'm watching her as closely as possible. I want you all to be on the lookout for anything suspicious. Has your PI reported anything yet, Declan?" I asked my oldest brother, and he shook his head.

"No, nothing yet, but I'll make a note to call him as soon as I can get a chance. We need all the ammunition we can get about her and her mother."

Oliver's next words had me snorting. "I'm with Kai. Leave me out of it as well. Harlow and I have a connection, no matter how unexpected it might be. There's something different about her, and I'd like to get to know her a little better. Not just for Dad or Nana or Poppy, but for myself."

"Bullshit, the only connection you feel is the one that's ruled by your cock," I snarled at him before gauging my other brothers' reactions. Declan nodded his head in agreement, and so did Jaxon, but I could also see the doubt in his eyes. I knew he felt something for her. He couldn't shut up about the beautiful girl he'd met when he'd been in Connecticut. He'd had a sparkle I hadn't seen for a while, and the fool was already making plans to go back to see if he could find her again.

The faintest whisper of regret touched my heart, but it was quickly overshadowed by jealousy. Sharing Dad was one thing. Although I'd always been the only girl, it wasn't like I'd ever really had Dad to myself. But sharing Jaxon? My twin had always been my strongest ally, the one I could count on when Nana, Poppy, or Dad, even through no fault of their own, just didn't have the time for me. I couldn't lose both Dad and *Jaxon; something within me would break if that ever happened.*

I took a sharp breath, trying to center myself and get some semblance of control over my expression. My brothers were never fooled by the ice princess exterior, but I could cover up some of the anxious, twisted mess that was inside of me while I waited for Jaxon to speak. My brother had leaned forward, his mouth parted like he wanted to talk but was weighing his words carefully.

"He's not wrong. There is *something about her that just draws you in. I was ready to try to find her next time I was back at the club in Hartford. You know me, I don't go back for seconds."*

Again, I snorted, needing to convince him that there's nothing he needs from her, needing to hide the fact that on the inside, I was just that same scared little girl he'd always needed to protect. "That's only because you got interrupted before you got firsts. It's the one that got away syndrome." He frowned but didn't deny the accusation.

"I guess it doesn't matter anyway. She's not wanted, and she needs to go," he finished, but Kai growled at him.

"You three are the only ones who really don't want her here. Maybe you need to take a good look at why. If we didn't have money, would you be reacting like this?"

We went around in circles for a while, but for the first time in years, we were a family divided.

I'd done a lot of soul searching over the last few days, especially with the news of being put on suspension from the company. A tiny part of me is saying that maybe I was too harsh and I should get to know her. Especially since we have a lot of the same interests, and I might be able to admit I like how fiery she is. But then that insecure side tells me that she's going to replace me in the hearts of the most important people in my life, and, well, that tiny part that wants to get to know her, the one that almost longs to have a sister, gets smothered.

As the limo continues up the driveway and the Aston Martin disappears, I'm feeling a little smug. "So, Oliver, change your mind about her now?"

He's frowning, and Kai snorts. "Dude, are you really surprised? Dad's going to make us all pay for that little stunt even if we weren't actively involved. He's not going to believe that we didn't all know about it, and it's going to be guilty by association. I can't say we don't deserve this, and I don't think you can argue that either."

"No, I guess not," he grumbles, slumping back on the bench seat next to Kai. "But my car!" he whines, the sound of his voice throwing me back to when we were younger and he didn't get his way. It almost makes me smile or let loose a laugh, but I hold it in, refusing to give an inch to anything associated with her. The car falls back into silence as we all contemplate Kai's words. Holden and Thomas' brows furrow even further as they worry, and I find myself chewing my lip over what else Dad might do to me as well, but I shake it off. I don't care. *I can't.* I stand by what I did, and I will continue until I see Harlow Stubbs out of our lives for good.

"Come in, sit down, and *don't* say a word." Dad's orders are said in a tone I've rarely heard, like an approaching thunderstorm. When all the pressure builds up in the air and you can feel it pushing down on you. The only way the pressure will cease is when that storm breaks and the rain comes pouring down. The seven of us quickly take seats, and I notice that Nana and Poppy are in the room as well but Cecelia isn't. Thank God for that, I don't really need her to see our utter humiliation; she would hold that over us for years. That's another bitch we haven't been able to get rid of yet, and I'm pretty sure she thinks her position in this household is more secure than it is. Dad won't ever look at her as anything other than a PA, and she's going to be bitterly disappointed when she doesn't get any further than that.

Dad paces back and forth in front of us, his face a storm of anger and disappointment, causing more of that nasty guilt to roll through me. He's given us so much, and knowing that I'm mostly the cause of that look on his face is causing a sharp pain. Then he stops and clears his throat, his gaze cutting like a laser to the seven of us.

"I know I said it the other night, but I think it

needs to be said again. I have never been as disappointed in all of you as I am now. That night, I didn't see my mature, successful, and confident heads of industry that the seven of you have become. No, that night, I saw a bunch of insecure, catty, and scared children. The kids you were when you first arrived here, with all your bumps and bruises and shaken self-esteem. The ones that Nana, Poppy, and I worked so hard to bring out of their shells, to instill love and confidence in." Dad's words hitch a little, and my stomach ties itself in even more knots.

"I say it's sad because although you all started off in shaky situations, you landed on your feet with relative ease once you joined this family. You've had advantages and privileges that countless parents wish they could give their children, that kids all over the country dream of having. Harlow has had to fight tooth and nail to get ahead in life for a lot longer than any of you. Although she was fostered with a good family, that damn woman still had a place in her life, one that wasn't deserved at all. Don't you understand the guilt and devastation I feel that she had to go through that? That I could save all of you from horrible situations, but I couldn't save my own blood? I can't understand how you don't recognize Harlow as being a kindred spirit, similar to your younger selves. Instead, you feel threatened and see competition. I brought her here so that she could have a family, so that I could develop a relationship with her that wasn't above any of you, but equal. Even though it might be too little, too late, I wanted her to know what it was like to be welcomed into our family as my daughter. Haven't I proved to you all how much love I have in my heart? What have I done as a father to make you think one person could so easily steal away all of my love for the seven of you?"

He stops in the attempt to let all his words sink in, and I can see it's working with the softer half of my siblings. That God awful hint of doubt is back in my twin's eyes, hardening my resolve. Damn it, she really must have had an impact on him if these cracks keep showing. I need to nip that in the bud quickly, but I'll wait until the two of us are alone before I work on him.

The boys all start to say something, but I just sit back and wait. I know Dad, and he's not going to listen to them at all. He thinks we stepped over the line, and he may be right. Bringing the business into it might have been taking it too far, but I'm not sorry. Even though it didn't have quite the effect I was aiming for, aka her leaving, it was more than satisfying, and I hope it's a step in the right direction. She's going to realize that she can't muscle her way in so easily.

Nana and Poppy have sat quietly while this has been going on, disappointment on their faces. It's weird to be in the same room as all of my family and not have Nana fussing over one of us. With the softness she can show her grandchildren, it's sometimes easy to forget that Nana was an integral part of building Neighpalm into the mega company it is now. Well, there's no way of forgetting that right now. Her face is lined with sharp creases, and she has a frown that I'm sure many a businessman has cowered before. It's certainly disconcerting to be on the end of that look now.

Dad holds up his hands. "I don't want to hear any excuses. It's not me you have to make it up to. You need to make it right with her, but I've already told her she is under no obligation to listen to any of you. I've told her she doesn't even have to look at you or be in the same room as you if she's not comfortable with it."

"Does this mean we can come home?" Declan shoots to his feet, a hopeful look on his face. "Princess must need me; she's getting close to having those kittens."

I roll my eyes, making sure he doesn't see. He's such a damn hard ass in every other part of his life, but that damn cat could tell him to jump and he'd ask how high. It's sweet but annoying.

"Yes, you can, but stay away from Harlow unless you intend on making an effort at getting to know her," Nana warns us all while Poppy stands beside her, his arms crossed. He wears that look that he reserves for people he thinks are idiots, and I feel a bit ashamed at the fact that he's aiming it at us. Usually, it's outsiders who get the look, not family.

"Just before you got here I was on the phone with Hope, arranging for her to show Harlow the ropes of each individual business." Again, all of the boys try to say something, and I join in this time.

Hope is Neighpalm Industries' head of PR. She knows all the ins and outs of each business and has a huge team of people under her. Guaranteed, she's the one who supervised damage control since the billboard incident.

Again, Dad makes his signature gesture for this unfortunate conversation. "No, I told you to sit there and shut up. Harlow will be learning about the businesses whether she decides to be involved in them or not. You know what the press are like as well as the people that are in our social circle. They will eat her alive if she comes across as anything less than knowledgeable, and you've all given her a severe disadvantage in making a strong first impression."

"You guys will go about your lives as normal and *stay away* from Harlow. If she approaches you, fine, but unless you are groveling for forgiveness, I don't want to see you near her." The boys now completely silent, he turns to me, his eyes filled with disappointment.

"Jacinta, I told the press that you were taking a break to design the next line for Neighpalm Couture, which you can do, but in reality, we're going to get a couple of designers in to supplement you until you can get your shit together." His words are a knife to my heart, each stab of pain a reinforcement of what my new "sister" has already cost me.

"Sweetie, I think maybe you need to see your therapist again. It's been a long time since you did, and I thought you were doing well, but it seems like maybe some old issues have been triggered by Harlow's arrival. Take this time to think about what you want from life, whether Neighpalm Couture truly makes you happy or if you would rather be doing something else. I know you hate the limelight, but you love designing. Maybe we could make someone else the face of NC, and you could just take a role as chief designer if that would make you happier." I hear what he's saying, but I can't believe it.

"*Give up my company?*" I ask, confused, but then the anger surges through me. "Like fuck will I give up my company! The company that I made and put my own stamp on. Like fuck I'll give that up. I will see the fucking therapist, and maybe then you'll trust me with my own goddamn company again."

Not wanting to hear another word out of his mouth, I stand up and leave, heading toward our wing of the house and the comfort of my own room. I have some serious planning to do, plus, I need to make a fucking appointment to see my therapist.

The echo of footsteps has me turning, and I

stop, waiting for my brother to catch up. I know it will be Jaxon. It's always Jaxon.

"Are you okay, J?" He wraps an arm around my shoulder as we continue to our wing. "Dad is just worried about you; you know he didn't mean that he'd take your company away from you permanently." I growl, waving my hand around to cut him off.

"I know that! That's not what I'm worried about. I'm worried about *you*. Are you softening on that bitch? Can't you see how upset she makes me? Don't you want to get rid of her so I can be happy again?" He stops, and fuck, I think I might have just layed on the guilt trip a little too quickly. After what our mother put him through, Jaxon's always been a bit sensitive to women telling him what to do. I've almost always been the exception, something my therapist tells me I need to respect, appreciate, and tread carefully with, but sometimes even I can trigger him if I come at him too aggressively.

He growls at me, eyes narrowed. "You know I would do anything for you, but I will not go against Dad again. He saved us and gave us the life we have. There might have been a little bit of wiggle room before, but he's specifically told us to leave her alone now. I won't interfere with whatever you have planned, but I don't want to be involved either. I won't go out of my way to make her comfortable, and that will be for you. I personally want to see what she's going to do from here on in, and I'll make my judgment from her actions. It will come out eventually why she's really here, and if she's here for the money, we *will* crush her then."

His eyes soften, and he pulls me in for a hug again. "You know I've got your back in almost everything. It's you and me versus the world, and I've always been okay with that, but I really think we might be wrong this time. Call it a gut instinct but I think your therapist might agree, J. Mom's bullshit is really where all this is stemming from. It's time to let it go, Jacinta. Stop looking back and start looking forward. Who knows? Maybe one day, when she proves she's genuine, she could be another person who has your back."

His decision about Harlow is not surprising, but that doesn't lessen the sting. Jaxon has always been the one who tried to keep the peace. He got in between our mother when she was laying into me, physically and emotionally, and he's always played the referee when my fiery temper got the better of me as a teenager. I think if he hadn't had that run-in with Harlow at our club, he might not have even sided with me in the first place. I mean, what are the odds that they run into each other there and not a week later, she's staying with us? My brother has been burned as much as the rest of us, and I might have played on that history a tiny bit. There's a piece of me that finally feels a little hint of guilt. Out of everyone, Jaxon is the person I want to hurt the least, so I nod my head in agreement, needing to rein in the part of me that wants to rage and scream.

I will still try to protect my brother from her, but sometimes I guess I also need to protect him from *me.* Isn't that a sobering thought?

He presses a kiss to my temple as we continue on, both of us quiet, lost in our own thoughts.

Chapter Four

Harlow

The car drives like a dream, and my ride back to the city is filled with Sanctuary of Chaos playing at levels that are probably doing damage to my ears, but I sing along anyway. I park it in the visitor's parking lot at Shane and Alex's place and make my way upstairs to their apartment, bypassing the doorman with the entry code Alex had given me.

The elevator opens directly into the foyer of their penthouse apartment, and as I step out, I call out to see if anyone's home.

"Alex? Shane?" My words echo around the seemingly empty apartment. When we had left this morning, Shane was still in bed. He'd had a late night at a fashion shoot, not arriving home until the early hours of the morning, so we'd left him there when Alex took me out to Dad's place. I'm not sure what his plans were after he'd dropped me off, but I thought he had been coming home. The poor guys hadn't had any alone time since they rescued me from the premiere.

Shrugging, I head to the room that they gave me and start to pack away all my crap into a bag. The day after the premiere, Nana had dropped off some things so that I wouldn't be without clothes and toiletries or my laptop. The boys had offered to buy me replacement items, but letting them be my white knights was about my limit. I couldn't accept anything else from them. They'd already offered me a permanent place to stay if I didn't want to return to my dad's; it was only Alex's equally thirsty desire for revenge that made him give in when I explained that I needed to go back to Dad's place. Keep your friends close and your enemies closer, after all.

And boy, did I have plans. Once the horses were gone, I was going to make sure that Jacinta wished she'd never crossed me by making myself invaluable to Nana and Neighpalm Couture. I didn't have one fashionable bone in my body, but Alex had promised to be my fashion guru, and with his help, I was sure I could pull this off. Declan and his precious Princess were also on the list. By the time I was finished with her, she was never going to want to leave my side.

As for the rest, well, I'd just have to see where their passions lay. A noise in my doorway has me looking up at a sexily rumpled Alex wearing nothing but a pair of sweats and a cheeky grin. *Fuck, I must have interrupted them.*

"God, I'm sorry," I blurt out, but he waves his hand at me.

"No, don't apologize. I'm more than satisfied with our alone time." He winks at me, and I don't know whether to blush or be insanely jealous. It's been way too long since I had any worthwhile "alone time" of my own. "And I'm dying to know what happened. Are you back in?"

Shane appears behind Alex, a matching grin on his face that solidifies my choice: jealousy it is. Damn, these men are sexy. It's a shame they feel more like brothers to me than anything else. It would be the ultimate revenge if I managed to turn their eye from Jacinta, but I just can't do it, and I'm pretty sure they're not interested. Despite her actions, I think they both still want her, but it's going to take a major gesture on her behalf to erase their disappointment in her.

"Yes, Dad really didn't want to take no for an answer, and we already knew me going back there was the likeliest choice. If I'm being honest, even if I didn't have an ulterior motive, I don't think I could've hurt their feelings by staying away. They're not stupid though, Nana especially. In fact, Nana actually suggested that she could help me, but Poppy put a stop to that, and he's not wrong. They're pissed off now, but I don't want them to alienate the kids. I told them that much, so I'm just going to hope they stay out of the way."

"Harlow, I just can't get over how nice you're being. I would *not* be so forgiving," Alex muses as Shane wraps his arms around him from behind.

"That's because *she* is a classy lady," he says over Alex's shoulder, and I grin at his compliment.

"Yeah, not that classy. I'll get my revenge, just not at the cost of their relationships with Dad and our grandparents. If that happens, I really am no better than the kids have suggested. I'm just going to keep this between the younger generation. It's more that I'm so disappointed in Oliver and Jaxon if I'm honest. I've thought about it, and I can see how it might seem to Jaxon, but I didn't even find out Mom had died until *after* I'd met him. That night we just clicked." My core nearly clenches at just the memory of his body against mine while we danced. Even if we had had to put that heat between us on hold, we could've been friends. It would've been nice to have a friend among these wolves. Anyway, I know I could spend forever lost in the what ifs of that night, so I push myself to keep going.

"We talked for ages about weird and wonderful things, and then once we hit the dance floor, the chemistry was off the charts, and that was something I hadn't felt in such a long time. We were headed out the door to indulge in that chemistry when Max stopped me. If he'd just given me a fair chance and talked to me about all of it, I could've cleared this whole thing up, I'm sure. Instead, he'd rather just be his sister's puppet."

"And Oliver..." A sigh leaves my mouth at the memory. "He pinned me against the wall at NI and ravished me when we were there for tattoos. He also had me pretending to be his girlfriend to ward off the artist he was interviewing. I thought he and I'd clicked too, that maybe we could explore what it meant, yet he just threw me under the bus as well. Talk about mixed fucking signals. And they say women are complicated. Nope, fuck them all, each and every one of them could have given me a warning, but their family 'loyalty' stopped them." The anger is there, sure, but this time there's a tiny bit of longing that I won't admit to anyone but myself. It's hard to think about them and not want… something. Their bodies? Their company? Just to know that I don't have to be alone in that giant house? I'm not sure what it is, and I'm really not in the mood to dissect it right now.

"It looked like Kai didn't actually know it was happening." Shane's comment has me thinking back to his reaction that night. He *had* seemed pretty mad, and I hadn't gotten the impression that he was a natural liar. Maybe he hadn't known the exact details, just that something was going to happen? He would be the one sibling who I'd consider forgiving, if any. He'd been kind and friendly from the start, not like the others who were either downright hostile or aloof and disinterested like Holden and Thomas.

I shrug as I finish packing my shit. "We'll see what happens. If he tries to make amends, I may consider it. Like you said, he had looked blindsided by it, and he was friendly." *It doesn't hurt that he's sexy as well*, whispers my mind. I frown at the thought, not liking… or maybe liking too much… the train of thought that follows. *God, he's not the only one who is.* All six of those men are hot in looks; it's a pity the attitudes that come with them stink. I don't understand how I can still find them all attractive. *There's got to be some kind of issue here.*

"What's wrong?" Alex pushes when he sees my frown.

I roll my eyes before I respond, not ready to dig into the emotional aspect of what the hell is wrong with my taste in men. "Just my overactive libido playing the devil on the other shoulder. I'm really going to need to get laid if I keep thinking about how sexy they all are. Not to mention, I'd have to choose."

Shane laughs, and Alex shakes his head enthusiastically. "Girl, you'd have to be dead not to notice what a hot bunch those brothers are. Who cares if you find one or all of them sexy? Please, multi-partner relationships are the new 'in' thing. Love is love and all that jazz. Embrace it and take advantage of it if you get a chance. That could even be part of your revenge!" His eyes sparkle with excitement, and he wiggles his eyebrows comically. "Make each of those brothers fall for you and then smash their hearts to smithereens."

He jumps up and down on the spot in excitement, and Shane drops his arms from around his waist, rolling his eyes at his partner. "I don't know, Alex. Only a psychopath would be cold-hearted enough to not actually develop some kind of feelings doing something like that, and I really don't think that's Harlow. She'd be hurting herself just as much as she hurt them, not to mention that might be playing a bit too dirty for her dad and grandparents to forgive."

Shane's points certainly bring some caution to the forefront of my mind, and he might be right, but I'm not taking the idea off the table. *Yet, anyway. That's one to heavily think about before diving in.*

"Come on, you two. Let's have some lunch before Harlow heads back to the estate," Shane says, trying to rein us in. And likely get his boyfriend's mind off of any revenge-driven matchmaking. "How did you get here?" he asks, leading the way out to their kitchen as Alex and I follow behind.

"Oh, get this!" I nearly squeal, already riding a high at the mere thought of the beauty waiting for me outside. "Dad gave me the keys to Oliver's Vanquish." I take the keys out of my pocket and wave them around, my body doing what can only be described as the world's most awkward happy dance. "Says I can use it to get around. I think he knows how much it's going to piss Oliver off. You should have seen his face as I drove down the driveway with it when they passed me in a limo. That thing drives like a freaking dream."

The boys both laugh at me gloating over my small victory before deciding it's time for lunch. Throughout the fun meal, Alex and I toss around more plans for revenge, the ideas getting more ridiculous each time, while poor and ever-patient Shane does everything he can to temper our crazier schemes.

"We want them feeling sorry, not dead," he finally ruled, but still Alex and I cackled like crazies.

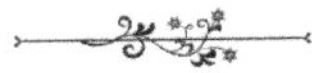

When I finally return to the estate in the late afternoon, I drive around the back toward the stables instead of pulling into the garage, needing to check on the horses. *It makes more sense to do it now than have to come back out later.* I pull the Vanquish to a stop in front of the barn and jump out. I'm just about to head over to the yards when Josh comes out of the stable block followed by a familiar, unexpected, and definitely unwelcome face.

Luke, one of Chuck's stablehands follows him, an oily grin on his face. *What's he doing here? Chuck never said anything about the horses being accompanied by a groom.*

"Hey, Harlow, look who turned up here not half an hour after you left this morning." Josh is looking at me with a smile, but I can tell by the curious gleam in his eyes that he's wondering why Chuck or I hadn't warned him of this.

"Oh hey, Luke. What a surprise. Chuck never said anything about you coming out as well."

"Hey, Harlow." He steps up like he's planning to hug me, but I quickly move away from the gesture and head out to where I know the horses are, giving them no choice but to follow.

"Why are you here? I thought I was working the horses until they went to set. I was ready to stay with them until Max could join them." My voice is a little harsh, but Luke has always given me the creeps. *And what if Chuck sent him because he doesn't trust me to get the job done?* Shaking my head, I quickly ditch those thoughts. *No, Chuck wouldn't do that to me. He knows how insecure I can be.* Before I can create another reason in my head, Luke speaks up.

"Mr. Boston sent me because he was worried that the horses would take up more time that you should be spending with your new family," he tells me. The last little bit sounds like he's attacking me, though when my eyes meet his, he's smiling and showing no signs of animosity. His words make sense since that *is* something that Chuck would think of, but I'm still a little surprised that he didn't let me know.

I rest against the white wooden fence, and the two guys lean next to me as we look out over the Summers Estate. The sun is starting to set, and the temperature is dropping slightly as I watch my charges eat the fresh hay that has been thrown over their fence.

None of the three in this paddock pay one lick of attention to me, but as I move to the stallion yard to check on Samson, he lifts his head and whinnies before trotting over to the fence to say hello.

I give his silky soft muzzle a rub and a scratch behind the ears, a nagging feeling still poking at me. I feel like I'm missing something, but I don't really have time to deal with it now. Maybe I'll message Chuck later and ask. Shaking away my concerns, I address him again.

"Okay, well, let's start working them in the morning. I'll meet you out here at seven, and we'll put them through their paces in the indoor arena," I tell Luke before turning to Josh. "If they need a run, do you think you could show us the cross-country course? I would love to try it out."

Josh grins at my question. "Absolutely, I'm even happy to ride one of them for you if you want, and I'm sure one of the Summers kids will take the other."

I frown at that second comment, which he

notices and quickly corrects himself. "Or even Brad would probably be happy to help out."

His alternative brings a smile back to my face, and I almost roll my eyes at my own emotional yo-yoing. "Yeah, that's a great idea! I'll ask him this evening. Now, if you wouldn't mind showing me where Jenny and DS are? I'd love to give them some cuddles before I go inside."

He gestures for me to follow him, Luke trailing after us, but a shout from the direction of the back patio has me lifting my head to find one very angry Oliver Summers headed in my direction. A small smile crosses my lips at the sight of him. His blue hair is tousled like he's been running his hands through it, and his glasses are sitting a little crooked on his face, like he was in such a hurry he hadn't bothered to straighten them. There's a scowl on his face, and his eyes flash with fury. Seriously, he's the hottest thing I've seen in a long time, and it amuses me that his anger makes me happy and horny. *Fuck, I really am messed up*. I'm going to blame that all on my mother.

I quickly drop the smile as he gets closer, but he storms straight past me and the other two, proceeding directly to his car so that he can inspect every inch of it. I roll my eyes and follow Josh toward the stable block, more than fine with letting Oliver continue this on his own. Inside, most of the stalls are free except for one that has Jacinta's pretty pregnant palomino quarter horse mare in it. She sticks her head over and nickers at me, so I go over and give her a pat. She seems calm and happy, munching on her food, so I leave her alone and move to the only other stall that's occupied, finding my two terrors doing the same.

"I brought them in here for the night. I thought they'd be safer in here than out in a paddock. It's rare, but occasionally a cougar or a bobcat is spotted in the area, and the mini would make a tasty meal."

I laugh at his observation, though I'm grateful for his smart thinking. "Thank you, Josh, but I'm sure you've figured out by now that it'll be a brave bobcat or mountain lion that tries to take on DS."

He runs a hand through his hair and smiles ruefully. "Ah yeah, she tried a few things like you warned me."

I look around the stables for Luke, but he seems to have disappeared. "I'm sorry about Luke. Had I known, I would have told you. I'm surprised Chuck didn't let you know. He's usually really good with that sort of thing."

He shakes his head, that easy smile back on his face. "No problem, Harlow. I've got him bunking in the loft. There's a small room with a cot, and he can use the bathroom down here in the office. I've told him to head into the kitchen to grab breakfast in the morning like I do, and I've informed Gretchen that we have one more mouth to feed. We're all organized, and it's not like it's forever."

Before I can thank him again, I hear Oliver shouting my name. Josh makes a face and quickly disappears as I open the stall and let myself in. Maybe he won't look for me in here. Though I doubt I'll be so lucky; he's not that stupid.

Keeping an eagle eye on DS, she seems occupied with her food, so I just wrap my arms around Jenny's neck when he appears in the doorway.

"What the fuck, Harlow? Who said you could take my car?" I roll my eyes at his angry outburst. I know he knows that Dad said I can take it; otherwise, where would I have gotten the keys from? He's just ready to pick a fight, so I ignore him.

I rub Jenny's ears, whispering sweet words to her while she nuzzles into my armpit. But Oliver's not happy with me ignoring him, so he opens the door and steps into the stall, reaching out to grab me. *Big mistake, dick head.* Turning my face, I hide the wicked smile that crosses my mouth as he steps too close to DS and her back end.

CRACK! "Ow, fuck!" Oliver's shout of pain has me giggling and thanking God for ornery mini ponies.

When I turn around, Oliver is bent over, rubbing at his calf, his look of fury aimed at the taffy-colored mini that's still calmly eating her food.

"I see you met Devil Spawn," I say calmly, a snort almost escaping when he turns his back to her again. Before he can say anything, she whips around, teeth bared and charging for his ass.

"FUCKKKK!" He spins, ripping his ass cheek out of her teeth and growling at her. Her ears are flat back, and she bares her teeth at him again, but I step between them, not wanting to risk any more injuries.

As soon as I do, he unbuttons his jeans and drops them to the ground, neck straining to see what his ass looks like. Before he makes a full rotation like a dog chasing his tail, he looks at me with pleading eyes.

"Can you see if she broke the skin, please?" This time, I can't help the snort that escapes, the sound threatening to turn into a full laugh when he growls at me. I don't break my staredown with him, trying to show how much I don't care, but my heart beat increases at the thought of seeing an almost naked Oliver. Stupid ass is so freaking sexy.

I push the angry mini back toward her food since she knows better than to try me, and I look to where he's rubbing his butt cheek.

"I'm going to have to lift your boxers," I tell him, and he just nods his head. I can see he's in pain just by the tightness around his eyes, and a *tiny* part of me feels almost 0.5% bad about using DS to hurt him. Pulling aside his boxers, I look at his nicely formed ass and wince at the sight of the damage. Damn, she must have gotten a nice mouthful; the skin is already turning purple, and there are perfectly shaped mini teeth marks. *Hmm, karma at its finest.* DS might have gotten to him first, but it won't be the last time he gets bitten on his ass. My bite may be a little more permanent. Trying to hide a smile, I let the band of the boxers snap back, earning a yelp that does make me laugh this time.

"Yeah, you're going to need to ice that, but there's no broken skin," I tell him before patting both animals and leaving the stall.

I can hear him hurrying to pull his jeans back on, and by the time he gets them done up and follows me out, I've started the Vanquish. With a wave goodbye, I drive away, leaving him to hobble back to the house. *Well, it's not like he could have sat down anyway.* He's going to need a cushion for the next day or two, and I chuckle at the thought all the way to the garage.

Chapter Five

Harlow

Instead of heading straight to my room, I go in search of something to eat, my stomach rumbling so badly I can't ignore it. I'm sure they were planning on making me too uncomfortable to take meals with them, but I don't plan on giving them the satisfaction. Dumping my bag and things in front of the door to our wing, I head toward the main living areas where I can hear the sounds of a meal taking place.

Murmured voices and the *clink* of silverware on china echo down the corridor, and my steps slow. *Do I really want to face them all now?* I mean, it's one thing to wave and smile at them as I drive past in one of their cars, but to be within feet of them all? Shaking my head, I take a big breath and continue walking. *I can do this. Those assholes have got nothing on what I've already been through*. My pep talk seems to work, and by the time I arrive to where everyone is sitting around the dining room table, I'm feeling confident and ready to face anything.

The atmosphere is tense, and the small amount of chatter dies instantly the minute I enter the room. Looking around the table, I can see everyone but Oliver is here.

"Harlow, honey, come and sit next to me." Nana pats the empty chair next to her and smiles encouragingly at me. I hadn't actually planned on staying, but the sour look on Jacinta's face is reason enough for me to change my plans, and it provides the perfect opportunity to rub a little salt into the wound.

"Thanks, Nana, I think I will. I'm starving," I tell her, sitting down between her and Kai who shoots me a hopeful smile, which I return briefly.

"Did you have a nice afternoon with Alex and Shane?" Poppy asks as Nana piles some food on my plate and everyone else continues to eat. I can see out of the corner of my eye that they're all watching me warily, and Jacinta's scowl gets even deeper at the mention of the two guys.

"Yeah, I really did. They've been so great. One of the best parts of my trip was meeting the two of them."

I'm laying it on a bit thick for Jacinta's benefit, but I'm not lying. They're great friends, just not in the way I can see everybody assuming they are.

"How did the horses settle in?" Dad asks, taking a sip of his drink.

"Really well. I'll start working them tomorrow. I'm not sure how long it will be until they're needed on set though. I'll have to give Chuck a call and get him to call the director."

"It's one of our films, isn't it?" Dad asks, and I shrug.

"I'm not sure, actually. I think that's what Chuck said. I know the one that Maxine is working on at the moment is." Dad looks from me to Declan who's scowling down at his plate but obviously listening in. Everyone is. None of the previous conversations have resumed.

"I'm sure Chuck said it was. Do you know, Dec?" Dad asks his oldest son. Declan looks up from his food, putting down his knife and fork and wiping his mouth on his napkin before replying.

"Yes, I'm almost certain it's for that middle ages epic that Shaun Walsh is working on." He looks from Dad to me, and I nod my head. *God, this is so fucking awkward.*

"Yes, that sounds like what Chuck had told me too." Declan's eyes narrow, but he doesn't look at me for too long before Dad's speaking up again.

"Give him a call tomorrow, will you, Dec? See what's going on. That's not great for us if he's running behind; the budget's going to blow out. When you find out, you can let Harlow know so she has a better idea about when they'll be needed on the set."

Declan keeps his face neutral as he nods his agreement to Dad, but I can see the tension in his muscular frame. He doesn't like being told what to do for his own company, and he definitely doesn't like that his marching orders are in any way for my benefit. That just makes me smile internally. Anything I can do to ruffle this one's feathers is a win-win situation for me.

Before anyone can say anything else, Oliver hobbles into the room, groaning in pain and holding his butt cheek.

Nana jumps to her feet, ready to do whatever he needs. "Oh my goodness, Oliver, are you okay?" she asks as she goes around the table to help him over to the couch. The other siblings are on their feet too, all of them looking between me and Oliver suspiciously.

"What did you do to him?" Jacinta growls at me, but I raise my eyebrows in shock. *Wow, didn't think she'd be game enough to blame me so soon.*

"Jacinta," Dad snaps at her, "why would you even think Harlow had anything to do with this?"

I wipe my mouth with my napkin before turning to Dad and wincing dramatically.

"Well, actually, I kind of did... indirectly." His eyebrows shoot up in surprise at my confession as I turn to Poppy. "Oliver met DS," I tell him, shrugging, and Poppy starts to chuckle.

"Oh no, did he get too close to the menace?"

"Yeah, he made the mistake of assuming she was harmless because of her size. He came into her stall uninvited."

Even Nana has a smile on her face as she places a cushion under his ass before helping him to sit. The other siblings still look confused, but I don't owe them any explanation. Instead, I get up calmly and head through the swinging doors to the kitchen.

In there I find Mrs. Hayton bustling around, tidying up after dinner preparations.

"Harlow, Liebling, there you are." She hurries over to me, drying her hands on her apron before pulling me into a hug. "Oh, my sweet child, those children were Arschlöcher. Are you okay?"

"I'm okay, Mrs. Hayton," I reassure her, but she still looks me in the eye, searching my gaze. She must see what she's looking for because she nods and pats me on the cheek before stepping back. "You wouldn't happen to have an ice pack I could borrow, do you?"

"But of course." She hurries over to an industrial fridge freezer. I guess with a family this big you need one. Returning back, she's wrapping a dish towel around it. "What have you done?" she asks, worry in her eyes while handing it to me, but I shake my head as I take it.

"It's not for me. It's for Oliver. He made the

unfortunate mistake of getting between me and my mini pony, and she took exception to it."

The worry clears while understanding fills her expression, and she nods her head, a small smile crossing her lips.

"Yes, how unfortunate." She pats my cheek again and returns to the dishes as I head back to the living area.

Marching up to Oliver, I hand him the ice pack. He tries to grab my hand instead, his eyes imploring me to talk to him, but I quickly drop it into his lap. It lands heavily, and a breath escapes his mouth, but I say nothing as I return to the table. When I peek back at him again, he has a hurt look on his face, but I have no sympathy for him. He's the asshole who played me for a fool. He deserves all he gets as far as I'm concerned.

Dad and Poppy are still chuckling. "Oliver, you know better than to put your back to a strange horse like that," Dad admonishes, and Oliver groans as he removes his jeans before placing the ice pack on his ass.

"But she's this tiny cute thing! I assumed she'd be as sweet as she looks." He sighs with relief as the ice starts to numb his embarrassing wound.

"No, Devil Spawn is a tyrant. Everyone at the Bostons' place knows to be wary, and Harlow has a sign up: *beware of the pony*. Not many people believe it until they suffer the same fate as you. She has a thing for biting people on the butts." Poppy just barely makes it through that last sentence before breaking out in laughter, and Nana's lips are twitching like she's just barely holding back her own.

"What are your plans for working the horses?" Dad asks me, changing the subject.

"Tomorrow, I'll work them in the indoor arena, practice some of the moves that may be required during the movie, then, if you don't mind, the following day, I'd like to take them for a big run. Josh has said he'd take one, and now that Luke is here, he can take another. I was wondering if you'd like to join and maybe show us the cross-country course. All of them are jumpers."

A huge grin crosses Dad's face, and he nods his head enthusiastically. "Yeah, I'd love that."

My eyes move to Jacinta, catching her scowl, and when her eyes meet mine, I feel a little guilty. I can see the hurt in them, but that quickly disappears before it's replaced by hatred. *Damn it, girl, you started this shit. Did you really think I was just going to roll over and take it?*

I ignore the look and keep eating, my eyes moving to Declan and Jaxon who are sitting next to each other just down from Jacinta. Both are staring at me with hostility, but Jaxon's eyes also hold a hint of confusion. His frown seems more like he's trying to work me out more than anything. Well, too bad. He trashed his chance when he so fiercely accused me of being a money grabbing ho.

Ignoring the two of them, I move around to Thomas and Holden. Neither of them have been outright hostile, but neither have been welcoming like Kai either. In fact, you'd think that I was a non-entity and not worth their attention, but they both hold a slight bit of interest in their eyes now. They seem genuinely interested in what's panning out around the table. I guess being smacked on the nose like little puppies wasn't to their liking, and they're trying to decide which way they want to go with this. Whether they're going to join Jacinta, Jaxon, Declan, and now Oliver, I guess, in their outright hostilities or they're going to be like Kai and try to get to know me. I don't have a clue which way they're going to go, but it will be interesting to see how it all plays out over the next week or so.

"Harlow, honey, I've organized for you to meet Hope, our PR representative, at Neighpalm Couture the day after tomorrow. I will accompany you, and I thought we'd start there since you have some experience with it. She'll show you around and give you the run down before you and I interview a couple of people for some open positions."

Jacinta's head comes up at Nana's words, and she pales slightly. "New people? You were serious?!"

"Yes, dear, we are interviewing some new designers since you have made it abundantly clear that that business doesn't mean as much to you as we thought." Nana's tone is icy, and the atmosphere gets even more tense as a frown crosses Jacinta's brow before she starts to argue.

"But I thought you wanted me to concentrate on the next line," she stammers, sounding a little confused and hurt. It's obvious that she's surprised, and there's a small pulse of satisfaction at this first crack in the ice queen's facade.

"Yes, but it doesn't mean we're going to use it. You have to prove to me that you want this." Dad's eyes show his disappointment although he doesn't allow any emotion to leak into his voice. You'd think he was talking to a business associate right now, not his daughter.

Again, her gaze comes to mine, and I keep mine neutral despite the obvious venom in hers.

"Is that good with you, Harlow?" Poppy's voice breaks the tense silence, and I nod quickly, happy to keep the conversation moving on.

"Yes, that's great. Tomorrow afternoon I'm actually going to explore the abandoned house next door."

Poppy chuckles, knowing all about my love of abandoned buildings. "Going to make yourself a YouTube channel?" he asks with a smile on his face.

I shake my head, the barest hint of a blush heating my cheeks. "No, but the building is basically calling my name, begging me to explore, and I just can't resist."

"Be careful," Dad warns me. "There used to be a caretaker on the estate, but I think the old man passed on a few years ago, and I'm not sure if another was appointed. Try not to get arrested for trespassing or anything," he jokes, but I see the worry on his face.

"Oh, don't worry, Dad, I haven't been arrested in years," I reply brightly, hiding a smile. Nana and Poppy snort, but Dad's eyes bulge out of his head.

"You've been *arrested*?"

"Yeah, our senior year of high school, we were at a party that got raided by the police, and Maxine's asshole boyfriend at the time left without us, so we ended up being arrested," I tell him, a little sheepish at the admission because we'd been drunk as skunks, very loud, and had woken the whole house once we got home. Maxine's grandparents and Nana and Poppy had unfortunately been to visit that day. The disapproving looks that I had received from the senior Bostons are forever etched in my memory, but Nana and Poppy had just been amused, and luckily so were Chuck and Melinda. "But all charges were dropped once Chuck arrived."

Kai laughs beside me, the rumbling sound reminding my body how close he is to me. "Well, Dad, looks like you're zero for eight on the children getting arrested front."

My eyes widen as I turn to look at him. "*All* of you have been arrested?"

He nods his head, no shame on his face. "Yep, for a variety of things over the years."

I look around the table, and amazingly enough, all the siblings are wearing the same sheepish look that I must be. Well, what do you know? We *do* have something in common.

The table returns to quiet conversation, and as I finish up my meal, Kai leans into me, whispering in my ear. "I had no idea they were going to do that, Harlow. I swear, I would have told you if I had." His words are rushed, like he wants to tell me before I stop him.

I turn to see his golden brown eyes imploring me to believe him, and the butterflies in my stomach twitch, but I hold firm. Instead of answering, I stand up, pulling away from him.

"Thank you for dinner. I'm going to head to bed and check my emails and things and then read for a little while. It's been a long day." I look at Dad, Nana, and Poppy when I say, "Hope to see you in the morning." They smile and wish me goodnight while the rest of the table is silent.

Before I can leave the room, Kai calls out to me, "Sleep well, Harlow." But I don't turn or acknowledge him, I just keep walking. His whispered words confirm what Shane and Alex had thought, but I'm still not ready to play nice, and he'll just have to deal with the brunt of my emotions.

They tried so hard to break me, but they need to realize, I was broken a long time ago, and it's going to take a lot more than that for me to shatter.

When I get to my room after grabbing my

things, the door is cracked open. Seriously? They couldn't just let it go. Popping my head through the cracked door, I scan the room, but it looks like nothing is out of place. In fact, Princess is firmly ensconced in her place on the bed with her eyes open. As I step in and close the door behind me, a loud purring sound reaches my ears, bringing a smile to my lips.

Putting down my things, I rummage around in my backpack, looking for the thing I bought on the way home today. Once I've got the pack of cat treats out and a couple in my hand, I head over to the bed and climb up next to Princess.

She butts her head against my hand in thank you, gobbling down each of the treats that is *so* not a bribe. This is exactly why I became a vet. That unconditional love and affection from an animal with no expectations. Unlike humans who always have some kind of goal in mind.

Smiling again, I quickly put away my things and shower before checking my emails.

There's one that starts my heart racing. I have an interview with the MacGinty Sanctuary, a privately run zoo, for their intern position. It's near San Diego, so not horribly far away. Carefully putting my computer down, I jump off the bed and do a little happy dance. When that's worked out of my system, I hop back on the bed and send an affirmative response. It's in three days time, which works well with my plans. I just hope the director doesn't require the horses that day.

Putting the laptop away, I snuggle down in the bed, the cat lulling me to sleep with her soft purrs. *At least things are starting to look up.*

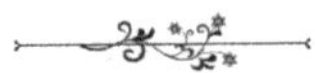

KAI

I'd thought we were doing okay when we'd all had a laugh about Dad's children all being arrested, but Harlow's green eyes were cold and distant when she turned to me after I'd whispered in her ear. The hurt that I saw punched me in the gut. This time, Jacinta has gone too fucking far. And I'm not going to stand around and just let her issues get in the way of me having a life.

I just have to find a way to get through to Harlow, to convince her I had no idea about Jacinta's final plan. I get that I fucked up because I should've tried to stop it in the first place, but I have no idea how to fix that part now aside from convincing her to give me a chance.

My mind totally not prepared to tackle that challenge right now, my gaze goes to my brother, the pathetic one moaning and groaning about his ass on the couch.

This is all his fucking fault. Something happened

between him and Harlow when they had the tattoos done after their bet. The glare she gave him when it all happened, not to mention the middle finger as she drove past in his car today tells me everything I need to know. Now I just need to hope that whatever shit he pulled isn't added to the pile of things I need to make up for. Why do my siblings have to be such assholes?

I think my best chance is to separate myself from them. I love them, but if they're always hanging in the background or just a few seats down the table, Harlow will never stop being reminded of what they did to her. An idea pops into my head, the thought so perfect that I barely manage to stop the smile that wants to spread across my face. If I don't keep it hidden, they'll start getting into my business like they always do.

I really want to invite Harlow to come to Hawaii with me when I go on the weekend. Especially since I know she's never been allowed to go anywhere, that her bitch of a mother stopped her from going on vacations with the Bostons. I want to spoil her like she deserves, and this kind of trip will do both that and help us get to know one another.

I just need to come up with a way to approach her without her immediately going on the defensive. Maybe I'll ask Nana if she has any suggestions.

Chapter Six

Oliver

My butt cheek is burning as I lower myself onto the cushion Nana has put out for me, the wicked woman not hiding her chuckles at my misfortune when Harlow describes what happened. How could something so cute and sweet be so damn vicious? *I swear I've been bitten by a velociraptor and not a mini pony.* Leaning to one side to take the pressure off the bruised cheek, I remember the heat in Harlow's eyes as I dropped my pants, showing she's not as indifferent as she pretends to be. I still have some hope. *Though the question still is, how does one apologize for what we've done?*

Suddenly, she appears in my view, holding out an ice pack. She has that aloof neutral look on her face, like she doesn't care, but she went and got me an ice pack, and those aren't the actions of someone who doesn't give a shit. I try to grab her hand, wanting to show her how sorry I am with my eyes, but she ignores me and pulls away, dropping the ice pack in my lap. Fuck, now my dick hurts too, but I won't give her the satisfaction of letting anyone know. *Probably should start with saying the words first, goddamnit.*

Dinner finishes up very quickly with Nana wrapping me a plate of food for when I feel like eating, but I think I'll be hobbling for a few days, and right now, I'd rather take a painkiller or two. I guess it serves me right. I'd gone out there with the intention of blasting her about the car even though I knew Dad had given her the keys and permission, but I just needed to see her, and it was a perfect excuse. I hadn't expected her to be so cold. I wanted to see the understanding, feisty girl I know is in there, the one who kissed me back so thoroughly at the studio that day. I've been thinking about that day over and over again, especially in the shower, reliving the way she made my heart race and my cock rock hard.

I feel so bad that I didn't stop Jacinta's plan. Unlike Kai, I knew what she was going to do, but I let it happen, and I think Harlow realizes that. No, the fact that she didn't warn me about the demonic mini with a taste for ass means she *definitely* realizes that. If she never forgives me, I won't be surprised. But damn it, I haven't been this interested in a woman in years. I learned in high school that girls would say what they thought you wanted to hear instead of being real, but I get the feeling that there is nothing fake about Harlow. By the time I tried to stop Jacinta, it was too late, and now I've ruined whatever we could have been.

"Oliver!" Jacinta snaps, dragging my attention back to the room. Looking around, I see that it's just my brothers and sister left, and they're all standing around me.

"Come on, let's go outside." Holden waves his hand, showing me the joint he's holding, and Thomas holds up a couple of beers.

"This will help with the pain." He laughs, and the others join in... except Jacinta. She still looks furious. God, her pettiness is really beginning to piss me off. I'm so sick and tired of dealing with the fallout from her insecurities. All of us are, even Jaxon who has infinitely more patience with her out of misplaced guilt.

When we're all situated outside, a cushion still under one of my butt cheeks, I take the offered beer from Thomas and drink down half of it. This little sibling ritual started many years ago when we were all in high school and realized that bottling everything up inside was neither healthy or helpful. We started doing this once or twice a month, using each other as sounding boards for all the drama in our lives.

We sit there, chilling, Kai telling us about how his extreme team is about to retire and the scouting process for new athletes. "I think I want a summer and a winter team this time round. And not just all guys. I need to scout some girls, bring them into the mix. Seriously, girls are fifty percent our demographic too, and I mean, who doesn't like a woman who's into extreme sports?" His eyes move to the parental wing of the house where I know Harlow is presently tucked into bed.

I hold in the sigh that wants to be set free. I'm sure once she gets past her anger, which I deserve, I can tease out that interest she showed at Neighpalm Ink. If she rejects me even after I find a way to make amends, then I don't know what I'll do. My stomach lurches at the thought, and I shudder. I can't go through that again. I haven't taken a chance on too many people in my life, and the last time I thought I had something worth keeping, it ended in me being tossed aside. Despite being for "good reasons," the rejection just made me incredibly reluctant to try and create something worth keeping again. *And now's not the time for* that *horrible trip down memory lane*, my heart scolds. Knowing it's right, I shove those feelings back and check in with what my brothers are saying.

"I agree. It was stupid not to have a few women on your teams; it's limiting yourselves." Thomas nods, his slight Irish accent coming out now that he's a few beers in. It's not often we hear his accent anymore. It was strong when he first came to us, but he deliberately made an effort to sound more American. It's sad, really, but it was one of those things he was teased about as a child. No matter how much we all told him it didn't matter, he went through a period of time where he didn't talk much at all, especially in public. He became known as the strong silent one, and fuck, the girls went crazy trying to draw him out. After his ex fucked him over, what had become a role he played to keep people at arm's length actually reverted back to his original insecure self.

"We've been going about this all wrong," Jacinta says suddenly, completely off-topic. In the silence that follows, Holden hands me the joint, his hand brushing against mine. A spark of familiarity hits me, but I push that feeling down and lock it away again. No need to tempt fate or put myself through any extra heartache. I take a deep drag, holding it before blowing it back out and letting that relaxed feeling wash over me. The pain dulls, and the guilt in my mind seems to wash away.

"What do you mean?" I ask her, passing the joint to Kai. The big guy's frowning at Jacinta, a furrow to his brow like he's already unhappy with whatever's going to come out of her mouth.

"Are you talking about Harlow? Still? For fuck's sake, Jacinta, haven't you done enough damage? I've never seen Dad so angry at us," Kai growls at her, and he's not wrong either. "You've basically lost your business as punishment. Do you want to make that permanent? To drag the rest of us down with you?"

"Exactly! It's her fault that happened in the first place," she hisses, waving the joint away when it's offered to her. *God, she needs to relax. Wish she would've taken it.*

"Yeah, I'm not sure that's right, sis. That's all on you. Had you not been trying to get rid of her, none of it would have happened." Thomas' statement has my eyebrows raising, and I'm not about to jump in the middle of this now. He and Holden have been fairly indifferent the whole time, neither committing to either Team Harlow or Team Jacinta, which was actually kind of unusual. They're usually happy to let Jacinta do whatever she wants, and even if they don't get actively involved, they never get in her way. It looks like he's finally picking a side, and Jacinta is furious.

My sister might have her polished veneer down flat, that cold but beautiful mask that makes her the perfect face of Neighpalm Couture, but that's nowhere to be seen now. As her brothers, we've always been both blessed and sometimes cursed to have complete access to the authentic, unfiltered Jacinta.

"I don't care either way." Holden's eyes are slitted and his words mellow as he lights up another joint he's pulled from the stash in his pocket. Holden does like his recreational drugs. Before he was responsible for Neighpalm Records, he went off the rails for a while, though he tends to stick to just weed these days. "Work is kicking my ass, and I just have no time to indulge you in your games, Jacinta. I think we need to give her the benefit of the doubt at this point. So far, she's done nothing but let a mini take a bite out of Oliver's ass."

Jacinta screams quietly, but then her eyebrows rise and a smile crosses her lips. "Well, sure, okay, that might work with my plan anyway. I think the problem is that she was expecting us to be hostile from the start. Her guard was probably up before she finished freeloading off Dad's plane service. What we need to be doing is earning her trust and friendship and then smashing it. Then she'll know not to mess with the Summers family."

My stomach drops at her words, and I can see Kai is shaking his head. "Fuck no, you leave me out of it. I like her, and until she does something that proves she is what you accuse her of, I'm going to do my hardest to make friends with her. For real, Jacinta. I'm not going to be part of this, and I'd appreciate you not trying to use me to strike back at her."

Declan and Jaxon have been very quiet through the whole conversation, but after getting the same kind of response from Thomas and Holden as Kai gave, she turns to them.

"Well? Are you in or out?" Her eyes narrow on her brother. Poor guy doesn't stand a chance; he's always allowed his sister to walk all over him. It's a guilt thing left over from their abysmal childhood.

He gives her a small nod, but I can see in his eyes he's not so sure about it.

"And you?" She turns to Declan, eyebrow raised and eyes already glinting with challenge. "She's basically stolen your cat." She throws the words at him, but I have my suspicions about that. He's always been a huge softy regarding his cats, and if he thought Princess was more comfortable in Harlow's room and wanted to be there, I don't doubt that he'd let her in there. That cat is the one woman in his life that he'll bend over backward for, even if it irritates him to no end that she's choosing a stranger over him.

But instead of telling Jacinta this, he nods his head. "Yes, we need to get rid of her. I'll call my PI next time I'm in the office; god knows the man asks for enough money that we should've had *something* by now. I don't want to do it from here in case Dad overhears," he tells her, but that just seems like a cop out to me. It's not like there aren't places Dad wouldn't hear him. I don't think Jaxon and Declan are as indifferent or as disgusted by Harlow as Jacinta thinks they are. Jaxon already admitted to having a connection with her when they met that time in the club. I can certainly see what attracted him to her in the first place, and it's not only her looks. She's funny and interesting, someone I wouldn't mind getting to know better.

I'm not even jealous that my brother is interested in her either. Nana's suggestion about sharing her is appealing to me more and more. I mean, what are the odds that we would each find a partner that got along with everyone? Plus, with our collective total of horrible relationship experience, having more than one of us with her would give Harlow someone to rely on when the others had fucked up again.

Shifting, the pain in my ass making me wince, distracting everyone. They laugh at my misfortune, but it's not enough to distract Jacinta and she turns on me. "What about you? You in or out?"

"I'm out. I like her and want to get to know her better, though I'm pretty sure I screwed that up already. I'll do whatever I can to make it up to her. Leave her alone, Jacinta, and worry about getting your own shit together. From what I can see, you're doing a good job of blowing it up without any help from her at all. What are you so afraid of? It can't be just because you think she's after our money. There's got to be a deeper reason for you to be acting so extreme. No one in the past has caused you to go off the deep end like this. You need to think about the answers to those questions. You're my sister, and I love you...."

I get to my feet, the beer and the weed making the pain more bearable. "But don't come crying to me if you screw things so badly that Dad never forgives you."

With that parting remark, I hobble to my room wishing that I was hobbling to Harlow's instead.

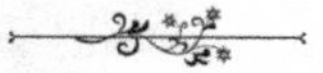

The next morning, I'm up early, having made a plan last night. I want to see if I can get Harlow to talk to me again, and to do that, I need to be where she is. So that means I'm watching her work her horses this morning. I may even offer my assistance. I mean, how different can it be to working a normal horse? Each and every one of us knows how to do that, even if I don't ride as often as my siblings.

After examining my ass in the mirror and discovering a rainbow-colored bruise that still hurts, I make my way downstairs to breakfast, thinking I might be able to get Harlow on her own before she goes out. Would she forgive me if I had the bruise made permanent in a tattoo? A forever reminder to never be a dick unless I want to get bit in the ass. Snorting in amusement at my own idea, I head toward the main living area.

But when I get there, it looks like I'm not the only one who had the same idea. Every one of my siblings is there, all dressed casually, looking like none of them have any intention of going into their respective offices today.

Nana gets me a plate of food when she sees me wincing, ruffling my hair and giving me a kiss on the cheek as she places it in front of me. Out of the corner of my eye, I notice Harlow coming into the room, but I'm too busy listening to Nana. She whispers in my ear, "Make this right, boy" before going back to her place.

My eyes meet hers, and I nod, the wordless response bringing a smile to Nana's face, and at least I can rest a little easier knowing that she's in my corner.

Chapter Seven

Harlow

The alarm wakes me early the next morning, Princess following my socked feet as I quietly make my way to the kitchen, carrying my boots. I guess she's decided to spend the day somewhere other than my room. Though I won't be surprised if my sleepover buddy is back in my room just in time for bed.

When I hit the living area expecting to find nobody, I'm surprised to see everyone is not only awake, but they're also having breakfast.

"Morning, Harlow." Dad's cheery voice is followed up with a round of grumpy grunts and head nods from all the various siblings. "We only use the formal dining room occasionally, so most of the time you'll find us in here," he explains, obviously seeing my surprise.

What the actual fuck is going on? Did everyone get bodysnatched by aliens overnight? I mean, they're not friendly, but they're not acting downright hostile like they usually are.

Shaking off my confusion, I mumble back a greeting as I get a cup of coffee from the side cabinet before sitting down. Princess has followed me the entire time, and when I sit down, she quickly jumps into my lap before I can pull my chair in.

"Stolen my cat, have you, Harlow?" Declan's tone is *almost* neutral, but the tightness of his eyes tips me off to the undercurrent of bitterness that tells the truth.

I run my hand over her back before taking a sip of my coffee and smiling at him. "Sorry, dude, I can't help that I keep finding her in my room. Someone must be letting her in because I always find the door cracked open."

Nana frowns at my reply, and I can see Declan flinch slightly. *Would he really let his cat into my room just so he has a reason to bitch at me? Petty level 1,000.* I study his face but then shake myself mentally. No, he wouldn't do that; he dotes on the cat. Picking Princess up, I walk around to his side and dump her gently in his lap so that I can get myself some food. "You should take better care of a queen who's about to give birth. It's almost time to lock her down in a room so she doesn't give birth in some random place," I suggest to him.

With barely enough room to take a breath, he

snarls, "I know. It's not my first time doing this. I've had other cats that have had kittens." But then he turns back to his cat, and out of the corner of my eye I watch as he snuggles into her, rubbing his face against hers as she does that ragdoll thing and flops into him, her purring louder than I've ever heard. The sight makes me smile, so I quickly turn, not needing to show any extra ounce of connection to my asshole "siblings." It would be cute if he wasn't such a dick. *Who am I kidding? It's cute even though he's a dick.*

When I've got enough food, I sit back down at the table and look around. The atmosphere is relaxed, and nobody seems to be in a hurry like the last breakfast I attended. It's then I realize everyone is wearing casual clothes. *Duh, Harlow, it's Saturday.* Damn it, I assumed I'd have the place to myself. Well, no matter, I've got a busy day planned. I can't wait to get the horses worked so that I can go on my little adventure.

Quickly finishing up my breakfast and coffee, I wish everyone a good day and take my plate through to the kitchen before putting my boots on and slipping out the other door. I've got to get all four horses into stables, brushed and tacked up, and that always takes a while when you're working with more than one animal.

But when I get down to the yards they were in, they sit empty, and I finally remember that Luke is here too. I guess maybe that's not a bad thing. He, or maybe Josh, has already stabled them for me, and that's going to save me a small amount of time.

So I head over to the stables, the sound of horse hooves banging on the floor bringing a smile to my face. Someone is impatient this morning.

Cross-tied in the middle of the stable walk way is the pretty white mare, Delilah. She's being brushed by Josh, and a couple of feet behind him, Luke has Hercules saddled and ready to go.

"Wow, look at you guys go! That makes my life a little easier."

Josh smiles at me but Luke just nods, his eyes scanning up and down my body in a way that makes me feel weirded out. *And that's why I tirelessly avoided him whenever possible.* Hiding a grimace, I turn to Delilah and run my hand over her muzzle.

"Brad called down last night and asked for me to give you a hand. He says you've got plans for later this afternoon." My heart warms at my dad's thoughtfulness. I'm pretty sure he thinks my fascination with abandoned buildings is a little weird, but it's nice to know he supports it whether he understands it or not.

"And it's not like I'm all that busy. This really is the cushiest stable manager's position I've ever had. When any of the Summers actually ride, they do everything themselves. All I really have to do is feed them and ride an occasional horse if one of the others doesn't have time. Oh, and look after

Prada." He nods toward the palomino mare. *So that's what her name is. Figures.*

"Thank you anyway, I really appreciate it. Do you know what the driver did with my safety gear?"

"Yeah, I put it in the tack room," he says, waving his hand in that direction.

Giving Delilah a final pat on the neck, I head over to grab my things. The door sits open, and when I enter, the rich smell of leather fills my nose, making me smile. There's nothing better than the smell of freshly cleaned tack.... except maybe Oliver's car. *Stupid man, why did he have to go and ruin it?* A smile crosses my face, though this time it's driven by a twist of wicked satisfaction. *I wonder what his ass looks like today*. See, if he hadn't gone against me like that, I could've been kissing it better for him right now. Maybe even distracting him from his pain with a bit of pleasure. Stupid man.

Needing to focus on anything besides Oliver's ass and all the things I wish I could be doing to it, I shake my head like I can fling those thoughts away. My bag is on one of the shelves, and I dig out my safety vest and my helmet, eager to get going. I pull on my vest first, making sure it's fastened correctly before securing my helmet on my head. Lying on the floor in front of me are a couple of practice jousting lances and my padded jousting jacket. Looks like Chuck wants me to practice jousting too. Maybe that's why he sent Luke. Though I am a little reluctant to do it again so close to my injury. I'll leave it as a last resort.

Heading back out, I approach Luke and Hercules, a large Holstiener chestnut gelding, a little on the heavier side. Makes him a perfect horse to carry around a knight in armor, which, given the jousting equipment, might be pretty likely for this movie.

"I noticed the jousting lances, but I don't think we'll work on that today. Maybe later in the week," I suggest, and his eyes widen slightly, looking worried, before nodding his head.

"Yeah, okay, sounds good." I almost snort out loud at his obvious concern. Luke doesn't usually work the horses through their stunts; he's strictly exercise work, but I may as well use him while he's here. Plus, Chuck's been trying to give him a better range of skills, so this will be good practice for him.

I unclip Hercules and walk him out of the stable block through the tunnel that leads to the indoor arena on the other side of the stable. The smell of sawdust meets my nose as I walk into the large covered grounds and look around, a whistle escaping my mouth. Wow, I thought Chuck's was fancy, but this is *amazing*. It's at least the size of two dressage arenas, and on one side there's tiered stadium-style seating for viewing purposes. On the opposite side to the seating, the wall is covered with mirrors, making it easier for the rider to see what their horse is doing. Over near the stands I can see a bluetooth docking station.

Smiling, I pull my phone out of my pocket and pick out one of my favorite playlists before heading over and putting it into the dock. Immediately, my warmup playlist comes through the speakers, and Hercules' ears prick up, the horse throwing his head and snorting. He knows it's work time and is ready to go. I'm just about to head over to him when a hand on my back has me jumping almost a mile high. Turning around, Luke is right there in my face.

"Holy shit, Luke! I didn't even hear you come in," I tell him, my breathing a little fast with the adrenaline now flowing through my system. He laughs but removes his hand from my back.

"I just thought I'd give you a leg up since you hurt your knee before you left," he answers, holding out his hands.

"Oh yeah, good thinking. I was wondering if I was going to be able to get up there. He's so freaking tall." My knee has been feeling pretty good, especially after lying around and wallowing in my misery with Alex, but every now and then I get a twinge that reminds me I shouldn't over strain it. Luke's offer is very thoughtful even if the thought of him having his hands on me grosses me out.

I gather up the reins in my hand and step onto Luke's waiting cupped hands. With a boost, up I go, throwing my leg over the saddle and slipping my feet into the stirrups.

"Thank you, that was much easier than doing it on my own." I smile at him, and he beams back. For once, the moment between us isn't weird.

"I'll just go and get Zeus and Samson ready," he suggests.

"Sounds like a plan! I really appreciate the extra help. You're saving me so much time."

He leaves, and I nudge Hercules with my heels so he starts walking around the indoor arena. In my head, I'm already planning what I'm going to do today. Hercules has been trained to do a number of moves on command, but instead of practicing those, I'll just work him through a walk, trot, and canter dressage routine with some lateral movements. After that, maybe a few flying changes, all used to keep up his fitness and flexibility for when he's doing big chase scenes, joust scenes, or even if he'll be required to die for the cameras. It can be quite taxing on a big animal, so we keep them as fit as possible.

As Hercules walks around the arena, I drop the reins and use my legs to guide him, not that he really needs it. Stretching out, I warm my body up too. Windmilling my arms and twisting my torso, I take some deep breaths in and out, my body going with the flow of the animal. I haven't ridden since I came off Samson awkwardly, and I don't want to be stiff. After a couple of rounds, I gather up the reins, and when a faster-paced song comes on, I nudge him into a trot.

A feeling of freedom and relaxation flows through me, and a huge smile crosses my face. Ever since I arrived in California, I've felt off balance and like I'm two steps behind, scrambling to keep up. But right now, with this powerful creature between my legs, doing what I love... Right now, everything seems to have centered itself. I feel in control and steadier, and it feels *good*. Like taking a breath of air after being underwater for too long. The ache in my chest has gone, and my mind is clear and focused. I really hadn't realized how bad it had gotten until right now. And right now, while everything is crystal clear, I promise myself to take better care of myself.

I've been so focused on revenge and the anger that Jacinta inspired in me that I really hadn't acknowledged that it was fucking with my soul, not just my feelings. That's not really the type of person I am, and as much as they hurt me, they really aren't my priority. Brad and Nana and Poppy are. They're who I'm here for. Yeah, it would have been nice to gel with his other kids, but it really isn't important, and if I start a war with them, then I'm no better than them. I mean, if I get an opportunity to get a little bit of payback, I'll probably take it, but I think the ridiculous things that Alex and I came up with under the influence were going a little too far. Using sex as a weapon? Manipulating their feelings? No. I'm not my mother, and I never want to be like her. I close my eyes for as long as I dare, taking a deep breath to refocus myself in the freedom of the moment. Shane was right trying to rein us in. I'm just glad I didn't put any in to action just yet.

Now that we're both warmed up, I put Hercules through his paces, moving from trot to canter then back to trot and walk. First making large circles and smaller circles then moving to half pass movements across the arena and figure eights with flying change in the middle. We follow that by doing sliding stops, finishing by moving from a standstill directly into a canter. Hercules does it all with ease. Once he's done, I put Delilah and Zeus through the same kind of routine, and by the time Luke returns with Samson, I've been working with them for three hours and need a break.

Sliding down off of Zeus, my knees threaten to buckle once I'm on solid ground, but I manage to stay standing. *8/10 for dismount.* Once Luke and I exchange reins, me taking Samson's and Luke taking Zeus', I take a minute to check out the spectators that have gathered throughout the morning.

Somehow, Dad, Nana, Poppy, and all of the Summers siblings have made themselves comfortable in the stands. They must've drifted in at their own pace because I might get a bit oblivious to the world while I ride, but they're a large crew. I definitely would've noticed if they'd come in en masse.

"Dad, could you come and hold Samson while I get a drink?" I call up to him, and a wide grin covers his handsome face as he stands up and comes down the stairs toward us. He reaches out for the reins and Samson snorts, throwing his head, but he quickly brings it back down so Dad can stroke his velvety soft nose.

Following him down, Nana hands me a bottle of water before stepping closer to inspect Samson.

"Thanks so much, I was just going to stick my head under the tap in the bathroom. I didn't think to bring anything out," I gasp in between guzzling the entire bottle.

"There's a stocked fridge in the stables if you need something, as well as one at the top of the stands," Nana literally points out.

As my eyes scan the stands, Poppy smiles and waves, Kai doing the same, but none of the others make an effort. I can see Jacinta and Jaxon whispering furiously to one another, and Declan has his phone in his hand and appears to be reading something. He and Holden seem to be chatting about something. Both Oliver and Thomas are staring at me, the former's eyes sparkling with heat as well as a touch of annoyance. I can see he's sitting on a cushion, and I can't help snickering quietly in amusement. Thomas, on the other hand, has a look of contemplation on his face, like he's considering something he never has before.

The absence of hostility being directed at me

like a heat-seeking missile is both refreshing and perturbing at the same time. Maybe they're biding their time? I'd be a fool to think that one slap on the wrist from Dad would be enough to calm their thirst for blood.

When I turn back around, Dad is looking carefully at the saddle. "What's this thing for?"

When I look at where he's pointing, I notice that Luke has saddled him with his trick riding saddle. It's similar to a western saddle, but it has a long pole sitting where the horn would be. "Oh, that's the trick saddle. I didn't realize he was putting that one on though. I'll get him to change it."

Both Nana and Dad's faces light up with excitement. "Do you think you could give us a demonstration?" Dad asks, looking like a little kid on Christmas.

Nana adds her own eager pleas, seeing the immediate hesitation on my face. "Oh, please, Harlow! That would be so exciting."

"He's all warmed up for you, Harlow. I had him on the lunge outside while you were finishing with Zeus," Luke calls from the entrance to the arena. He's holding the long whip in one hand and has obviously returned Zeus to where he belongs. Crap, my knee is a little achy now, but as I scan the stands again, I can see them all watching me, Jacinta with a smug look on her face. If I say no, they're going to think I'm intimidated by them.

"All right," I reluctantly agree, taking the reins

back from Dad as Luke enters the arena, carrying the whip.

I hand the reins to Luke, and he heads to the other end of the arena from me as I move into the middle.

"What are you doing?" Dad's eyes are sparkling with curiosity, and there's a part of me that's almost preening to be the center of his interest. Chuck was always hands on with me, so I didn't miss out on having that fatherly interest growing up, but it's nice to know that Brad is also invested in what I can do.

I wave him and Nana away. "Go back and sit down so you're out of the way. I don't want to worry about where you are," I tell them and start rolling my shoulders and arms, warming up the muscles. This move I have planned always wrenches them a bit.

They hurry back into the stands, and once they're seated, I nod to Luke. Seeing my signal, he waves the whip at Samson, the Friesian cantering toward me at a rapid pace. His hooves thunder across the ground, causing a ripple of vibrations that can be felt through the soles of my boots, his long black mane flying behind him.

I need to time this just right, and as he goes to pass me, I reach up and grab the pole, using his forward momentum to pull me up and over his back. I land smoothly in the saddle then circle him back around to the cheers of Nana, Poppy, Dad, and Kai. The others look stunned, and if I'm reading Jacinta correctly, there's the tiniest drop to her jaw, like she can't believe I did it. Before I can be sure of what I saw, she snaps her mouth closed, lips pressed in a firm line. *Still in the negative on bonding points with that one.* Thomas, Holden, and Oliver all join in with the applause while the other three continue their stony silence, but I can see the hint of admiration in both Declan and Jaxon's eyes.

I circle Samson a couple of times before getting him to do a sliding stop in front of them. Using the correct cues, I have him bowing down, earning more enthusiastic applause from the spectators.

Next, he rises up onto his back legs to a soundtrack of gasps, but before I can give him the cue to drop, the saddle shifts. Without warning, it's sliding down off his back and I'm falling with it.

Thankfully, I'm able to kick myself clear and land with a thud on the ground, the sawdust digging into my back where my shirt has risen up. Quickly, I crawl out of the way as the saddle gets stuck around his back legs. Samson doesn't like that, and he takes off down the arena, saddle dragging, until he finally gets clear. He canters back toward the stable, and I just hope Luke or Josh catch him when he gets there.

"Oh my god, Harlow! Are you okay?" Nana rushes over to me followed by some of the others. Of course when I look up into the stands, the terrible trio haven't moved. In fact, they all watch on with amusement, Jacinta's face made ugly by a smug smile.

Holden holds out a hand to me with a concerned smile, and without comment, I accept it so he can help me to my feet. Dusting myself off, I wave them all away as I head over to the saddle. I can't believe Luke didn't check it to make sure it was done up enough. Most horses have a habit of blowing themselves out, and the girth has to be tightened after you've started working to make sure it doesn't slip. This is everyday procedure for readying a horse, and frankly, if he's making mistakes that basic, I might need to put in a call to Chuck.

Picking up the saddle, I dust it off and start to undo the still closed girth, but I notice something. The leather girth is *broken*. The saddle didn't slip; the girth snapped, and it got tangled. That's unusual; our equipment is all well looked after, so it shouldn't have been able to wear through, but when I look close, the rip is too clean.

It's been cut. Someone has cut through far enough that the natural movement of the horse did the rest.

"Is that what I think it is?" I look up at Dad's question to find him staring at the same thing I'd been studying, his jaw clenched.

"Yeah, it's been cut."

"Oh my god, but who would have done that?" Nana gasps in surprise, looking between Dad and Poppy. Behind them, Kai, Oliver, Thomas, and

Holden all look at one another before turning to look at the stands.

My eyes follow theirs, and when I get to the three who stayed behind, a wave of anger rises. Jacinta is staring right at me, arms crossed, cold smirk on her face. I can't believe she just did that. My pride and reputation are one thing, but my physical well-being is another. That's hitting an all new level of low.

How can her animosity be so great that she stoops to *hurting* me like this? *I thought* I *had issues...*

Chapter Eight

Holden

Watching in silent amusement as Harlow manages to ruffle my older brother's very polished feathers, I can't help but smile, though I quickly hide it behind my coffee cup. Declan strives so hard to be in control all the time, and sure, he can let loose and have fun, but he doesn't show that side of him in public. No, he shows the public the cold and icy demeanor he's known for: the powerful head of one of the most elite production and talent companies around. Women flock to him, and he enjoys their company, but none of them ever have an emotional impact on him. Watching Harlow elicit any kind of reaction is interesting, and to be honest, I think it's good for my brother to have someone who isn't scared of him, who isn't willing to roll over and show their belly the minute he growls.

She's such a delicious surprise. I'm finding I like her assertiveness, and that's usually not what appeals to me in a partner. I like submissive, pliant people who are easy to control. But Harlow... well, she's different, and I'm dangerously intrigued by the idea of having a partner like her. There's something about her that makes *me* want to submit, and that's such a novel idea that I don't know how I can't pursue this. Even right now, my cock is showing how much it appreciates her, and I'm thanking god I'm sitting at the table and no one else can see.

I watch as she quietly eats her breakfast. She's wearing a t-shirt that says 'My other ride is a Friesian' and a pair of black riding pants that hug her gorgeous figure in just the right way. Her beautiful blonde hair is pulled back into a braid, and she hasn't got a scrap of makeup on.

The first time I saw her, it struck me how beautiful she was. How beautiful and completely different to the usual women in our lives. Instead of artificial and made up, she was fresh-faced and natural, and the way she put Jaxon in his place after he'd attacked her had made my cock hard, but I ignored it for the sake of my family. The minute Jacinta declared war, I knew I wouldn't have a chance with her.

Our sister's determination to make Harlow's life

hell was a surefire way to get her to hate us whether we wanted that outcome or not. The way Jaxon and Declan cave to her demands all the time drives me nuts. I understand they never want to see her hurting like she used to when she was little, but I think they took it too far this time, and I'm thankful Dad has put his foot down. Now I can get to know her, and none of them can say anything about it. Even if they do, I'm not going along with anything anymore. I had to give up the most important thing to me when we came to this house, and I refuse to give up anything else just because someone might not approve or it might upset my sister. Nope, it's time for me to have the things I want, and what I want is to get to know Harlow better. I'll beg for her forgiveness if I have to. I just want a chance.

When Harlow finishes breakfast and disappears from the table, Dad turns on us, all smiles having disappeared the moment she did.

"You will come out there and watch her today and show her some support," he growls, pinning us with a gaze that tells us he doesn't want any arguments, but of course Jacinta and Declan both have to give it a shot. Jaxon, the third musketeer, is strangely quiet.

"But, Dad, I don't need to see…" Jacinta starts, but her voice trails off when Nana holds up her hand.

"It's not like you have anything else pressing, do

you, dear?" Nana's brittle smile and icy question make her meaning clear; she loves us, but she's *never* hesitated to put us in our places. Jacinta stops immediately, her eyes flashing with the annoyance that she's no longer voicing.

Declan tries his luck next, the fool. "Dad, you know you wanted me to call and find out what's delaying the set and when the horses will be needed?"

Dad frowns before raising an eyebrow, his expression clearly saying that he's not buying where this is going. "Yeah, and so what?"

"Well, I was planning on going into the office to do that and get a few more things done." *Yep, he really just tried that. Oh, there's Dad's eye roll. He got the frown* and *the eye roll. Just quit while you're definitely not ahead, big brother.*

"You've got a phone, son, and we have a perfectly good office here. You can go and sit in there if you need quiet. Don't give me any of your bullshit trying to get out of this." He looks around the table, another wave of disappointment crossing his face. "I don't think you guys understood me. Even if you can't accept her as a sister, I want you to try and be *friends* with the girl. She will be in your lives for the rest of it, and I want her to feel comfortable coming and going as she pleases, not turning down invitations to Christmas and special occasions because the seven of you are childish."

Poppy hasn't had a lot to say, but I can see things running through his mind. "Your father's right. We don't expect you to embrace her as a sister. That was never our intention, and I think you may find that if you get to know her, she's a funny, kind, and beautiful person. No matter what life threw at her, she picked herself up, dusted herself off, and just kept going. If you all gave her a chance, she would be able to fill a role each and every one of you have been searching for." His words are kind of confusing, and when I look around the table, it's clear I'm not the only one feeling like that. Oliver's the only one who doesn't seem as confused as the rest of us, but I can't imagine what secret *he* knows that the rest of us don't. *Did something happen between him and Harlow when she spent the day at Neighpalm Ink?*

A blinding wave of jealousy courses through me at the thought of Oliver and Harlow, but that soon fades to something else. Clenching my fists under the table, I bite my tongue so that the words I've been dying to say don't come flooding out and ruining everything. How is it that even after so many years I still feel this way? Maybe I always will. Maybe it's time to have another conversation with him and get all of it out in the open.

"Anyway, finish up! When you get a chance, head on out to the arena, please." Dad's words are final. Nobody bothers arguing this time, having realized resistance is futile today.

The three older adults leave the table and disappear, leaving me with my siblings. Jacinta starts to grumble the moment they're out of sight, but Kai holds his hand up, stopping her. "Just fucking stop. I don't want to hear it. Leave me out of anything you have planned because if I don't know I can't tell Harlow."

"You'd choose *her* over me? Someone you don't even know? Wanting to stay out of it is one thing, Kai, but you'd actually give her a heads up?" Jacinta sounds surprised, but I'm not. I know Kai is fed up with the way the others are always chasing off women. He wants a relationship, not just one night stands. Even more than that, he wants a family, but our sister doesn't make it easy for us even if she is right most of the time. It's not like this is the first time he's made it clear that he wants no involvement; Jacinta has just always had a way of hearing what she wants and throwing the rest out as she pleases.

"It's not a matter of choosing her over you. I just want the chance to get to know her. I want to make my own decisions based on my own opinions, not on one you formed in five seconds flat. You saw a beautiful, intelligent woman, and your claws came out. I bet if she wasn't attractive, if she was mousy and quiet, none of you would have looked sideways at her." He's angry as his gaze moves from Jacinta to Declan and then lands on Jaxon. Holy shit! The easy going one is losing his shit. Kai's always so chill and relaxed most of the time; nothing really ever fazes him. To be having this kind of reaction tells me this means more to him than I thought.

Unlike Oliver, the only history I have with Kai is that of a brother. While I'm not entirely sure how I feel about the latter's clear interest in Harlow, I know I'm not immediately unsettled or uncomfortable in Kai's. While I'm lost in my own head, the others are still going back and forth, and I tune back in right in time to hear what he's dishing out to Jaxon.

"And don't get me started with *you*. She didn't even know her mother had died when she met you, so she wouldn't have known who her father was let alone his connection with you. You think too much of yourself, and you always have."

A scowl crosses Jaxon's face, but he doesn't say anything. Kai stands up from the table, and this time, his gaze includes Oliver, Thomas, and me. "Don't make me choose this time. You might not like what decision I make." He strides away, each step a thud that telegraphs how unhappy he is with us right now, and nobody tries to stop him.

Thomas leans back in his chair, looking our sister directly in the eye. "Look, I don't want to see this family divided, but the guy's not wrong. We're not those led by our dick teenagers anymore, Jacinta. Each and every one of us got burned, and we all learned from our mistakes."

Tears well in her eyes. I don't think any of us has ever gone against her like this before. That, combined with losing her business, even if it is only temporary, must really be a blow to her confidence. I genuinely feel sorry for her, and it's obvious Thomas does too. His voice gentles, and he reaches out a hand to grab hold of hers.

"We love that you want to protect us, but you're going to have to let us make our own mistakes. We're big boys, and Dad's not stupid either. You may think that he's not using his smarts because his emotions are involved, but I guarantee you he is. Not to mention Nana and Poppy have known the girl for years. They wouldn't steer us wrong; both of them are fiercely protective of this family."

She swallows down her tears and nods, not saying anything else, but I can still see that glint in her eye. I'm not sure if any of this has helped or if it's just made it worse.

Before I can say anything, my phone rings, a smile crossing my face when I realize it's Hope, calling me. I didn't have anything scheduled with her, so I wonder what she could want. Hope and I have been friends since college. In fact, you could say she's my best friend apart from my brothers. Put together as part of a group project, Hope and I did most of the work and ended up bonding over mutual frustration with our lazy group members. Despite her being one of the only women I trust, neither of us ever felt romantically inclined toward the other. We regularly act as wingmen for the other or rescue one another when dates get too clingy. It's worked well, and Hope is one of the few females Jacinta accepts and is friendly with as well.

"Morning, Hope, what can I do for you?" I ask, getting up from the table and walking away from my siblings. I'm not sure if that conversation is going to erupt into chaos or not but better to put some space between us.

"Fuck, Den, have you looked at the gossip rags today?" Hope's question has my heartbeat speeding up as I head back to my room and open up my laptop.

"No, I've only just had breakfast. We've had some family drama, so I'm a little behind on things. What's going on? Which one of our highly paid idiots has made a fool of themselves now?"

I swear, managing a record label is like trying to herd cats. Trying to convince our artists to keep all the dramatics behind closed doors is a nightmare. Most are pretty good, but we've got a few who I'm seriously considering dropping thanks to the headaches they regularly cause us.

"Ninja Starfish." Surprise has me almost pulling the phone from my ear as though a little distance from her words will help it all make sense.

"Really? That's not who I thought you were going to say at all." I can't hide the shock that I feel, and she laughs at it.

"Yeah, it's not the usual suspects for a change. Turns out that there are more issues than just the members not getting along. Jessie and Cash got into it at a club last night. There are photos of the brawl, and then they were both arrested, but thankfully, no charges were pressed. They were released a few hours later," Hope explains, the echoey quality to her words telling me she's on the road with the call on speaker.

"What was the fight about?" I ask as I run my fingers over the keys of my laptop, bringing up the main gossip pages. Sure enough, splashed across the screen are the two members of Ninja Starfish. Can't see the other three though, so that's a bit of a relief.

"I'm not a hundred percent sure, but it looks like it's about a girl."

"Fuck my life," I groan, and she just laughs. She's always been the bright one of the two of us. Even though their drama is as much her headache as it is mine, she has a way of keeping herself smiling no matter what shit she needs to do to keep Neighpalm as clean as possible.

"I'm going to organize a meeting with them later on in the week. Give them a few days to cool down then bring them in to explain their actions and see if we can get to the bottom of it all."

I run a hand through my hair in frustration while reading the story. Ninja Starfish was put together by a reality TV program that Declan's company ran a few years ago. There's always been a little tension in the group since they were kind of forced together in the beginning. All five of them auditioned as solo artists and weren't expecting to have to work with others, but I thought they'd become good friends. There have been a few issues recently, but I thought they had sorted through them. I guess I was wrong.

"Yeah, okay, sounds like a plan. I also got a call from Jeremy. He wanted to set something up; the guys have something they want to talk to me about. Do you think you could be available for that too, just in case?"

"Sure, get your PA to send the appointment to my calendar, and I'll work around it," she tells me. "So... how are things at home?" she asks carefully, her voice lowering at the delicate topic.

I blow out a deep breath before flopping down on my bed. "Tense. I think we really screwed up this time."

"You think?" The sarcasm isn't hard to miss. "What was Jacinta thinking?" Hope had been the one to organize the press conference the day of the billboard, and she also knows the mechanics of our sister's brain very well. No matter how we played it to the public, Hope knows this has Jacinta's name all over it.

"I don't know. Dad is *so* mad at us. In fact, I have to go and do some family bonding as per his orders this morning." She snorts, completely unsympathetic to my fate.

"I thought he was going to have a coronary that day. I have never seen your father that mad, ever."

"No, me neither. He's usually so calm and collected, but then I guess he had reason to be. That's his daughter splashed across the billboard, branded a gold digger. I understand Jacinta needing to do something; I mean, she is who she is, but I think making a public move was really crossing a huge line for him."

After a few more words, I end the call and sit up. Putting my phone in my pocket, I head out to the riding arena, quietly excited to watch this gorgeous woman. *Though I think I'd much prefer she be riding me instead.*

The rest of my family is already sitting and watching by the time I make it into the arena, and I'm greeted with another fatherly frown when I grab a seat with them.

"Sorry, Hope called with an emergency," I explain, and his face clears.

"Okay, grab a seat."

I climb up the stairs and take a seat next to Thomas. Oliver and Kai are on the other side of him, with Declan, Jacinta, and Jaxon behind us one step up.

"Where have you been?" Thomas asks mildly, his eyes never leaving the horse and woman down in the arena.

Harlow is on the back of a large bay, easily

putting him through his paces. They're beautiful to watch, their bodies moving fluidly in sync, and for a moment, I can't tear my eyes away, but Thomas nudges me to get my attention. A full smirk and raised brow greet me when I turn to face him, so I answer quickly to get his mind going in a different direction.

"Oh, ah, Hope called. Ninja Starfish hit the tabloids last night."

He frowns in surprise, echoing my own skepticism when I heard the news.

"Yeah, that's what I thought. I've got a meeting later in the week to see what that's all about." He smiles and leans back against Jacinta's legs, relaxing into the contact in a way that he only does with family. She smiles down at him, ruffling his hair, but her gaze quickly returns to Harlow, narrowing as soon as she's in her sights.

"So glad I don't have that kind of shit like you, Dec, and Jacinta. Artists and models can be so temperamental."

I turn back to watch as she brings the horse to a stop. Dad, Nana, and Poppy erupt into applause, and I automatically join in with the others.

She gives the animal a pat on the shoulder, talking quietly with him before sliding down to the ground. There's a quiver in her legs, and my mind remembers that she was injured before she came here. I'm just about to stand up, wanting to head down to help, when she manages to stand her ground on her own. By the time she's got herself collected, a guy I don't recognize enters the arena, walking a prancing black Friesian toward her. He's eyeing her like she's a snack he'd like to eat, and a wave of jealousy rolls through my body, surprising me.

A whistle out of Jaxon's mouth takes me away from having to analyze that uncomfortable reaction. "Now, *that* is a magnificent animal." He's leaning forward with interest, but a nudge from Jacinta has him sitting back again. God, he lets her walk all over him. I know it's survivor's guilt or whatever, but dude, man up. My eye roll is in no way hidden, earning me a scowl from my very bitter sister, but I learned a long time ago to not let Jacinta's moods hold me down.

"You're going to end up very sorry if you keep going," I warn her.

"Shut up, Holden," she hisses so that the parentals can't hear.

A ping on my phone has me looking at it to check who's sending me a message now, but it's just an automated one confirming the meeting for the following week. I tap the confirmation button and tuck it back into my pocket.

"Is that a trick saddle?" Kai asks, sounding excited, and Poppy turns around to answer. Given the guy runs our extreme teams, it's safe to say that he likes anything with a little twist of action or adrenaline. If she nails all these tricks, she might just be the woman of his dreams.

"Yep, they use them when training certain movements. It's safer for the rider, but in the actual film they use proper saddles."

Kai nods with enthusiasm, leaning forward for a closer look. "So we're going to see a few tricks?"

"I guess so, though she did look surprised to see it." Poppy shrugs, the little crease between his brows giving away that he's not feeling 100% enthusiastic about this idea. "I hope her knee is okay for this."

It feels like ages ago, when in reality it's only been a week. Even if she's not using the crutches she had when she arrived, there's a decent chance she's still in some kind of pain or discomfort.

Harlow walks to the middle, rolling her shoulders, as Nana and Dad come back to the stands. Her face shows nothing but focus, and there's this ease to the way she moves that says none of this is a big deal to her. She's in charge down there, and the rarely-present sub in me is sitting up and taking notice again.

"What's going on?" Oliver asks, a small amount of concern in his voice. He's been very subdued since they spent time at the shop, apart from having his ass bit by the pony yesterday, and it's not quite like him. He's not one to be affected by a woman. I can't help the little twinge of jealousy that prickles just under my skin at the thought. Declan snorts behind me but I don't turn around.

"Harlow's going to give us a demonstration," Dad says before shushing us all with a wave of his hand.

By the time she finishes the first trick, we're all applauding, amazed at the feat of agility. Kai whoops, impressed with her athletic ability no doubt.

After a couple of circles, she slides the horse to a stop in front of us, digging a groove in the arena floor, and I hear Jacinta tut over it but ignore her. Josh will fix it up when she's done. It's not like Jacinta has to do the work herself. The horse then bows down in front of us before it rears back on its hinds legs. Nana sucks in a breath, but my eyes are on the beautiful blonde, and I see her gasp in shock as she slips slightly. Suddenly, the saddle and Harlow are sliding backward, heading for the ground, and I jump to my feet waiting for the impending disaster.

She kicks herself free but still hits the ground with a thud as the horse takes off, bucking himself clear of the saddle before disappearing. I'm the first one to move, but before I make it down the steps, I hear Kai hissing behind me, "You better not have had anything to do with this." I turn back and see him staring daggers at Jacinta, but her face looks as shocked as the rest of us. Either she's a really good actress, or she doesn't know anything about this.

Nana is already to Harlow by the time I get to her, and I hold out my hand, with a smile, to help her out of the dust. She takes it but quickly lets go and stalks over to the saddle, either not wanting that much contact with me or too rattled to stand still and be coddled. I find myself hoping it's the latter, which is another sign that I might have more interest in this woman than I should. She stares at the saddle, Dad saying something to her too quietly for me to hear, but her response comes through loud and clear.

"Yeah, it's been cut." Her voice is flat, almost too flat to be believable. She's got to be even more rattled now. It's one thing for her to almost get hurt by mistake. For this to be a set-up? I mean, I'd be feeling pretty fucked up right now if I were her.

"Oh my god, but who could have done that?" Nana gasps, and as one, Oliver, Thomas, Kai, and I swing to look in the direction of our sister. Her face shows a myriad of emotions, shock and concern amongst them, but then it swiftly moves to amusement as a smirk crosses her lips. I'd like to think Jacinta wouldn't have done this, but the messages are a bit mixed right now, and I definitely need to sort through this to figure out what's the truth.

"She has gone a little bit too far this time," Thomas murmurs to me, and I nod my head in response. "Someone is going to have to keep an eye on her. Maybe we shouldn't let Harlow be alone anymore," he suggests. "If Jaxon isn't going to do anything about this and Declan's going to keep playing along too, we might have a real problem on our hands."

I don't answer, still shocked at the fact that Jacinta could possibly hurt Harlow like that. I think my sister might be losing her shit.

Chapter Nine

Harlow

After my fall from Samson's back, I really should have brought him back to the arena and kept working him, but I'm a little shaken, understandably so, with the knowledge that someone deliberately tried to hurt me.

As I leave the arena, Dad's shouting echoes behind me. He hadn't pointed specific fingers, but he'd whirled on his children and started shouting at them, his face red with anger. Their denials were fast and just as loud, and I hadn't wanted to stick around, so I carried the saddle back to the tack room, leaving it with Josh. He assured me he'd fix it, but honestly, I'd rather buy a new one than have to look at that one again.

"Josh, have you ever explored the house across the road?" I ask, my need for distraction getting the better of me. It's much more pleasant to think about than my narrowly avoided injury. He carries more gear back into the tack room while Luke finishes brushing Samson for me. When he returns, there's an amused smile on his face.

"No, I haven't. There's a huge fence around it, so I'm not even sure you could get in. I know there was a caretaker for a while too, paid by the lawyers for the estate, but I'm pretty sure he passed a few years ago." He leans against one of the empty stalls, eyeing me curiously. "Why do you ask?"

I laugh, sheepishly looking down at my feet, my cheeks turning pink in embarrassment.

"I have this thing for old abandoned buildings. I find them fascinating."

"Well, it's not really abandoned, more that it's empty, being held in trust for any living relatives that can be found. I mean, after this many years, I'm pretty sure the count and his son aren't planning on returning, but you never know, a relative may pop out of the woodwork."

"What's the story there? Nana told me some but not much."

"One day, the count and his son just disappeared, no word, no sign of them. The son had had a girlfriend, and she was brought in for questioning, but they had to let her go since they had no leads. Even now, nobody really knows what happened. There are all sorts of rumors about drugs and the family having illegal ties to the mafia, but I don't know. It all sounds like something out of one of Declan's movies, but then, how do two people disappear without a trace?" He shrugs. "Anyway, the zoo was disbanded, the house shut up, and the staff dismissed, so now it just sits empty." His words cause a shiver to roll down my spine followed with a bolt of excitement. This is exactly what I need, a distraction from the shit that's happening in my real life.

"Harlow, you've got a gleam in your eye. Now, I don't know you well enough to know exactly what it means, but be careful," he warns, and I pat him on the shoulder.

"Thanks, Josh, and don't worry, I'm just going to go for a walk. Maybe take my GoPro and do some exploring. I appreciate the info." Waving goodbye to him and Luke, I head inside to get changed and see if I can get some snacks to put in my backpack so that I don't have to leave too early if I do find a way in.

The stone wall surrounding the property is covered in ivy and has large trees overhanging it, blocking out the sun. As I walk along it trying to find a way in, goosebumps cover my skin, and I shiver from the chill the shade brings. I had changed out of my riding clothes and put on a pair of denim shorts and a tank top because it was so sunny and warm, but now I'm wishing I'd brought a sweater.

Strapped to my chest is a harness for my GoPro, leaving my hands free for any climbing or exploring, and I've got my stocked backpack hanging from my shoulders. Not sure what conditions the grounds will be in on the other side of the fence, I have my hiking boots on to protect my feet. I don't want to make it easy for any snakes that might be hiding in long grass.

So far I've walked most of the front side of the property, and there's no way in. The wall is solid and impenetrable, with the entrance gates locked tight. It doesn't look like I can climb it either, and my heart sinks at this realization. *Damn it, maybe I won't be able to explore at all.* At the corner of the wall, I expect it to stay the same, but the wall turns into a high wire fence topped with razor wire. Where the two materials join, it looks like someone used bolt cutters to cut a hole large enough for a body to get through.

Looks like I'm not the only person to have this idea. I'm not the kind of person who would ever damage someone's property in order to get a chance to explore, but I can't say that I won't take advantage of someone else doing the deed. Slipping through the fence, I notice it's in a perfectly hidden spot too because there's a large hedge on the other side. It must be there to hide the sight of the wire fence from the inhabitants of the home. I can still push my way through, albeit with scrapes and scratches to my arms and legs before I'm finally in.

My heart races with excitement as I scan the estate. Unlike the well-kept manicured grounds of the Summers estate, this property has become wild and overgrown. The grass is long, and the various bushes dotted here and there are unkempt and scraggly. There are lots of large willow trees with long dense overhanging branches. So dense that I can't even see the trunks. The inner child in me thrills at the sight, imagining hiding away from the world under one of those. I'd set up a daybed and use it as my special reading nook.

My eyes move on from there, following the overgrown and uneven driveway up to an honest to god gatehouse. The mansion is surrounded by a now dried up moat that disappears behind the massive building and must be at least fifteen feet wide. A large wooden drawbridge, which is currently down, allows access to the main building.

I make my way toward it, marveling at the unbelievable sight as I make a pit stop in the gate house. There's an intercom system in the wall, long since abandoned if the layers of dust are any indicator. It must be so that people inside would know when to lower the bridge. Why on earth you'd have a drawbridge and moat in modern times, I have no idea, but Nana did say the count was *slightly* eccentric.

I make my way across the drawbridge that's

wide enough to fit cars, but there's no room for parking on the other side, so I'm guessing it's foot traffic only. *What kind of parties did these people have that they needed this much space for their guests?* The bridge creaks and groans as I cross it, like I'm the first person to do it in a long time. And, if the little I know is to be believed, I guess I am. Stepping out onto the ground on the other side, my eyes hungrily scan upward. Towering over me, like something out of a dark European fairytale, is a gothic masterpiece of a home.

Dark stone is covered in green ivy, accented by contrasting white trim around the window frames. Plenty of lead-lined dusty windows that must let in plenty of light when cleaned. Spires and turrets, crosses and gargoyles, dotted here and there in a mismatched masterpiece of engineering. Bay windows and doors jut out along the frontside of the building, and at the very top of the central turret, a balcony with wrought iron trim sits, allowing someone a bird's eye view of all that is going on. *I wonder if you can see the Summers' place from up there.*

My eyes drift back down again, and I move toward the house and up the steps to the front porch. *Abandoned explorer rule #1: Always check the front door before you try more… creative ways of getting into the building.* I try peering through one of the nearby windows, but the dirt and grime build-up is so bad I can see nothing but shadows. The front door is a large wooden structure with ornate door knockers, gargoyles holding the rings in their mouths, similar to one in that David Bowie movie, *The Labyrinth.* They're so life-like I expect them to start talking. Hands almost shaking with excitement, I slowly reach out, grasping the handle and giving my best shot at getting it to turn. Locked! Well, I guess I hadn't really expected to be able to waltz right in.

Heading back down the steps, I make my way across the front of the building. Each and every window is either covered by grime or closed drapes on the inside. As I continue exploring around to the side, my eyes swing to the moat. It looks to be as deep as it is wide, and it continues toward the back of the mansion, so I follow its line. There are no entrances on this side, only more covered windows. *How curious. Only one way in and one way out?* The lawn in the back of the house is equally overgrown and long, and the garden beds that line it are barren and dry. The only thing that seems to be surviving and thriving is the climbing ivy. I stumble over the uneven ground and get too close to the moat where the edge crumbles slightly, tumbling into the bottom. *Shit, that was close.* My knee sends out a jolt of pain at the sudden jarring, but it fades quickly enough that I can't convince myself to turn around.

Righting myself, I keep following its path, the moat opening out into a dried up lake with an island in the middle. The island has the same large weeping willows on it that the front of the house does, and there seems to be a building on it, but as I look around, I can't find any way over there. Unlike the front, there isn't a bridge connecting it to this side. Must need a rowboat to get over. Or maybe you could swim if there was water; that would be fun on a hot summer day. I can just imagine it, races to see who could get to the island faster, splashing around for hours to beat the heat. Maybe a servant rowing across with a lunch basket. Picnic blankets spread out under the shade of the hanging willow branches and lazy afternoon naps. Scanning the shore on this side, I find a small dock and boat house further down from where I am. There's an old row boat sunk into the mud over there, but it doesn't look sea-worthy at all.

Turning my back on the lake, I head back up to the mansion. There, large doors lead out to a large entertainment area with an empty pool that looks like something out of the Playboy mansion. Surrounded by lush overgrown tropical plants, there's a large rock wall that looks to have a slide carved into it, and a possible cave. I'd have to get down into the empty pool to have a look, but I think I'll leave it for another time. There's so much to explore, and I haven't even been inside the place yet. *Abandoned explorer rule #2: Don't go overboard on the first day.*

Passing it by, I step under the large patio area which is covered by overgrown wisteria, with low hanging branches waiting to snatch at hair or exposed skin. The wooden floorboards are worn out and rotten in some spots, and the sunken hot tub is cracked and has leafy debris in it. There's no patio furniture, just a large empty space. Once I move closer, I can peer through bi-fold doors, which must be capable of opening to allow the flow of people in and out, but again I'm thwarted by window coverings. A quick and frustrating rattle of the door handle gives me the same verdict as before: locked.

My heart sinks in disappointment, and I blow out a big breath. I'd been excited to explore it, not even considering that I wouldn't be able to get in.

Turning back around, my eye catches on the building on the little island. *Maybe they weren't so attentive to that place? Abandoned explorer rule #3: Don't give up!* Walking back the way I came, I carefully step down into the empty lake. I was worried it was going to be muddy and slippery like it looks near the little dock, but the ground is hard and compact underneath my feet.

The ground slopes down as I move across the lake before sloping back up when I get closer to the little island. A sweet scent starts to tease the air, my eyes tracing the source of it back to a flowering creeper that's hugging the little stone building. Once I reach the island, I somewhat clumsily climb up the slope, hurrying over to the lonely building the second I'm on solid, flat ground once more. Built with the same stone as the main house, this one looks like the equivalent of a pool house. Glass windows on three sides give the occupants a view of the mansion to one side and behind it. Unlike the big house, this one hasn't got anything covering the windows, but I can see that the room is empty and the door on the wall with no window is closed so I can't see beyond it. But there looks like there are more living space beyond that.

Disappointment flows through me once again as I pull a bottle of water out of my backpack and take a long sip. Just about to give up for the moment and sit down for a quick break, something catches my eye. On the back side of the building, at the other end of the island, is another bridge leading over the moat on the other side. This one only looks wide enough for one person at a time, maybe two. So I guess this little pool house was a way station of sorts, a place for people to chill and spend some time if they didn't feel like continuing on to whatever attraction lies on the other side of this next bridge.

So I hurry around, dodging the longer of the grass and pushing willow branches out of the way. When I get to it, I can see that it looks like it's quite rotten as well, but I'm left with no alternative this time. On this side of the island, the walls of the moat are steeper, more of a straight up and down rather than the slope I'd used to get here in the first place. Sure, I could probably get down without hurting myself, but I'm pretty sure I wouldn't be able to get back out on the other side. I would have to walk back around to the other side of the island, and the tired part of me that nearly stumbled when getting off the horses today doesn't really love the sound of that extra effort right now.

Carefully, I step out onto the bridge that creaks and groans in dismay, but it holds my weight. Cautiously and quickly, I move across the fifteen-foot span, breathing a sigh of relief as I make it to the other side. Before I can even really understand what I'm seeing, I gasp, my heart beating faster. The estate must slope downward at the back of the property because this couldn't be seen from the front at all. Before me, dotted amongst more overgrown foliage, unkempt bushes, and large trees, looks to be a zoo. Large cages nestled amongst vegetation and more natural settings. Footpaths lead from cage to cage, overgrown grass disrupting their natural flow.

Goosebumps rise across my skin as I remember Nana had mentioned something about a menagerie, but it hadn't occurred to me that it would look like this. Josh had called it a zoo as well, but I'd just assumed the count had some kind of makeshift set up like I do at the Bostons'. This looks professional, and a thrill of excitement runs through me. Now, *this* is interesting, and so in my ballpark.

Hurrying forward, I take a look in the first cage. It's large enough to have been some kind of aviary, and there are double doors on the opposite side from where I am, lending more clues to it being that. There's a plaque on a sign near it, but it looks like whatever was on it has been ripped off. The smell of dusty grounds and overgrown plants overpowers any scent left behind from any long gone animals.

Skipping forward in my excitement, I try to calm myself down, needing to be careful as the paths are uneven and overgrown and I don't want to trip over anything.

The next enclosure I come to isn't actually a cage. There's a waist-high fence with an empty plaque again, and then there's a bit of greenery before the ground dips away into another moat, separating the animal from the public. Wide enough for no animal to leap across and low enough that if they could swim they couldn't leap up on to the other bank. It's much like you would see in zoos nowadays, very progressive for one that's at least twenty years old.

I marvel at the sight and speculate what he might have had in there. Maybe big cats or a bear? Behind the enclosure is a rock wall with gates in it, probably to let the animals in and out like a normal zoo, so there must be enclosures and things behind it as well.

I continue to walk through the now empty zoo, and there looks to have been plenty of large animals in this private collection if the size of the enclosures are anything to go by. Maybe there's a manifest somewhere that says what was in here.

There must be ex-staff members who I could get information from. I'll ask Dad if he knows anything when I go back to the house later.

A clattering of animal's hooves have me jumping and hurrying forward. When I round the bend, a herd of deer are running away from me in the opposite direction, a buck with massive antlers leading the way. A huge smile spreads across my face. *Wow, they must be leftovers from the zoo or escapees.* I hurry after them, but they quickly disappear amongst the cages. I'll leave them be; I don't want the buck coming back and defending his territory.

The building to catch my attention next has me squealing a little in joy. A big frosted glass enclosure is in front of me, likely a butterfly house. A few of the glass panes are broken now, and when I walk through the front double doors, the sun beating down on the glass still lends some heat to the space, but it's missing the tell-tale humidity usually found in one of these. There are some misting pipes running over the roof and down the walls, and in the middle is another dried up lake surrounding a cute little gazebo sitting on an island. I can just imagine large carp living in the water, swimming under the little white wooden bridge that is now faded gray and missing a plank or two.

Exiting the glass house, I glance around, finding myself baffled. *Is that a pool?!* A frown crosses my brow, figuring there's got to be some kind of clue

I'm missing. Surely, he didn't have any aquatic animals.

There are some stands next to it that give it a little seating area and a platform on the other side, but that can't be right, can it?

Puzzled, I walk over, past the stands and what looks like a little concession booth, and up to the edge of the pool. There's a little sunken beach area that's maybe a foot and half deep. I step down into that and walk the fifteen or so feet to look down into the pool, taking careful, measured steps so that I don't go tumbling down the deep slope. I can't even guess the depth, maybe forty feet, and when I crouch down I can see there are tunnels with gates over them over the otherside. They must lead to another pool somewhere else.

Brushing off my hands, I start to get up, but a shadow appears over me all of a sudden. Before I get a chance to turn and look, I feel a pair of hands on my back, giving me a shove. With my heart in my throat, I tumble over the edge and slide down the long slope, head first.

Chapter Ten

Harlow

Thank god it was sloped and not a straight up and down; otherwise, I would have gone head first into the tiled bottom. Wind rushes past, a thunderous sound in my ears as I slide, trying to find something to grab onto to stop my descent, but my fingernails can't find purchase on anything. When I finally slide to a stop, my heart is beating a million miles an hour, and my exposed skin is scratched up. *Oh, that's likely going to hurt in the morning.*

Thank god it hasn't rained. Would just add insult to injury if I had to splash down into some soupy, muddy mess. Catching my breath, I scramble to my feet, turning around to see who did this, but all I can see is their shadow.

"Hey, help? What the fuck did you do that for?" I shout up at them, but the shadow backs up and disappears. *Would the ice princess really follow me out here? She messed with my saddle, but stalking me over to the property, just waiting for the perfect chance for a second try to hurt me…* I'm honestly not sure.

Looking down at my GoPro, I'm immensely relieved that it looks like it's held up quite well. *At least that's a win!* It might sound stupid to get sentimental over an easily replaced piece of technology, but my GoPro was my first real investment in this hobby of mine, and I would have been devastated if it had broken before I'd even had a chance to really use it. Brushing myself off, I scan where I've landed.

There's a ladder near the side of the pool, maybe forty feet from the bottom of the tank, so it's way too far out of reach. Useful when the pool's full of water? Sure. Any good to me while I'm stuck at the bottom of this drained monstrosity? Not at all. There's also a glass viewing area, the kind that lets visitors watch what the animals are doing underwater. Still not sure how anyone could get away with having this on their property, no matter how rich and eccentric they were, I keep investigating. My eyes catch on the huge gates that block two tunnels on either side of the pool, opposite from where I am. Maybe I can lift one of those because I can't see any other way I can get out of this section.

Trying to keep my mind busy so that I don't

panic over what's likely going to be a complete failure, I run through ideas of what could've been kept in this pool. Dolphins? They could definitely fit, but I feel like the owner of this place might've gone for an animal with more flare. Sharks? Eh, likely too ordinary. My mind races, finally halting on what would've been a show-stopper. Holy shit! Is there any way he could've had some kind of whale?

By the time I hit that point in my brainstorming, I've reached the gates. With a deep breath, I do my best impersonation of Superman, desperately trying to get them to budge. As expected, nothing moves except me, and my heart sinks. I'm going to have to call someone to get me out. But before I can pull my backpack off, I hear the whining sound of a golf cart or some kind of vehicle, so I start shouting.

"Hey, help me!" My shout echoes around the space, loud in this dry prison of mine, though I have no idea if the sound is traveling out. "Help please, I'm stuck down here!" I shout even louder.

The noise disappears, and of course, I have no way of knowing whether they've stopped or just gone past my range of hearing. My heart sinks even further, and I collapse to the floor, readying myself to pull my phone out of my backpack. I just don't know if I have it in me today to face a round of Summers smirks when my "siblings" hear about me needing to be rescued. I close my eyes, taking the deep breath I need to get this over with, but suddenly, a voice on the other side has my eyes snapping open and looking up. The sun is directly behind the person so I have to shield my eyes from the glare. A woman, maybe my dad's age, is standing there, hands on her hips and a frown on her face as the wind tousles her brown hair.

"What are you doing down there? This is private property, and you're trespassing." Her tone is harsh and unimpressed, and a wave of embarrassment floods me, any lingering thrill from my expedition faltering under the weight of her reaction.

"I'm so sorry. You're right. I just wanted to have a look around, and I didn't intend to cause any trouble. Did you see anyone else up there?" I change the subject, hoping she'll forget about the whole trespassing thing. "Someone pushed me in here." Her frown deepens as she scans the area.

"No, I didn't. No trouble for years and then two people in one day," she angrily mutters to herself. "Going to have to get a dog."

"Could you help me out?" I ask, and her eyebrows rise in surprise.

"You can't get out?"

"No, there's no way," I tell her. "Unless you can open those gates and there's some way down those tunnels."

She just shakes her head, eyes narrowing as she inspects the space. "The pool on the other side of this does have a shallow end, but the gate mechanism doesn't have any power running to it. So we're going to have to figure another way out."

"What about a ladder?" I ask, but again, she shakes her head.

"Not one long enough. There used to be a cherry picker to do the windows on the front house, but it hasn't been needed in years, and it's not much good to you down there," she explains. There's silence for a moment, and an idea hits me. Still not an idea I like, but I was just about to give in and call someone anyway. Maybe help will get here faster if she just takes a trip there.

"Could you go to the house across the road and tell them what's happened and ask if they could help?" I cross my fingers, hoping she's desperate to get me off the property and not vindictive enough to leave me down here.

"The Summers' place?" Her voice rises in surprise, and I nod.

"Yeah, hopefully my dad or Poppy might have an idea. I'd hate to have to call rescue to come and help us. That would be *so* embarrassing," I groan.

"You're one of the Summers kids? I don't recognize you from any of the media things I've seen." She sounds suspicious now, and I don't blame her. The others are always in the gossip columns or business news for some reason or another, so it's not ridiculous to assume I could be some weird hanger on, trying to get close to them in the most convoluted way possible.

"Yeah, I've just recently found out that Brad's my dad. Neither of us knew the other existed." Her frown softens at my admission, determination taking its place.

"Okay, hang tight. I'll go and see if any of them can help us."

"Thanks. I'm Harlow, by the way. What was your name?" I ask, not wanting to be rude. I mean, she *is* saving my ass right now. Can't hurt to be friendly.

"Emma, I'm the caretaker for this place. I do a drive around twice a day; you're just lucky I heard you. Otherwise, you would have been stuck until tomorrow."

I laugh and show her my backpack. "I was just getting ready to call someone for help when you showed up."

She waves her hand at me. "Good luck with that. The reception back here tends to do what it wants. Anyway, hold tight, Harlow, and I'll go see if I can get us some help. Hopefully, they have some equipment to help us get you out of there." Emma disappears, and the sound of the vehicle can be heard driving away.

Blowing out a breath, I sit again in the bottom of the tank. God, I hope none of the siblings are around when she gets over there. But then one of them already knows I'm down here. Or at least that's the only explanation my mind can come up with. Who else would be here? Who else has it out for me this badly? A shiver of disbelief courses down my spine. I think I need to confront her; it can't keep going like this. Two near misses in the space of a couple of hours, that's some serious fucking hate, and I don't know what to do to get her to back off. To let her know that I'm not so easily intimidated.

I run a hand through my hair. God, Dad is going to be so upset if I have to go to him to get her to stop. I really don't want to be that person, but she seems to be escalating.

Pulling my ever-present paperback out of my bag, I continue reading from where I left off to fill my time instead of focusing on all the hate that surrounds me. I'm not sure how long it's going to take for her to find someone to help me.

About half an hour later, the droning sound of the vehicle returns, and my heart rate speeds up in anticipation. Did she find someone to help?

"Harlow, honey, are you okay?" My dad's voice has me looking up and nodding my head sheepishly.

"Yeah, a bit scratched up and a lot embarrassed, but apart from that, I'm fine." I put my book back in the bag and stand up, brushing off. Voices behind Dad have him turning away from the edge of the pool.

"Harlow, Kai's just getting his rappelling equipment set up. He's going to rappel down, hook you into a harness, and they're going to pull you back up."

So, Kai's here, but who does he mean by 'they'? Before I can ask, Thomas and Holden both appear next to Dad, trying hard to hide their amused expressions, not that it's going well. The minute Dad turns and walks away to supervise Kai, I guess, their grins break free as they both chuckle.

"Hey, Harlow, you are the furthest thing from a whale that I can think of," Thomas shouts down to me, his accent strong with his uncensored emotions. I'm not sure I've yet seen him this gleeful since I got here. *Though it's a pretty damn good look on him.*

"More like a mermaid or a siren, I would say," Holden teases, smiling down at me.

Their easy going manner is a direct contrast to what the two of them have been like in the past, and my hackles rise a little bit. Is this the part of the program where they try to be friends with me just to destroy me once my trust in them is secure?

They must see the wariness in my eyes because the chuckles drop. "But seriously, are you okay?" Holden's concern seems genuine, but I don't know enough about any of them to be sure, not after Oliver. I'd thought the moment between us was genuine but look where that got me. "Emma was saying you thought you were pushed in."

Bringing my hands to my hips, my temper rises. "Do you think I'm making this shit up, Holden?" I snap at him. "Or was this morning's little accident a part of my imagination as well?"

They look a little taken aback at my anger, and Thomas starts to shake his head. "Surely you can't think any of us had anything to do with that?" His accent is still thick, his emotions changing from easy going amusement to what sounds like a healthy dose of shock in his attempt to defend himself and his siblings. Unfortunately for me, the sound has butterflies flipping around where they have no business flipping when I'm this angry.

"I saw the way you all looked at Jacinta when it happened. You suspect it was her too! Really, with the way you have all behaved since I arrived, I wouldn't put it past any of you." Kai appears next to the two brothers, his mouth downturned as he hears the last of my words.

"Harlow, I swear to you I knew nothing about any of it." He places his hand over his heart, and though I can't see his eyes, I have a gut feeling he's telling the truth. Last night, he'd insisted the same thing.

I scan down his body, noting he's ready to climb down into the pool. He's wearing a type of harness around his legs and ass that has a carabiner attached to it and a length of rope behind him, along with a helmet on his head. In his hand he has a matching harness that I guess must be for me.

"Look, I hear you. For now though, just come and get me and we can talk about it later." I'm starting to feel worn out, and I hadn't realized how late it had gotten until just now that I'm noticing the sun has started to drop. Even though I didn't get to look in the house, I must have been exploring the back of the estate for hours.

With the sun dropping behind the large trees, shade slowly covering the pool, the air is starting to get as chilly as it was in the willow-covered front lawn, and goosebumps appear across my skin.

I watch as Kai exchanges some quiet words with his brothers before shooing them away. Thomas turns and leaves with a scowl on his face, but Holden argues a little longer before he too throws up his hands and disappears out of sight.

Dad steps up next to Kai, a reassuring smile on his face. "Don't panic, Harlow. Kai knows what he's doing; he's very experienced with rock climbing and rappelling. We'll have you out of there in no time!" Dad's gentle words wash over me, bringing a sense of warmth. How sweet is he? I'm not going to burst his bubble and let him know that I'm more cold than anything. Rappelling or rock climbing is nothing compared to leaping onto the back of a 1200 pound horse when it's coming at you at great speed. If I can handle that, I can handle this.

"Thanks, Dad." I wave up at him, not wanting to discourage that gentle nature. It makes a nice change to the normal parental interaction I'm used to from my mother.

He disappears, and Kai starts to edge himself

over the side of the pool. Once he's got secure footing, he pushes off and slides down the rope before landing against the side again. Two more times he does this before he's at the bottom. I make my way over to him, and he unhooks himself from the rope before running his eyes over me, looking for damage. He takes in all the scratches, but I wave him off. Nothing is deep or even in need of a bandage, just a good wipe over with antiseptic.

Finally, his eyes meet mine, the relief in them staggering. He reaches out and pulls me in tight, those damn butterflies coming back without any invitation from me. "I'm so sorry about all of this. I'll put a stop to it," he whispers before pulling away. My ear tingles where his words had brushed across it.

Blinking in surprise, I smile up at him. "The thing is, Kai, you can say that, but the person or people responsible are fucking adults who need to own up to their actions and accept that the consequences may be retaliation ten-fold." I'm growling at the end of my response, and he nods his head, sadness clouding his eyes. There's something about him that just seems more… open than his siblings. The rest of them have masks. I'm pretty sure I've seen each one hiding their true self already, but Kai has this openness about him that threatens to lure me in against my better judgment.

"I don't blame you in the least, Harlow. Today's actions could have gone too far. They're lucky you weren't hurt worse than you are." He tucks a stray hair behind my ear, the sadness in his eyes replaced with something a little more cheeky that has my heart skipping a beat. The smile that crosses his face is big and bright and dangerously dazzling.

He waves the harness at me. "Let's strap you into this and get you out of here. Holden was right; you may be pretty enough to be a mermaid, but with no water you're pretty much high and dry." I roll my eyes at his cheesy attempt at humor as he helps me into the harness, making sure it's correctly fitted before attaching me to the rope.

"Now, it might be best if you walk up the wall as they pull you. Otherwise, you'll bang into the side and hurt yourself further." With those instructions, he tugs on the rope and the tension increases as I turn and face the wall. Suddenly, I feel myself start to lift, so I put my feet against the wall and start walking up the steep incline. I move quite swiftly, but that's no surprise with Holden, Thomas, and possibly my dad on the other end.

When I finally make it to the top, Dad hurries forward and assists me over the ledge. On my hands and knees, I breathe out a big sigh of relief before I let him help me stand.

Holden moves over to me, and without breaking eye contact, undoes the rope from my harness. "Incoming," he shouts to Kai before launching it back over the edge. He still has a hand on my harness, though I can't figure out why he's not letting go. I can see a small frown on his face, his face creasing with concern as he studies me.

"We'll get to the bottom of this, Harlow. I promise." Right now, especially in the wake of Kai's strange openness and that dangerous smile, I'm honestly tapped out, so I just smile my thanks before I step out of the harness and walk over to where Dad is standing with Emma. Now that I'm closer, I can see she's gorgeous, and by the look in Dad's eye he thinks so too. Seeing me safely out of the pool, he apologizes to Emma, thanking her for what seems like not the first time for being kind enough to help me out.

"He's right, and I'm sorry. Abandoned buildings are my weakness, and when I saw this one, I couldn't help myself. Had I known there was a caretaker, I would have found a way to ask if I could explore. Thank you so much for going and getting help." I hold my hand out, and she smiles, shaking it in return.

"I don't think anyone realizes there is still a caretaker. My father was the one before me, but he passed on a few years ago. We actually lived in the caretaker's cottage on the far side of the mansion. He was sick for a long time, and I moved home to care for him. I guess I just continued the job once he passed on because I just didn't have anything else to go back to."

"Oh, no family or kids?" I not so sneakily fish for info for my dad.

"Harlow," he scolds, but she waves it off.

"No, it's okay. I'm divorced, and unfortunately, my ex didn't want children. I would have loved a house full of 'em, but I guess it's too late for me now." Studying her, I decide she can't be much older than early forties. I'm about to say there's still a chance, but I can see a blush on her cheeks and a slight sheen to her eyes with her admission. I didn't mean to make her upset, so I quickly change the subject.

"Will you come to dinner tonight as a thank you?" I look to Dad for an okay, and he eagerly jumps in. *Best wingwoman ever.*

"Yes, please do! I wouldn't want to think what could have happened if you hadn't been around." She laughs and rolls her eyes, all signs of discomfort gone.

"Well, she would have called you, of course." He looks kind of sheepish but doesn't say anything. He just ushers her in the direction of the golf cart. Turning back toward us, he shouts, "Kai, you and Harlow can jump in the cart. Thomas and Holden, you can walk back."

Turning, I see that Kai is now back up top and organizing his gear. He quickly piles it onto the seat between us and sits down next to me, his body all too close to mine. As the golf cart takes off up the path through the zoo, its quiet humming is the only noise to be heard. Thomas and Holden wave good-bye, the two being surprisingly good natured about needing to walk back on their own. I just nod my head in return. I appreciate their help in getting me out of there, but I'm not ready to make overtures toward them just yet. Who knows if they're genuine or not, and my sense of self-preservation says we need to look before we leap.

Chapter Eleven

Kai

During the ride back to the house in the golf cart, Harlow is quiet and subdued. Up front, Dad and his new friend Emma are chatting casually about various things, but I can't bring myself to pay too much attention. Though I *did* notice how animated Dad had become before my attention was drawn back to Harlow. Honestly, it's about time the man had some companionship. Maybe the siblings and I can play the wingmen and help this happen. Maybe I won't mention it to Jacinta quite yet. Wouldn't want her to get her panties in a bunch and chase her off before Dad even gets a chance to get to know her.

My focus now locked on the gorgeous woman next to me, I can't help but study her face out of the corner of my eye. Although she apologized for trespassing, she had still looked thrilled at having been able to explore the place.

"Did you record everything?" I ask her, gesturing to the GoPro on her chest. Deep in thought, she jumps, startled by my question, but her face lights up with a huge smile.

"Yes, I did. I'm so excited to watch it back and see all the things I missed out on the first time round. I'm just disappointed I didn't have a chance to look inside the house."

"Well, I can fix that," Emma calls back over her shoulder, her eyes on the driveway, dodging the worst of the potholes as she heads back toward our place. "Why don't you come over later in the week, and I'll give you the grand tour? We'll have to do it during the day because there's no power in the main house, but I promise it will be worth it. The house is amazing."

"Really, you can get in? And you'd let *me* in?" Harlow's voice rises in excitement, and I smother a smile at how cute she looks, her eyes wide and sparkling.

"Yes, of course, I have a key in case the estate sends a cleaner or needs maintenance done inside the house."

"And do you know the history of the place? Can you tell me all about what kind of animals he had in that zoo? Is there a record somewhere? Or maybe some old staff members I can speak to? Surely something that big would need a team to take care of it, right?"

Her questions pour out one after the other, and she's practically bouncing on the seat, but before Emma can answer, Dad is holding up his hand to Harlow.

"Whoa, sweetie, slow down." The little cart is approaching the house now, having traveled quite quickly up our maintained driveway unlike the one in the other estate. "I'm sure Emma will share everything she knows with you in due time. Let's not harass her as soon as she's helped you out of a sticky situation." A gentle pink starts to color Harlow's cheeks, the firmness of Dad's words adding a little more embarrassment to her likely bruised ego.

"Yeah, you're right, Dad. Again, I'm so sorry, Emma, and thank you for helping me out. It's such a shame you didn't see who pushed me in."

My heartbeat increases again with that reminder; I'd temporarily put it out of my mind that she hadn't gotten down there on her own. "Did you really not see or hear anything?" I ask her, and she frowns as she thinks about it.

"No, I really didn't. I was so caught up in my head, speculating about the big pond and imagining what the whole place looked like, that I didn't notice a thing. I guess I could have captured something on this." She points to the camera strapped across her chest, drawing my eyes to her rounded breasts which are made even more obvious by the harness. Clearing my throat, I drag my eyes back to hers, the cheeky raised eyebrow and amusement sparkling in her eyes telling me that she knows exactly what I was focusing on. Thank fuck she didn't get offended. I'm really happy being the one person she seems to trust at the moment, apart from Dad and the grandparents.

"I'll help you go through the footage when we get back. I mean, if you'd be okay with that," I offer, and she smiles her thanks.

"That's a great idea," Dad says, turning in his seat as he's speaking. "Even though we have Dec's production team, Kai does a lot of the editing for the sports teams' videos himself. He's got a real eye for detail. If anyone is going to see anything, he would. That being said, Declan's another good one to ask too." Harlow cringes a bit at that, and Dad holds up his hands, eyes widening as if he's worried it's now his turn to piss her off. "No pressure, just a suggestion." Her cringe turns to a small grateful smile, and he turns back around.

"You know he's really making a real effort for you," I whisper quietly in her ear.

Her eyebrows turn down in confusion again, and I nod toward Dad. "The man's the CEO of one of the largest companies in all of America; he's used to getting his own way no matter what. The fact that he's letting you move at your own pace and not forcing us all together says heaps. He's not a man who's used to hearing no, though he *is* getting better as he gets older, more mellow so to speak."

Her frown clears, and her eyes widen in understanding. The next few moments, the two of us just face forward, quietly spending time with one another while Dad and Emma have a hushed conversation. Suddenly, they break off, Emma calling over her shoulder again as we approach the house.

"Harlow, I know how excited you are for that video footage, but I'm going to have to ask you to keep it private and not post it anywhere online. Otherwise, I'm going to have to get the estate lawyers involved." There's a firmness to her comment that hints at her being just as confident in her requests being followed as Dad is. Even though he owns a giant company and she's the caretaker for an abandoned house, it looks like she's got as much of a strong sense of backbone as he does.

"The estate has made a huge effort to keep the fact that it's vacant out of the press, squashing any aspiring news reporters that might poke around. They don't want hoards of explorers arriving on the doorstep, and I think that strategy is one of the reasons it's in such good condition. They still live in hope that the count will return or an heir will come forward."

My dad's head turns quickly to look at her, his

eyes blinking in an odd way that seems almost… suspicious. *Well, that's a little odd.* I frown at his reaction; my father usually has an extremely good poker face, so something she said must have surprised him.

Harlow's easy smile drops at the request not to post the footage anywhere, but there's a slight slump to her shoulders that tells me she's going to go along with it. I'm pretty sure she had her heart set on putting it on YouTube. "Okay, Emma, I won't post it anywhere. I wouldn't want to cause the estate any harm. There will be no need to involve lawyers." I can hear how disappointed she is, so I reach out and give her hand a quick squeeze, surprised when she doesn't immediately pull away.

The cart comes to a halt directly in front of the large house, and she turns the thing off, the humming noise dying and bringing back the sounds of nature. A horse whinnies somewhere behind the house, and a bird swoops down in front of the cart to land on the large fountain in the middle of the circle.

We all climb out of the cart, me lugging all my equipment. Harlow swings her backpack over her shoulder and takes the coil of rope out of my hands as I juggle the harness and other gear.

"Let me help you. It's the least I can do after you saved me from such an embarrassing predicament," she says as Emma and Dad disappear into the house in search of dinner.

Leading the way, I feel her follow me up the steps as we enter the front foyer, and I take a left toward our wing of the house. When I no longer hear any noise behind me, I turn to see Harlow frozen in the hallway, staring in my direction with dread plainly on her face.

"Come on, it won't be as bad as you think it is, I promise." I step back and take her hand to drag her forward, keeping my grip light in case she wants to pull away. "I didn't take you to be a chicken," I goad, and I see her straighten at my taunt, taking a deep breath before shaking off my arm.

"I'm not. Lead the way." She gestures for me to go, so I make my way into our wing, her by my side.

When you enter our wing, you enter into a plush entertainment/lounge room. Basically, it's where we all chill out if we're home and not spending time with the older generation.

Fat comfy couches with plenty of throw pillows take up most of the room, but we also have some large therapy pods that we use as well. None of us need them for anything specific, though I'm sure we all take comfort in them. Plus, they're *really* fucking comfy. In front of that is a cinema-style setup with a huge screen taking up most of the wall.

But Harlow's eyes drift to the other end of the room, my sister's favorite place in our wing. Tucked away into a little corner is a small library. Unlike the library in the main part of the house, this is a cozy setup with a daybed surrounded by shelves and a curtain in case she wants to block out the sound from the tv. Harlow looks at it with longing, and I realize that she and my sister have so much in common. I bet if Jacinta could put away that petty animosity brought on by her underlying issues, she and Harlow would be tight. In fact, I shudder to think about the things the two of them could get up to against us all.

"You know you're welcome over this side of the house anytime you want. You have a room in this wing too if you want it."

Her gaze moves from the reading nook back to me, scoffing in disbelief. "And put myself directly in the firing line? I don't think so. I think I'll stay where I am for now." I don't even bother arguing. Her mind is made up, and I can't really blame her. I've got better things to talk about anyway.

"Come on, my room's this way." I lead her away from the living area and bypass the small kitchen, heading toward a staircase. This wing is three stories high, the main floor with communal areas and the next two with bedrooms and bathrooms spaced out across them.

Climbing upward, I bypass the next floor. Declan, Jacinta, Jaxon, and Oliver have their rooms on that one, so we keep climbing higher. I share the top floor with Holden and Thomas, and that's also where the spare bedroom is that would have been Harlow's if she had decided to stay on our side. By the time we reach my door and I open it wide, turning back to welcome her into my sanctuary, I manage to catch the wince she's obviously trying to hide. Hurrying, I drop my gear just inside the door and reach out for the coiled length of rope she's carrying, taking it from her hands, and then help her to my bed.

I scan my room, just to make sure I left it clean this morning. Apart from a basketball on the floor, everything's in its place, although I haven't made the bed. Usually, I've hit the snooze button a few too many times and need to hurry, so the bed doesn't get made more often than not. It's also a little fuck you to my previous home where a disorganized room would have been grounds for a beating. *How messed up am I that some wrinkled sheets feels like a rebellion even all these years later?*

The third floor rooms all have super high ceilings and exposed beams, and my room is on the end of the house, so I've created a climbing wall up the brick side, my harness hanging neatly on the side of the room. I also have some hooks in the beams high above us for other things, but thankfully, she hasn't noticed them. I wouldn't want to scare her off before I even get a chance to woo her.

"Are you okay?" I ask, making her take a seat. She grimaces but allows me to help her down, groaning when she finally hits the soft mattress.

"Yeah, I think the day is just catching up with me. Falling off Samson, then all that walking before sliding into the pool next door, and then climbing the stairs. It just set off my knee that I banged up before I arrived."

Kneeling down in front of her, I reach out to touch her, stopping right before I make contact. *Look but don't touch. At least until you get permission.* I consider myself to be a pretty respectful guy, consent being king and all that, and I've never had more trouble following that simple respect for personal space as I have with this woman. "May I?"

She nods, the slight chewing on her lip the only indicator of her unease, and I slide my hand up her bare calf to her knee. It looks like it's starting to swell, so I feel around a little bit. I have no clue what I'm doing, but this is what I've seen our team doctors do, and it doesn't hurt that her legs are silky smooth and soft.

"How about we check out the footage quickly and then have dinner with everyone else? Afterward, we can hop in the hot tub and soak away all of today's stress," I suggest, my hand still on her calf. I'm reluctant to remove it, and I can see her eyes brightening with amusement as she looks between me and my hand, but she doesn't shove it off. *I'll take the wins where I can get them.*

"Actually, that sounds really good. The heat from your hand was already a small relief, so a hot tub will probably work wonders."

My dick twitches inside my pants at the thought of my heat warming *other* parts of her body, but I quickly clear my throat and step away, hoping she doesn't notice now that it's practically eye height for her. Heading to my nearby desk, I open up my computer and sit down at the chair. "Why don't you pull the memory card out, and we'll have a look at the footage?"

I hear rustling behind me, so while my computer loads up, I turn to look back at Harlow. She's trying to get herself out of the GoPro harness, her struggles pulling up her shirt and exposing the smooth expanse of her stomach. Just a little bit higher, and I'd really be in trouble. A glittering catches my eye, and it's drawn to her belly button where a bright pink gem sits nestled inside and just above. My dick twitches at the thought of swirling my tongue around the piercing before moving lower on her body.

"Can you help me?" Her muffled voice has my eyes moving upward, and I laugh when I get to her head. She's become all tangled with her shirt and the harness and is now stuck, her exposed lacy pink bra making her breasts look absolutely biteable. *Fuck me, I need to get my head out of the gutter.*

"I don't know... This is a pretty good view for me." I chuckle as she growls at me.

"Kai, it will be the last view you get if you don't help me out of here." *Gotta get my ass in gear. Can't have that.* I help her untangle herself, and as she pulls her shirt back down to where it belongs, I remove the GoPro from the harness before taking out the disk and inserting it into the slot in my computer.

When the time stamp pops up, I realize it's going to take a lot longer than I thought. A hint of heat and a firm touch on my shoulder have me turning around in the chair, Harlow automatically adjusting her position as I face her. For the moment, she's trapped between my legs, her breasts now at my eye level.

"There's a lot of footage here. We're not going to have time to run through it before dinner. Why don't you leave it with me, and I'll have a look tomorrow. I know you're spending the day with Nana and Hope at Neighpalm Couture, and I don't have any plans until the weekend."

Her eyes light up at my suggestion, and it's not escaping my notice that she's making absolutely zero effort to remove herself and put some distance between us. *That's at least three signs that she doesn't mind me being so close. I'm totally her favorite.* "That would be great, thanks. That'll give me time to have a quick shower before dinner, wash off some of the sweat and dust."

"I'll see you at dinner then. Have you got a bathing suit for the hot tub?" I waggle my eyebrows, figuring I can ease into her good graces with a little humor. "Because nudity is always an option."

"Oh, nudity? Okay, that sounds great," she says to me, and my mouth drops open as she turns and saunters to my door.

"Really?" I squeak, sounding like a teenage boy.

"No, silly, but I liked your reaction." She shoots

me a wink back over her shoulder before opening the door and heading toward the other wing of the house, slightly limping. Swallowing my reaction, I run after her, sweeping her into my arms. She gasps in surprise before her arms come up around my neck, and I'll be damned if I don't make the most of this moment.

"What are you doing?" she demands a little breathlessly. A smug feeling rolls through me at her reaction, but I push it away, not wanting her to start associating me with my all too smarmy brothers.

"What kind of a man would I be if I let you hobble down the stairs?"

We make it to the second floor, and just as I reach the next set of steps, Jaxon's bedroom door opens and the man steps out.

"Kai, what are you doing?" he asks, his eyes narrowing on me and Harlow.

"Harlow's a little banged up, so I'm giving her a hand down the stairs." His eyes widen in concern before he tries to hide it, but it's too late. I've already seen it. Brother dear is pretending way too much. I'm always seen as the friendly, outgoing one, but my siblings never really give me credit for how observant I can be too. Extreme sports, or any kind of competition really, is all about strategy and making use of all the details around you. I notice much more than they give me credit for. I just usually decide to keep those things to myself, not needing to bring any drama to the table since most of my siblings manage that well enough on their own. It might be worth starting a little drama if it means I get to keep Harlow though. He starts to hurry toward us, but another door opens and Jacinta steps out this time. Even though her back is to him, her presence completely stops Jaxon in his tracks.

"What's going on? What happened to you?" she asks, sneering at Harlow in my arms, but before she can answer, I butt in.

"Like you don't know, kind of like her accident this morning," I snap back at her, and she flinches. What looks like genuine shock crosses her face, and her eyebrows turn down in a frown. Is she surprised that I'm calling her out in front of the "enemy"? Or does that surprise mean that she really has no idea? I love Jacinta, but sometimes she's really damn hard to read, no matter what cues I pick up on.

"You can't seriously think I had anything to do with that, and I have no clue what you're talking about now."

Looking down at Harlow, I see a frown cross her face at Jacinta's denial, but my sister doesn't stop there. "I might not want her here, but I don't want her hurt or anything. That would just upset Dad."

"And what you're doing isn't going to have the same result?" Jaxon mumbles from behind her. She flinches with the all too accurate barb, but she doesn't reply.

"Well if you didn't do these things, who could

have done it?" My words echo through the hallway, a solemn silence following them. Does that mean Harlow has someone else after her? This gorgeous woman is a whole different kind of trouble than I ever expected.

Chapter Twelve

Harlow

Dinner with Emma was pleasant, a refreshing change from the dramatic Summers mealtimes of the past. Everyone was in attendance again, and for the first time, it was a rowdy affair. Conversation flowed, and everyone was on their best behavior. Everyone except Cecilia. She had arrived just before the meal, claiming that she had some things for Dad to sign, and she basically invited herself to stay for dinner. Every time Dad asked Emma a question, she would dive into the conversation, trying to monopolize it. Luckily, Emma managed Cecilia's interruptions like a pro, and Dad's not so covert admirer eventually fell into a sullen silence, obviously not happy that Dad was captivated by our new friend.

Afterwards, much to Cecilia's disgust if the

look on her face was anything to go by, Dad escorted Emma back to the caretaker's cottage across the road. Meanwhile, everyone else disappeared to do whatever it is they do in the evening, and Kai and I headed out to the hot tub. I'd put my bathing suit on under my clothes before dinner, so it was just a matter of stripping off and climbing in.

Settling back against one side, the warmth of the water and the pressure from the jets has my aches and pains easing instantly, leaving my limbs languid and relaxed.

My eyes hooded, I watch as Kai strips down, pulling his shirt over his head, exposing muscles that ripple with every movement. Although I can't hear the sound of his zipper over the noise of the hot tub, the moment feels like it's in slow motion when he pulls it down and peels his jeans away from his legs. His thigh muscles bulge as he steps out of them, throwing them off to the side. His tight black boxer briefs are the only thing covering what looks like an impressive package hidden beneath. Forgetting myself, I wipe my mouth to make sure that no drool escapes, my eyes greedily scanning his entire body. Jesus, the man is cut. He looks like he's as fit as one of his extreme athletes.

When my eyes reach his, he's smirking. The cocky asshole knows what he looks like and the effect it has on the female species. Pushing his hair back off his face, he steps up and into the hot tub, settling down next to me and covering that all too distracting body under the bubbling water.

Leaning his head back, he closes his eyes and groans. “God, that feels good.” His voice is all deep and rumbly with his appreciation, and it sends a shiver down my spine. Not dissimilar to the reactions I had to both Oliver and Jaxon. What the fuck is it about the Summers men that is so damn potent?

He rolls his head lazily in my direction. “I haven't done any climbing in a bit, and today I used muscles I haven’t in a while.” He’s smiling lazily as he says this, the total lack of discomfort in his expression making me snort in disbelief.

“Dude, you’re ripped! I’m sure there isn't a single muscle on your body that you don't regularly work out, let alone forget.”

His lazy grin just gets wider, but he shifts a little closer so our thighs are touching under the water. My core clenches at the feel of his skin against mine “Maybe, but still, it reminds me that I haven’t taken the time to indulge in a bit of climbing in a while. I need to change that… and you should come with me,” he suggests, and another shiver flows down my spine, this one a completely different feeling to the other.

“After today, I think I’ll avoid anything that requires climbing or falling.” The thought that someone deliberately pushed me into that pool, that

I could still be stuck down if it hadn't been for Emma... *God, what a nightmare.*

I shudder as I remember the conversation from before. Jacinta was fairly adamant that she hadn't pushed me into that empty pool. She'd argued with us all the way down the steps from their wing, claiming her innocence for both that and the cut in the saddle. Honestly, I was even wavering by the time she was finished, but she had gotten angry and stormed away before we could properly discuss it, so I don't know what to believe now.

He sits up and reaches over the edge of the spa, opening what I thought was a storage box for towels but is in fact a mini fridge full of drinks. I gratefully accept the one he offers me. Twisting the top, he hands it to me before reaching in and grabbing one for himself. He tosses both tops back into the box and closes it before sitting back.

"I'm inclined to believe her. Jacinta is a lot of things, insecure and childish being the two main ones, but she has *never* been violent. I think she suffered enough at her mother's hands for it never to be something she has ever wanted to be. As to who it could have been, who knows? Maybe some punk kids were doing exactly the same thing as you and were worried you'd see them and report them. I'll go through that card this evening and see what we can find out." He shrugs, taking a sip of his beer. "And as for the saddle, maybe it had happened before it even left the Bostons' place. Just be mindful of your surroundings, and if anything else happens, make sure you tell me."

Taking a long swallow of my beer, I slide further down in the water and mull over his words, letting my body truly relax. Although I've always been so independent all my life, I like this feeling of being cared for. Don't get me wrong, the Bostons were always loving, but this is from someone new, someone not "obligated" to care for me, and I can't say the feeling isn't addictive. That feeling combined with the warmth of the spa and the cool slide of my beer helps me to release the tension that has been a constant through my body for days now. Allowing my eyes to close, I feel my mind drift from that to other things, and it's not until Kai says my name that I realize he'd been talking to me.

"Harlow, I need to fly to Hawaii this weekend to check out a couple of surfers I'm thinking about adding to one of my teams. I was wondering if you'd like to come with me?" He sounds a little nervous, and the look on his face tells me he's worried I won't accept, but Kai has been nothing but sweet to me. Accepting and friendly from the start, talking to me when everyone else pretended I wasn't even at the dinner table. Why wouldn't I want to spend some time with a kind and sexy man? In Hawaii! I've always dreamed of going, and I'd love to see how he scouts his athletes for his teams. It would also give me a break from all the drama without Dad thinking I'm giving up. Seems like a win-win situation to me.

"Yeah, I would love that. I should tell you I have a big week coming up though. Apart from going with Nana tomorrow, I have an appointment the following day, *and* I also asked Dad to go riding with me on Wednesday. I guess it depends on what Declan finds out this week about the horses. If they go to the set before the weekend, then absolutely. If not, I may have to skip the trip." Disappointment stirs, and I almost sit up straighter, surprised to realize that that's what I'm feeling. I want to try to examine why I feel that way, but if I look too closely, a whole heap of other worries are going to surface. I'm too relaxed to deal with all of that now.

His smile drops, and his disappointment is almost enough to break my heart. He looks like a little boy who's had his favorite toy taken away from him. But that look quickly clears until he's smiling again. "Fair enough, but I hope that they've gone by then." His heated look has my pulse spiking, and a thrill flows through me at the thought that he wants to spend time with me. I can't say I don't feel exactly the same way and discreetly cross fingers in hope. *Maybe third time's the charm? Sometimes the nice guy does actually get to win.*

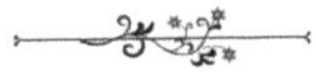

The next morning, I wake up early to prepare for my day at Neighpalm Couture with Nana and Hope. She's going to be my guide to all things Neighpalm Industries, and I'm actually a little excited and a little wary to meet her. At dinner last night, Holden was saying that she's one of his best friends and has known the family for years. That had my heart skipping a beat, because what if she was just like Jacinta? Thankfully, Kai whispered in my ear that she doesn't approve of Jacinta's games and will have nothing to do with them. That made me feel a lot better about today. It also didn't hurt to have his lips that close to my ear or the heat of his body pressing just so slightly into mine.

Staring at my closet, I chew on my lip as I contemplate what to wear. Nana assured me that I didn't need to worry, but I'm not sure if what I feel comfortable in is really the best choice.

"You're a Summers now, Harlow, and we can do whatever we want." Her haughty advice rings in my mind, the twinkle in her eye letting that good humor of hers shine through. Nana means every word she says. She *does* believe that Summers can do whatever they want, but her good nature has always stopped her from being a tyrant to anyone who didn't deserve it.

"Meow." The quiet call out from the very pregnant stowaway on my bed makes me realize

I've been staring at my clothes for the last few minutes.

Pulling out a pair of three-quarter capris and a nice top from Melinda that I haven't had a chance to wear yet, I lay them on the bed.

"Do you approve, Princess? Or do you think that they'll all look at me like I don't belong there?"

"Like Nana said, you're a Summers now. First step to keeping others from thinking that is to stop yourself from saying the same." Looking up, I jolt in surprise at the almost kind words coming from the man in the doorway. Almost immediately, my eyes narrow in suspicion.

"What do you want?" I growl as he steps into the room. Why the hell does that door keep opening? I swear I'd closed it. Either the latch is faulty or the jackass has ninja skills.

"Just came looking for my cat. Wanted to make sure that she was okay." Declan's eyes cloud with sadness as he looks at the pregnant feline. "It seems I've been replaced as her favorite."

A smug feeling flows through me to hear him say that, *damn right, you have*, but then it's followed by a shadow of guilt. Princess seems to be the only creature he shows any kind of softness toward, apart from his siblings. I watch as he sits down on my bed and lowers his face to hers, muttering quietly to her. I strain to hear what he's saying, but I can't make out the words. Rolling my eyes at my inability to hold a grudge, I throw him a bone.

"Why don't you take her with you? I'll be gone all day today, and I'm staying in town at Shane and Alex's tonight." I gesture to my packed overnight bag, and his eyes narrow again as he stands back up.

"Are you dating one of them? *Both* of them?" He tries to sound gruff, but he doesn't quite pull it off. Instead, he sounds nosy. *What the hell?*

"Not that it's any of your business, but no, they're just my friends. To be honest, the two of them are kind of keen on your sister. There's no accounting for taste, I guess."

His frown deepens as he runs a hand through his hair, pushing it back before he lets out a big sigh. "Look, it's not my place to tell the story, but Jacinta had it rough before she came here, then again when she was a teenager. Things happened, and her ability to trust or even see reason is sometimes a little... skewed."

"So what's *your* excuse then?" I cross my arms, staring him in the eye. "What did I do to you that was so offensive? You've been nothing but nasty since the minute I walked through the door! None of you gave me a chance. Except maybe Kai. I thought the fact that you were adults would have made things easier, yet I feel like I'm back in high school."

Declan breathes out another deep sigh, and his shoulders slump like all the weight of the world is on them. "You're right. We have been awful, and you didn't deserve it."

What did he say? Did he just agree with me? This has me blinking in the ensuing silence, a little shocked at his admission. He keeps stroking the cat and avoids looking at me as he continues to talk. "It's a little like a pack mentality. We all kind of circle around her when she lashes out; it's what we've always done. Me and Jaxon more than the others. I was the only one Brad had adopted by the time they arrived, so it was just me and the twins, and they were both shy and reserved, and I felt like it was my duty to take care of them. I was a big brother, and it was my job to make sure my new brother and sister were ok, especially my sister." He looks off into nothing as he recalls his memories, the smooth stroke of his hand down Princess' back the only movement he makes.

"I remember the first time I saw them. She was smaller than him, this pale skinny fragile thing that looked like she would blow over with a stiff breeze. She was huddled behind Jaxon like he was the only thing protecting her from the world, and I don't know what came over me, but I vowed to protect her from everything in life even if I'm only protecting her from herself. Though I guess I haven't been very successful at that last part..."

He shakes his head, his scowl returning as he brings his mind back to the present. "Look, I know this might seem stupid to you because you're also

Dad's daughter and I should feel the same way, but like you said, it's different now that we're adults. I'm sorry that you've gone through shit in your life just like Jacinta did, but I look at you and see someone who can handle herself. Jacinta's not like you, not yet. Maybe part of this is my problem or even my fault, and there's no reason I should be that overprotective big brother anymore, but I just can't go along with something or someone who puts that look back in my sister's eyes. So, unless she changes her mind, I guess you and I are enemies."

He's very quick to hide it, but I see the disappointment in his eyes and can't miss it in his voice. However, Declan is nothing if not a man of his word, scooping up his cat and heading out of my room. "You and Nana are getting a lift in the helicopter with me this morning since the interviews for the new designers will be held on the Couture floor at Neighpalm Headquarters. I'm leaving in an hour. Don't be late, I won't wait."

The cold demeanor is back as he leaves my room, those cryptic words floating behind him. What does he mean, he won't wait?

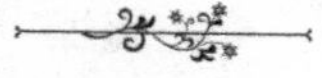

Declan

As I walk away from Harlow's room with Princess under my arm, I thank god she couldn't see the tent in my pants. She's so fucking sexy when her eyes are flashing in anger, and her nipples had pebbled under her top, drawing my eyes right to them. A quiet groan leaves my mouth as I stalk to our side of the house and upstairs to my room. I want to support Jacinta, and I still think there's something suspicious about how her mother just conveniently overdosed, leaving a perfect opportunity for her to find her birth certificate. She'd never tried to find it before then? Never wondered who her birth father was? I love my father and grandparents, but that doesn't stop me from thinking about, and getting lost in memories of the family that I used to have. No matter how amazing the Bostons were to try and compensate for her disastrous biological mother, I really can't believe that she had never tried to find out who her real father was.

But no matter how perplexing the woman is, she's gorgeous and she challenges me like none of the air head actresses I usually date do. They're all so narcissistic and only want to hear how pretty and talented they are even though most of them are as dumb as a box of rocks. There's a kind of safety in that, isn't there? If I can easily outwit my partner, then I'm the one ahead. There's no way that they can get the advantage and find a way to use me or my family. Instead, I can use them for what I want and then move on. Or at least that's what the therapist said the time Dad talked me into speaking with one. I'm not saying they're wrong, but what does it mean that I'm now spending so much time thinking about Harlow? I don't know if it's my brain or my dick leading the charge on that one, and with the added complication of Jacinta's feelings, it's really just best for everyone if I don't get involved in any shit with her.

Placing Princess down on my bed, she does a couple of turns and flops down gently. Satisfied she's back where she belongs, for now at least, I rush to get ready and down for breakfast. It would be no good for me to be late when I've just told Harlow not to be. I don't get the impression that she'd lord it over me like Jacinta would, but I want to make sure I'm staying that step ahead anyway. Stripping off, I climb into the shower, my cock still standing at attention.

I almost refuse to give in to the urge to do something about it, but the way Harlow's eyes flash when she's angry is such a fucking turn on. My siblings would be the first to tell anyone that I'm the biggest control freak of us all, and that's served me well in business. If I can control the situation, even others' emotions when possible, I can figure out a way to work things to my advantage. So, knowing that spark is in her eyes is because of me, knowing that I was able to push her just that tiny bit, well, that just makes this all the more satisfying. Maybe it makes me a little bit like that boy who pulls the girl's pigtails because he can't admit that he likes her, but if I can't make her eyes spark with some other kind of emotion right now, I'll grab those little sips of control where I can.

Taking my thick length in my hand, I stroke it with a tighter grip than normal, the friction from the water adding extra sensation as my mind goes to the night of the premiere and how she'd looked in that dress. All those long limbs encased in purple silk, her cleavage perfectly framed, those pouty lips slicked with that sexy plum-colored lipstick. My first thought was how that shade would look when smeared along my dick, Harlow on her knees at my feet. My own knees buckle slightly as the images work to send my pleasure even higher, and I put my other hand out to steady myself against the wall.

Closing my eyes, I continue speeding up my strokes while a movie reel plays through my mind, all the times I lashed out at Harlow and she gave back as good as she got. My toes curl against the tiles as a tingling starts at the base of my spine. I want to know what all that passion would feel like when put to a completely different use than fighting. But then again, I do like a good anger fuck. With those last thoughts, I'm moaning her name and painting the tiles with my cum.

No sooner than my cum washes down the drain do the feelings of guilt and disappointment hit. As much as I'd like to explore my visceral reaction to Harlow, I also feel that if I gave into these feelings flowing through me it's almost like I'm betraying my sister. *And isn't that the worst mood killer.*

My head flops back against the tiles as I lean on the wall, the water sluicing over my shoulders and down my back as my mind whirls like it hasn't since I was a teenager. When I failed to protect my sister and hadn't noticed that something was going on in her life, so absorbed in the woman I was dating at the time. She had me so wrapped around her finger I blew off Jacinta's messages, thinking nothing in her life could be as important as the women who kept me occupied with blow jobs and hot sweaty nights. When the night of their sixteenth birthday had come and everything that followed came to light, I finally woke up to the fact that I had failed her. Had let her down when she needed me the most, and I swore up and down that it would never happen again.

But here I am, once again finding myself led by my dick and the softer emotions I feel when I look at Harlow. I know she doesn't deserve everything that is being done to her, but what can I do? I don't know if I can pay the cost of treating her the way she deserves.

Blowing out a sigh, the cold water and the depressing thoughts have successfully gotten me off to a bad start. Turning off the water, I step out of the shower, grabbing a towel to dry myself off.

Time to get dressed and make my way downstairs, preparing for the next round of exchanged barbs between Harlow and me. And just like that, the thought of all her feistiness has my cock starting to twitch once more. *I'm so fucked.*

Harlow

Deciding to take him at his word, I hurry through my morning routine, lost in thoughts about Jacinta and Jaxon's life before my dad, desperately wanting to know what they went through. Maybe, like me, they suffered at the hands of a drug-addled mother, but unlike my refuge with the Bostons, they didn't have anything until Dad found them. My heart pings a little with sympathy, knowing the kind of things they may have gone through first hand; without the Bostons, I may have very well ended up bitter and twisted as well. I could've been just as guarded and aggressive toward strangers. He *did* mention an incident later in life that helped mold her, so who am I to judge? I just hate that I'm at the end of her firing squad at the moment. I guess one positive of the situation is that I just got a different glimpse of Declan. I almost admire him for sticking to his guns and honoring a promise he made as a child, but really, she's an adult. She's able to defend herself now, as everyone witnessed at the premiere, and I really am no threat to her or any of them.

Making sure I have everything thrown into my backpack, I hurry to the main wing of the house to find the breakfast table empty of everyone but Nana, Poppy, and Declan. I didn't notice before, but he's dressed in black suit pants and an emerald green long-sleeved button-down shirt with a silver tie. The shirt brings out his stunning green eyes, which meet mine as I rush into the room.

"Finally, you're here. We can get moving." He's lost any sign of the slight warmth he showed early, a more gruff and cold exterior already in place. Draining his coffee mug, he stands up, grabbing his suit jacket from the back of his chair and putting it over his shoulder. A black leather satchel is snatched from a nearby chair, also thrown over his shoulder, before he goes out the back door, heading for the helipad we used on the night of the movie premiere.

"Sorry, dear." Nana waves a hand in his direction, her eyes rolling. "He's in a hurry this morning. We'll get you something to eat and a coffee at the office." She too is dressed in a pantsuit and armed with a designer handbag, her eyes raking over my outfit. A smile comes to her lips when she's looked her fill. "You look gorgeous. Don't let anyone tell you otherwise." Her words ease some of my insecurities, knowing that I've got her in my corner.

Giving Poppy a kiss on the cheek, she hurries after Declan.

"Give them hell, Hally." Poppy salutes me with his cup of coffee and goes back to reading his newspaper as I follow after the two.

Nana's waiting for me just outside the large glass doors, and she tucks my hand under her arm as we walk toward the helipad. "Now, I wanted to tell you how much Brad actually wanted to be doing this, but he's concerned you'd feel like he was trying to force a relationship with you. He's so worried that he's going to scare you off that he's being overly cautious." Nana's words sound similar to what Kai was saying the other day. "Don't think he's not interested! Say the word and he will jump in with both feet. I told you before, the man is a brilliant businessman, but his social skills are not great. Though Emma seemed to bring him out of his shell last night." When I take a peek at Nana, she has that scheming look in her eye, and I breathe a sigh of relief that it's aimed at Dad and not me. *God knows my life is complicated enough right now.*

The helicopter blades are already spinning as we get closer, and conversation becomes too hard over the noise. Looking at the cockpit, Declan's cryptic words finally make sense. Sitting in the pilot's seat with a headset on is none other than the man himself.

Chapter Thirteen

Harlow

Stopping suddenly, I look between him and the house, wondering if it's not too late to go back and drive in. It would mean I get to drive that awesome car of Oliver's again, so I'm seriously considering it, but Nana must see what I'm thinking.

"Hurry up, dear! We need to get moving." I start to follow her into the backseat, but she shakes her head.

"Why don't you sit up in the front with Declan? The view is so much better," she yells over the sounds of the engine, her eyes twinkling with mischief and voice loud enough that I can't pretend not to hear it. Damn it, what is this woman up to now? She knows well and good that he hasn't been welcoming. Why would she force us together? I start to shake my head, but she pulls the sliding door closed, giving me no option but to climb into the passenger seat next to the pilot.

There's a headset on the seat as I pull the door open and climb up, thanking God and whoever else is up there that I hadn't worn a skirt or a dress today. The thing would have been around my neck with the wind rush. My eyes meet Declan's, the almost permanent frown still on his face, as I pull the headset on.

"About time," he grumbles to me, and within moments, the helicopter is moving upward.

"Now, now, Declan, we never confirmed a time with Harlow, so I think we can let it slide, don't you?" Nana's voice holds a hint of steel in it, and she quickly changes the subject, the queen of keeping her grandchildren in line. "Anyway, I'm pretty sure you were a part of the reason she was held up. Didn't I see you hovering around her room before you made it to breakfast this morning?" The steel turns to a teasing lilt, and my head shoots to Declan. Crap, Nana saw him. Damn woman is going to get the wrong idea. *Even if I tell her otherwise. Especially if I tell her otherwise.* Declan blushes slightly at my attention, but the frown doesn't leave his face.

"Just trying to see if I could get my cat back," he tells her, and I hear a tiny scoff in the headset before she changes the subject yet again.

"So, you're staying with Alex and Shane tonight? They're such nice boys and so handsome. What do you think they're going to do with you?" Nana's question sounds more suggestive than it should, and when I turn to look at her, there's a huge grin on her face. Rolling my eyes at her, I shrug.

"Not sure, but probably just stay in because I have that interview tomorrow." This time, Declan's head turns quickly to me, his eyebrows lifting in surprise.

"Job interview?" he prods, but I don't engage. Instead, I watch the world go by until we reach the towering building that is Neighpalm Headquarters.

Once we touch down on the helipad on the roof, Declan is busy shutting down the helicopter while Nana and I hop out right away, making our way to the elevator. Once inside and away from the noise, she starts to give a run down of the day's schedule.

"Okay, I'm going to take you straight to Hope. She's going to take you down to the ground floor and work your way up. She will give you a tour through each of the different business levels and explain a little more about each. Then, after lunch, you and I are going to be interviewing a few people for temporary design positions within Neighpalm Couture."

My heart jumps at that. Jacinta actually got

punished for her behavior; honestly, I was expecting Dad to have caved, but it seems that he's really going through with this. I feel a little guilty, but the feeling barely registers before Nana pushes the pause button on the elevator.

"Now, Harlow, you of all people don't need to feel guilty. Jacinta deserves what she got. Between you and me, she probably won't lose her position permanently, but she needs to be made aware there are consequences with her actions, especially when her animosity is aimed at you. If it had been someone else, we probably would have cleaned it up and moved on, and yes, I realize how bad that sounds. However, saying that, she's never done something so extreme before either. We just want her to sweat a little bit, and she's always talked about bringing in more designers to work with her. So really, we're doing her a favor. She just doesn't know it yet. As far as the interviews go, the prospective designers are being told they will be working alongside Jacinta. It's only her that thinks she's being replaced. In a few weeks, we'll bring her back in as CEO."

With that, Nana pushes a button and the elevator starts to descend once more, directly to the ground floor. A small smile creeps across my face, the guilt receding as I contemplate Nana's admittance. They really are devious, and I'm pleased her behavior is not being overlooked.

When the doors open to the ground floor, I'm able to take a better look at the lobby than I did the night of the premiere. We all rushed through here so quickly that I didn't get a chance to look around.

Center stage in the foyer is a large reception desk with a marble counter and two very polished secretaries sitting behind it. Behind them on the wall is the Neighpalm Industries symbol of the palm tree and horse.

Poppy had told me the story on the plane on the way over. It was a witty play on words that had originated because of a dare. A drunken colleague of his father had dared him to change the company in the late forties, and being one to never back down from a challenge, he did so. Summers' Industries forever more became Neighpalm Industries, and the horse head and palm tree were immortalized into a symbol that's now recognized world-wide.

Scattered around the foyer are a few comfy-looking couches for people waiting on meetings. Nana had told me that no one was allowed beyond the foyer until their scheduled meeting time, established clients of Declan or Holden, or one of Kai's sponsored athletes, being the exceptions. Everyone else has to wait until called upon.

My eyes peruse the already half-full couches, wondering if any of these are here for our interviews, but then I throw that idea away. That's ridiculous; they're not until after lunch. But even with that thought my eye catches on one individual, sitting over in a quiet corner. A swath of icy white-blond hair cut short at the sides and long on top hides his face from me, but I can see a sketch book in his lap, and I have a feeling I might be seeing more of this guy later.

"Grace, it's so good to see you! It's been ages." A fresh voice has my attention turning back toward Nana. Exchanging a warm hug with the woman in front of her, Nana replies quickly.

"Hope, dear, it feels like you haven't been out to the house in ages! That needs to change." The dark redhead is about the same height as me, but as I scan her body I notice she has three inch heels on. She's wearing a royal purple pencil skirt with a black sleeveless turtleneck that accentuates a slender figure more suitable for showing off Jacinta's clothes than running the PR department for the whole company, but who am I to judge a book by its cover.

Once they finish their pleasantries, they turn to me, but before Nana can say anything, Hope pulls me into her arms. And if that isn't surprising enough, the words tumbling out of her dark red lips are a shock for sure.

"God, Harlow, the Summers kids can be such assholes. I'm so sorry for the way they've behaved, and if you need any help plotting revenge, like I know I would if I were you, I'm *all* in."

Stunned by her offer, I just stand there as she hugs me, Nana's chuckles filling the silence. "Jacinta has run so many women off from those boys, and mostly she's been right, but I can't support her this time. Just say the word, Harlow. I want in." She pulls away with a friendly smile on her face and an earnest look in her eyes.

"Hope had to get past her fair share of Jacinta's antics, but when she realized there was nothing between her and Holden, nor did she have interest in any other of the boys, she let her past the great golden gates," Nana explains as Hope walks us both back into the elevator.

"You know what? I'm going to hold you to that." I pull out my phone and hand it to her. "Your number, please. I'm starting to feel a little claustrophobic, and although Shane and Alex have been wonderful, a little female company would be great right about now."

Hope grabs my phone and enters her number before handing it back. "Okay, let's get this tour started, shall we?" Hope's cheerful attitude is infectious, and I find myself excited for what's to come.

Nana is left behind on the Couture floor, claiming other things need to be attended to before our interviews. Hope and I continue to the top level which houses the administration block for Neighpalm Energy Drink. Stepping out into a light and bright reception area, Hope waves her hand around like a game hostess.

"This is probably the most boring of the businesses," Hope says as I look around the room. The walls are decorated with action shots of athletes, and apart from one woman behind the desk, there is no one else in sight. "The factory pretty much runs itself and has people that oversee the production. This place is used more for looking after Kai's extreme sports teams. The people here are in charge of booking events and photo shoots and all the things the team needs like accommodation and travel arrangements. What you need to do is familiarize yourself with the athletes on his teams so that if you're asked any questions, you'll be able to answer them."

She walks over to the reception desk and grabs a tablet from behind it, returning and handing it over before leading me to a nearby sofa. "This is your official key to the businesses. All the siblings, Brad, Grace, and Howard have one. This is where all the daily information from each business comes. That can be anything ranging from information from my department, to official sales reports, to anything in the media that is tagged with the various business tags. It's how you are able to keep up to date on everything that is going on. Just do a quick scan every day, and urgent things will be highlighted in red. Really, you don't need to know about sales figures and stuff, but you *will* need to keep up to date on things such as which artists are trending, which athletes are winning, and the scandals and gossip circulating about them all." She stops as a woman approaches us with a tray containing coffee and pastries, and after she places them on the coffee table in front of us, she quietly departs without a word.

"Nana messaged me from the chopper and said you hadn't had a chance to have breakfast because Declan was being a douche," Hope says as she pours coffee into two mugs and passes me one.

"I'll be honest, unless you plan on doing a lot of social things which involve the paparazzi like a lot of the others do, you probably won't be harassed." Her eyes narrow as she considers me, searching my face. "That is, unless you plan on trying to muscle your way into one of the businesses."

Unfortunately, I'm taking a sip of coffee when she says this, and she just about ends up wearing it as I choke at her comment.

"Fuck no. Jesus, it blows my mind that none of you have actually asked me what I want," I snap at her, finally sick and tired of everyone assuming I want to work at Neighpalm. Preparing to stand up and leave at this latest insult, she quickly holds her hands up in a defensive manner.

"Hey, whoa, slow down. Okay, I'm sorry, but I just wanted to double check. Holden's my best friend, and I get a little 'Jacinta-like' if I feel he might be threatened."

I roll my eyes in annoyance, anger simmering just below the surface as I grind out my next words.

"Hope, I am a fully qualified veterinarian. I could be running my own practice back at home; I'm just weighing my options right now. Tomorrow, I have an interview for an internship at a zoo. I can't even express how much I don't want any of these damn businesses. The thought of being stuck inside at meetings and mixing with the kinds of people that go along with running big high-profile businesses makes me feel ill. I much prefer animals to people, and after the last week, I am more than sure my instincts are correct."

Hope's mouth has dropped open in utter amazement, and I can practically see her computing what I've just told her. With a snort of amusement, I reach for a pastry. I may as well enjoy the yummies in front of me while she has her mini stroke.

"You're a vet, and nobody actually knows this?" Her voice is incredulous, and again, I almost choke on my pastry when I see the look on her face.

"Well, Nana and Poppy know, so I'm assuming Brad does, but everyone else just jumped to the gold digging conclusions. They all think I work for the Bostons, training horses, which I do, but I've also got other skills. Ones I worked extremely hard for over the last eight years. I figured if they didn't care to ask, I wasn't going to burst their delusional bubbles. They'll figure it out eventually. Or not." I shrug, my anger dissolving as the coffee and sugar hit my system.

Hope flops back in the chair. "So what are you doing here?"

I shrug my shoulders again. "Dad asked, and who am I to deny him? Plus, extra knowledge never hurt anyone. Especially now with the whole bill-board disaster, which you thankfully managed to squash quickly."

This time, Hope snorts. "Ah, yeah, I might have squashed the original billboard, but have you seen the new one? The one that was supposed to go up in the first place." My stomach sinks at her words, and I quickly shake my head as she sits up and grabs me by the hand before dragging me over to the window. Across the street and further down on the building opposite us is a billboard.

Holy shit!!! It's another shot of Alex and me with the other model, all of us wearing the required underwear and nothing else. You can't see the guys' faces, but mine is wearing a look like I've been well satisfied. The slogan says, "Neighpalm Couture. For a lady who knows what she wants."

"Well, maybe they won't put two and two together. Let's face it, that's not how I look every day."

Hope rolls her eyes and drains her coffee. "Come on, let's get moving. I'll give you a quick tour. The Summers kids are idiots. Hold me back if we see Holden! I may slap him upside the head." My heart speeds up a little at the thought of seeing any of them. Obviously, I know Declan's here, but it hadn't occurred to me that the others might be too.

"There isn't a Neighpalm Ink floor, is there?" I ask as we get back into the elevator. Oliver is the last person I want to see. At least all of the others were assholes or indifferent to begin with. His behavior hurts the most.

Hope gives me a look that I know is going to kill my hopes. "Yeah, there is. Because he's making it a chain across the country, he needs somewhere to have them order all their equipment from and to standardize practices and advertising and merchandise." She sounds a little curious but doesn't push for more, and I'm not ready to explain, knowing how close she is with Holden. "But I don't think Oliver is in. Apparently, he was interviewing another artist at his flagship shop because he had a bad interview the last time."

My heart races at the thought of his last interview and how I felt when the girl propositioned him. That was before, when I thought he was truly into me. If I were there now and she did the same thing, I'd tell her to have at it. Hell, I'd even toss her a condom.

The elevator closes, and I grab Hope's hand. "Please don't say anything to them about me being a vet. I want to see how long this whole thing goes on for. I'm hoping they all feel like idiots once they eventually figure it out, and I have no desire to make it easy on them."

She sniggers and squeezes my hand, the twinkle in her eye akin to the one that so frequently appears in Nana's. "As long as I get to be there when you tell them. With my phone in hand to record the whole thing." I smile and drop her hand as she presses the next floor down, feeling at home for the first time since I met Alex and Shane.

Chapter Fourteen

Harlow

The next floor is Thomas' and Neighpalm Airlines. There's really nothing to see here, but it's a large bustling office. Apparently, there are two floors; this one is corporate, and the one below us is commercial bookings and sales. Word on the street, aka Hope, is that Thomas and Dad are in a meeting discussing a small commercial European airline that's in trouble. They're considering buying it and consolidating it into NA. The two of us spend a few minutes peeking through the boardroom's glass window as Thomas and Dad watch a pitch by the European airline's executives, trying to sell why it would be a good idea to invest. Cecelia is also there, and she notices me first, but she doesn't do anything to let Dad know I'm here. She just studies me with those eyes that glare in such a similar way to Jacinta. Seriously, what did I ever do to her? I'm the man's *daughter*.

Eventually, both Dad and Thomas see me on their own. Dad's eyes light up as he stands, stopping the presenter, and he says something before walking out altogether, giving the presenter no chance to reply.

"Harlow, honey." He reaches us and pulls me into his arms, giving me a kiss and a hug before stepping back and doing the same to Hope. It's easy to see that she's considered one of the family, making me feel even better about my possible new ally. "Good morning. How's the tour going? Is Hope being good to you?" He narrows his eyes in mock anger, and Hope and I laugh before I reply.

"Hi, Dad. The tour has been interesting so far, and yes, she's been wonderful." His smile gets broader at my reassurance, and a little bit of tension relaxes in his shoulders.

"Good, that's excellent. I'm sorry I can't join you, but this meeting is important. How about we have lunch before your interviews with Nana?" he suggests, including Hope in the invitation.

"That sounds great, actually," I tell him, but Hope turns him down.

"Thanks for the invite, Brad, but I've got a few things I need to do, and I'd also like to follow up on this meeting with Thomas. I'd like to see if there's anything the PR team needs to do regarding the merger."

"Yes, good thinking. Okay, I'll let Thomas know to call you when we're done. I need to get back, but I'll see you a little later, Harlow."

He returns to the room, and as I follow his tall back, my eyes meet Thomas'. He's not paying any attention to the speaker, or at least I assume he isn't considering he has his gaze locked on me instead.

His red hair is tousled like he's been running his hand through it already, and his shirt sleeves are rolled up to his elbow, showing off his forearms. What is it about a man with his shirt sleeves rolled up? My eyes scan his body, and when they return, he's still watching me closely. I would give anything to know what he's thinking right now, but he has an incredible poker face, absolutely no emotion showing. He seems to have perfected the art of not giving anything away, unlike his other brothers and she who shall not be named.

"Hmm, girl, what's with the eye fucking?" Hope whispers in my ear, startling me, and when I look again, Thomas has turned back toward the meeting.

"Nope, *zero* eye fucking," I quickly assure her.

"Ah no, I disagree. I haven't seen Thomas show that much interest in the opposite sex in a long time. Still waters run deep in that one, and he was burnt badly. Hasn't so much as looked at another woman since his ex-fiancée stole company secrets and sold them to their closest competitor."

My eyes widen at Hope's insider information,

and it occurs to me that I may just have access to someone that has all the Summers' dirty little secrets. She must notice my look because she smirks. "Oh yes, girl, the things that I know and can tell you. Come on, let's keep moving." We walk toward the elevator, once more on our way to another floor, and I take a moment to consider what I want to know from her first.

"What can you tell me about Jacinta and Jaxon from before they came to be with Brad? Everyone keeps saying that her past trauma dictates her current behavior, but no one will tell me what it is. If I can work out why she's like this, maybe I can find a way to get through to her. I'm not here to wreak havoc, and as much as I'm determined not to let her beat me down, I'd rather spend my time building relationships than defending myself. I promise I won't use it against her. I just want to get to the root of the issue."

She studies me, and I guess I pass some test because a smile crosses her lips. "Ok, what are you doing tonight? This is going to be a conversation that needs good food and *copious* amounts of alcohol."

"Damn it, I've got plans with Alex and Shane."

Her eyes light up when I mention them. "I love those two, so freaking sexy and nice. Wow, between me and them, you really hit the friend jackpot." She bumps her hip into mine as we reach the next floor and gives me a knowing smile. "Or is it more than that?"

I shake my head. "Nope, we are *definitely* in the friend zone. Though I'm pretty sure Jacinta thinks it's more."

"Oh yeah, shit, that's not good." Hope steps out of the elevator, and I follow her before coming to an abrupt stop. This reception is way different than the other two we've been in. Where the previous floors were all light and breezy colors, this one is dark and moody with sexy photos of rockstars and musicians all over the walls as well as gold records and signed guitars. There's quiet music playing over some hidden speakers, and the receptionist behind the desk is a little younger than the last two and has bright pink hair and a septum piercing.

"How about tomorrow evening after your interview? We'll have drinks and dinner, and I can give you the rundown on all the siblings." Her offer has my heart pounding, though there's a tiny twist of guilt that I have to force myself to ignore. Do I feel bad about possibly using this info against them? No. Do I feel bad that using this info against any of them would make me a liar to my new friend? Yes, that's something that I'll have to think about. Can I reconcile possibly hurting a friendship with Hope in order to get my revenge on the others? I'm honestly not sure what I should let the Summers cost me. What price will be too much?

"Deal!"

"Come on, let's go find Den. I've got a few things I need to talk to him about." Hope strides across the foyer, her heels clicking on the dark marble-like tiles, straight past the reception desk. She waves at the receptionist on the way, but the girl just stares her down, her face not moving a muscle. *Okay, strong silent type.*

"You'll find that Holden's, Declan's, and Oliver's secretaries are catty cows. Don't give them the satisfaction of knowing they upset you if they try something. Unfortunately, they're good at their jobs and none have gone far enough, yet, to warrant being fired. Jaxon's PA is by far the worst. But between you and me, they've had an on again/off again thing for a while, so her bad attitude might be the most reasonable. I think they're off at the moment."

I gape at her, her words bringing a stabbing pain to my chest, thinking about how Jaxon and I made out and possibly would have hooked up if things had gone differently that night. "How long have they been off?" I grind out between clenched teeth, and she turns to look at me while she keeps walking.

"About two or three months, I think. I'm hoping it's going to last this time; she's a raging bitch, deserved or not." My breathing eases at the news. I would have had to kick him in the nuts if it had been recent.

My eyes skim the walls, taking in all the

different artists, easily spotting the boy band Ninja Starfish. Sanctuary of Chaos, one of my and Maxine's favorite bands, has a few shots of each of the individual members as well as a group shot. *Fuck, they are smoking hot.*

There are a couple of pictures of Daisy Dallas, a young country singer, and then there are some pics of Wicked Sirens, an all girl group. Further along, there's also some of a K-pop-looking band I don't know the name of. So many famous artists, and Holden is responsible for all of them. I think if I were interested in any of the businesses, this would be it. Or Ink, but that's soured for me now.

We finally reach the end of the long door-filled corridor we've been walking down, stopping at a dark double wooden door with Holden Summers CEO inscribed on a nearby gold plaque. Not even bothering to knock, Hope launches the door open and steps into the room.

"Hope! Missy just informed me you were here. You really need to stop tormenting my secretary. Let her do her job." Holden chuckles as he says this, standing up and walking over to her. She shrugs as he gives her a kiss on each cheek, and I almost don't know what to do. In just these sixty seconds, I've seen more genuine affection from Holden than I have yet.

"I would play nice if she did, but she doesn't, so screw her."

Holden moves from Hope to me, that look back

in his eyes again. That look that I definitely need to ignore. He leans in, his fresh appley scent washing over me as he brushes his lips across each of my cheeks, lingering slightly before pulling away. *Well, that's certainly friendlier than we've really been before now.*

"Hi, Harlow. Fancy meeting you here." He's still smiling when he heads back to his desk, my head feeling a little light at the scent of him. *Damn, these Summers boys pack a punch. How is it that every one of them is single? Oh yeah, their raging attack dog of a sister.* Hope is smirking at me as I not so smoothly shake my head to clear the fog, and we both take seats in front of his desk.

"So, what do I owe this pleasure?'

His hazel eyes burn into me even though he's speaking to Hope, and I can't seem to pull mine away from them. Why has Holden started to show interest in me? He was so indifferent when I first arrived. Did Dad put him up to this, or is it something else all together? It's all I can do to stop from squirming under his intense gaze. Thank god for Hope, because she clears her throat and he turns toward her, breaking our strangely intimate staring contest.

"I've set up the meeting with Ninja Starfish for tomorrow, but their manager wasn't very forthcoming with information regarding the cause of the brawl," Hope tells him once he's focused on her. "In fact, she was downright evasive, so I'm afraid we're going into the meeting blind."

Her words have him sitting up straighter, a frown creasing his brow. All signs of attraction disappear as he goes into work mode.

"Who's their manager again?" he asks, shuffling through the paperwork on his desk as if looking for the answer.

Hope huffs before replying, "Her name is Giselle. Remember, she was a new hire right around the time that we ran the competition that ended with Ninja Starfish. We gave them to her because we weren't sure how they would go, but they exploded, and well, then we couldn't really change it. Don't get me wrong, she's been good at her job, but there's just something about her that rubs me wrong. She's around the same age as the guys, I think mid-twenties at the oldest, and I'm just not sure if it was the right decision."

"Oh yes, I remember now. I almost didn't hire her because she batted her eyelids at me through the whole interview." He stops shuffling his papers, looking at Hope with an eye roll that's recklessly attractive. *I need to get laid. Definitely something wrong with me.*

"Yes, I remember," she said wryly. "But she came with some impressive recommendations, and there was also the family connection. I'm pretty sure she's a distant relative of Chester Mercury."

"Ah yes, that's right. Chester gave Dad a call and hit him up to give his great-niece a chance."

Holy crap, Chester Mercury is the lead singer to

the legendary rock band Garden of Sin. I hadn't realized they were under the Neighpalm Records label.

"Damn it. Okay, we'll do some more digging, maybe send someone to ask around the rest of their staff. They're not doing any recording at the moment, are they?" Holden pushes, and Hope shakes her head.

"No, they're due back in the studio in a month or so. They've been on a break since their world tour finished a month ago."

"Alright, I guess we just have to wait and see what happens." He turns away from her, focusing on me. *Wonderful, where are we going with this?*

"So, Harlow, how has your day been so far?" His voice takes on a more relaxed tone now that he's not trying to figure out his band's latest issue. "Is my bestie treating you well? If not, I might have a few stories to turn that around." The teasing that ends his offer has an effortlessness to it, like this is who he's really meant to be when he's not being dragged down by his siblings' bad attitudes, and it's a good look on him. There's a little smile in his eyes and that twinkle that makes me see how he and Kai could be similar even though there's no biological relation. Apart from a few stilted conversations previously and that short moment when I was stuck in the pool, this is the first real interaction we've had. I've got to say, it's nicer than I thought it would be. Not wanting to waste this moment, I throw the guy a bone and respond in kind.

"It's been good. Hope is a fountain of information. In fact, you could go as far as saying she's the best thing that's happened to me just recently." She and I exchange a grin, and another frown creases Holden's brow as he looks between the two of us, his eyebrow raising in what might be genuine concern.

"I hope you're not telling Harlow any exaggerated tales about me. I wouldn't want her to get the wrong impression."

Hope stands up and gestures for me to follow, giving Holden a wink in the process. "Holden, I really think you don't need me to tell her anything. You've already made a bad impression if the rumors I've heard are true, not to mention that billboard debacle. I still can't believe you didn't stop Jacinta," she scolds, and he immediately hangs his head with a wince.

"I know, I know. You're right, and I plan on making it up to her." His eyes meet mine as he says this, and I can appreciate this part of him. Holden, away from his siblings and any of the games, with a helpful bestie to call him on his shit… that Holden is one that I might be able to forgive.

And Hope snorts. "Well, have you even apologized for letting your sister railroad you? You know I love you guys, but come on, she's not an insecure teenager anymore, and you have *got* to stop letting her make these kinds of decisions."

Amazingly, Holden's cheeks grow pink with embarrassment as Hope continues to chastise him, and he twitches in his chair like a child being lectured. I almost speak up about how he and Thomas hadn't actually done anything, but then think again. They must have known she had something planned, and even if they weren't outright encouraging the behavior like Jaxon and Declan, they're just as guilty of complacency as Oliver.

To my amusement, Hope continues to rake him over the coals while I just lean back and soak it up. Seriously, from the look on his face, this is almost punishment enough, but I think I can get something more out of it.

Leaning forward, I interrupt her tirade. "Do you really want to make it up to me?" I ask, my eyes narrowed as I watch for *any* sign of duplicity.

"Yes, of course," he's quick to assure me, no sign of deception to be seen. Well, this could work in my favor.

"And are you prepared to do whatever it takes?" I nearly hold my breath, not sure what he's going to say.

I can see Hope out of the corner of my eye, waiting with baited breath to hear about what I want him to do. There's a kind of sadistic spark in her eye that tells me she's enjoying seeing her bestie squirm.

He gives me a quick nod, and I can see the caution in his eyes, but he breathes deep and gives me a more decisive nod this time. He fucked up, and he knows he has to pay the price. I've got to say, that makes me a little hot, that he's recognizing he fucked up and now wants to make amends. It certainly gives me another picture of the spoiled billionaire's son.

I'm not sure why, but the thought of Holden being my bitch makes me squirm in a much more pleasant way than he is now. To have him at my beck and call, this strong, capable man entirely submissive to me, just lights a fire inside of me. Some small sadistic part of me really wants to see him, all of them, really, grovel for my forgiveness. I'm not sure where it comes from, probably some fucked up interaction with my mother, but the need is real.

"Awesome, from now on at home and in public when strangers aren't around, I need you to refer to me as mistress. You will be at my beck and call twenty-four seven, catering to my every need. Is that understood?" There's a hint of steel in my command so that he knows that I'm serious. Sitting back again, I wait for the fall. Wait for him to rant and rave and declare me crazy. He didn't have the balls to stand up to his sister before, so will he have the balls now? I can only imagine how she'll rip into him for showing any signs of *obedience* to me, and something inside me just loves the idea of her knowing I've "taken" one of her brothers from her. If I make it to that Hawaii trip with Kai, that'll be two of her allies I think I could now call mine.

His jaw clenches, the only sign of a negative reaction. His eyes, which had been deliberately blank, then begin to heat with something I hadn't expected. *Desire.* Well, well, well. Who would have thought Mr. CEO would like the idea of being bossed around? I had honestly just been thinking about making him my bitch at home, but now *all* kinds of possibilities are coming to mind.

The room is thick with tension and a growing sense of a sexual... something, so when Hope clears her throat, both of us startle. Getting to his feet and coming around to our side of the desk, he holds out his hand to me. I take it, making an extra effort not to glance down at anything that may or may not be happening there, and he pulls me to my feet before kneeling in front of me. "Mistress Harlow, if this is what you require of me, then I will be yours to command." With a bow of his head, he waits for me to respond.

Holy shit. Over his head, my eyes meet Hope's, and she's fanning herself and mouthing "Hot."

I shake off his hand and step away. "Well, good. I will see you at home then, pet."

Without another word, I stride out of his office, leaving him kneeling on the floor. I can hear Hope's heels as she hurries behind me, but I don't stop until I hear the door click closed. Breathless from his response, I need to take a moment to calm down. While I'm totally lost in the hot mess of my hormones, Hope steps up next to me, her hip bumping mine again.

"Jesus, I don't know what's going on between the two of you, but that was some *steamy* shit right there. I just hope you make him work for it before you give in to the lust."

Shaking my head to clear the fog, I blink at her a couple of times. "Huh?"

"Oh, come on, the sexual chemistry between the two of you was off the fucking charts. Holden's not backward in coming forward with his sexual interests but submitting to a woman has never been one of them. He prefers for women to submit to him." She starts moving down the long corridor, dragging me by my arm, keeping her voice low so that it doesn't carry to the receptionist in front.

"Not to mention the eye fucking Thomas and you just gave each other too," she adds in, and I nod, admitting she's not wrong.

When we pass her on the way to the elevator, we both wave and smile broadly, getting no reaction from the sour-faced young woman. Giggling together, I wait for the door to close to respond to her.

Collapsing back against the elevator walls, I sigh deeply again. "The problem is he's not the only one I have chemistry with. Jaxon and my chemistry was off the charts when I first met him before all this. Not to mention what happened with Oliver when he gave me my new tattoo, and I also find myself attracted to Kai. Which, to be honest, seems like the safest bet. He's the one who's been nothing but kind to me since the very beginning."

The words come tumbling out of my mouth, the confession feeling like a release, and I hadn't realized how much the worry had been building up inside me. I run a hand through my hair before meeting her gaze.

"How do I know that the rest won't continue to support her? Because I can guarantee from the look in that woman's eyes, she is *not* done with me yet. I was so determined to get payback for how they treated me. Spent hours with Alex and a bottle of wine plotting all sorts of crazy schemes, but now it all seems pointless. It's just not in my nature, and some of them seem to be coming around and acting like mature adults instead of childish teens. Maybe I can still get a little taste of that revenge without it making me resort to something ugly. I must admit making Holden my bitch is going to be fun."

My stomach swirls with butterflies and disappointment. On one hand, I love the thought of spending more time with Kai, but I feel guilty as well because I want to be spending more time with all of them. At least the nice versions of them that I only get these little peeks of. If we can move past their initial hostility so that I get the real versions of them full-time, what am I supposed to do then?

Hope's eyes are wide with surprise at my confession, but it doesn't take her long to recover and start addressing some of the rambling I've just dropped on her. "Dude, who says you have to choose? You're young and single, and it's not like you're trying to trap them into marriage, are you? You might be the perfect piece to fit into their not-so-normal puzzle. Things don't need to be conventional to be right."

Her words have me pausing. "No, I guess not… This is probably my own family baggage talking, but I guess I've always just thought it would be nice to have someone to rely on. That traditional future of a man to cook dinner with and watch Netflix."

She shrugs, looking entirely unfazed. "Why not a few someones? The world is a different place than it was for our parents, Harlow. Who says you have to pick just one? Arguably, I'm closer with Holden than the rest of them, but I don't think that ordinary would ever work for the Summers. They're just so close-knit and protective of each other, and god knows their family legacy adds a million layers of complication. Let's face it, they're all very busy men and often travel on business. I can guarantee you, you will spend *a lot* of time on your own if you settle for just one." Her eyes sparkle with her next words. "But if you had more than one, it would guarantee that someone was always around. You would never have to feel lonely again."

Her words touch something deep inside, resonating with and appealing to that desperately lonely inner child who has never felt like she really belonged to someone or somewhere. We're both quiet while the elevator opens on the next business, Hope allowing the message to sink in before she steps out.

Holden

My eyes are glued to her ass as she sashays out of my office, Hope following behind wide-eyed and fanning herself. I snort a little, wondering how long it will take for my bestie to get back in here and launch a barrage of questions at me. She's a much warmer person than Jacinta, not that that's hard to accomplish, but I've never seen her so bubbly around a new friend as she was around Harlow. I've always thought that Hope was an excellent judge of character, so this is just one more piece of evidence stacking up to say that I was a royal asshole.

The door slams shut behind them, and I push up off the floor, adjusting my cock now that there's no witnesses to me reacting like an overwhelmed teenager. There was something about the heat in her eyes as I got down in front of her and lowered my head that almost had me coming in my pants.

Only once before have I had this reaction, and when that went bad, I promised myself I would never voluntarily be vulnerable again. It's amazing what promises you'll break for the right reward. I think I… trust Harlow, which is either a huge leap for me or a huge lapse in judgment. I'm thinking it's the former, and there's a tiny bit of me that might be healing from this silly little game that started between us today. If I can do this, if I can be vulnerable and have it all be okay, then maybe I can start to heal those old wounds. Something tells me that Harlow would never abuse the control I'm willing to give her.

Straightening out my clothes, I return to my desk and look over the various contracts I have to review and all the other boring day to day crap that comes with running this business. I miss scouting new talent, and I miss the rush of going out and having a good time. For so long now, I've been stuck behind a desk or attending boring ass meetings, behaving myself and never overindulging in any way that would put the company's reputation at the slightest risk. I miss the music, I miss performing, and I miss the *rush* of it all.

Sighing, the noise loud in my otherwise soundproof room, I pull up my emails and notice one from Paul, the head of the A&R department.

Hey, man, found this band in that new goth club that's just opened up. Attached is a sample of them live. I really think they've got something. I've set up a meeting with them and their manager the night of their next show. Let me know what you think.

Pressing play on the link, the music comes through my surround sound system installed for exactly this reason. I lean back in my chair, letting the sounds flow through me. A male and a female voice harmonize perfectly, bringing goosebumps to my skin. This sound needs to be heard by everyone on this planet. My pulse races, and I start to feel more alive than I have in ages, not counting that moment of giving myself over to Harlow.

Once the song finishes, I sit up in my chair and shoot an email back to Paul.

Neighpalm Records needs them. I want in on that meeting. Let me know the details.

A rush of adrenaline flows through my body. This is what I need, an outlet for all the built up tension in my body and my growing feelings for Harlow. And maybe while I'm at it, Neighpalm Records may also be finding the next big thing. The moment my reply is sent, I'm already messaging Hope, needing my bestie to know that I'm feeling alive once more.

Chapter Fifteen

Harlow

Over the next forty-five minutes, I see the Ink offices, the Production offices, and, with somewhat of a relief, I don't see either Oliver or Declan. I'm already so confused that I don't need to see them to add to it. Thankfully, it's almost time for me to meet Nana on the Couture floor, but we still have Jaxon's domain standing in the way. My brain knows he treated me badly, but my heart speeds up when my traitorous body remembers our dance. Stupid organ, who needs it anyway?

There's no one at the reception desk when we walk past it, thank god. "Come on, Jaxon's office is this way," Hope points out, directing me down a nicely decorated hallway. "We'll go and see if he's around. He's just secured another property; it's beachside in Hawaii, and it was a rundown dump, but he's in the middle of gutting it and renovating. It's a fun process, and we get to see all the decorating samples." Hope's voice rises with her excitement, and I smile even though I can't bring myself to feel that same thrill over wallpaper and paint samples as she does.

The office door is open when we get to it, and there sounds like quite a heated conversation going on inside. We exchange a glance and pause just outside to listen in, the two of us both making faces that say we don't want to get in the middle of this shit. Thank goodness there's carpeting in this hallway and they haven't heard us approaching.

"*No*, Raquel, I don't want to do this anymore." Jaxon sounds weary, like he's sick of saying the same thing over and over again, and I feel a pang of sympathy for him before I quickly shut that shit down. "We're done, and it's exhausting how you keep trying to change my mind. I'm not interested; I've moved on."

"But, Jaxon, why?" The voice is whiny but breathy at the same time, and I'm impressed someone can achieve that level of annoying while still managing to simultaneously sound sexy.

I shrug in Hope's direction, that sort of "what do we do now?" gesture, but she just rolls her eyes and continues to eavesdrop. *Okay, so we're all up in this right now.*

"Is it because of your bitch sister? Poor little

orphan girl, so easily deceived then thrown away. Clinging on to her brother like he's her only hope." The sheer venom in her voice almost makes me gasp, and I can only imagine how those words are striking him. He has been an all-around asshole, but if I've been able to understand anything about him by this point, it's how much he loves his sister. If this girl is truly trying to be a fixture in his life, she's barking up the wrong damn tree.

With a sigh, I resign myself to getting involved. No matter what we have between us, no one deserves to be spoken to like that, especially because it's his right to decide who he does and doesn't want to be involved with. Already hoping I don't regret this, I push Hope out the way and march into his office, adopting that cold look that Jacinta has perfected and worn around me basically every time I've seen her.

"Jaxon, are you ready for lunch?" I ask him, totally ignoring the curvy woman who's sitting on his lap. Both of them jump as I approach the desk, not having heard me enter. Standing in front of his desk, I stare down at them, feeling powerful. "Get rid of the help so we can go." I'm striking a low blow, I know, but it's really only a return volley after all.

"Who the fuck are you?" The words practically fall out of the woman's mouth as she scrambles off of his lap. "And I'm not 'the help.' I'm Jaxon's girl-friend." Her face is red and eyes blazing in annoyance as she stands there, her fists clenched by her side.

"Yes, honey, I'm sure you are. That's what all his *friends*,"—I say bitingly, lifting my fingers in emphasis—"call themselves. You seem to have a lot of them, Jaxon." I raise one eyebrow at him, and he narrows his eyes in return, but no matter how he feels about my interference, it seems to have worked for the better, mostly. The girl screeches her disgust and hurls herself at me, slapping me across the face.

Shit, that escalated quickly.

"Yes, security, could you make your way up to the Hotel and Resorts floor? We need to have someone escorted from the building." While I rub at my stinging cheek, Hope's already handling this shit show in an official capacity. It's been a while since I've been slapped across the face, not having happened since I grew bigger than my mother, but I can still take a punch and stay standing.

"Yes, get out and stay out." Raquel, if I remember her name correctly, sneers at me, but Hope steps up to my side, shaking her head.

"Oh no, honey, you assaulted one of the members of the Summers family. You just lost your job. Pack up your shit and get out." The girl instantly pales as each of Hope's icy words strike into her, her eyes widening with panic as her easy ticket to a spoiled life disappears right before her eyes.

"No, no, you can't do that!" she appeals to

Jaxon, her eyes pleading, but he's got that cold imperious thing down perfectly. In fact, it's the same look I saw the day I arrived, and I start to feel a little sorry for the girl, though the heat in my cheek makes that quickly disappear.

When he says nothing, her pleading turns to fury as she growls, "You'll regret this" before she storms out.

"Phew, never a dull moment around here, is there?" Hope tries to lighten the moment, but I'm on pins and needles, waiting for the fallout from everything that happened. Jaxon looks like an atomic bomb waiting to explode.

But what comes out of his mouth is very different from what I expected.

"Thank fuck for that." His breath escapes in a whoosh, hands running through his hair. "I didn't know how to deal with that without ending up with a sexual harassment suit on my hands. Harlow, you just helped me out, thank you."

"Gee, glad I could be of help," I mutter, continuing to rub my still stinging cheek. The girl put some force behind it. I seriously can't win in the damage department at the moment; maybe I need to be wrapped in bubble wrap. *Guess I should count myself lucky she wasn't wearing a ring.*

"Jesus, Jaxon, it's what everyone has been telling you for a long time. Don't shit where you work."

"Hmm, classy, Hope," he drawls. "But I've

learned my lesson. No more office romances, I promise."

"Thank god, because that would have been a PR *nightmare*. I mean, the least you guys can do is keep yourselves out of the tabloids. I have enough problems dealing with all the temperamental artists. Seriously, my PR team doesn't get paid enough for you to add more work to it."

She's wandered over to a coffee table on the side that has a jumble of what looks like fabric samples spread out over it. But it's the three-dimensional model on a pedestal on the other side of the office that draws my eye. Walking over to it, I discover what must be a model of Jaxon's new hotel. It's small and boutique-looking, not like the five-star monstrosities they're known for. This one only appears to be five stories high, and from the looks of the windows on each floor, there are maybe four or five suites on each level. The grounds are lush and tropical, with a number of intimate swimming pools dotted here and there through the foliage.

Hope sees where I'm looking and bounds over to it, Jaxon following close behind. "I'm so excited about this place! It's completely different to what we normally own. It's going to have themed floors," she tells me, practically giddy over the idea. "And it's aimed at the adult market. Each room is stocked with adult supplies which we source from Sugar and Spice. It's like a mini bar for sex!"

Whoa, okay then. Sugar and Spice is an

upmarket sex toy chain dotted around the country. Totally not something I expected Neighpalm to be involved in, but the idea is… intriguing.

Jaxon takes over the explanation. "It's going to be a fun place for adults to play and live out their fantasies. Very exclusive, and we're thinking about making it membership only. It's something I'm discussing with my great-aunt."

His great-aunt? "That would be Poppy's sister?" I ask carefully, and they exchange a glance before grins break out over their faces.

"Have you not heard that story yet?" Hope asks, dragging me over to the seating area and shoving me into a chair that's as amazingly comfortable as it looks. Jaxon follows behind again with an indulgent smile on his face.

Wow, the look on his face almost has me speechless. I had forgotten what he looked like when he was relaxed and enjoying himself. It causes my heart to stutter slightly, the beat growing more and more erratic as I imagine the twinkle in Holden's eye, Kai's easy smile, and the softness in Declan's whispers when he speaks to Princess.

"Well, in my defense, there's a lot I don't know about this family yet, nor have I really had the time to ask. I did hear that there had been a family falling out and that's why she sold the property across the road to the Transylvanian dude."

"Yes, but it wasn't Poppy and Aunt Merideth that fell out. It was their father and her," Jaxon adds in, our momentary truce apparently extending to the sharing of family stories. “The old coot actually croaked not long after she moved away, so it’s never been a thing.”

“What happened? And what has she got to do with your new hotel?”

Hope's face gets all animated, and she leans forward, practically bouncing in her seat. “Well, Aunt Merideth wasn't interested in being a part of the Neighpalm Industries company; she was a groundbreaker and wanted to establish her own business.”

“Well, that’s awesome, I guess. I mean, it might have been a little daring back then, a woman CEO, but why wouldn't her father support it?”

“It wasn't actually that he didn't want her to run a business; he offered her half of Neighpalm Industries, after all. It was the nature of the business she wanted to run.” Jaxon rolls his eyes as Hope drags out the explanation, her smile telling me just how much enjoyment she gets out of this.

“Aunt Merideth realized, long before a lot of people, that sex is profitable,” he casually says, shrugging his shoulders.

"She's the CEO of Sugar and Spice Enterprises and the original owner and Madam of the Sugar and Spice brothel in Las Vegas.”

And just like that, my mind is blown. Whoa, first Nana and Poppy are talking about polyamorous relationships and now this revelation. I really do come from a sexually adventurous family. *And I definitely don't need to think too far into that aspect of the family tree.*

"And she also has family problems of her own," Jaxon says wryly. "Her daughter ran off years ago and hasn't been heard from since. She's spent thousands of dollars searching for her, but it's like she just disappeared into thin air. She was a little bit younger than Dad and flighty as fuck from what he tells us. It's sad, really. Aunt Merideth is a blast, but her eyes always look a little haunted now."

"So this is a sex hotel," I deadpan, and they look surprised. Immediately, they both jump in, trying to convince me that it's all above board and blah, blah, blah. They look so worried that I can't keep my face straight, bursting into laughter. "Relax, I don't care, sounds fun. Do you have samples of the 'gifts' that are going to be available to the guests?"

Hope's eyes light up and she turns to Jaxon, probably because she wants to know too, but his eyes have narrowed on me, his previously pleasant manner disappearing quicker than snacks at a Weight Watchers meeting. *Ahhh, there he is. I was starting to wonder who this pleasant person was.* I guess saving him from a sexual harassment suit only earns me so much leeway. The ice has returned, and he spins on his heels and heads back to the desk, the moment gone.

"You can see yourselves out. I have a lot of work to complete."

Exchanging glances, Hope shrugs before we both make our way out.

"And close the door," he shouts, so Hope grabs the handle and slams it shut behind us, clearly telegraphing how we both feel about his sudden Jekyll and Hyde routine. Before we can dig into his return to assholeness, the scene that greets us is enough to distract us.

Raquel is at her desk, fingers flying across the keyboard, and from here it looks like she's copying and pasting files into emails, sending them on quicker than I can even emotionally process what's happening.

"What the fuck?" Hope dashes over to the desk and grabs Raquel, yanking her backward and away from the desk. But the bitch isn't going down without a fight. She turns and tackles Hope, and together, they go down in a tangle of arms and legs and squeals as hair is pulled and slaps are exchanged.

While she's distracted, I head over to her desk to see if I can work out what she was doing, and sure enough, the sent emails contain files on all the properties that Neighpalm Clubs and Resorts is looking at for future investment.

Right then, three things happen. Their yelling gets louder, and Jaxon's door flies open before he storms out then stops, stunned and slack-jawed. At the same time, the elevator opens, and two security guards step out. Also momentarily frozen, they leap quickly into action when Jaxon shouts, "What the hell is going on?"

The burly guards separate the two women who are still spitting insults at each other. Neither of them has come out unscathed. Hope has a red handprint across her cheek, her hair is askew, and her top three buttons are ripped off. Raquel is similarly disheveled and has lipstick smeared across her face while her shirt is missing an entire sleeve. Bright red drops of blood drip from her nose, splattering on the pristine white of the ruined blouse. Hope must have gotten a solid punch in, so I'd call that a win. *Definitely bestie material. I can't fault Holden's taste in friends; I need a girl like this on my side.* I'm also hit with another spike of worry and maybe even the tiniest bit of fear at the idea of using any info Hope gives me to manipulate the siblings. If this is a taste of how fiercely she'll defend them, or at least their businesses, the risk might not be worth the reward.

"Raquel was emailing company intel to someone," Hope tells Jaxon, her breath wheezing out as she lowers herself into Raquel's vacated office chair, the security guard no longer restraining her.

The other woman struggles against her restraints but doesn't deny the accusations, sneering at Jaxon instead. "I said you would regret this."

Jaxon shakes his head, much less fazed than I would be. "Well, you must have really wanted those assault charges, and now we're going to add corporate sabotage to them too." Her face pales as she realizes how much trouble she's in now.

Jaxon turns to the unoccupied guard. "Please call the police and advise them of the situation. Then secure Miss Wells until they arrive and store her computer somewhere for evidence. Let me know when they arrive, and I'll come and speak to them."

The guards take away a still screaming Raquel, and Jaxon turns an accusing eye to Hope and me.

"Well, you didn't want a PR nightmare, so I suggest you clean up and get yourself together so you can deal with this mess." His tone is cold, and there is no warmth in his eyes. Hope hangs her head in shame, but a wave of rage flows up my spine. How dare he speak to her like that when she was trying to save his business! It was his fault in the first place. There he goes again, blaming another woman for his problems.

"How about a 'thank you, Hope'?" I snarl at him.

She whips her head in my directions and whispers, "Don't," but I ignore her.

"If it wasn't for her, you would've had no idea that Raquel had done that. You were arrogant enough to send her out here on her own and not supervise her departure, so that's on you. Now *you* can do damage control. Work out who she sent it to and how to fix it." By now, I've stepped up into his personal space, and that seductively spicy scent of his brings back vivid enough memories that my brain threatens to misfire, but I don't back down. I'm tapping my pointed finger against his chest in anger now.

"You don't get to talk to her like that and treat her like she's at fault. If anything, this is all on you, buddy, for not being able to keep it in your pants. It is *not* okay for you to project your anger at one specific woman onto Hope, or anyone else for that matter." Okay, so maybe I didn't have to throw that last part in, but that makes it no less true.

I'm so close to him now I can feel his breath on my face, and if I just leaned in a little more, I could mash my mouth against his. My body almost does move, involuntarily craving the feel of his lips against mine once more. My nipples are rock hard inside my bra as they lightly brush against his chest, and I pray he doesn't notice. His nostrils flare as his eyes sparkle with a dangerous light, and instead of taking a step back, he looks about to move closer. But another noise from Hope has me pulling away. Shaking myself out of my anger-induced lusty fog, I grab her gently by the arm and walk her toward the elevators.

"Where do you think you're going?" the growly voice asks from behind us.

"I'm going to find Nana, and we're going to help Hope clean up, and then she's going home for the rest of the day. Delegate this shit to someone else in her department. *Asshole."* That last word was muttered under my breath, but I guess not quietly enough. Hope snorts slightly but doesn't say a word, and neither does said asshole behind me. He must realize that it wouldn't be safe to push me right now. As we step into the elevator and turn to face him, I can see in his eyes that this confrontation isn't over; it's only been delayed. But I'm not scared. *Bring it, asshole*.

Chapter Sixteen

Jaxon

As the elevator door closes, I look around at the aftermath of the altercation. Sheets of paper are strewn across the room, and the computer is on the floor, the screen blank and cracked. One of them must have knocked it off the desk during the tussle. I can't believe she did this, risking everything just for some petty revenge. Now she's going to find herself with a whole heap of legal worries. God, why didn't I listen to Dad and stay away from an office relationship? *Because Harlow's right, and you're an asshole who creates your own problems,* a voice in my head jeers. Shaking my head, I pull my cell out of my pocket and call the IT department.

"It's Jaxon. Can you send someone up here? I need a computer and some specific emails looked at to see if we can determine where they went. We've had a security breach." Once I have assurances that someone will be here right away, I hang up and shove my phone back in my pocket, my hands running through my hair as I blow out a deep breath.

Inhaling again in an attempt to settle my mind, I catch the lingering scent of Harlow, and my cock twitches inside my pants. My anger drains away as I remember the words she threw at me. Jesus, she's right. I fucked up. Turning on my heel, I stalk back to my office, picking up the phone and dialing HR.

"It's Jaxon. I need a new PA, preferably someone older and married. Or a man."

The person on the other end snorts but assures me they'll get right on it. *Wait until Jacinta hears about this one. It's probably a good thing that Hope already got a few swings in.* Smashing the phone back into its cradle, I lean back in my chair, swinging it to face out the window and instantly regretting it. Across from me is a giant image of a half-naked Harlow rolling around on a bed with Alex and some other guy. Instantly, my anger rises again, and I clench my jaw, not allowing the growl that I feel inside to come out.

Why do I do these things to myself? I let women sink their hooks into me, and it's always the ones who want nothing more than my name, my money, my company. They don't want *me*, not really. If I'm being completely honest with myself, Harlow was one of the first women who ignited a spark in me. Sure, women think I'm attractive, but it's been so long since that first impression wasn't "helped" by my identity. When I met Harlow, she had no idea who I was. I think I have to admit that I believe that now. She could have been mine, all mine, and we could have been on our way to building something good, yet I let my sister get into my mind.

It's all fucked up, and I just keep making it worse. I can't stop these knee-jerk reactions that have been ingrained in my mind, to pull back and become cold the second I feel like someone might be more interested in what I can get them than who I am. Maybe I'm just doomed to be stuck in this endless loop of suspicion and scorned women, my sister and Nana as my only consistent female companions. *Fuck, that's depressing.*

My eyes scan the golden skin covered in colorful tattoos. The sexy full sleeve that drew my attention in the first place as well as the others scattered across her body are captivating. But the one that has me intrigued is just in the crease of her underwear. I can see a cute little penguin peeking out and curse my behavior because I could have been tracing that penguin with my tongue. Instead, I'm sitting here with a hard dick, and Harlow is angry at me once again. How am I going to make this better?

Picking up the phone again, I press the button for Kai's cell.

"Hey, bro, what's up?" Kai's permanently cheerful voice comes through the speaker loud and clear. I roll my eyes at his sunny disposition, but a smile forms on my lips. That's one thing I've always begrudgingly appreciated about Kai; he never fails to make a bad day better.

"Did I hear you telling Dad that you were taking Harlow to Hawaii this weekend?" His silence after my question has me rushing ahead. "Because I need to inspect the new resort, and I thought I would grab a ride on the jet with the two of you."

He blows out a breath which echoes through the phone. "Look, man, I don't think that's a great idea. You haven't exactly been welcoming to her, and I really wanted to make the trip fun and relaxing. She deserves it after that shit with the billboard, not to mention the riding accident and being pushed."

"I know, I fucked up. I let Jacinta get into my head, but she swears she didn't do those other two things. She said she hadn't had a chance to do anything else, and I think losing the business was enough to give her a kick in the ass. Especially since Nana invited Harlow to have input into the new designers. Every time I've seen her over the last day or two, apart from at meals, her head is over her drafting board and her pencil is flying furiously across the paper. She's a woman with a mission, and Harlow has become an afterthought for the moment."

"So why do you want to come? Because, man, I got to tell you... I really like this girl."

"Shit, Kai. I just want to make up for my behavior," I admit, and since I'm being honest right now, I may as well lay it all out to him. "Harlow and I had a connection that night, and I want to see if there's anything remotely salvageable. I just want a chance to actually get to know her as much as she'll let me." I run my other hand through my hair, the urge to get up and pace riding me hard, but I stay still.

"Fine, but I'm not backing away. You blew your chance, and now it's mine. If you even look at her funny, I swear my fist will be in your face." It looks like it's going to be may the best man win, but he does deserve the opportunity to see what might happen with her. Part of me can't deny it as much as another part hates to admit it, but he's earned this chance. Kai's really one of the best of us, if not *the* best, and even though it might be to my own loss, I can't take the chance of something good away from my brother.

"Yeah, okay. How about we stay at the new hotel? I'm afraid I really put my foot in it… again. Yeah, I know, hold the groan until I hang up, please. Hope brought Harlow to the office, and we told her about the new property and a little bit of Aunt Merideth's involvement, but when she asked about samples of the products that we're going to offer at the hotel, I was a dick. My mind immediately went to another person trying to get something out of me, but of course that wasn't the case. She was trying to be friendly." I huff in disgust at myself. *So many damn issues… maybe Jacinta isn't the only one who needs to go back to therapy.*

Taking advantage of Kai's silence, the guy probably stunned by my capacity to be a dick without even trying, I keep rambling, trying to sell him on the idea. "A few of the suites are functional, and I have a skeleton crew there to tidy up after the builders and designers. We can stay in one of the little bungalows with the pools. I can check it out, you can do your scouting thing, and we can take her out for dinner and dancing or even out on the water. We should let the captain of the boat know we're coming, just in case. I'll be nice Jaxon the entire time, I swear. If I'm any sort of dick at all, I'll willingly walk into her demon mini's stall and let it add bite marks to my ass too."

Kai ignores my last comment, probably because he won't believe it until he sees it. But he does consider the rest of what I said at least. "Already ahead of you with the boat, bro, but the hotel sounds like a good idea. I was just going to stay at my house, but I'm dying to see what you've done with the new one. I'll let my housekeeper know not to bother dusting."

His chuckles have a smile crossing my face, and a sense of relief flows through me. I have some *serious* groveling to do. I'm just not sure how but I'm going to make up for my atrocious behavior toward her, but it's going to have to be good if I want to even get close to where we had started.

Kai hangs up after hashing out a few more details, and I dial another number. Turning back toward the billboard, my eyes roam her body and the way the two men are holding her. The possibilities are endless if I can convince her to give me another chance. Maybe Kai and I can persuade her to roll around on the bed with both of us. I don't like the thought of stealing the girl my brother likes; I'd much rather share her so we can both be happy.

I don't see why either of us needs to be selfish with a woman like Harlow. Both of us are busy men, and knowing someone can look after her when I'm at work and vice versa is a comfort rather than a disappointment. Nana always made sure that we could feel comfortable talking about sex and other topics as we grew up, and she's never shied away from talking about our main airline hostess Jilly and her polyamorous relationship.

Wishing that she too had been strong enough to make that choice when she was younger.

Most people might find it awkward to talk about that kind of shit with their grandmother, but there's just something so straightforward about Nana that takes the drama out of it. Like her bluntness takes away your ability to be embarrassed before you can even think twice about talking about threesomes and sex toys with her. Now, Poppy's another story, but the man has definitely learned not to get in the path of Hurricane Nana. If she wants to talk about threesomes and the best positions for sharing a partner, then that's what's being discussed. In any case, before I get myself into more issues of the romantic kind, I'm afraid I have to man up and take care of my friendship first.

The cell stops ringing, and it goes to voicemail.

"Holden, can you get your PA to send Hope a bunch of flowers from me, with just the words 'Sorry, I'm an asshole' on the card? She saved my ass today, and I'm afraid I wasn't properly appreciative. Maybe have her book her a table at a nice restaurant on me too."

Hanging up, I place the phone back down, more gently this time, and walk over to the model that Harlow had been so fascinated by. At the moment, I'm ignoring my sister's voice whispering on my shoulder like the devil itself. Asking me what the fuck am I doing and why I'm betraying her. Nope, I'm just going to worry about it when it actually happens.

Wiping at a smudge in the glass, I admire the model. I'm really proud of my collaboration with my aunt, creating something that people can use without being afraid of being shamed. Hope's PR team has got a great campaign ready to go once we make this project public. It's one we've kept very quiet about due to America's broad-ranging views on exploring your sexuality. We're not going to market it to the general public, but we have got a lot of interest from the wider BDSM and sex club community. Eventually, I'd like to open it up to anybody and make it a membership thing, but for now we'll stick to marketing within Aunt Merideth's gentlemen's clubs as a trial run. Unlike her clubs, we won't be providing "entertainment" due to Hawaii's laws. People will have to bring their own partners, but I think it will be a great way for them to vacation and indulge in their kinks at the same time.

According to my psychologist, my own kinks come from being unable to control what happened to me and my sister when I was younger. The over the top attention our mother lavished on me was a stark contrast to how she treated Jacinta. But I shake away those triggering thoughts and imagine what Harlow would look like wrapped up in silk ropes suspended from the ceiling, bound for my enjoyment. Maybe this Hawaii trip really will be perfect. Kai has some of the same interests as I do.

Groaning as my cock pushes against my tailored pants, I quickly adjust when there's a knock on my door. Quickly sliding behind my desk, I hide the evidence of my arousal and try not to look like a complete mess. "Come in," I call out, cursing Raquel in my head again. I'll need them to send me up a temp until they can find me a permanent solution.

Declan enters, a frown on his face as he looks

between me and the empty front desk. "Where's Raquel?" I groan at my older brother's question, knowing he's going to pull the whole *I told you so* shit. Even though he's been involved with clients too, so there isn't much room to hold this particular mistake over my head.

"Raquel was propositioning me and not taking no for an answer when Hope and Harlow paid a visit to the floor. Harlow apparently didn't like hearing her try to take advantage of me, so she stormed in here… There was a scene. Long story short, she slapped Harlow, and Hope fired her ass before I could even get a chance to. When the girls left, there was another scene because they caught Raquel sending out confidential company files." I rub a hand across my face as my brother's eyes get wider and wider as the story goes on. "There was a brawl, and we just had Raquel escorted out by security. They're waiting for the police to arrive and arrest her for company sabotage and assault. So, today has been a shit show."

Declan drops down into the seat across from me, mouth gaping like a goldfish. I can see everything running through his mind before his mouth twitches slightly. Sure enough, he bursts into laughter, and I have to wait for him to get his chuckles under control. He's practically wiping tears from his eyes by the time he's finally able to form a sentence. "You really know how to pick them."

"Fuck you! You're not much better. In fact, none of us are. Look at Thomas and the she bitch."

He settles, and a curious look crosses his face. "I wonder why Harlow came to your defense. You've been a complete asshole to her."

A growl escapes my mouth before I can stop it. "It's not like you haven't been too."

He sighs deeply, an uncomfortable look crossing his face. "No, you're not wrong, but I'm struggling. There's something about her that draws you in, and I'm getting sick of keeping this cold and aloof thing down. I like the woman. I like that she's not cowering in the corner crying, that she's ignoring all our shit and trying for Dad. That says a lot to me. Plus, I know you assholes will laugh about this, but my cat loves her. As much as I want her to love me more, it says a lot that Princess is so fond of her. The more I get to know her, the more I feel like she's above board and that we need to stop with the aggression. Dad will never forgive us if we don't, so that means reining Jacinta in. Maybe if my PI confirms there's no skeletons in the closet, we can get her to calm down."

Well, well, Mr. Cool and his icy shell are starting to thaw. This is a surprise. Declan doesn't let anyone in. Ever. He always has this perfect media persona where he's friendly and approachable and dates the gorgeous stars his company represents, but in reality, that's not the case. He may date them, but that's just about public image. He never brings them home, and he never introduces them to the family as anyone other than his client. Unfortunately, some of them don't realize and think the date might lead to more, so that's led to a few awkward moments in the past. Sure, he's no angel. He sleeps with quite a few of them, but never does he imply that it means more than a quick fuck for him. The fact that he's even saying something nice about Harlow is a huge step for him, and it makes me think that Mr. Cool is also falling for our new sister. *Okay, no, fuck you, brain. Let's not call her sister ever again.*

Realizing I've been sitting there in silence, just looking at him, for far too long, I blurt out, "Yeah, I was just having the same kind of thoughts. She's sexy, smart and interesting, and I was already attracted to her from before. Seeing what her personality is like just makes things that much harder."

"So we're in agreement then? We'll let her be for now? How about Jacinta?"

A frown crosses my face along with a nearly painful sigh. "She's going to be harder to convince, but she's distracted for now. I say we just run interference. Eventually, she's going to come around. She did with Hope, and she will with Harlow in the end too. In any case, I've already drawn a line with her. She knows I won't actively stop her, but I'm also not going to help her. I just need to keep it a bit more under wraps if I'm giving Harlow a real chance." I'm trying to sound confident, but we both know our sister really is a loose cannon. Mom did a real job on her.

Declan stands up and gestures to the door. "Shall we head down and wait for the police? Probably should call the legal department too, and you need to find a temp. Preferably one with a bald spot and a beer belly."

My big brother just can't help himself; he has to feel like he's got a handle on everything, or he spirals. I completely understand how he feels, so I'm happy to let him share the burden if it makes him feel more in control.

"I've called HR but forgot to ask for a temp." I grab my cell phone out of my desk drawer. "I'll call legal on the way down to security." Stepping away from the desk, I take one last glance at the billboard, and with that image fixed in my mind, I follow my brother out of my office to deal with what's hopefully my last mistake.

Chapter Seventeen

Harlow

Hitting the button for the Couture level, we head down one floor, and when the doors open, I gently assist Hope out of the elevator. A sudden snort, definitely not the quiet kind, has me looking up at her. She's staring at my hand on her arm, a bemused and amused smile on her lips. I raise an eyebrow before removing my hand. "Sorry," I mutter a little defensively.

"Oh no, it's fine. It's just that I had four foster brothers in one of the houses I grew up in, and that little scrap was nothing compared to the brawls we all got into when I was a kid."

A horrified grimace must cross my face because she is quick to reassure me. "Not that they beat me or anything. We'd wrestle, and things would devolve from there, so I learned very quickly to hold my own. The dirty moves they taught me definitely helped too. Raquel didn't stand a chance!" She tries to straighten herself out, but it doesn't make her look less disheveled.

"Hope, my goodness! What on earth happened to you, child?" Nana comes rushing over, frowning in concern, but Hope just brushes her off.

"Just taking out the trash, Grace. If you'll excuse me, I'm going to go and raid the Wardrobe, then I have a few things to attend to. I'll leave Harlow in your capable hands." She turns and tugs me into her, hugging me tightly before pulling away again.

"Thank you for being concerned. Don't forget to call me tomorrow! We'll have dinner and drinks, and I'll tell you everything you want to know."

Nana raises her eyebrows at this, and Hope puts her hands on her hips. "Harlow needs to know everything, and I'm a neutral party who can tell her without it looking like I'm taking sides." Nana's eyes soften, her shoulders relaxing in a sign of trust.

"Yes, dear, that… that would be wonderful, thank you."

With one last smile and a wave goodbye, Hope disappears down another hallway, looking for a change of clothes, I guess.

"Brad tells me you're having lunch with him." Nana eyes sparkle with joy, not looking disappointed in the least that she and I won't be spending the time together. "Come on, I'll show you where he had it set up." She follows the same path as Hope, bypassing the receptionist with a smile. We pass a couple doors before she pushes one open and steps through into a tropical garden delight.

"Holy crap!" The words fall out of my mouth before I can stop them, but Nana just laughs.

"How do you get everything to grow so well inside?"

The room is wall to wall plants. Hanging baskets, pots, plant walls, and an actual garden bed in the middle. The room has floor to ceiling windows that let through so much natural light. The room is also a little humid, so I'm assuming the lights above us are heat lamps and grow lights to help achieve this tropical look. Somewhere beyond the foliage, there's the faint trickle of some kind of water, and I'm so tempted to explore and find the source.

"Come on." Nana leads the way through the room, along the clear path laid out before us. Stepping around one large pot, the area opens out to a clearing. There's a table and chairs set for lunch, and Dad is waiting for me with a smile as big as Nana's. He stands up as we approach, coming around and giving us both kisses on our cheeks.

"Perfect timing! Lunch has just been delivered." He waves a hand at the table which is covered in a spread of meats, cheese, and crackers. There are a couple of salads and a basket of bread as well.

My stomach rumbles at the sight of all that delicious-looking food, earning an exchange of amused glances between Nana and Dad. I blush a little but shrug my shoulders. I'm starving, and there's no point in denying it.

"Are you joining us, Mom?" Dad asks her, but she shakes her head.

"No, I'll leave the two of you to it. I'm going to check on Hope... make sure she's okay and find out what it was all about."

Dad frowns in confusion, so I help him out. "I'll tell you all about it while we have lunch," I assure him, and his frown clears.

Waving goodbye, Nana leaves as we sit down to lunch. Nerves roll across my skin followed by excitement. This is the first real alone time we've had, and I'm really looking forward to getting to know my dad. Everything I've seen so far shows me he's a caring and fair man who loves his family. I'm dying to see if that's the truth or all just an act. My mother could show a loving and caring side in front of the right people when needed, so I'm reserving my judgment until I can see for myself and make my own decisions.

"What would you like to drink?" Dad asks as I study what he has to offer. "There's water and soda, or I can probably find a bottle of wine somewhere." He starts to stand up, but I hold up a hand, stopping him.

"Soda is fine, thanks, Dad." He hands me a can

to drink, and we're quiet as we help ourselves to all the food.

"So how has your morning been? Getting a feel for how everything works around here?" Dad asks once we've finished serving ourselves.

"Yes, it's been really good. Hope has been so kind, and having that"—I gesture to the tablet she gave me—"is going to make keeping up to date on everything Neighpalm-related easy." While I can feel an easy smile on my face when I mention Hope, there's no denying some of it dims when I mention the rest.

Dad puts down his silverware, a serious look crossing his face. "Harlow, I know this hasn't been easy, and I hope you won't hold that against us. I also know your interests lie elsewhere, Mom and Dad have made that very clear, so don't feel like you need to give up your dreams for me. I would never make you do that. Like I said before the press can be a real issue. It's better that you know whats going on then for them to speculate why you don't know as much as you should. It's part and parcel of being part of this family."

A wave of calm flows through my body. I had been fairly sure that was the case, but to have him confirm it is a huge relief.

He shifts a little in his seat and grimaces. "I know this is the first time we've really spent some alone time together, and that was partly because I'm socially inept, but it's also got to do with how guilty I've been feeling." I go to say something to reassure him, but he quickly holds up his hands.

"No matter what you say, even though I didn't know about you, I am forever going to feel guilty over the way you suffered at the hands of the one person you should have been able to trust the most. I'm so disgusted with what Mom and Dad have told me, and I really just don't know what to say or do. Nothing is ever going to make up for that, and I-I'm truly sorry for that." His eyes shine with unshed tears as the words come tumbling out of his mouth.

This really wasn't the way I was expecting lunch to go, but for as sad as he looks, there's something about him that almost seems a tiny bit lighter, like these were words he *needed* to express to me. The hair on my arms rises as I absorb everything, a wave of hope-filled love rolling through me. Could this man be any better? I love the fact that he's trying to find a balance between smothering and not overly interested and that he really is making an effort not to force his way into my life.

I reach for his hand in my attempt to reassure him. "I can't tell you how much it means to me to hear you say all of that. Growing up wasn't easy, but things did get better when the Bostons stepped in. And although I did still have to deal with her regularly, I learned techniques and ways to manage her. For you to feel guilty is sweet but really not necessary. Neither you nor I had any control over the situation. So let's leave all of the fault firmly at the feet of the person responsible." He squeezes my hand in what I think is a reflex when I allude to my mother, but he doesn't let go, his hand tightly in mine. "Thank you, and I appreciate everything you've done so far, but it's okay. *I'm* okay. I'll tell you if you're getting too pushy or whatever. Same as I have no problem telling your children to kiss my ass if they really go too far. Yes, what happened at the movie premiere upset me, but I really should have expected something. And I was more upset for reasons that link to my chosen career rather than being ashamed of what was up there. I mean, I got to say, I looked amazing."

He smiles as I try and lighten the mood, but he shakes his head.

"Please forgive my ignorance, but how would the billboard affect you becoming a vet?"

Ah, so he does know. "It's more because I'm trying to get an internship and they do background checks. Something like the billboard can reflect negatively on me, especially with all the speculation that came with it despite the press conference. All those whispers about who I was really did make me look like I was your mistress."

His cheeks turn red at my explanation, and he can't hide his embarrassment. "But we did the press conference to straighten that out."

"Dad, come on. People are idiots, and they're going to believe what they want to believe."

"Well, just tell them to call me. I'll straighten it out with anyone who needs a character reference."

"While I'm grateful for that, I want to get the job on my own merits, not because you put a good word in for me. I know you're used to being able to call the shots and provide for all of your other children, but I've always had to be a bit more independent than that. I truly appreciate the offer, but for better or worse, I have to stand on my own two feet and resolve any issues on my own." He frowns, not happy with my decision, but I quickly change the subject before CEO Dad can talk me into changing my mind.

The conversation moves away from more serious subjects, Dad and I spending the next hour getting to know each other's likes and dislikes, and the two of us find we have a lot in common. By the time we make it to the background of what happened to Hope, we're both more relaxed.

"I never liked her. Don't know how many times I cautioned Jaxon about mixing business with pleasure, but you can't tell my kids anything. They have to learn from their own mistakes. You would have thought he'd know better after Thomas' experience," Dad grumbles. I almost push him on what happened to Thomas, but he changes the subject quickly enough that I get the hint that he's not ready to share, probably doesn't want to betray Thomas' trust.

"I'm looking forward to coming riding with you

on Wednesday. I didn't get a chance to tell you after the incident with the saddle and the big black horse, but you're one hell of a horse woman, Harlow, and I couldn't be prouder. I can't thank Chuck and Melinda enough for taking you under their wings and loving and caring for you when I wasn't there to do it." He reaches out and squeezes my hand, his mouth opening and then closing as he clears his throat, seemingly overcome by those emotions welling back up again.

Happy to try and rescue him, I offer, "I can't wait to see what your cross-country course looks like, or even just go for a run. This is the longest I've gone without doing it, and I've got to say I'm starting to feel a bit antsy. My life has always been so physical, and well, I've felt practically lazy since I've been here." He laughs at my confession, that brightness reigniting again.

"Well, there's the gym and the pools at the house anytime you need to use them. And of course once Chuck's horses go, you're welcome to use any in the stable. No one will mind. The kids are good with letting Josh know when they're going to ride, so he knows which horses need riding and which don't."

"Yeah, Josh has been great. He's been spoiling Jenny and DS too. DS thinks he's the next coming of Jesus; he always has some treat in his pocket for her."

The door to the conservatory unexpectedly

opens, and Nana walks in, carrying a box. Declan and Jaxon trail behind her, and all my relaxed energy disappears as I'm instantly on alert. To my great surprise, neither of them are aggressive or nasty. They take a look at all the leftovers on the table and grab seats next to me and Dad before wordlessly piling food onto plates.

"Help yourself, boys," Dad says dryly, and they both just nod, focusing on all the food.

"Thanks, I'm starving. Dealing with the police was not exactly how I thought I'd be spending my morning," Declan grunts without stopping what he's doing. Jaxon, on the other hand, shoots him a look of aggravation, which he misses.

"Ah yes, Harlow told me what happened. I hope you've learned your lesson, Jaxon?"

He holds up his hands, eyes wide. "Dad, I have *absolutely* learned my lesson. It will never happen again, I promise."

"Thank God," Dad grumbles. "No need to give the lawyers even more work to handle. God knows poor Hope is already busy enough."

"Here, Harlow, this was left at the security desk. It's addressed to you." Nana hands me the box she was carrying before pouring herself a cup of coffee.

Surprised, my eyes scan the prettily wrapped box in front of me. It's not large, probably four or five inches, and a wide red bow is wrapped around it. Looking up at the table, everyone is watching me, waiting for me to open it. It's got my name on the card taped to the top, but it's typed so no hint as to who it might be.

"Did they say where it came from?" I ask, pulling on the red ribbon.

Nana shakes her head. "No, apparently they didn't even see who left it on the counter. It was left while they came upstairs to escort Raquel from Jaxon's office." Nana glares at Jaxon, who has the grace to look embarrassed again.

Lifting off the lid, I gasp in shock at what I see. It's a picture of DS with a sniper rifle scope over the top of her.

"What the hell?" I tear my eyes away from the threat and find Jaxon's. "What the fuck is wrong with your sister?" I demand.

Frowning, all three men stand up and Dad reaches over, pulling the box into the middle of the table so they can all see.

"Oh my word," Nana gasps, a hand coming up to grip at the necklace around her neck.

"That's not Jacinta," Jaxon declares, and Declan nods his head in agreement. "She would never threaten one of the horses. Ever."

"She also adamantly denies tampering with the saddle or pushing you into the pool," Declan adds in, and Dad frowns at them before looking at me.

"You really thought it might be Jacinta doing those things?" He sounds a little surprised, and I shrug my shoulders, my heart still thudding in my chest from the threat against DS.

"How was I to know? She hasn't exactly been welcoming, and the billboard was all her."

Dad and Nana exchange a glance, but before they can say anything, Jaxon quickly rushes to her defense. "I get how you might think that, but I never suspected it was her. She has done some crazy shit in the past, but it's never devolved to physical threats or violence."

"I'm afraid I'm going to have to agree with Jaxon." Dad runs a hand through his hair, looking severely uncomfortable with this entire line of conversation. "Pranks and catty comments are Jacinta's MO, I will readily admit that, but she would never do this. I'm sorry you thought it was her, and I hope you two can get to a place where a suspicion like that wouldn't cross your mind again. This seems like someone has an agenda against you, and we need to get to the bottom of it before it escalates further. The two incidents yesterday were already too far, but I had other things on my mind at dinner last night. I should've pushed for us to call the police then, but I have to insist on it now."

"Yeah, okay, I think maybe that's not a bad idea," I agree, my breathing easing with the suggestion.

"Can you make the call? We should also have security pull up surveillance tapes so that we can look out for whoever delivered the box," he adds, looking to Jaxon and Declan.

The latter is already standing and pulling his

phone out of his pocket, his brow creased in concern. "I'll go right now. Don't worry, Harlow, I know a local detective. I'll get him to come over and take your statement, then you don't have to go down to the precinct."

He rushes out of the room without saying anything else, and my mind is left reeling with everything that's happened in the last few minutes: my anonymous "gift," the news that Dad doesn't believe it's Jacinta, Declan being… nice? That last one might be the strangest pill to swallow right now, though that might also be my mind's way of avoiding thinking of the threat made against my poor DS. Nana pats me on the hand reassuringly, a small smile on her lips.

"Come on, dear, we still need to interview those few designers. Let's go and do that so we can keep your mind occupied until the police get here."

"What about that?" I gesture to the offensive box.

"Just leave it there. They may be able to get some fingerprints or something off of it," Dad tells me as I stand up.

I say goodbye to both Dad and Jaxon, the two men waving distractedly as they discuss who might be leaving threats and why. From what I overhear as we walk away, they're talking about people they may have pissed off business-wise. But then why target me?

Nana pats my arm, giving me a squeeze before

she lets go. "You can worry about all of this later. Let's not worry about it for now."

Shaking my head, I focus on the task ahead of us. "So what exactly does one look for in a designer? Why are we doing this if you're not replacing Jacinta?"

Nana scoffs, "We'd never replace her unless she wanted it, but we *are* looking to add someone else to the team. She will remain CEO and head designer, and the person we hire will work closely with her. We'll look at their portfolio, but it's more about us trying to gauge what kind of person they are and whether they will be a good mesh with Jacinta."

I grunt, not thinking that this sounds fun at all. "So do we have any prickly cacti interviewing today?"

Nana's peals of laughter echo down the corridor as we make our way back to the reception desk.

"Who knows? Maybe."

Chapter Eighteen

Harlow

Two hours and countless designers later, my head is pounding and my brain has ceased to exist. Thank fuck Dad doesn't actually want me to be a part of one of the businesses. I think I would shrivel up and die if I had to deal with such shallow, vapid creatures every day.

Nana handles it like a pro, fluffing their egos and getting them to engage, but so far we've picked one woman. Personally, I thought she was a stuck up cow, but Nana really liked her drawings even if her personality was lacking.

"Jacinta is strong enough to deal with all of that," she assures me. "Don't forget this is her chosen business. She helped build it from the ground up, and although she doesn't enjoy dealing with the egos, she's a pro at it. We'll give her a trial."

The woman was a little older than me, maybe in her early thirties. Her chestnut hair was pulled back in a severe bun against the back of her head, and her blue eyes looked cold behind her artfully applied makeup. Her painfully thin body was wrapped in a pencil skirt and a beautiful off the shoulder top teamed with sky high heels with a range of buckles and straps. But her smile looked like a sneer, and I could see her judging me when she scanned my body as I stood up to shake her hand. But that quickly cleared when Nana introduced me as her granddaughter who was filling in for Jacinta while she was on a break.

I clenched my teeth through the whole interview as Nana asked Rowena questions about her qualifications and experiences, and she responded in an overenthusiastic and insincere way. To be honest, I only agreed because I think she's going to give Jacinta hell, which she certainly deserves. At least it's only a trial, so she can be let go at the end. Who knows? They may get on like a house on fire. We'll have to wait and see.

Our last interview of the day has just been escorted into the room. He's cute with shaggy ice blond hair that's short at the sides, long on top, and styled to look like he's just gotten out of bed. He has on a pair of wire-framed glasses over eyes that make me look twice because he has one blue and one hazel. Moving on from there, I scan his body. He wears his clothes well, his jeans hugging nicely shaped thighs and his t-shirt stretched across a broad chest. On his feet he has a pair of Doc Martin boots. Instantly, I like this guy. Everyone else we saw was dressed in suits and designer clothes. This guy looks like he's dressing for no one but himself, and I can appreciate that. He has a large sketch pad under his arm and a pencil tucked behind one ear.

A shy smile is on his face as he shakes Nana's hand before they both turn to me. "Jace, I'd like to introduce you to my granddaughter Harlow. She's helping out with interviews today."

When the guy turns to me, a memory from this morning flashes through my mind. "You were sitting down in the lobby this morning. Have you really been here all day?" I ask, and a blush crosses his cheek as his warm hand engulfs mine.

"Ah yes, I'm from out of town, and the bus got in early this morning." His brow creases in concern, and his eyes dull with worry. His southern accent is strong, but he's not hard to understand. "I had nowhere else to go, and I know no one in the city, so I just came straight here. I hope that wasn't a problem."

Instantly, my heart feels for this guy. I know exactly how it feels to be the odd person out.

"Oh no, not a problem at all," Nana assures,

gesturing for him to take a seat. He does so then slides his sketch pad across to us.

"So, tell us a little about yourself, Jace," Nana encourages as she opens up his sketch pad and starts flicking through the designs on the pages.

Now, I am the first to admit that I know nothing about fashion, but the pictures in front of us render me speechless. Gorgeous dresses fit for movie premieres or royal galas line the pages. Sumptuous fabrics and beautiful lines that scream to the inner princess inside of me. As Nana flicks further forward, the dresses change to lingerie. Jewel tones and sexy cuts are prevalent, and what impresses me even more is that he's drawn them on a range of different figures. Not just the stick-thin models that have graced every other designer's portfolio today, but on regularly shaped women as well as women who move into the fuller figure category. I'm seriously impressed at this guy's forward thinking because he's made every one of them look gorgeous and sexy, and I can just imagine there's a big market for such a large size range.

"Well, I'm from New Orleans, and I tend bar in the local club. Growing up, my mom was a huge fan of old movies, and she made me watch them with her. I've always had a passion for drawing, and whenever I saw those beautiful dresses in black and white, I'd want to draw them in color. My school didn't offer any kind of design classes, so I took art and watched YouTube tutorials in my spare time.

I've always wanted to work for a fashion house, but with no qualifications or experience under my belt, no one has even been interested in looking at my portfolio."

Nana and I exchange a glance. I'm almost sure we're thinking the same thing, that people are idiots, because training or not, this guy has a gift.

"Jace, I've got to say I really like what I see. Would you be interested in doing a three-month trial run with the company to see if you would be a good fit? Paid, of course, and we could even provide you with accommodation so you wouldn't have to commit to a rental in case it didn't work out."

His eyes light up at Nana's offer, and a warm glow infuses my body. This feels right. Giving an underdog the opportunity to succeed. That's what I love about Nana; she's open to giving people a chance, just like she did with me so many years ago.

"Seriously? Th– that would be amazing, thank you." He stutters slightly, fumbling his words, but he quickly gets it together.

Nana's smile is full of warmth as she continues. "Have you got somewhere to stay tonight, and would a week be long enough to get organized to relocate out to LA? You said you took the bus here? We can fly you home. Just let me know when you're ready to return, and we can send the jet for you."

His eyes just about pop out of his head at her suggestion, and he starts to argue, but Nana, force of nature that she is, just holds up her hand. "No,

Jace, don't argue. I insist! After all, you are uprooting your life to come and work for us, so it's the least we can do."

"Thank you, Mrs. Summers, I appreciate it. I had just planned on finding a hotel for the night, but I don't have anything booked yet."

Nana nudges me at his words, and I jump in. I'm not quite sure why, but I'm pretty sure she wants me to offer him a place to stay tonight. Crap, I hope Shane and Alex don't kill me. I'll have to text them before we leave. "Nonsense. You can crash with me at my friends' place tonight, and then I'll order you a lift to the airport in the morning. I'm sure that's enough time for Nana to reserve one of the jets to return you home."

She nods and stands up. "If you just give us a minute, I'll get you some contracts to look over when you go home. Please feel free to consult a lawyer if you need to. You can just sign them when you're ready and bring them when you return. Harlow, come with me."

We leave him looking a little shell shocked, the two of us moving into what I now know is Jacinta's office.

"What was that?" I hiss at her, confused at her behavior. "You better hope that Shane and Alex say it's okay."

She waves her hand at me, the woman convincing me that she's unflappable no matter what situation she's in. "Pshh, if it's not, then you can both go to the company hotel and use a room or two there, but I have a good feeling about that man. Never have I seen such raw talent like that except maybe in your sister when she first started." I startle at the word sister but let it go. *That's a battle to fight some other time.*

"Talent like that cannot be taught, and I can't wait to see what he can bring to the table. We may make an exclusive line of evening gowns designed by him. Not to mention the lingerie! Such creative thinking by catering to all body shapes instead of being stuck in that stick figure crackwhore thinness that so many designers favor. Unrealistic and unattainable." I blink at my Nana in surprise. *Yes, she just said crackwhore. That's Nana.*

She gathers some contracts, not bothering to review the details or fine print, so I guess there must be some kind of standard deal they offer. "This one he must sign today. It's a standard NDA, but the rest he can read over and bring back to us."

The door opens behind us, and Dad walks in, looking far more relaxed than he did at the conclusion of our lunch date. "How did it go?" He looks between Nana and me, and we exchange a glance.

"Really well! I think we've found two that are going to work perfectly," Nana tells him. That's an interesting way of phrasing it, and by the look *they* are now exchanging, they have something up their sleeves.

"Hang on, I know this look," I comment,

gesturing between the two of them. "What are you two planning?"

"Nothing for you to worry about, dear." Nana pats my hand, the taps just forceful enough that I know she intends for me to follow her lead. "Just a way to bring Jacinta back into line."

They smirk at each other, and I shudder, hoping I never get caught in the middle of their scheming.

"Here." Dad throws something at me. "I know you flew in with Declan this morning, but you're going to need a car for your interview tomorrow, so I drove Oliver's in for you. I'll catch a ride back in the helicopter."

My mouth drops open at his thoughtful news, and I throw myself at him, pulling him in for a tight hug. A woosh of air escapes before he chuckles and returns the squeeze. "Thank you for thinking about me," I whisper, and his arms tighten a little more before we step apart.

"Always, Harlow, you will *never* be left behind again," he swears to me. "Promise me something. Promise that if you ever, *ever* need anything, you'll come and see me. And if you don't feel comfortable with that, ask Mom or Dad. You know they'll move heaven and earth if you let them. He presses a kiss to my head and then pulls away, his smile turning into a frown. "Now that we have that out of the way, that detective is here to speak to you. Can you finish up with that designer and then meet us in the security office?

An hour later, I've gotten a yes from both Shane and Alex about bringing Jace to their place. The two seemed excited and totally unbothered by the request, especially when I explained he'd be a new designer for Neighpalm Couture for the next three months. I could practically feel Alex vibrating with curiosity through the phone.

"Come on, Jace! Let's head out," I suggest after Nana accepted his signed NDA and gave him the rest of the forms in return. "If you don't mind waiting in the lobby while I quickly do something, we'll be on our way right after."

He smiles at me, picks up his portfolio, and gestures for me to lead the way. "No problem, Ms. Summers. I left my backpack down at the reception area, so I need to grab that before we head out anyway."

What is it about a man with manners and a southern accent that just has you smiling? It's a bit like when you see Matthew McConaughey in a movie. There's just something about him that appeals to you.

I lead him toward the elevator, both of us having said goodbye to Nana already. "Oh no, my last name isn't Summers, and Harlow will be fine. I don't actually work for the company. I was just helping out today."

We step into the elevator, and he tilts his head, a thoughtful look on his face. "Yes, I was wondering about that. I had expected to see the other Ms. Summers."

Crap, what should I say? "Oh yes, Jacinta is working from home for a few days. Just taking some time away from the office, hoping it helps with her creative block."

My excuse sounds pretty flimsy, but he seems to believe me. Or he's willing to buy it at least. *Note to self: let Hope handle things like that whenever possible.* Within a few moments, we get down to the lobby and head to the reception area.

The smiling receptionist looks up when we approach the desk, her eyes sparkling as she runs her gaze down Jace's body and back again, ignoring me completely. "Hi, you're back!" She sounds excited to see him, her voice all bright and perky.

"Hi there, Shelly, thanks so much for minding my bag for me." I can practically see cartoon hearts pounding from her eyes as she sighs at his accent. Snorting my amusement, she finally recognizes someone else is standing in front of her.

"Oh, sorry, can I help you?"

"Could you point me in the direction of the security office?" I ask her politely, and she indicates a door to the left of the desk with the word *Security* across it. *Yep, definitely on a roll. Could have figured that one out myself.*

"Thank you. I won't be long." I reassure Jace,

and he simply gives me an easy going grin and nods.

"No problem, Harlow. I'll just chat with Shelly here. She was awful helpful before while I was waiting for my interview, telling me all about things to see and do in LA while I'm here." He's laying it on thick now, and she's falling for it hard. *Not such a sheltered country boy after all. Seems the man has game.*

"Oh, I'm sure she was." Chuckling, I head toward the office.

Knocking on the door, I enter, finding the small room crowded with four large men. The two security guards from before and Declan, plus a man who must be the detective. He's an older gentleman, growing gray at the temples, but like many of the people I've encountered in LA, he's handsome and fit.

"Harlow, this is Detective Scott James. He'd like to ask you a few questions." Declan gestures for me to take a seat then positions himself behind me, his hand on my chair. There's an aura of reassurance that seems to flow between his hand and my back, sort of an "I've got your back" message that I'm blown away to feel. But Declan has admitted to being very protective of his family, and I guess at this very moment he considers me a part of that. I shiver with an unknown emotion, but Declan must think it's from fear because his hand moves from the chair to my shoulder, giving it a reassuring squeeze before letting go.

"Declan informs me that you seem to be the target of a stalker." His voice is a little gravelly, but he doesn't sound skeptical or anything. *Huh, I can't believe Declan followed through and actually found me someone to take me seriously. I guess the Summers name could account for that, but it's nice that he made an effort to make me feel a little safer.*

I detail the two incidents from yesterday while he takes notes, and then I gesture to the box on the table which came today.

"I can't think of anyone I've upset enough to warrant wanting to hurt me," I explain, leaving out the animosity in the Summers' house. I trust Dad enough to believe that it's not Jacinta who's been targeting me. While I'd easily believe that her brothers would defend her to the death, I've seen zero reason to think Dad would overlook my safety, and I *know* Nana wouldn't.

"What about your mother's death? Was there anything suspicious about it?" He pauses his note-taking while I think about my answer.

"No, I don't think so. As far as I'm aware, it was a drug overdose. I can give you the names of the two detectives that worked on that case if you would like to check with them." I pull my cell phone out of my backpack, and he copies the information down before asking a few more questions then flipping his notebook shut.

"We'll have a look into your mother's death, and we'll run fingerprint analysis on the box, but at the moment, there isn't a lot to go on. According to the security footage, a courier dropped the package off, and when they were contacted, it was a dead end. I'm sorry I can't offer any more suggestions right now except to watch out for people you may recognize in places they shouldn't be. I think it's also not overly cautious to advise that you don't go anywhere alone for a while."

With those discouraging words, he grabs the box, which is already in a sealed evidence bag, shakes mine and Declan's hands, gives a nod to the security guys, and shows himself out. I deflate in the chair I'm sitting in. I didn't think he would have an answer yet since it's so soon, but I thought he might have some ideas.

Thanking the security guys, I get up and turn to leave, smashing into a solid chest since I've completely forgotten that Declan was behind me. He grabs my arms to steady me, and when I look up into his eyes, they hold a hint of worry.

"Where are you going now?" he asks gruffly, the grip on my arms remaining steady. "Are you ready to head home?"

"I'm staying at Shane and Alex's tonight, and I have an appointment tomorrow," I inform him. With that, Declan abruptly lets go of my arms and steps back, the worry I saw in his eyes replaced by the usual ice king look. I roll my eyes internally. Of course he would assume the worst. He's only ever been surrounded by fickle women. He could ask the question he's dying to know, but instead, he's stubborn and ignores it. *It's not like I haven't defended my honor to him already. I'm not going to keep insisting we're just friends only for him to believe what he wants to regardless.*

"I spoke to Sean Walsh, and he confirmed that the horses need to be on the set on Thursday. I've organized for our truck to be at the farm Wednesday afternoon, so we can load them and drive them down on Thursday."

"*We?*" I ask, and he nods, the cold look not thawing.

"Yes, I told Dad I would check in and see why the movie keeps getting delayed, so I might as well come down with you then. I can drive the truck." He turns and leaves without waiting for a reply.

Jesus, what did I do? For a moment there it almost looked like he cared... and then he just flipped his bitch switch. Again.

Men. Seriously, who can keep up with their mood swings?

Chapter Nineteen

Harlow

The drive over to Alex and Shane's was pleasant, Jace and I passing the time by chatting about fairly safe things. He told me about New Orleans and the bar he works in, and I told him a little about me as well, but I managed to keep most of the conversation focused on him.

Pulling the Vanquish into a guest spot in the underground parking garage, we head toward the elevator where I put in the code for the penthouse. We head straight up without stopping, and when the elevator opens into their apartment, I call out for them. *God, I hope we haven't interrupted them again; that would be awkward as fuck.*

Jace follows hesitantly behind me, his backpack

over his shoulder, eyes wide as he takes in the beautiful apartment. The guys are nowhere to be seen, but I can hear some thumping music coming from down past the bedrooms.

Kicking off my shoes and dropping my backpack on the couch, I gesture for him to do the same. "Just drop your bag there for now. Let's go see if we can find them." He does as I say and follows after me, his hands jammed deep into his jeans pockets, a little frown creasing his brow.

"Don't stress! My friends are really easy going. It will all be fine. They already know you're coming." The frown lessens slightly, but the poor guy still looks uncomfortable.

We head in the direction the music is coming from, the sound getting louder the closer we get until I push open a semi-closed door and find the guys hard at work in their gym. Alex is on a treadmill, singing along to the music, and Shane is doing bicep curls on one of the benches. Neither of them have their tops on, their torsos glistening with sweat. I just about swallow my tongue at all that exposed muscle but quickly come to my senses when Shane notices us.

He reaches over, turning the music off, though Alex is completely unfazed, continuing to sing the next couple of words before stopping.

"What did you do that for?" he grumbles, looking at Shane. His boyfriend nods his head in our direction, putting down his weight, and Alex turns off his machine before swiveling to face us.

"Harlow, honey, you're here." He jumps down and rushes toward me, and I hear Jace quietly curse.

"Holy shit!"

Alex is about to scoop me up in his sweaty arms, but I hold up my hands until he freezes. "Eww, no, gross! Don't touch me."

The grin that appears on his face could never be described as anything other than cheeky. "Are you sure you don't want me to make you wet?" He winks and then turns to Jace. "Hi, welcome, I'm–"

"You're Alex Winters," Jace interrupts, a kind of reverence in his voice. "And he's Shane Silver," he says, pointing at Shane who has a small smile on his face. "I had no idea where we were going when Harlow said I could stay with her and her friends. I cannot believe I'm here. Thank you so much for having me," he all but gushes before turning on me with a scolding look. "God, Harlow, you never told me we were coming to stay with fashion royalty!" He can't seem to look anywhere except between the two of them, even when he's talking to me. *The idol worship is strong with this one.*

"Really?" I look at him, a little confused. "I knew Nana said you were popular, but I didn't realize it was *that* big."

"Poor Harlow here has no idea about the

fashion industry; we've taken her under our wing," Alex whispers out of the side of his mouth to Jace while running his eyes up and down his body. "And you're the new talent that's going to cause tidal waves down at Neighpalm Couture."

Another frown crosses Jace's face, and he finally looks at me. "What does he mean?"

Before I can answer, Shane grabs a towel off the bench next to him and wipes off his chest before throwing it at Alex's head. "Ignore him, Jace. Come on, I need a drink. Let's grab you a beer or something."

Shane moves Alex out of the way and pulls a shirt over his head, pushing past us and heading to the kitchen. Jace turns and follows him, while Alex grabs hold of my arm. "Now that's a tall glass of sweet southern iced tea."

"Settle, tiger." I roll my eyes at him and follow after the other two. When I get to the kitchen, Jace is telling Shane about his interview with Nana and his job offer. He waves a wine glass at me as we get closer.

"Fuck yes, it's been a day." Jace stops, but I wave my hand at him. "Sorry, continue. I'll order us some food, and then we won't get interrupted again until it comes. Everyone happy with Chinese? Anything anyone doesn't eat?" Shane and Jace both agree with the food decision, neither being a picky eater.

Alex saunters into the kitchen, still shirtless.

After grabbing a beer out of the fridge, he hands me some takeout menus from a drawer before taking a seat at the kitchen island. "Start from the beginning again! I want to hear the story too." Jace's eyes almost bug out of his head, the poor guy swallowing nervously before I turn and walk away, smiling. Alex is a lot to take in, but I'm sure Jace will be fine.

The voices fade as I grab my backpack and take it to "my" room. Throwing my bag on the bed, I follow closely after it, a huge breath of air escaping as I settle in with my phone and the menu. God, I'm tired. Between the drama, interviews, the box, and the police, today was *so* long. Rubbing my cheek, I notice that there wasn't even enough power behind her slap to still hurt. Damn woman had spaghetti arms, similar to my mom's, but at least hers had the power of whatever drug she had taken for the day behind them. *Was coming out here a mistake? Should I have just continued on, pretending I never found out about Brad?*

The questions resound in my mind, taking on a life of their own until something else breaks through: that feeling of sitting at lunch with Dad today. I really enjoyed our time together, uncovering tiny snippets of what kind of man he is, what kind of father he seems to be. Something inside me settles the tiniest bit, and I'm really looking forward to going riding with him on Wednesday.

Shaking off the mood, I call the Chinese restaurant and place an order, making sure I grab enough for three hungry guys. They can always eat leftovers tomorrow if it's too much. With that done, I change into a pair of yoga pants and a tank top, getting rid of my bra. There's nothing better than taking off your bra at the end of the day. It's just instant relaxation.

Heading back out to find the guys, I realize they've moved from the kitchen to the sofas in the living room. The three are chatting like they've been friends for years, their conversation pausing and all eyes on me when I approach.

"Come here." Alex pats the couch next to him, and I collapse into the space. He wraps an arm around me and pulls me closer, placing a kiss against my temple. I can see Jace looking at us out of the corner of his eye, but I can't bring myself to care. From what little time I've spent around him today, he's given me none of the vibes that the Summers kids have. I think he's someone I could trust. "Tell Uncle Alex all about it," Alex coos at me ridiculously. I push him away with a laugh before reaching for my glass of wine. It has condensation built up on the outside, but it's still nice and cold as I take a sip.

"Well, yesterday was a complete disaster..." Another few minutes and a half glass later, they're up to date on my accidental trip into the abandoned estate's pool and Kai's rescue maneuvers. Though I *might* have left out the hot tub. Not sure if

I want to unpack that yet. Seeing Alex just bursting to comment, I put a hand over his mouth, needing to get the rest out.

"As for today, where do I start? You know that I had a tour of the offices today." Both Shane and Alex nod, but Jace looks confused. Deciding to go with my gut, I fill him in on the back story. "I only recently found out that Brad is my biological father, as did he. Neither of us knew each other existed, so I'm here to get to know him, and by extension, his adopted children. Today was my induction to all things Neighpalm." Alex scoffs, and I amend my statement. "Most things Neighpalm." I leave out the whole previous drama with Jacinta since I'm sure he'll find out soon enough.

"I'm as new to this as you are," I say at the end. "In fact, even newer. You at least have an idea of fashion. More than an idea if your drawings have anything to say." I gesture to the portfolio that's sitting on Shane's lap, and both he and Alex nod with enthusiasm.

"Much more than an idea! These are spectacular," Shane gushes, and Jace ducks his head, cheeks pink with embarrassment.

When they turn back to me with expectant eyes, I dive back into the details of the day. By the time I'm finished with the bit about Raquel, all three of them have open mouths.

Alex laughs as he takes a sip of his beer. "Shit, girl, things just happen around you, don't they?"

In the silence following his question, Alex and Shane look at each other before glancing at Jace, and I wave my hand to halt where their concern is taking them. "He's signed an NDA which says he's not allowed to talk about anything but Neighpalm Couture to the press. Anything personal is off-limits, so you can talk in front of him."

"Do we think it was Jacinta that did any of those things?" Alex asks, a frown on his face.

"Ms. Summers?" Jace sits up straight, eyes wide. "Why would she do that?"

With a deep breath, Alex, Shane, and I explain everything that's happened since I first found out I'm a Summers, starting with my mom's death.

"So basically you know everything now. And no, we talked about it at lunch. Jaxon, Declan, and Dad agree that she wouldn't do anything like that, and she swore black and blue yesterday she hadn't done those things either. I think I believe all of them too."

"You had lunch with your dad?" Alex asks, eyes bright with excitement. "On your own?"

"How was that?" Shane asks gently, interrupting Alex.

Smiling at his concern, I reply, "Really good. It was nice to sit down one on one and get to know each other. He asked me questions, and I got to learn more about him. But then Nana, Declan, and Jaxon arrived." I tell them about the box that had been delivered, and their faces turn from amused to concerned in an instant.

"Yeah, that's not good, Harlow. It sounds like someone is obsessing over you," Shane says, eyes dulling with concern. Alex shivers where he's sitting.

"I had one of those once; it's not fun."

"No, I know. Dad and the guys are taking it really seriously. They called the police, and a detective came and spoke to me before we came here."

Alex shudders and puts his arm around me, hugging me tightly again before releasing me. "Well, don't go anywhere on your own until the police can find them."

"I won't," I promise, giving his arm a squeeze. The easy affection from Alex and Shane is something I didn't even know I needed. It's nice to have more friends than just Max. *Shit, Max!* I'm going to have to call her and fill her in. Who knows if she'll be on set by Thursday. God knows I'm already going to hear an earful for having so much I haven't told her. It's just been so easy, *too* easy, to get caught up in all of this Summers drama.

"Oh hey, Alex, can you or Shane please give Jace a ride to the airport? Nana is sending him home in style." I smile at our new friend. "He needs to pack up and take some extended leave or something and then come back. Nana is going to put him up at the Neighpalm Hotel for the duration of his trial. I would, but I have that interview tomorrow."

Jace is already shaking his head by the time I finish asking. "No, it's okay. I'll just call an Uber or something."

Shane and Alex exchange a glance. You know, the one where couples basically do a mind meld thing and it's almost like they're speaking telepathically.

"Nonsense," Alex declares, breaking his stare down with Shane. "What kind of friends would we be if we let you do that? Both of us are off for the next few days. Not only will we take you to the airport, we can come with you and help pack up your things. It will be fun! I could do with a vacation. Where are we going?"

"New Orleans, Louisiana," Jace stammers, stunned at the offer. I swear Alex's eyes light up as he whoops. *Well, Jace is definitely getting a quick introduction into what life will be like in LA.*

"Laissez le bon temps rouler," he says in a sexy French accent, and Shane rolls his eyes, an amused smile on his lips while Jace swallows nervously again. *Should I rescue him or just leave him to take care of himself? Definitely more fun to just watch and see what happens.*

"And not only will we do that, but you can have the other spare room here if you want it," Shane offers. "Staying in a hotel for three months would wear on anyone, and you're part of the Neighpalm family now." And that, in a nutshell, is Shane and Alex.

Jace, wide-eyed, shakes his head in a totally futile attempt at refusal, but Alex won't let him. "Come on, I'll show you which room is yours." He holds out his hand to Jace who looks at it and then at me. I smile at him encouragingly, and he takes Alex's hand, letting the over-enthusiastic man pull him to his feet. When they're chest to chest, I can see that they're basically the same height. Alex stands there, his nostrils flaring slightly before turning and flouncing off in the direction of the bedrooms. His hand is still in Jace's, dragging the poor man along behind him.

Well, that was interesting. Turning to look at Shane, he has an amused smile on his face. He doesn't look upset, so I don't say anything. If they're going to insist on giving him a home for a couple of months, who am I to argue?

"So you've got your interview tomorrow? Are you excited?" Shane's arm comes up on the back of his sofa as he relaxes into the cushions.

"Yeah, I really am. This is something I've always wanted. I know it's a long shot, but they must have seen something they liked when they read my resume."

"Oh, Harlow, they'd be lucky to have you! Are you going to come back here tomorrow night?"

"No, I'm going to go out for dinner and drinks with Hope, and then I'll probably drive home. I'm going riding with Dad on Wednesday morning, then on Thursday I've got to deliver the horses to the set. And then on Friday—" I pause, blushing a little, and Shane's eyebrows jump.

"What? What's happening on Friday that has you blushing?" he pushes. Alex and Jace come back as he asks, so of course Alex jumps on it.

"You're blushing? Oh, now I *need* to know what that's about." He collapses onto the sofa and yanks Jace down next to him. The man yelps, startled, but quickly rights himself, also looking eager to know what's going on.

Crap, should have just kept my mouth shut. Nosy bastards. The last thought hits me with an unexpected bit of comfort, like a fuzzy blanket being wrapped around my shoulders. It's nice having so many people care about me. "I'm flying to Hawaii with Kai for the weekend to check out a couple of athletes for his new team." The words fly out of my mouth in a rush with the vain hope that we can just quickly move on from the subject.

There's silence that's broken by the sound of the intercom. "Mr. Silver, the food you ordered is on its way up," a disembodied voice announces, filling the living room. *Phew, saved by the bell, literally.* Jumping to my feet, I grab my purse which I had laid on the coffee table and hurry over, opening the door to wait for the delivery guy.

I can hear a whispered conversation going on behind me that's hard to miss. Rolling my eyes at their lack of discretion, I find it amusing how much they remind me of gossipy old women the minute my back is turned. Even Jace is putting in his two cents. It's funny how he's just slotted right into the friendship like he's been with them for years.

I take the food and pay the young guy, giving him a decent tip before turning back to face the music. All three have stopped their little powwow and are looking at me, so I brace myself for what they're about to say.

"Good for you! Kai is hot as hell, and you deserve some fun after the last couple of weeks," Alex says to me, a smile on his face. I breathe a sigh of relief at the refreshing lack of drama.

Bringing the food over to the kitchen island, I start pulling out containers. The guys all join me, Shane grabbing plates for all of us and finding silverware too.

"Well, to be honest, all of them have been a lot less hostile over the last couple of days," I admit quietly. "Except maybe Jacinta, but I haven't really seen her."

Alex wraps his arms around me from behind and gives me a smacking kiss on the cheek. "I'm happy for you, honey. I'm sure your dad gave them a swift kick up the ass and they've all begun to realize how amazing you are." He steps away and starts dishing up his food while Jace does the same, but Shane just looks at me, his eyes narrowed with tension.

"Are you still planning on revenge?" I shrug my shoulders, not wanting to tell them about my deal with Holden. Something about that arrangement feels too… personal to talk about right now, and I honestly don't know if it's going to be about revenge or maybe another way he can pay me back for letting his loyalty to his siblings hurt me.

"If an opportunity presents itself, maybe, but I have to admit that some of the immediate fiery anger might be calming down as I get some space from it all."

"You're not going to make them fall for you and then break their hearts, are you? That would be too brutal. I know that they hurt you, and they deserve to make that up to you, but I don't want you to use them and then wind up proving to them that they were right not to trust you." The other two stop what they're doing to listen to what I say.

"No, that's just not the kind of person I am, and to be honest, if I let them get that close and then destroy them, I'm no better than my mother or any of the horrible people I've come across in my life. No, my plans of revenge have died a fast death, but I'm not trusting them instantly. They'll still have to earn that. And who knows? Between Jacinta still hating me and them needing to work through their own issues, it might be more torturous for them to earn my good opinion than it would be for me to strike out at them."

Shane nods, looking happier about the situation

than he has in days, and we finish serving up our dinner. The rest of the evening is filled with good food and great company, and I'm grateful Nana pushed the idea of me bringing Jace here. I know he'll be in good hands if I leave him with these guys.

Chapter Twenty

Harlow

The next morning, nerves flutter in my stomach as I get ready for my interview. Nana had made me choose something out of the Wardrobe at Neighpalm Couture, ordering my choice to immediately be steamed and delivered to Alex and Shane's apartment. While I was hesitant to borrow something from the business, I have to admit that Nana didn't steer me wrong; the black pants, navy blue top, and small pair of heels make me look professional and together. I've styled my long blonde hair into a low bun at the back of my neck, and a swipe of mascara and lip gloss completes the look.

Looking at myself in the mirror, I'm pleased with what I see. I could fit in at Neighpalm Industries looking like this. My stomach lurches at the thought. Looking like I could fit in at Neighpalm and actually having to spend my future there are very different things. I'll take the borrowed outfit, but I'll have to decline that path in my future. No, if I can't get into a program, I'll just return home and work for either myself or for Doc Davies. I want to achieve my dream of being a vet too badly to give it up for an easy alternate career path with Dad's company.

Grabbing my backpack off the bed and the keys to the Vanquish, I head for the kitchen. I'm not sure if the guys are up this early, but I need coffee before I head out. When I went to bed last night, the three of them were still up talking and didn't look to be stopping any time soon.

The kitchen and living area is quiet when I get there, and I flick the switch on the coffee machine before opening the fridge to grab out the creamer. My stomach is rolling too much to eat, but I grab an apple to put in my bag for later just in case.

I'm halfway through my coffee when Shane wanders down the hallway. He's shirtless, his hair is in disarray, and there's a flush all over his torso. I don't think he's noticed me, so I clear my throat and his head comes up. Raising an eyebrow, I smile, receiving a smirk in return. "Good evening?" I ask him, and a wicked smile crosses his face. Before he can answer, I hear a loud shout from the bedroom, followed by a moan.

My mouth drops open. If Shane's out here, then

who was that? He winks at me before I can even ask the question. "You could say it was a *very* good evening."

I'm momentarily speechless. "Jace and Alex?" I ask when I come to my senses. "And that doesn't bother you?"

"Why would it? I was in there until just now when I smelled the coffee and realized you were up."

"Oh, okay." He comes over to me, a whiff of musky sex hitting my nose, almost making me moan. God, it's been too long since I got laid. He kisses me on the head, making sure I'm looking him in the eye before he says anything else.

"Alex and I love each other, and we are a solid unit. If we invite another partner into our bed occasionally, male or female, well, neither of us is going to be upset if we're both in agreement. And let's face it, did you see Jace? You'd have to be dead not to be attracted to the man."

I drain the rest of my coffee as Shane pours himself one. "Well, I've got to say, I'm immensely jealous, but I'm happy for you all. Just don't let Jace be late for the plane. Nana messaged me, saying it's scheduled for eleven. She said she would message Alex the details, so make sure they come up for air at some point."

"Don't worry, we'll be there on time. Alex is determined to help him, so we'll be away for a few days. You have a key to get in if you need the place," Shane reminds me as I grab my things off the counter. "Good luck today. They'd be stupid not to realize what an asset you are. And if they *are* that stupid, I can always get you work modeling."

I laugh and wave goodbye, hurrying out the door. "Say goodbye to the others for me, will you?" I shout over my shoulder.

A little later, I'm heading toward the corporate offices of the MacGinty Sanctuary. It's an almost two-hour drive from LA with the traffic, and if I do get this job, finding somewhere to live nearby will be a priority. I can't drive this distance every day, nor would it make sense to use one of the helicopters. *Did I just say that? Have I accepted the fact that I'm a Summers and have access to that sort of thing?* Luckily, I'm stopped at a light when this thought occurs to me because otherwise, I might have driven off the road. A blaring horn has me shaking off the distraction and moving again.

I'm still contemplating the fact that I've accepted being part of the family when my phone rings through the car's entertainment system. Max's name flashes up on the screen, and despite knowing what's coming, I pick up.

"Girl, I haven't heard from you *for days!* You better have a damn good reason why." Max's voice comes through the speakers, her annoyance echoing, and I roll my eyes. Of course I couldn't just be busy.

"Hey, Max, how's it going?" I reply, keeping

things light and nonchalant. *Does mentally crossing your fingers count for good luck?*

"Oh no. Last time I spoke to you, you were a mess. You don't get to pretend everything is okay! You don't get to put on a fake smile and try to reassure me you're fine." She sounds angry, and I'm kind of surprised she even realized that's what I'm trying to do. She's never really noticed in the past. I love Max, but sometimes she doesn't dig too deep.

Blowing out a deep breath, I proceed to tell her everything that has gone on. She's lucky this traffic is horrendous because that's a lot to unpack.

"What the fuck!" Max explodes after a moment of stunned silence. "And you're just telling me all this now? When I see you on Thursday, I'm going to kick your ass. Are you okay?"

"Actually, I think I am," I try to reassure her. "Look, I've got to go. I've got that interview, and I finally got here. We'll talk more on Thursday. Can't wait to see you. I miss you, love you." And I wisely hang up before she can say another word. I really don't have time for Max dramatics at the moment, no matter how well-meaning they are.

Disconnecting my phone from the car system, a text comes through. A whole heap of angry emojis followed by a few middle fingers then Max wishing me good luck and promising that this conversation isn't finished.

Smiling, I throw my phone into my backpack before checking my reflection in the mirror of the car. After I hop out of the car, all that's left is straightening my clothes and taking a deep breath before I walk inside.

A polished-looking secretary looks up from her computer with a polite smile and asks, "Can I help you?"

"Ah yes, I'm Harlow Stubbs. I have an appointment with Rose Smith regarding an opening in your veterinary residency program."

The woman frowns and looks down at her appointment book before looking back at me. "If you could just take a seat, I'll make a call." My stomach sinks at the frown on her face. It doesn't look positive at all.

I take a seat while she makes a hushed phone call. Straining, I try to hear what she's saying, but the music pumping out of the speakers is loud enough that it blocks out her voice. Any other time, the rainforest sounds might be pretty zen, but not today. After a few moments, she hangs up the phone and stands up.

"Someone will be out here to see you soon." She won't meet my eyes as she says this, sitting back and out of my sight fast enough to somehow make me feel even more awkward than I already do. Taking a deep breath, I prepare myself for the worst. I mean, it just wouldn't be right for my life to go as I'd hoped. There's always been something to shit on it. Whether it was Mom hanging around to ask for more money, or the asshole kids at school that Max called friends, or any number of other things that had happened to me over my lifetime, things just don't run smoothly for me. I guess I'd just hoped it would be different this time, that my luck had finally changed.

The *click click click* of a pair of heels can be heard, and my head comes up, bracing myself for what's to come. An older woman appears from behind a frosted glass panel. Probably close to Nana in years, she's tall and thin and has a slightly disapproving sneer on her face which smooths out as she reaches me. "Harlow, I'm Rose Smith, the director of the MacGinty Sanctuary and Foundation. I'm sorry to have wasted your time, but unfortunately, we are no longer in the position to offer you a place within our team. Someone should have called you to let you know."

"But, but… why?" *Is this another cruel joke?* I look around the room to see if maybe Jacinta is here, waiting to watch the fallout, but no.

"Well, as you know, we take into account more than your grades and academic achievements. We also examine your personal and private life. It has come to our attention that you have been in the media just recently, being portrayed in... shall we say, a not so rosy light."

My hopes come crashing down. I knew that the billboard would hurt me in the end. No matter what embarrassment Jacinta had hoped to bring me, this right here is the cruelest result.

"But that was a mistake and was quickly cleared up by Neighpalm Couture," I try to explain, but I can see that she has no sympathy for the situation.

"It's not even just that. Our goal is to care for our animals, first and foremost, and as a sanctuary, part of our funding comes from the generosity of our donors. We can't take on an employee whose notoriety might outweigh our donors' attention to our cause. Perhaps, with the public record of the company correcting their billboard's statement, we could have discussed overlooking it. However, the new one doesn't exactly show you in a light that portrays family entertainment either. We like to hold our employees up to exemplary morals, and let's face it, you rolling around on a bed with two men doesn't exactly portray that, does it?"

Oh, now she's done it, the prudish cow. I can't believe she's slut shaming me and anyone else who enjoys an "untraditional" relationship. Fuck her. I put a smug smile on my face and adopt my best impression of Jacinta, that looking down at you like you're not worth spitting on if you were on fire kind of sneer.

"No, that just makes me fucking lucky." Turning my back on her gasp, I leave her clutching her pearls and don't look back. If that's the kind of place this is, I don't want anything to do with it.

Despite my surge of bravado lasting long enough to get me out the door, I feel a tear roll down my cheek once I hit the parking lot. I hurry to the car in the hope that they're not looking out the glass door, waiting to see if I break down. I tear out of the driveway, my eyes stinging with tears, but I manage to keep them from falling until I can find another parking lot to pull over in. There was no way I was going to sit in my car and cry in front of the other one.

Pulling to a stop, I apply the emergency brake. "Fuck, fuck!" I bang my hand against the steering wheel and let the tears fall. In one fell swoop, my dreams have just been destroyed, and I can't even blame it all on Jacinta. They had a problem with the billboard period, no matter which slogan it was. Prudish cocksuckers. How dare they judge me! On the other hand, why hadn't I thought about it when I agreed to do it? I was so busy trying to get one over on Jacinta, I didn't even consider that the billboard could have consequences. Would I have done things differently?

This hurts, knowing that I've missed out on even the chance to earn this position, but if I try to look at it objectively, I can honestly say I wouldn't want to be a part of that organization. A company with that kind of mindset is ready to jump and judge at the tiniest infraction, and being a Summers makes it a larger possibility that I could be in the media for really any reason. One wrong step and I would have been out on my ass anyway. I guess better to lose the chance in the first place than to start shaping my life around a position and have it tugged out from under me.

I wipe my eyes, searching the glove box for a tissue so I can blow my nose. Pulling down the visor, I study my face. I look a mess, but there's nothing I can do about that now. I'll just tidy myself up when I get where I'm going. Blowing out a sigh, I dig around in my backpack for my phone, plug it into the onboard system, and dial a number, calling the one person who could make me feel better right now.

"Harlow, is everything okay? I thought you had your interview right now. Have you finished already?" Nana's gentle tones come through the car speakers, the warmth and caring in her voice soothing an exposed nerve.

"No, Nana, it was a disaster." I hiccup as I blurt out, "They didn't want me because of the billboard. They implied I was bringing the wrong kind of morals to the team." I sob a fresh load of tears at her quick inhalation of air.

"Those assholes. Shall we buy the zoo and fire them all?" The fact that this isn't just a grandmother siding with her granddaughter almost makes me burst out into laughter. Nana's deadly serious, and the level of disgust in her voice tells me that she might already be looking into the funds to do so.

"Really, Nana? Could we afford to do that?" I ask, a little curious.

"Honey, we could buy and sell it ten times over *and* employ and fire whoever we want. You want a zoo that badly? We will get you a zoo and find the best vet possible to train you." Hmm, that explains so much about why the Summers kids are the way they are. Nana is a fierce grizzly bear when it comes to protecting her family, and I'm sure Dad and Poppy are no different. "I'll get legal on it right away."

"No, stop. Nana, just stop." The tears have turned to giggles, and I wipe my eyes and face once more, throwing the tissues on the floor of the car. *Poor Oliver, he's not going to be happy about that.* And that thought cheers me right up. "I'm okay. I don't want to work for a company that will slut shame me and judge me on choices I make in my private life."

"They slut shamed you!" Nana shouts into the phone, and I turn the volume down slightly so people walking past can't hear her. "They only wish they were so lucky," she mutters, and I giggle.

"That's basically what I said too," I tell her, and she huffs.

"Well, come back and have some lunch with me. We will make some inquiries at other zoos. There are a few in California, and if we have to look at other states, we can do that. Although I want you as close as possible, it's not like I haven't got a plane at my disposal to visit whenever I want. Same with Brad and the boys."

"Boys? What do you mean by *boys,* Nana?"

There's some muttering in the background, Nana murmuring back in a little bit of a growl.

"Poppy says come to the offices and he'll give you a big squelch and not to worry about the job. You didn't want to work for them anyway. He's just done some quick research, and it looks like they might not be in the best financial situation," she says, ignoring my question. "Are you sure you don't want us to buy it for you?"

"I'm sure, Nana. Tell Poppy I'll be there for lunch and I can't wait for one of his hugs. I really need one." I hang up before she can come up with any more crazy ideas to buy me some happiness. Talking with them was really all I needed. My tears and sadness are gone, replaced with amusement and warmth at the joy of having a family who has my back... *and* a little bit of indignant anger at that woman and the assholes she works for.

Chapter Twenty-One

Harlow

Nana and Poppy must have told Dad what had happened, because when I arrived at the Neighpalm offices, I was immediately swarmed by the three of them trying to reassure and comfort me. My heart just about exploded with happiness, and I quickly forgot about the rejection from someone that didn't matter, basking in the love and acceptance of the people who did.

We had lunch and discussed our plans for riding the next day, deciding a nice trail ride would be perfect since they'd be off to the set the following day. By early afternoon, I couldn't decide whether I should wait around the offices or go and find something else to do, so I checked in with Hope. A few texts later, we had a plan set.

I would go check in with Nana on the Couture

floor, possibly borrow something to wear, and then Hope would meet up with me after about an hour. While the clothes I'm wearing are suitable for a job interview, they're not really *me,* and I want to find something more comfortable.

Waving hello to the secretary, I wander down the corridor toward Jacinta's office where I know Nana is located, but before I can get there, I find Lindy, Jacinta's PA, and the new hire Rowena standing just outside the office.

"You!" Lindy gasps, and I raise my hand to give her a little finger wave.

"Yes, me!"

"But, but …. You were supposed to be an intern. That's what Alex said," she stammers, clearly remembering the way she treated me when I met her if her nervous expression is any indication. *Definitely knows who I am now.*

"Did he say that? Or did you take one look at me and assume? You really need to not judge a book by its cover. Nor gossip about things you have no idea about," I tell her, remembering very well how happy she was to indulge in gossip about the Summers family when Jacinta wasn't around. She lowers her eyes in embarrassment, and I turn to the painfully thin woman next to her who has a grimace on her face like she smells something bad. "What are you doing here? I was under the impression you weren't starting until next week."

"Well, I had nowhere else to be, so I showed up

this morning and offered to start right away. Of course, Grace was so impressed with my work ethic, she immediately accepted," she sneers. The longer I look at her, the more I'm thinking this is her normal voice. I can't understand how someone can sound so disdainful all the time, but it's apparently possible.

"Oh wow, she even asked you to call her Grace? She must have been impressed." She blanches slightly, and I know I hit the nail on the head, but I don't call her out. I just let her stew a little in the fact that I know Nana would never have given her leeway to call her anything but Mrs. Summers until she gets to know her.

Pushing past the two of them with no further words exchanged, I let myself into Nana's office. She's on the phone but smiles when she looks up, waving a hand at the chair across from her, so I sit and wait for her to finish.

"Yes, Jacinta, I know. No, I won't forget." She pauses for a moment and listens to what my adopted sister has to say, a frown crossing her face. "Well, maybe next time you try and pull a stunt like this, you'll stop and think about the consequences. Now suck it up and take your punishment with true Summers grit. An apology probably wouldn't hurt either." Again, she stops. "No, not to me, to Harlow, you daft girl." Nana slams the phone down in frustration and shoots an apologetic look in my direction. "Sorry, dear."

I wave my hand at her. "Don't be, let's just leave it between me and Jacinta to sort out now. We're both big girls, remember? We'll be fine." I quickly change the subject when it looks like Nana is going to say more. "Can I raid the Wardrobe? I'm going out to dinner with Hope, and I don't really feel comfortable going in these interview clothes."

"Of course you can. All staff have been given a memo declaring who you are and that you are able to make use of whatever you wish to. If you have any problems, just let Hope know. She will sort it out." Nana's attention is drawn back to the papers in front of her, not a purposeful dismissal but a sign that she's definitely overwhelmed by all that needs to be done.

"Thanks, Nana, I'll leave you to it," I say, making my way back toward the huge office that has been converted into what's called the Wardrobe. Basically, anything ever designed and produced by Neighpalm Couture exists in this room, in a variety of sizes, ready at the drop of a hat to courier over to a celebrity in need of an outfit for something special, if Neighpalm Productions needs something for one of their movie sets, or Neighpalm Records for one of their music videos. The way every one of these businesses interacts with one another is nothing short of astounding, and it's really amazing that Dad's company has grown into this web of success.

Lindy and Rowena are still talking outside the

office, thick as thieves already, but I ignore them when I move past them. Making my way down the hallway, I hear them stalking after me, both wearing hideously high heels that click and clack with every step. Whatever could they want now? Pushing open the door to the Wardrobe, I step inside, breathing out a sigh of relief when all that greets me is quiet.

Looking around, I marvel at everything that's available. There are racks and racks of clothes, all with labels sitting above them to tell people what is what. I bypass the evening wear and lingerie until I find the label that says street wear. I've never been one to get overly impressed by clothes, but even I have to say I'm astonished when I flick through the racks. They must have had a goth run as there are short plaid mini skirts and waistcoats and velvet dresses. Moving past those, I discover the jeans, all with strategically ripped holes in them, and I find a black pair in my size and pull them out. Wondering if it's going to be dressy enough for where we're going tonight, I shoot Hope another message.

Me: Are we going fancy or casual?

I wait a few moments before she quickly replies.

Hope: Jaxon got us a reservation at a new Korean fusion restaurant that's supposed to be amazing as an apology for his behavior yesterday. Let's dress up a little bit. Are you in the Wardrobe?

Me: Yeah, I'm just getting changed out of what I wore to the interview.

Hope: Okay, I'm wrapping this meeting up now. Don't decide on anything without me!

The messages go silent, and I look between the jeans and the rest of the racks. If I get dressed quickly, Hope will just have to deal with what I'm wearing, but disappointing my new friend is not what I want to do, so letting her dress me up is really no big deal.

Flopping into a chair to wait for her, I pull my book out of my backpack and read in silence for a few minutes until my peace is shattered once again. *I knew it was too good to last.* The door to the Wardrobe opens, and Lindy and Rowena clomp in.

"Of course you're welcome to use the Wardrobe whenever you want. As head designer for the company, that's one of the perks."

Well, Lindy seems to be getting ahead of herself. She also seems a bit fickle in her loyalty. If she's Jacinta's PA, why is she already fawning over the new girl? She might be a shit sister so far, but everything Shane and Alex have told me indicates she's an amazing boss and is kind to most people she works with. That's why they were surprised at her animosity toward me. I consider saying something, but it's not really my place. I'm sure Jacinta will set everything straight when she comes back and then Lindy can fall all over herself to get back into her good graces.

Barely a moment passes before I'm hit with a little strike of guilt about that decision. Yes, she's been horrible, but that little voice in my head keeps asking me if I want to be like her or rise above her. *Can't believe I'm about to do something to help out the ice princess.*

"Wow, Lindy! You sure are doing an amazing job of welcoming our new *trial* employee. I'll be sure to tell Jacinta what a great job you're doing." Lindy blanches at my words, while Rowena narrows her eyes at me and curls her top lip. With the absolutely blatant lack of shame in her facial expression, it's pretty clear that she's got her sights set on making it big in the company, even if it means she has to compete with our resident Couture Queen. *Good luck with that, Jacinta. Do I bother bringing this up with Nana?*

"So I read that you're a long lost daughter who was recently reunited with her father. It must feel like you won the lottery," Rowena says, her hands on her hips, towering above me in the chair. Does she think I'm going to be intimidated? She's got another thing coming if she thinks that's the case.

"I guess you could say that," I reply noncommittally, and I can see that she's bothered by the lack of juicy gossip. Not that it would be any use to her with the NDA she signed and everything.

Nervously eyeing the space between us, Lindy drags her away from me and they start to browse through the clothes. Rowena is throwing subtle passive-aggressive shade about everything she puts her hand on, Lindy mindlessly agreeing with each comment. Rowena doesn't even seem to care that I could have input into whether she keeps her job or not. She mustn't consider me important enough, which I'm not, really, but I'm pretty sure at least Nana would listen if I had something to say. Honestly, I think I don't have to worry too much. Jacinta doesn't seem the type to put up with that kind a shit. *Note to self: bring popcorn to snack on when Jacinta comes back and meets her.*

I block them both out and continue reading my book, but my ears perk up when I hear Declan's name mentioned.

"Is he in the building very often? Are any of the guys here?" I pretend to keep reading, but I'm very interested in what Lindy has to say.

"Oh yeah, they're here all the time. Especially Declan and Holden. Thomas does a lot of flying all over the world, but I think he's gay. He hasn't dated a woman in years, and …." She breaks off as the door to the Wardrobe opens and Hope strolls in. Lindy scowls at her and quickly stops gossiping, suddenly on her best behavior. Hope looks around, her eyes lighting up when she sees me, but they sparkle mischievously when they flick to Lindy.

"Oh hey, it's Jacinta's shadow," she mocks as she walks over to them. Her gaze switches to Rowena, and as she scans her body, I can tell she's not all that impressed. "And this must be Jacinta Jr. I'm Hope, head of PR here at Neighpalm Industries." She holds out her hand, and Rowena reluctantly takes hold of it, not even trying to put in any effort. How one can give an apathetic handshake, I have no idea, but Rowena's managing to do it.

Lindy scowls and sneers at her, "At least my nose isn't so far up Holden's ass I can't see where I'm looking. Have you managed to land that yet, Hope? Whoops! No, I don't think you have."

Hope wrinkles her nose, a ridiculous grimace on her face. "Ew, gross! No, he's like my brother. But good try at the burn. You'll get there eventually." She pats Lindy on the shoulder, only laughing more when Lindy tries to slap it away.

Putting my book down, I quickly interfere, not ready for another cat fight like the day before.

"Hey, Hope, how about you pick me out something to wear tonight? I thought maybe these, but…"

That gets her attention, her eyes widening when she sees the jeans I'd picked out. Leaving the other two alone, she quickly makes her way to the racks and flicks through them, tension releasing from her shoulders the further she gets from Lindy. "Last year we had a great range of body con dresses that could be dressed up with heels and jewelry or dressed down with a pair of sneakers and some leggings underneath. And with your figure you would look *hot.*" She continues to flick through them, stopping at the tartan mini-skirt I saw before.

"Oh no, hang on!" She looks me up and down then back to the skirt. "How about we step out of our comfort zone a little? There's this great little club I want to go to after dinner. It's kind of goth, but the music and atmosphere are great, and I could really do with letting off some steam. I'm betting you could too." I'd texted her about the disastrous interview in between hugs from Nana and Poppy during lunch, and I'm extremely grateful that she didn't blurt that out in front of the vultures who are still in the room. "Want to pretend to be someone different tonight?"

"Fuck yes," I reply. She has no idea how much that appeals to me right now. I just want to get out of my head and blow off some steam. Maybe find someone to blow off some steam with. If I can spend a little time with a guy who's not battery-operated, I'm sure I'll feel better in no time.

A huge smile crosses her face as she pulls out the tartan skirt followed by a mesh top. She goes over to another wardrobe and grabs a pair of knee-high platform boots with plenty of buckles from another display. She turns back to me, a devious smile on her face. "Okay, so... a bra underneath or do you want to be daring and go without?"

I look at the mesh top in her hand. It's dark enough that if we're in a club, I'm sure you'd barely see the shadow of my nipples. "Fuck it. Tonight I'm pretending to be someone else. Let's go without."

She squeals with excitement and runs to another section of the room before coming back with a wig that's a short black bob. Raising her eyebrows at me in question, I nod before she throws all the clothes at me and turns.

"I'm sure you ladies don't mind coming back later!" She ushers the two women out of the room without another word, closing and locking the door behind them. Blowing out a huge sigh once it's closed, she finally looks completely relaxed.

"God, I hate that woman. She tried to play some underhanded tricks to force a wedge between me and Jacinta not long after she started. Luckily, we were able to see through them. If she wasn't so damn good at her job, Jacinta would have fired her. I think she's crazy for trusting her, but she's willing to take the risk. She's so protective over who the guys trust, but she's not nearly as good at taking care of herself." She shakes away her annoyance and waves at me. "Come on, get dressed! We'll blow this place and go find us some food and fun."

Chapter Twenty-Two

Harlow

"Ok, I promised you the low down on Jaxon and Jacinta, but I might as well fill you in on everyone," Hope says once the waiter takes our drink order. "Especially because Nana basically gave me the go ahead. If you wait for anyone else to tell you, you'll be waiting forever. They're all so tight lipped that I never even heard about some of this from them. Once she saw how close I'd gotten to Holden and the others, Nana sat me down and filled in some of the blanks in their pasts. She knows how… difficult they can be, and she wanted to make sure that I gave them the benefit of the doubt if they ever did anything that might run an ordinary person off. That woman loves her family, and she just wants them all to have the best lives they can, even if she has to bend a little on respecting their privacy."

I had driven us over to the restaurant in the Vanquish with the plan that I was going to have a couple of drinks and then stop so I could drive home later. There's nothing enjoyable about a hangover when you're bouncing around atop a horse running full throttle. No way I'm spending my and Dad's ride with a killer migraine.

She's quiet while our drinks are deposited in front of us, but she starts as soon as the waiter is out of hearing. "God, I don't know where to start. Maybe we'll just go in order of adoption? Declan was Brad's first. I think he was about ten when he was adopted. His story is tragic but not as traumatic as some of the others. His parents were killed in a car accident, and he had no living relatives so he went into state care. I don't think he was there long before Brad got him, so he didn't have to go through the foster system. As far as I'm aware, they were loving, caring parents, but he's got a bit of survivor's guilt, I think, driving that overprotective-ness. I didn't know him when he was that young, but I've been told that he used to be pretty anxious, worrying that things would happen to Brad, or Nana, or Poppy whenever they traveled for work or left for too long. I never could understand why, but he seems to blame himself in some way." She takes a sip of her drink as I contemplate that. Yeah, okay, I can see how that could happen.

"About a year after he was adopted, Brad was approached by a woman. Nobody knows the details of the arrangement, but I have a feeling this one wasn't done through proper authorities. When she left, she left behind the twins. Jacinta and Jaxon were about five, I think. Both were shy, and Jacinta showed signs of abuse, emotional *and* physical. Jaxon seemed like he'd been spared a lot of what Jacinta went through, but whatever he witnessed made the two of them extremely close, and you've seen first hand how protective he gets. Unfortunately, that only got worse when him and Declan teamed up."

"Okay, but that doesn't explain the hostility toward me. In fact, the twins should be able to relate to me a lot more than most."

"Yeah, but it doesn't end there. The woman that dropped them off was their mother. She was a mentally unstable junkie, and she'd always tell Jacinta that she was just a useless girl and nobody had any need for her. That she'd never be as good as her 'darling Jaxon.' Apparently, he looked just like their father, so their mom had some weird kind of fascination with him. As far as I know, it never amounted to anything beyond overt favoritism toward him, but that might be something Nana wouldn't have wanted to share."

Hope pauses, taking another sip and staring into her drink like she's deciding what to say next. Meanwhile, my mind is racing. Though I feel bad for what Declan lost, his story didn't hit me the same way the twins' is. And to be honest, I'm kind of annoyed with myself because the more I hear, the more I feel myself taking a closer look at Jacinta. I meant what I'd said to Hope. Jacinta and I should have been able to connect with each other, that bond of knowing someone else has survived a taste of what you've gone through, and a part of me is actually a little hurt.

I could have had a real sister in her, someone to talk with who would have understood me on a level that Max never could, no matter how hard she tried. I've resigned myself to the fact that Jacinta is out to hurt my reputation, my chances of getting to know Dad, and finding a place in the Summers family. What I wasn't expecting was to feel this kind of pang, the hurt of a missed opportunity.

"Anyway, Jacinta thrived in the house under the love and care of Brad and your grandparents, but when she was fifteen, her mother made her way back into her life somehow. One of the stipulations for Brad taking them off her hands was zero contact, but I guess she couldn't resist what she saw as an easy pay day. She spent months manipulating Jacinta into thinking they were developing a loving mother/daughter relationship, but it turned out she just wanted a way to break into the Summers' house and steal from them with her boyfriend and his feral gang. They robbed the place and even killed the one employee they could find after using

Jacinta's key and some stolen security codes to get inside. The poor guy was gunned down in cold blood. He'd just been unlucky enough to be sick that day, so he hadn't joined the rest of the staff and family at the twins' birthday party. Since everyone else was at the sweet sixteen, no one was there to save him or stop them. When the security footage was played and it was discovered who had done it, Jacinta changed. She went from a friendly, kind girl to the seemingly cold and definitely untrusting woman you've had the displeasure of meeting. She built walls to rival the Great Wall of China, and *nothing* gets through them."

The waiter comes over then, interrupting her to take our dinner order. While Hope takes care of it, my mind reels with the information she's just given me.

Oh my god. That explains so much, and I feel a lump of sympathy in my chest for her. I'm pretty sure that I would be similar to Jacinta if my mom had managed to do something like that to the Bostons. Luckily, they wised up early on, and she never had the chance to steal from them a second time, let alone murder someone in their home.

"So what happened to the mother? And what about a father? Where is he in all of this?" I ask.

She shrugs. "She and the gang disappeared. There was a man hunt for ages, but eventually they gave up. They're still at large, but there was no more contact with Jacinta after that night. As for the father, they never knew who he was, and neither of them care. Brad's all they've ever needed or wanted as far as they're concerned. In any case, none of this excuses her behavior, but at least now you know why Declan and Jaxon are such suckers for her drama."

Not ready to possibly spiral into the memories and depression that will surely come from studying the parallels of our lives too closely, I move on for now. There's a lot to really dig into with all of this, and I'll never be able to let loose if I dwell. Dwelling is for later. "Okay, tell me more about the others," I push, wanting to know more about the other men who've so captured my attention.

"Two years later, Thomas and Kai were adopted, both ten at the time. Unlike Declan, they both came from dysfunctional families, so those details are a little bit darker. I don't know too much about their stories, and Nana didn't really give much away, so I can't help you out much there. Thomas has always been very quiet; after being teased pretty badly for his accent, he kind of gave up on talking. And I told you about his ex who stole company secrets..."

Her bringing up Thomas reminds me of what I heard in the Wardrobe, and I have to interrupt her. I can't get the thought of Thomas, that lilting accent, and those green eyes out of my mind any better than I can stop thinking about the others. "Actually, I was listening to Lindy gossip with the new hire earlier, and she implied he might be gay. Not that there's anything wrong with that," I quickly assure her, and she snorts loudly, almost choking on her drink. I have to pat her on the back a couple of times before she recovers.

"Gay? Fuck no! He's the biggest man whore out there; he's just a little more discrete. He's usually fucking one of his flight attendants... or all of them. Since his ex, he hasn't spent a lot of time at home. Instead, he flies all over the world, overseeing the different branches of Neighpalm Air. God only knows what else he gets up to because it can't all be Neighpalm business. He's the one who takes the most independent time for himself, and I don't know which of his siblings, if any, really know what he does with that time. In any case, the business gets taken care of, and the flight attendants certainly enjoy themselves."

"Well, that would explain the hostility on my flight over," I snark, and she raises her eyebrows.

"Oh really. Which one was it?

"Veronica, I think. Apparently Jilly was on vacation."

"Jilly is awesome! I can't wait for you to meet her. Veronica must be getting a little too big for her boots if she's throwing shade at the newest Summers."

"Don't worry, Nana put her in her place quite nicely."

"God, I love Grace. I wish she was my Nana."

Her eyes shadow slightly as she says this, but she quickly shakes it off.

"Ok, Kai, there's no gossip about him. What you see is what you get. He's my favorite of the Summers siblings after Holden. Though he did have anger issues when he was younger, he channeled all of that aggression into martial arts and any kind of extreme sport he could try, much to Nana's dismay. Neighpalm Energy Drink was his baby and has been since he was about eighteen." Speaking of Kai, my all too eager body almost prickles with goosebumps at the thought of spending an entire weekend with him in Hawaii.

She breaks off her story while our food is delivered to the table, sliding our glasses to the side so we can make room. We ordered a few different dishes so we could try a little bit of everything.

"Okay, then when the twins were about fourteen, Brad adopted Oliver and Holden. They were both sixteen and were already super close since they'd been staying in the same state-funded home. As the story goes, Brad had intended to adopt a younger child, but when he saw the two of them, he realized how small the odds were of one teenager, let alone two, getting adopted and couldn't bear to leave them there."

She looks sideways, not meeting my eyes. "There's more to that story, but it's really not my place to tell you that. And it probably doesn't even matter anymore since they grew apart. Although they grew to feel like they were family with the others, their prior relationship stopped them from ever feeling like brothers. Holden is still extremely conflicted about it, but he hides it well. Oliver channeled all his emotions into his art, while Holden lost himself in his music and some other… recreational choices. He's got himself under more control now."

I can feel my brows furrowing in confusion, a small frown appearing. What the hell is she talking about? Before I can question her, she quickly moves on.

"To sum it up before your head explodes with all this information, Thomas, Kai, Holden, and Oliver are all the same age but have been with Brad for different amounts of times. Declan is the oldest and the twins the youngest. That's pretty much it for the Summers. Now, let's talk you. What are you going to do now that this interview went to shit?"

"Fuck, I don't know what to do. Maybe I'll just finish up my visit and head home. Brad and I are establishing a pretty strong foundation, and I'm sure we can continue that long distance. I mean, there's Skype and Facetime, and he owns an airline, for God's sake. Maybe this is just another sign of it not being meant to be."

"Harlow, I don't think you should be going anywhere until the police have worked out this stalker stuff." Her eyes are creased with worry, and there's a small frown on her brow.

"Maybe all of that would stop if I just returned

home. Nothing happened until I came here." She shakes her head adamantly, the frown growing deeper.

"I'm telling you, Jacinta is a lot of things, catty and distrustful just to name two, but she's not a psycho. She would *never* have sent you that picture of your pony. Even if the creepy shit didn't start until you came to LA, that doesn't mean that the stalker is from here. Who knows what made them start acting out now? No, best you wait and see what the detectives can work out. In the meantime, I happily volunteer to chaperone all the dinner dates and club hopping you can stand!"

Conversation changes to much more mundane things after that. She tells me a little of her upbringing and how she and Holden met in college. Turns out they bonded over shared assignments and a love of music.

A few hours later, after we dragged out the meal, drinks, and dessert, where we talked enough to now feel like I have another bestie, we're walking back to where I parked the Vanquish when I notice a crowd of people surrounding the car.

"I wonder what that's about?" I say to Hope, a little confused. Oliver does have vanity plates saying NP Ink. Could it be paparazzi?

Hope pushes her way through the crowd of people, towing me along behind, her hand on my wrist. But both of us come to an abrupt stop when we see what they're looking at.

"Holy shit." The words hiss out of Hope's mouth as we both look on, stunned by the sight in front of us. Oliver's car is covered in paint. Words like whore, slut, and go home are branded all over the vehicle in red paint. The tires are slashed and the windows smashed. In short, the car is trashed.

"Oh my god, Oliver is going to *kill* me." My heart is racing with worry over both Oliver's reaction and this. Is this the same person who did all the other things? Just as I say that, a cop car pulls into the parking lot, blue and red lights flashing, and two officers hop out.

The crowd begins to drift away as the officers approach us. "Does one of you own this car?" one of the cops stops and questions while the other strolls around the vehicle, his flashlight shining into the windows.

"Ah, well, I was driving it, but it belongs to a friend." I stammer a little bit, still in shock at the vicious sight. I sink down onto the sidewalk, not caring if I'm flashing anyone in my short skirt, dropping my head into my hands. *God, this is not what I wanted to do tonight.* Seriously, this was supposed to be a night of no worries. I'm about to get back up and deal with everything, but Hope comes to the rescue. She instantly has her PR persona on and fishes around in her handbag before coming out with a card and handing it to the officer.

"I'm Hope Green, Head of PR at Neighpalm

Industries. The car belongs to Oliver Summers. I'm sure you can appreciate the fact that it's late and there is nothing to see here. I guess whoever did this is long gone. I'm just going to organize for it to be towed. While I'm taking care of that, could you please advise Detective Thomas James? He is investigating a possible stalker for Miss Stubbs here, and I'm sure this fits in with the rest of the incidents."

He frowns as he looks at the card. "If that's the case, it's better that we have it towed so that forensics can go through it. If you just give us a moment, I can ask you a few questions and we can get Detective James on the line to see what he wants to do. He may want you to stay until he can get here." Hope frowns but nods, and they move just over from me, leaving me to my freak out in peace and quiet.

My eyes can't leave the wreck that is the car. I'm pretty sure that's going to be classed as a write off, and I can only imagine how Oliver is going to react. Looking around, my brain prickles with that weird sense of an idea just out of reach, and I run my eyes over the scene again until I remember something. Hope had wanted me to use valet parking because of the stalker threat, but I hadn't wanted to waste money, so we'd compromised by parking in a well-lit spot. But now, both of the lights that had lit up the parking lot are smashed.

"Hope!" I call out to her, and she and the officer

look up. “Weren’t they working when we parked here earlier?” I point to the now dark lamps.

Her nose scrunches as she pauses, thinking, before she responds, “Yeah, they were. That's really weird.”

The two officers exchange a look, and one decides to expand his search outward from the car, flashlight shining behind and under other cars, hand on his holster. I scramble to my feet.

“There’s a good chance that the person who did this was waiting for you to return to the car and was going to use this for distraction. It’s a good thing there were people around earlier.”

“Holy fuck!” slips from Hope’s mouth before she exchanges a worried look with me. “I’m just going to get one of the Neighpalm cars to come and pick us up. The Detective I spoke to on the phone said it was alright for us to leave. He said he’ll catch up with you tomorrow.”

“That's a good idea,” the officer tells her. “I don't want you two wandering around on your own.”

Hope paces back and forth for a little while as I wrap my arms around me, trying to ward off the chill that's settled into my body.

“Jesus, they seem to be escalating. I better call your dad and tell him,” she says, pulling her phone out of her purse, but I quickly snatch it out of her hand.

“Please don’t, he’ll only worry. I’ll tell him in the

morning. Come on, now that I don't have to drive, I'm going to have lots of shots and just forget about everything for a while. I don't even care if I have to ride hungover tomorrow. Let me have this, please?" I beg. "I'll call an Uber later to get me home."

"You will *not* do something so stupid. Your stalker could be waiting for exactly that opportunity. The same car that takes us to the club can return and take you home. Midnight sound okay, Cinderella?" Her eyes still show worry, but she's smiling again.

"Sounds freaking perfect," I answer, my heart finally calming a bit as she makes a couple of calls.

Chapter Twenty-Three

Harlow

The club is loud and crowded and exactly what I need. As was the appreciative smirk and wink I'd gotten from the coat check girl when I'd turned in my jacket and revealed my mesh top. *Hey, I might not be interested, but that doesn't mean I can't appreciate the attention.* Smirking back at her, I take my ticket, realizing a moment later that I have nowhere to tuck it. With no pockets and VIP passes that get us free drinks, meaning no need for my wallet, I'm shit out of luck. While I'm feeling a little lost, Hope snorts and rolls her eyes before plucking it from my fingers and tucking it down into her bra. With her iron grip now on my hand, she pulls me deeper into the club.

She leads me straight to the bar, getting the attention of a nearby bartender. Leaning over, she shouts our order in his ear while I scope out the people around us. Hope wasn't kidding when she said it was a goth crowd; there are a lot of black boots and metal glinting through the crowd. When I turn around, scoping out another corner of the club through the flashing lights, I even see fake fangs and multi-colored hairstyles. Everywhere I look, there's something new and interesting and fun.

"This is awesome!" I shout to Hope as the bartender puts some shots in front of us. She picks one up and hands it to me, a devious smile on her face. I'm not sure what it is, but I trust her, and as we clink our glasses together she shouts, "To new friends!" Both of us throw the shots back, the familiar taste of tequila burning as it slides down my throat. Grabbing the piece of lime she's holding out, I shove it into my mouth and bite down, trying to fight the burn.

"Again!" she shouts.

We repeat the action, but this time I shout, "To new family!" Thank God this one goes down easier, though I still have to take a deep breath when I see the bartender immediately replacing our empty glasses.

"Compliments of the man down the end of the bar," he says, and while I pick up my glass, more focused on some very necessary drunken fun, Hope leans around me to check out the mysterious man.

Her eyes widen slightly before she smiles and nods in our patron's direction.

"What shall we toast to this time?" I ask as I turn back around to find her matching grin.

"To getting laid?" she suggests.

"Sounds fucking good to me," I shout, my inhibitions slowly leaking away with the intake of the alcohol, and we clink our glasses once more and throw them back.

"Let's dance." I put my glass down and drag her out onto the dance floor, feeling freer than I have since I got off the plane with Nana and Poppy.

There's a band playing, loud and hypnotic, with both male and female lead singers, their voices blending harmoniously while the thump of the bass and drums sends reverberations through my body. Before I know it, we're lost together in the crowd, my hips swaying and my hands lifting with the rhythm.

I'm not sure how long we dance for, but suddenly a set of hands wraps around me from behind. When I look down, I find black painted fingernails at the end of fingers that are spread across my stomach in a possessive gesture. The heat easily comes through the mesh top, sending a shiver through me. I'm just about to turn around when a whispered voice says into my ear, "Care to dance, Mistress?"

Spinning quickly, I'm surprised by what I see. In fact, I'm damn near floored. This man who was made up so nicely in a suit yesterday now screams goth bad boy. Like me, he has on a mesh shirt, but the mesh isn't as tight as mine, and his pierced nipples are easily visible. My eyes travel further down to follow his leather-clad thighs to thick buckle-covered shit kicking boots. Moving my gaze up, I take in the kohl-rimmed eyes and the eyebrow ring that wasn't there yesterday. Neither was the one in his lip. His blond hair is styled messily, and the cheeky grin on his face belies the hopeful look in his eyes.

"Holy shit." I'm a little stunned that this is Holden. Never in a million years would I have guessed this. Hope's laughter echoes behind me, loud enough for me to hear it despite the music.

"Did you tell him we would be here?" I ask her accusingly, but Holden puts a finger on my chin and turns my head back toward him.

"Now don't be like that. I was here to check out the band. I think we're going to sign them to our label." As he speaks, his eyes wander down my body, widening when he gets to my chest before moving further down. "Damn, Harlow, you're like all my wet dreams rolled into one." I lift an eyebrow and cross my arms, the cocky ass only smirking before leaning in, his warm breath tickling my ear. "Sorry, I meant *Mistress*."

Not wanting him to see that I'm surprised and a little thrown off that he's following through on our deal, I just turn around in his arms again and start to move to the music, silently giving him permission to dance with me. Leaving his hands on my hips, he moves closer, fitting his body to mine, and my heart skips a beat when I remember the last time I danced with a Summers brother. I just pray that this time doesn't go as badly.

Part of me is excited, but the other equally as loud part of me is cautious. Tonight is about fun, and there's an unexpected promise in Holden's eyes that tells me he might be willing to give me exactly what I'm looking for. What I need to figure out now is whether I'm okay with paying any cost that comes with that. At the moment, I do know that I plan to lose myself in this music and just damn the thinking for now.

We dance together for ages, his hands moving all over me as mine wrap around his neck from behind. There are no boundaries anymore, not while this music plays. My skirt is barely long enough to cover my ass, so when he brushes against the fishnets and feels bare skin under them, he suddenly stops. His breath is heavy in my ear, and whatever scent he's wearing, smelling like seduction and dark desires, hits my nose. "Are you not wearing any underwear?" The question is just rough enough to suggest it's coming out between gritted teeth, and I smile to myself.

"It's called a thong, Holden. Lots of girls wear them." He growls in my ear, and one hand caresses the globe of my ass as the other one slides up the inside of my top. "You are sinful temptation." His voice is still low and intimate in my ear, such a contrast to the noise around us. That caress tightens, his grip now firm enough that I can sense his determination to have me in his arms.

"This top is enough to bring a strong man to his knees. To just barely seeing those nipples peeking out when the lights hit just right… May I pleasure you, please, Mistress?" His teeth graze my ear as his hand palms my breast, our bodies pulled even closer together. He rubs his thick erection into my ass, and I close my eyes for a moment, losing myself in the music, the heat of his body, and the promise of release. My heart is of two minds. I shouldn't do this because he's still trying to work his way back into my good graces, but on the other hand, this is exactly what I wanted when I came here. To blow off some steam and not think about tomorrow. *Why can't I get what I want for once?* Unable to answer that question, I bite my lip and give him a quick nod.

His hand leaves my ass and moves around to the front, the crowd so thick and frenzied that nobody is paying attention to the hand that has slipped under my skirt. His finger teases around the edge of my panties, giving me barely enough time to gasp before he goes straight to my throbbing clit. Grinding back into him as he rubs with just the right pressure, I feel selfishly decadent, and I have no regrets. This isn't something that I would normally do, but I deserve to be pleased, to be given what I need by this man whose body is screaming that he'd be willing to give me more if only I asked.

His teeth gently bite at my neck, the little pinches of pain adding to the pleasure in a way that I'm surprised to enjoy. Unafraid of who might hear in the midst of all this hypnotic music, I moan and press down on his head, letting him know he can give me more. In no time, the pass of his finger over my clit and his teeth and tongue against my neck have me rising to my peak. When he pinches my nipple with his other hand, I detonate, shuddering through an intense orgasm, our bodies moving in sync the whole time. After a few moments, the waves of pleasure slow, and I turn to face him, wanting to… I'm not sure. Do I kiss him? Do I take this a step further and cross that next line into making this even more intimate? Before I can decide, the band finishes their last song and says goodnight. Groaning, he slumps against me, and I can't say that I hate the warmth that comes with his closeness.

"I've got to go. I've set up a meeting with the band and their manager." He places a small kiss against my neck. "Mistress, please, may I go?" he asks, the slightest of pouts sticking that lip ring out in a way that's entirely too tempting.

"Go. You'll pay for this later," I tell him, playing my part with no small sense of satisfaction.

Taking a step back, he smiles, his eyes sparkling with desire as he pretends he doesn't know what could've followed the moment we just shared. He sweeps my body one more time before his eyes rise to meet mine again. "What shall I pay for, mistress?" he asks.

"You know very well, and just remember, payback's a bitch," I growl at him, equally turned on by his actions and frustrated he's leaving me this way.

"Oh, I'm counting on it." With a wink, he turns, disappearing into the crowd.

I'm so worked up, I can feel the dampness in my thong and my nipples are as hard as diamonds against the mesh shirt, which is doing nothing to ease my arousal. *How can I still be this desperate after that orgasm?*

"Fuck." I head to the bar and wave down the bartender, asking for a bottle of water. He can't hide the admiration in his eyes as he returns with what I asked for, but I'm so wrapped up in how Holden made me feel that I don't engage with him. Not getting any interest in return, he walks away to serve someone else.

"Holy shit!" Hope flings herself at me, coming out of nowhere. I haven't seen her for a while, having lost her to her own dance partner while I was wrapped up in Holden. "I feel like I need a change of panties just from watching the two of you. I almost had a visual orgasm," she babbles, a huge grin on her face as she fans her hand against it. I roll my eyes at her, but she's not wrong, and it leaves me even more conflicted and confused. Not to mention severely determined to ignore that my new friend just saw her bestie's hand playing up my skirt.

I'm supposed to be going to Hawaii with Kai this weekend, and I'm pretty sure it's not a brother/sister bonding experience. I wonder how he would feel if he knew his brother just brought me to orgasm on the dance floor. Hope must see the anxiety in my eyes because she steps close and pokes a finger into my chest.

"Now you listen here, missy. I can just see by the look on your face that you're conflicted by what happened. Seriously, just Elsa it."

"Huh?" I'm not sure if it's me or the tequila or both, but I definitely am not following.

"You know, let it go." Oh, of course, a Disney reference.

"I told you this before. You don't know that any of them would be upset about the others. If they shared a relationship with one woman, that woman would have the attention of six men, someone always able to make up for whenever another is missing or fucks up or is an asshole. With these boys, all of the above is *guaranteed* to happen. Harlow, this could be a fucking fantastic thing, and I don't know if it's the shots or if it's just that you already seem like such an amazing person to me. Okay, it's probably both, but Holden and any or all of the rest of those boys would be *so* lucky to have you! Everyone else would let them get away with their shit, and that's not doing anyone any good."

I shake my head, all of this getting a tiny bit too real right now. "I don't..." She holds her hand up to my face, it waving slightly but finally managing to cover my lips.

"Nope, just think about it, okay? If it was me with the opportunity to have a harem, I'd be all over that like bees on honey. If I got the opportunity to see..." She trails off, looking wistful, likes she thinking of somebody or maybe a few somebodies in her past, but then she sways and shakes her head before returning her focus to me. "Never mind." She jumps slightly and pulls her phone out of her bra. "Oh hey, your ride is here."

"Okay. I got to pee and clean up first, then I'm out of here. What about you? Are you coming with?"

"Oh no, I'm going to find that couple I was dancing with and see if I can convince them to take me home for the night." I raise my eyebrows and laugh as she waggles her tongue at me.

"Well, okay then, have fun." I lean in and give her a hug and a kiss on the cheek before I reach directly into her bra. Her eyes widen at my move, a harsh swallow following next. Not able to hold in my laughter, I pull my coat check ticket out and wave it at her, sending her into an almost startled giggle.

Taking my bottle of water with me, I make my

way to the back of the club in search of the bathrooms. I pass a booth on the way, and Holden is there surrounded by the band, the group having an intense conversation. As I walk by he lifts his head, so I wave and mouth *I'm going*. Frowning, he nods before continuing his conversation.

By the time I make it out of the bathroom and get my stuff from the coat check, I'm feeling bad for the driver. The poor man's probably already worried that I skipped out on him, so I hurry away from the coat check girl, a smile on my lips as I head outside, thinking of the appreciation she graced me with again. It's a balmy warm night, and the limousine parked in front has Neighpalm on the number plate. I make my way over to the driver who is standing by the back door.

"Miss Harlow?" the guy asks, and he opens the door to the back seat with my answering nod. I slide in, and he's about to close it behind me when I hear a voice call after me.

"Wait up!"

Turning to look back, I can see Holden running toward the vehicle. "Thanks, Dan. I was going to stay in town, but if you're taking Harlow home, I might as well catch a ride."

"No problem, Mr. Summers."

Holden slides into the car next to me, and I move over slightly to make room as the driver closes the door and makes his way to the front. The privacy screen is up between us, leaving Holden and me in a little space that belongs only to us. Closing my eyes, partly from exhaustion and partly to escape the residual sexual tension that's still floating between us, I lean my head back against the seat. Unfortunately, it doesn't help much since I can still feel his eyes on me.

"Are you okay, Mistress?" Holden asks quietly, and a smile crosses my mouth. "Was… all of that, back on the dance floor, okay?"

"Yeah," I reply quietly, opening my eyes and finding his intense gaze on me like I expected. Leaning forward, I pull down the hidden zipper on my boots and slide them off my feet, a happy sigh leaving my mouth. Then I pull the wig off my head, groaning as I run my fingers through my own strands. "I'm tired and my feet are sore, but they're better now," I explain, leaning back again. I am totally OK with not discussing the dance floor right now. I won't hide from it forever, but right now, I want to just bask in some post-orgasm bliss and enjoy having these damn boots off.

He reaches down and grabs a foot, shuffling me so that he can put it into his lap. His thumb presses into the arch, pushing hard, and a moan slips from my mouth.

"Oh God."

"No, just Holden, even Den if you want. No need to call me God." His fingers continue to massage my tired and aching foot, and my eyes drift closed once more, reveling in the strength of his warm grip.

"Did you sign your band?" I ask, genuinely interested and enjoying this moment of peace. "They were really good."

"Yeah, I did." He sounds pleased with himself, but it doesn't cross that line into cockiness. Instead, it's a calm satisfaction at getting what he wanted. "They had interest from other labels but decided to go with us. They're coming in on Thursday to sign the contract."

"Hey, that's awesome. Congratulations." I open my eyes to look at him again, our gazes briefly meeting before one of his hands moves to my calf, massaging it. Another moan slips from my mouth, and I can't seem to tear my eyes away from him.

"What have you got planned for the rest of the week?" he asks softly.

"Mmm." I can't help the sigh that slips out before I answer him. "Well, tomorrow, I'm going riding with Dad." His face lights up when I tell him this, and that sheer happiness is a new look for him, a good look for him. A *very* good look.

"Dad couldn't stop talking about it at dinner last night. He was so excited about you having lunch with him too." I cringe at the thought of Jacinta and how she must have reacted. He must know what I'm thinking because he immediately shakes his head. "She didn't come down. Nana took something to her room. Apparently, the muse is riding her hard at the moment. I guess there's nothing like the threat of being replaced to make someone work harder."

Nodding, I let out a small sigh of relief that she was spared that experience; I'm kind of enjoying the lack of her attention, and I don't want something to spark her into coming after me again. "Then on Thursday, I've got to truck the horses to the movie set, and Max should be arriving at the same time we are."

"We?" he asks, raising an eyebrow.

"Declan is insisting on coming with me. He wants to see what the hold up is with the director, and he figures tagging along with me is a good way to do it, I guess." Nodding, he puts my foot down and picks up the other.

"Ah yes, my anal brother, the one who doesn't like things to be out of his control. Your arrival has got Mr. Cool unusually shaken. And what are you doing to his cat? You know it's driving him wild, right?" He has a wide grin on his face at the thought of Declan's discomfort. It's not malicious though, just amused, showcasing the easy camaraderie the two of them have.

"I swear I'm doing nothing. Someone keeps opening my door and letting her in!" I protest, and he snorts.

"It's probably Declan himself. I wouldn't put it past him. It's a way of being able to keep an eye on you if he can claim he's looking for his cat. And any plans on the weekend?"

I feel a blush spread over my face, but I'm sure he can't see it in the dim light of the limo. After dancing and flirting with him, I'm a little embarrassed and slightly confused about having to admit to him that I'm going away with his brother for the weekend. Feeling a little flushed, I slip off my jacket. "Actually, I do. Kai invited me to go to Hawaii with him. He needs to check out a couple of athletes for a potential new team." His hand stills on my foot for a moment before continuing.

"That sounds fun." He actually sounds like he means it, zero hint of any concern that I was grinding on him all night yet I'm going on a weekend getaway with his brother. Hope's voice comes to mind, and I can almost hear her singing, "*Let it go.*" Shaking it off, I tune back in to what he's saying. "I have meetings all weekend; otherwise, I would have liked to come too. Maybe next time."

"Yeah, that would be… good." I'm surprised at my response, but then he *has* gone out of his way to make an effort. Even though tonight was about fun, I also know myself. If I trust him with my body, even a bit, then there's something inside me that's made a choice.

Maybe I'm working on forgiving them all already.

Chapter Twenty-Four

Harlow

The rest of the ride home was silent but comfortable. Holden stopped rubbing my feet but put his arm around me, the two of us sitting closely together, my jacket long forgotten. It isn't until we pull into the driveway and I drop the partition to direct the driver toward the stables that Holden starts to talk again.

"Why are we going to the stables?" He sits up straighter, moving his arm from my shoulder. "And didn't you have Oli's Vanquish?" His body is tense now that he's realized something doesn't make sense about this situation, but I wait until the car stops to answer him so that I can make a fast exit. I quickly shove my feet back into the boots, hoping to get this over with as quickly as possible. *Yeah, blowing off steam time is definitely over with.*

"After yesterday's threat, I need to be reassured DS is okay," I tell him, getting out of the car and thanking the driver.

I start to walk toward the stable, his thick-soled boots thumping on the ground as he catches up with me. "And the car?"

I stop, my shoulders dropping with a sigh. "The car was vandalized while Hope and I were at dinner. It's now in police custody, waiting for forensics." His jaw drops as the sensor light outside the stable turns on with our movement. Turning, I slide open the door and flick the inside switch on, heading into the stable without waiting for his response. I'm about to clomp right over to DS's stall, but I come to a quick stop, the sight in front of me too shocking to comprehend.

"Harlow, I saw a limo drop you off and just wanted to come and see what the fuck has happened to my car." Oliver's angry voice easily travels into the stable, and normally, that tone would have me turning around in defense mode, but I can't turn away. A mirror shattering scream leaves my mouth, and I start to rush forward, but Holden wraps his arms around me, holding me back.

"What the hell?" Oliver's suddenly next to us, but I yank myself out of Holden's arms and run toward the blood-covered legs sticking out of an open stable. They have a pair of high heels on, and when I get closer, there's a horse blanket over the top of the body clad in a dress that I recognize as Jacinta's, her dark hair splayed out behind her and face hidden. Tears stream down my face as I realize what's happened. My stalker has escalated, and Jacinta is a casualty of his madness. Now she's truly a broken girl, and any chance of us ever changing the future between us is gone.

"Nooooo!" The anguished shout leaves Holden's mouth, and I turn to find the two of them directly behind me, Holden in Oliver's arms as tears stream down his face.

Stepping closer, I brace myself. I've seen my fair share of dead animals during training, but this is a whole different thing. My mind flashes back on the day I had to identify my mother, a roll of nausea threatening my resolve, and I take a deep breath to steady myself. Flipping back the horse blanket, a whoosh of air leaves my mouth and I blink, struggling to comprehend what I'm seeing.

It's a fucking mannequin. Just a fashion dummy dressed up to look like Jacinta. But aside from the "blood," there's another dark twist. A bullet hole is in the middle of her forehead, and a note lies atop her body. With a trembling hand, I reach toward the note, stopping myself when the thought that it might be evidence hits me. Instead, I lean forward until I can make out the words printed on it: *The real one is next!*

"Oh, thank fuck!" I breathe out a sigh of relief, and strangled gasps and sobs behind me have me turning again. Oliver and Holden, still holding onto one another, have stepped closer and come to the same conclusion; it's not really Jacinta. Suddenly, voices draw our attention toward the entry.

"Harlow?! We heard you scream." Kai bursts into the stable, Thomas close on his heels, the latter holding a gun like he knows what to do with it. They're followed by Declan, Jaxon, Dad, and even Jacinta, all of them sprinting. "Holy shit." Kai's hoarse whisper is echoed by his siblings, and Jacinta takes a surprisingly steady step forward. Meanwhile, the horses are freaking out, not appreciating all of the chaos.

"They're my shoes," Jacinta says, and I hear her step closer. "Oh my god," she gasps, and when I turn, she's wrapped in Jaxon's arms, her head buried in his chest. His eyes are tight with fury, that protective instinct of his definitely triggered by this sick display.

"This has gone too far," he says through clenched teeth.

"You're not wrong," Thomas adds in, tucking the gun in his hand into the back of his waistband and pulling his shirt over the top.

"Right, as of today, Harlow and Jacinta, you don't go *anywhere* alone," Dad announces, pulling out his phone.

"But I've got to take the horse to the set, and I'm going to Hawaii with Kai!" I blurt out, my heart racing. Right now, there's almost this strange bubble between me and the rest of the world. I'm lost in this feeling that this is all too crazy to be real, like I'm sitting back at the club, stuck in some tequila-inspired nightmare. It takes me a minute to realize that I need to get myself back into reality, and I almost feel like an idiot for what I just said to Dad.

My stalker… *our* stalker?... just left a death threat for Jacinta, and I'm worried about Hawaii and horses? Am I in some kind of shock?

The guys and Dad all glance around at each other, the looks passing between them for long enough that I'm convincing myself they're about to tell me that I've got my priorities real fucked up.

To my surprise, Declan breaks the silence, taking a step forward and drawing all our attention to him. "I'm going with her to the set, Dad, and Kai and Jaxon will be with her in Hawaii. I think she will be okay, and it might actually be a good idea for her to get out of here for a few days. Between the package at Neighpalm HQ and this, he's definitely got too much access to our usual places. Hopefully, Hawaii will be out of his reach. It's not like everyone has the resources to drop everything and fly there on a moment's notice."

Dad frowns, his shoulders slumping after a

moment like he's realized that any argument he might have made doesn't hold the same logic as Declan's reasoning. "Fine, you can do those things, but the boys *will not* let you out of their sight, and there will be *none* of the bullshit that's happened between you all here. I don't want anyone to have any reason to storm off and compromise your safety. *And* I'm hiring security for this place until this madman is caught."

He turns to Jacinta, his eyebrow raised and shoulders squared as if he's ready for his other daughter to make an argument for her crazy freedom too, though it looks like he has nothing to worry about on that front. Jacinta is still wrapped in Jaxon's arms, the streaks of tears on her pale cheeks catching the light as she shakes her head. "I promise I won't go anywhere. I'm happy here, drawing, at the moment."

That settled, my mind jumps to the threat I received yesterday, and my body makes the decision before my mind can, pushing everyone out of the way to rush to DS and Jenny's stall. Another scream leaves my mouth when I take in my beloved animals.

Both are just standing there, but they're covered in whatever the mannequin's body is coated in, making them look like Carrie at the prom. Totally unfazed, Jenny happily walks over to the gate and nudges my head. DS's ears are flat back, and she's shaking her head, trying to get the dripping stuff off of her. I'm surprised whoever it was could actually get close enough to do this without getting bit.

An arm around my shoulder has me turning and burying my face in the offered chest. I can tell by the scent that it's Kai. He smells like warm summer days, and his hand strokes over my head as he whispers in my ear, "Everything will be okay. We'll find the fuckers who did this, and they'll wish they'd never been born." A wave of warmth suffuses my body, and I want to snuggle in and let him take care of everything, but I know I can't do that. *Aside from the faux blood-covered animals, there's also the dance floor orgasm to worry about later. Complication, thy name is Harlow Stubbs.* I pull away from him and move to get the things I need to wash the animals, wanting to tackle the easiest obstacle first.

"What are you doing?" he asks as I bend over to fill a bucket with water. The rest of the family is talking quietly, Oliver still wrapped around Holden, and I'm starting to think there's more to that relationship than I first thought. There's something about it that just looks more intimate than a brotherly connection, and my mind thinks back to Hope's unexplained comment from dinner. *Control your curiosity, Harlow. Take care of your animals first, and then you can worry about orgasms, and too-close brothers, and all the other shit that's piling up on your to do list.*

"Harlow?" Kai's voice behind me has me snapping out of my dirty musings. Looking back at him,

I remember his question as I catch his eyes on my ass.

"Oh. Well, I can't leave them like that. I'm going to clean them up." The heat in his eyes is practically smoldering, and I'm thrown off for a moment. I mean, I know kinks come in all shapes and sizes, but I *really* didn't think there was a fetish for bloody animals. Maybe I shouldn't go to Hawaii after all. Some shit might just be too weird. That thought almost startles a laugh out of me, but Kai's started to respond, so I make myself focus back on him.

"As much as I like what's going on here," he says, a hint of a chuckle in his words as he gestures to my outfit, "maybe a change of outfit would be a good idea. Though please, keep this one for another time." He grabs my bucket of water as I straighten, my eyes wide and cheeks burning with what's definitely a deep blush. *Well, check "Dad seeing my nipples" off the bucket list I never wanted.*

"Harlow." The quiet voice catches my attention. "There are overalls in the tack room. May I give you a hand with washing them?" I slowly turn to Jacinta, schooling my expression before we're face to face. Her hands are twisting together like she's nervous, and she can't meet my eye. *Would it kill her to apologize to me?* I mean, really, we could put all of this behind us and move on if only she would own up to her mistakes. The last two days are really shoving my face in the fact that I have bigger shit to worry about than Jacinta Summers. In any case, I'm not going to let my animals be uncomfortable any longer than they have to be, so I'll take her assistance, apology or not. The animals always come first.

"Yeah, that would be helpful," I tell her, and her body loosens in relief as she makes her way toward the tack room to change.

"The police are on their way. They told me to not let you touch anything until they get here," Dad says to us all. "Let's go up to the house and leave everything like it is until then."

"But, but.." I try to argue, and he puts his hand up.

"It's not going to hurt the animals to stand there for another half an hour, Harlow. I'll get them to clear that area first, and as soon as they're done, you can wash them," he reassures me. I relent, not wanting to put anyone further on edge by having to argue with me.

The others leave, Oliver and Holden not touching anymore, though they do seem to be having a quiet conversation before they both follow Dad out of the stables.

"You go ahead," Thomas directs, the edge to his voice making me look at him closely. There's a calm authority to those three words that make me feel like he's not as rattled as everyone else. What has he dealt with as the head of Neighpalm Airlines that gives him such a cool head now? Who is this man? "I'm going to wait here for the police or in case Josh comes in for any reason." He drags a bale of hay out to the feed room and puts it next to one of the stable walls, settling his long body down on it. I can't help but notice he's wearing gray sweatpants and a black wifebeater, his feet bare and his red hair tousled like someone has been running their hands through it. I have to cross my arms over my chest to hide what his whole look is doing for me. *Damn these traitorous nipples.*

Jacinta walks over to follow the others, throwing a pair of overalls at me on the way. "Wipe your drool, will you?" she says quietly as she goes past, seeing where I'm looking. My eyes snap to hers, finding a very surprising amusement instead of the usual venom, but then it's like she realizes we're bonding and they cloud over again. Ending the moment, her gaze moves to the mannequin and she shudders before she breaks into a jog. "Wait for me," she calls out before disappearing through the doorway, leaving me with just Kai and a watchful Thomas.

"Come on, this'll give you a chance to get changed," Kai suggests, and I quickly take the overalls back into the feed room, hanging them on a hook. I haven't been in there before, but it looks to be well stocked with medical equipment too. There's an ultrasound machine in the corner, and the nerdy vet in me almost can't resist checking out the equipment, but it just gets added to the long list of shit I have to make time for later.

When I return to the others, Kai and Thomas are having a quiet conversation, their murmurs stopping when they see me. Kai smiles, but it looks a little strained. “Come on, let's go.”

“Can I bring you a coffee or something?” I ask Thomas as he watches me with those green eyes that seem to see so much. Thomas is always watching, taking things in. You never know what’s going on in that head of his. I guess all those years of remaining quiet around others taught him the value of looking and listening. I’m a little sad that he had to learn that lesson, but it makes me even more intrigued to find out what’s going on beneath his surface.

The pause seems to stretch for hours, a weird kind of tension or anticipation building between the two of us. I’m not really sure what the feeling is, but it’s definitely got a life of its own. A small smile crosses his mouth before he replies, “Yeah, that would be great. Thank you.”

Kai wraps his arm around my shoulders, and we make our way back to the house. The lights are blazing now, especially compared to the darkness of when we returned home. I’m not sure how everyone heard me from inside. Maybe Oliver woke them all when he saw me come home without his car? But then how would Dad have heard in the other wing? As I walk inside, my attention no longer occupied by the ghastly stable scene, I notice he's in a business suit, as are Declan and Jaxon. In fact, apart from Holden, Thomas in his sweats, and Jacinta in pajamas, they all are.

"What's with the suits?" I ask them, trying to distract myself from the scene in the stables.

"We attended a charity dinner tonight, and we had only just gotten home before you did. We were sitting having a nightcap on the patio until we heard you scream and followed Oliver out to the stable," Jaxon explains, pouring a cup of coffee from the pot on the counter and sliding it over to me.

Giving him a small smile of thanks, I'm about to ask what charity it was for, any kind of small talk to distract me from what happened, but Oliver prompts me again.

"You never said what happened to my car." His eyes are creased at the edge with worry, his gaze locked on Holden and the bottle of whiskey he's just pulled out of a cupboard. Holden pours a big slug into a glass before throwing it back without a flinch.

Hunching my shoulders, I avoid his gaze when it switches to me, the pause going on too long. "Harlow," he growls.

"Fuck, Oliver, I'm sorry, but the stalker was busy tonight. He must have trashed your car and then hurried back here to do what they did out in the stable."

"*Trashed my car*?" He bolts to his feet, the pitch of his voice rising in disbelief.

I swallow a big gulp of coffee before I meet his angry eyes. "Yes, he slashed the tires, smashed all the windows, and wrote graphic slurs across it in what looks like the same red paint that was used on the animals and the mannequin."

"I'm not actually sure that was paint," Kai interjects, and I shudder at the thought that it might be real. I was trying to avoid accepting that it could be, but it did have a suspiciously congealed consistency.

My eyes find Oliver's devastated face. "I'm sorry." He shakes his head and sinks down into his chair.

"It's not your fault. I don't blame you." His words are trying to send one message, but he's very quiet after that, the silence sending a much different one. I guess as far as revenge goes, this is above and beyond anything I might have attempted. I think he's probably suffered enough, but again, an apology probably wouldn't hurt from him either.

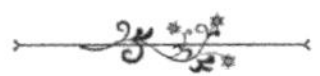

About half an hour later, the estate lights up with blue and red flashing lights, dragging my memory back to the day this all started. Brad gets up to greet the detective, leaving me with the siblings, minus Thomas. All of us have been subdued, conversation not really flowing, and the atmosphere is a little stifling. I guess we've all got a ways to go until we're all comfortable in one another's presence, or maybe it's just Jacinta. Jaxon tried to convince her to go to bed, but she insisted on staying up to both hear what the detective had to say and to help me wash off the animals.

Walking onto the back patio, there are big flood lights brightening up the back section of the estate beyond the entertainment area. I can see the outline of cops searching around the outside of the stables. Faint echoes of snorting and hoofbeats travel across the night air as the horses in the outside paddocks get spooked by the flashing lights. Blowing out a sigh, I've turned around to find someone to turn off the lights when a shadow steps out from behind a bush. Screaming, I throw my coffee mug at the person. Brown liquid flies through the air, but they sidestep quickly.

"Holy shit, Luke! You scared the shit out of me," I scold, my arms coming up to wrap around my waist in comfort and to hide my nipples. While I catch my breath, he moves forward out of the shadows.

"What's going on?" he asks, his hands deep in his pockets. "I heard the sirens and was worried there was a fire. But then I saw the police at the stables, and I didn't want to get in the way, so I thought I'd come up here and ask."

"Ah, yeah, someone broke into the stables and

vandalized some shit," I tell him, deliberately keeping it vague. He doesn't need to know everything else that has happened. Otherwise, he just might tattle to Chuck and Melinda before I can get a chance to tell them.

His eyes widen, but before he can say anything, a voice behind us has me turning. "Hello, Miss Stubbs."

It's Holden with the detective from yesterday. "Seems you've had a busy night." He tries for a comforting smile, but it doesn't work. "I've just got a few more questions, which shouldn't take long, while the forensic boys are fingerprinting and examining the crime scene. We should be out of your hair in no time."

"Have you had any luck finding a suspect?" Holden asks from where he is, holding on to his fourth whiskey. I'm surprised he's still standing because they have been *very* large whiskeys. He's obviously shaken, a lot more than the others, but I'm not sure why.

"We've been doing some background checks into the employees at Neighpalm Industries and the staff here as well, but nothing is jumping up and screaming guilty so far." He actually does sound sorry about it too. "We just have to keep looking for clues, and I'm hoping they somehow messed up and left behind something in the stable. But it *is* strange that he acted twice in one night. Especially because there's such a big distance between here and there.

We might have a look at the traffic cams to see if we can recognize anyone familiar using the highway between here and the city. Your father provided us with all the employees' photos and information." He shrugs like it's a long shot, and my heart sinks.

I head inside to answer his question, stopping and turning to invite Luke in, but he's already moving away. "You want to come inside?" I call to him, but he shakes his head.

"Nah, I'm going to see if Josh needs a hand settling the horses in the outer paddocks," he calls back and keeps walking. Shrugging, I follow the detective inside.

I don't know how long it takes, but I answer his questions, basically going over what I had already told him yesterday. He said he had called the detective back home to get his report on Mom's death but was waiting to hear back.

It was almost three in the morning by the time they packed up and left. I had changed into a pair of sweatpants and an old t-shirt when the detective and I finished talking, intending to take care of Jenny and DS before collapsing into bed, but I discovered that everyone had beaten me to the punch. While the detective had talked with me, everyone had left us alone and I hadn't questioned it, almost dead on my feet from the long day followed by dancing all night. When I arrived at the stables, I found Jenny and DS sparkling clean and smelling like roses, kind of. DS was even cuddling up to Jacinta, the traitor practically preening at all the attention she was lavishing on her. Bah, I knew that pony was psycho, and this just proves it.

Standing in the doorway to the stables, a feeling of belonging flows through my body as I watch them all band together and help make things right. There's a tiny part of me that's whispering, *Maybe this family is worth salvaging after all.*

Chapter Twenty-Five

Thomas

"Thank fuck that's over," Jaxon says, throwing himself on the sofa in the living room while Dad puts on a pot of coffee in the kitchen. Declan, Kai, and Oliver echo his groans as they join him on the couch, every single one of them shedding jackets, loosening ties, and unbuttoning shirt sleeves to get more comfortable. The only one missing is Holden. The lucky bastard had an appointment to see a band and was able to get out of the charity gala, much to his glee. Looking at my watch, I notice it's around midnight. *Is he coming home tonight or staying at the hotel?* I know he can look after himself, but I feel like I'm on constant alert after the threat Harlow received yesterday, worrying about who else might be caught in the crossfire of her deranged admirer. *Maybe I should text him?* Even odds he'll ignore it, but it might make me feel better to at least put the question out there.

Dad comes back out, smirking when he catches the tail end of the groans. "Don't forget we've got our annual family charity ball coming up soon," he reminds all of us, eliciting even more complaints. Oliver grabs a throw pillow and tries to smother himself with it.

"Fuck all of those grabby hands and toothy smiles. Jesus, I end up with bruises on my ass every single year from being pinched." Dad just laughs as the other guys join in, none of us showing him an ounce of sympathy. Though I guess with his still-healing bite, maybe we should run some interference for him. If he asks nicely.

"I'm heading upstairs to get changed," I tell them, needing to feel more like myself. They all wave a hand in my direction, and I make my way to my room in our wing of the house. Nana and Poppy attended the charity event with us, but they had stayed in town at the hotel. Normally, we would do the same, but this time, Dad had insisted on coming home because he was too worried he might be late for his riding plans with Harlow. Even took the day off work and ordered all of us to do the same thing. I think he wants it to look like it's our idea to go riding too so that Harlow doesn't realize he orchestrated this. As much as he's trying not to interfere, he can't help himself.

Neither can Nana, for that matter. She keeps

dropping hints about Harlow being the answer to all our needs, and wasn't that a fun surprise to figure out what the hell *that* meant. How one woman could quite easily be shared and loved and cared for by six very busy men, and how lucky that woman would be. I can't say I don't see the interest in my brothers' eyes, but I'll leave them to it. Harlow seems to be a pleasant woman, and she's sexy as fuck, but I have no plans to commit to anyone ever again.

Clarissa basically destroyed my soul when she left me for a competitor and took all the future plans I had outlined for Neighpalm Airlines. In retaliation, I destroyed her and her new partner, showing no mercy and no remorse. I enjoyed every moment of it. With the help of the Federal Department Of Counter Terrorism, I was able to have them indicted on charges of espionage and treason since the vindictive bitch also took plans for a new fighter jet that the government had contracted us to design. If she had kept them for herself to spite us rather than getting greedy and selling them to Neighpalm's biggest competition, she might have gotten away with it. She always was her own worst enemy. I would have given that woman the world if she'd only been willing to accept it.

Now, it might have taken some… less than legal means to get our proof, so even though I got what I wanted, I wound up with a bit of a debt to pay. The company doesn't operate only in California; in fact, they handle work for private clients all over the world. As head of Neighpalm Airlines, I was in the perfect position and had legitimate reasons for traveling often. So, in return for helping me get my revenge, I help them from time to time. I'm by no means a full member of their security team. The work I do for Neighpalm is real, and it does take up much of my time, but after I completed the security company's basic training, I had to make time to work with them too. The experience was brutal, much more than I was expecting, but I learned a lot, and it gave me an outlet and something new to focus on at a time I felt I was drowning.

As much as the occasional job with them puts me in danger, much to my family's unhappiness, the company became a lifeline for me. Now, between Neighpalm, looking out for my family, and my contracts with Federal Department Of Counter Terrorism, what do I have to offer a woman? Even if some part of me wanted to, what scrap of myself do I have left to give to her?

Pushing open the door to my room, I quickly shed the suit, taking off my shoulder holster and tossing it and the gun it holds onto my bed, and throw on a pair of sweats and a black wife beater. This stalker thing has got me all paranoid, so after a moment's debate with myself, I grab the gun, making sure the safety is engaged, and shove it into the back of my pants. Not since the incident with Jaxon and Jacinta's mom have we been worried about the security of our house. Never before have I felt the need to carry a gun at home, but the threats against Harlow have opened my eyes. Maybe we've become a bit lax; the tragedy with their mom and her gang was years ago, and even though Dad had private security on the grounds immediately after, he didn't renew their contract after a few years passed without further trouble. If he won't call someone in, I might just reach out to my own connections. What good are they for if not to help keep my family safe?

I contemplate staying here and just going to bed, but after every charity thing, we have a sort of debriefing to discuss who approached us for money, whether we committed anything, or if we were interested in supporting their chosen charity. If I put it off until the morning, everything will have become too vague for me. With a sigh, I head back to the living room.

When I get there, I find them all on the back patio instead, lights off, just sitting in the dark and enjoying the peace and tranquility. Being a part of the Summers family really does take a toll on the soul sometimes. People only want you for what you can give them as opposed to the person you are. I know each and every one of my brothers and my sister feel this keenly, and the need to escape and recharge hits us on a regular basis.

For me, just being able to get on one of our planes and escape to another country helps, but the

Summers name follows you, so finding hidden gems in foreign countrysides is a hobby of mine. I have a list of places I like to visit where the locals don't know me from the next tourist. It helps to settle the mind and makes it easier to breathe again.

"That's your coffee there, Tom." Dad points at the empty seat with a mug in front of it. As I move closer, I can see Jacinta has joined us. She's wearing a pair of flannel pajama pants and a tank top similar to mine. Bending down, I give her a kiss on the cheek and ruffle her hair, unable to resist that little bit of closeness with her. No matter how old we get, she'll always be my little sister, and right now, she's hurting a bit. She hadn't come to the event, not that she ever enjoys them anymore than the rest of us. She's still licking her wounds, and she didn't want to be bombarded with gossips trying to work out the real story behind her hiatus at Neighpalm Couture.

"Where's Oli?" I ask, noticing my brother is missing.

Kai snorts. "He saw a Neighpalm limo drive toward the stables and decided it can only be Harlow. He wanted to know where his precious car was, so he raced off to ask her."

Pulling out my chair, I move to sit down, but before I can, an ear-splitting scream has us all jumping up.

"Harlow!" Kai cries, taking off down the steps and toward the stables. I pull my gun out of my waistband and tear after him, everyone else on my heels. Jaxon's eyebrows raise in surprise at the sight of it.

"I've been carrying it around since yesterday's threat. Didn't think it would hurt to have something just in case."

When we get to the stables, we find Oliver with his arms wrapped around Holden, tears streaking his face, and Harlow, pale and shaky. My eyes go to the legs sticking out of the stable with what looks like blood covering them.

"Holy shit," Kai says next to me.

Jacinta says something before she steps a little closer and peers over Harlow's shoulder at the rest of the body, but the adrenaline has my gaze darting around the space, attention only half on her. "Oh my god," she gasps, turning to hide her face in our brother's chest as he grits his teeth, his face wreathed with anger.

"This has gone too far," he says through clenched teeth.

"You're not wrong," I say to them, tucking the gun into the back of my sweatpants.

"Right, as of today, Harlow and Jacinta, you don't go *anywhere* alone." Dad pulls out his phone and taps at the screen, likely calling the police.

I hear Harlow trying to argue with Dad about his restrictions, giving excuses about what needs to be done, but my thoughts aren't really on the conversation. My brain is trying to work out the puzzle. *Who would be targeting Harlow?* But I don't know enough about her to be able to have a clue.

Declan has just finished trying to reassure Dad about Harlow's safety when I grab him by the arm and pull him aside.

"Have you heard back from the PI?" I ask him, and his frown deepens.

"No, actually, I haven't. I keep meaning to chase him down, but things seem to come up, and I haven't had a chance yet."

"I need you to get in contact with him as soon as possible. Even if the police are involved now, he might be able to investigate things that they can't. Turn him away from investigating her and look at the people around her. She's obviously not doing this to herself, and I really don't think she has any hidden or alternative motives like we first suspected. I'll see what I can find out too."

I know what I said is a surprise since I'm usually the most suspicious out of everyone, even more so than Jacinta, but I have my own ways of vetting people... or getting rid of them if I need to. "Look, my gut is telling me we can trust her."

"Wow, okay then, you haven't said that in a long time. I'll give him a call first thing tomorrow." I nod my head in thanks, telling myself that I need to check with my own connections too.

"The police are on their way. They told me to not let you touch anything until they get here," Dad says, hanging up his phone. "Let's go up to the house and leave everything alone until they get here."

Harlow rises to argue with him, but he stops her, giving her a logical reason she can't argue with. Once she agrees, Dad leaves, followed by Oliver and Holden, their walls firmly back up again. It's sad to see that happen so quickly. I thought this might have been the kick in the ass they both needed to just throw away what's holding them back. Life's too short to not be with the person you want to be with, but now's not the time I guess.

I decide to stay and wait for the police, not sure I can be around the others at the moment. I'm a ball of built up aggression and anger at the thought of someone wanting to hurt my sister and, surprisingly, Harlow. *That's a thought to put a pin in.* "You go ahead," I tell them all, dragging a bale of hay out of the stables and putting it against one wall. "I'm going to wait here for the police or in case Josh comes in for any reason."

Looking up when I feel Harlow's eyes on me, that anger morphing into hot desire when the light shines directly onto her mesh top, giving me an obvious glimpse of her nipples. I can see a matching desire in her eyes, and she watches me closely. I keep my face disinterested though, not ready or wanting this complication.

"Wipe your drool, will you?" I hear my sister whisper to her as she throws a pair of overalls at her feet and shouts for the others to wait for her before rushing after them.

Harlow's eyes leave mine and snap to Jacinta, blushing slightly at being caught eye fucking me.

My brother puts his arm around her, and she looks even more embarrassed. But unlike any other woman, it doesn't bother me if she is interested in both me and my brother; in fact, I realize I don't care if it's any of my brothers. There's a sly voice in my head that says, *Imagine what she'd look like strolling across the green fields of Ireland, that castle you love as a backdrop. Then what she would look like spread out on the rug in front of the open fire, wearing nothing but a smile.* The worst part of it is that the voice doesn't sound like Nana anymore. It sounds much too suspiciously like my own. I run a hand through my hair as I look away. *Fuck, Nana really has gotten to me.*

"Come on, this gives you a chance to get changed," Kai suggests, and she quickly picks up the overalls and returns to the feed room as my brother and I exchange a look.

"I don't care if you're interested, but I'm not stepping away," he tells me quickly, and I acknowledge his statement with a quick nod of my head.

And it seems the time to decide is now. Better to throw my hat in the ring than miss my chance, right?

"Agreed," I tell him, feeling nervous for the first time in a long while. My gut says she doesn't have any ulterior motives, but it's not so sure that I'm ready to handle her. My head says I need to man up, be brave, and just commit myself to the chance. Unfortunately, I don't have the luxury of taking my time. Wait too long, and she could be stolen away by the others, not knowing that she needs to leave some room in that heart for me. Against all odds, this might be the most dangerous thing I've done in a while. Before we can talk about this in any real depth, she returns, ending our opportunity to speak.

"Come on, let's go," he says to her, but she stops in front of me, her long legs directly in my line of sight, making me wonder what they would feel like wrapped around my waist as I pounded into her from above.

"Can I bring you a coffee or something?" she asks, jolting me out of my dirty fantasies, and it's all I can do to slowly sit up in the hope of hiding the raging boner now tenting my pants.

"Yeah, that would be great, thank you." Giving her a smile, I hope it doesn't seem too predatory.

Kai directs Harlow back toward the house, leaving the stables silent once again but for the snuffling and snorting of the horses. Quickly getting up from the bale of hay, I pull my cell phone out of my pocket and start taking photos with the camera. It might not tell us much, but at least it's something I can give the PI.

Once I've taken the photos, I head into the feed room to raid the medical supplies. Grabbing a pair of latex gloves, I quickly pull them on before returning to the mannequin. I shudder at the sight of it wearing my sister's dress and shoes, the wig a perfect match for her hair. It's no wonder they thought it was Jacinta at first. Moving toward the head, I crouch down and carefully lift it up, trying to see an exit wound out of the back of the mannequin's head or if the bullet is still lodged inside. But no, there's an exit wound on the other side of the head and no bullet that I can see. Damn it, I was hoping there would be one for evidence to compare to other crimes.

Still crouching, I blow out a disappointed breath as my eyes search the rest of the empty stable. The floor is covered in straw, and it would take too long to search it before the police get here, but out of the corner of my eye, I see something glinting in the dim light. Lodged into the corner where the two sides meet is something metallic. Standing up, I move over to it, crouching down again and finding a bullet casing. Picking it up with my latex glove-covered hand, it looks to be a 9mm. That doesn't really help, but it's something more than I had to go on before. Dropping it back exactly as I found it, I stand back up, stretching out my back. There's nothing else to see, so I step around the dummy.

Backing out of the stable, I move to the other one with the animals in it. Harlow's donkey makes a noise and moves over to nudge at the hand I placed on the half door. It would be easy enough to coat this one in paint, but the mini is a whole other story. She comes charging at the door, ears flat back, teeth bared. I don't flinch, and when she gets to me, I put my hand out and grab her by the scruff of her mane, growling at her and showing no fear. At the sound, her ears come forward and she nudges the donkey out the way so she can get closer to me. She's not quite tall enough to stick her head over the door, but it doesn't stop her from trying. A smile crosses my face at her antics, but it shows me something else. Either the person who covered them in paint knew what they were doing when it came to horses, or they're possibly walking around with an injury. I'll have to keep an eye out on the employees and people around Harlow.

Pulling off the latex gloves, I throw them into a bin in the feed room before settling back down on the hay bale. The police won't be long, hopefully, and I've investigated all I can for now.

A few hours later, the police have left and Dad and the girls have gone off to bed. The six of us have gathered once again on the back patio to have the beers we would've cracked open had we not heard Harlow's scream. Holden has a joint lit and ready, and for the first time all evening my body loosens into a state of relaxation. The tension started with all the predatory women at the gala, and it only worsened when we saw the scene in the barn. I know I can hide that better than the others, but on the inside, I was a bit rattled. The slight discomfort in my shoulders tells me I was holding the stress there.

"This is fucked." Oh, Jaxon. Poor guy has been fidgeting all night. The threat against Jacinta has him worked up into a frenzy. "I wish Harlow had never come." When he feels like there's nothing he can do, nothing he can fix for Jacinta, he tends to lash out with his words. He needs to get some of that tension out of his body somehow to avoid later implosion. Listening carefully, I think there's less venom in the words than there would have been before. I think it's fear and helplessness that's driving him right now, but Kai's not as quick to pick up on that.

"Hang on a second. That's not fucking fair! This is *not* her fault."

Jaxon accepts the joint Declan passes to him and takes a big hit. I watch as the animosity leaks out of him and he deflates. He hands the joint to Oliver and runs a hand through his hair, heaving a sigh before turning to Kai with a frown on his face. "No, I know. I just need someone to blame. You don't know what it did to me, seeing that dummy laying there."

Holden snorts, but it's not in amusement. That's the sound he makes when he's out of patience. No idea what the fuck has him so pent up tonight. Normally he lasts longer than that. Then again, aside from Declan, Jaxon's always had a little chip on his shoulder as Jacinta's only "real" brother, feeling like that gives him more right to worry about her or protect her than the rest of us have. "Fuck yes, we do. She may not be our biological sister, but we still love her as much as you do."

I can see that they all need a more logical head to take over, so I step in before it turns into a fight. "I think we're in agreement that Harlow is not to blame and the only person responsible is the psycho that's stalking her. Right?"

All around the table their mumbles and nods of assent assure me we are on the same page. "Good. What we need to do now is lay off any of the petty shit that was going on with Harlow." I look toward Declan and Jaxon. Jaxon nods enthusiastically, and although Declan mimics the motion, he's a bit more reserved. "Our main focus now is making sure the two of them are never alone until whoever is doing this is caught. I'm sure with the six of us we can manage that around all of our commitments. Declan, you're going to deliver the horses with Harlow, right?"

"Yeah, we're bringing them to the set on Thursday since we're all going on that 'totally natural and not at all forced' family ride tomorrow."

"Good, that will be one less reason for her to be distracted. We need to find a way to monopolize her time after that. Dad would be heartbroken if he lost her before he's gotten a chance to really know her, and right now, she's more of a wild card than Jacinta."

"I'm taking her to Hawaii this weekend, and Jaxon's coming too. We've both got plenty of business we can involve her in, and then it should be easy enough for the two of us to keep an eye on her during the off time too," Kai assures us.

"I have an idea for the days following that but I need to run it past Dad," I tell them, and Declan frowns, crossing his arms.

"Care to share?" Of course my big brother doesn't like to be kept out of the loop. I might be the most paranoid of us all, but he's the most anal. I like to have information, but Declan likes to have control.

"Well, we need to inspect that new airline we just purchased in Europe. I thought we could make it a family trip. The likelihood that the stalker could get to them is slim, especially if we're changing locations so quickly from LA to Hawaii and then abroad with only a quick stop back home."

"That's a good idea, but it's still not helping us figure out who's doing this." Oliver's concern is not hard to miss and Declan leans forward, his beer resting on the table between his hands.

He turns to Oliver, replying, "I'm going to ask my PI to change his focus and look into the mother's background, and maybe the people who her mother associated with. Through her own admissions, we know they weren't the savory sort. Maybe that will turn something up."

"Okay, so we have a plan." Holden stands up, his eyeliner smeared and his stance looking a little shaky. "I'm going to have a shower and go to bed. I'm wrecked. I'll see you in the morning."

"Hang on! Sit down," Oliver calls out, and Holden flinches at his tone but sits nonetheless. "Has Nana had a conversation with any of you regarding Harlow?" I can tell by the bewildered looks on my brother's faces that she hasn't. With a sigh, I nod my head.

"Yeah, she had a few things to say to me," I admit, unsure whether I should be offended at the blatant surprise on Oliver's face.

"What are you talking about?" Jaxon has that frown on his face that always appears when he feels like he's missing out on something.

"Nana approached me the night of the premiere and had a few things to say about Harlow. She suggested the reason we had so much trouble finding the right woman was because we're always looking in the wrong spot. She also suggested that instead of trying to find six perfect women, we should find *one* who is happy to be shared by us all."

None of my brothers react in the way that I thought they would. I'd seen the signs of interest, but I wasn't sure if they'd all be able to share the same car let alone woman.

"None of you seem surprised?" I ask, looking around the table.

Kai shrugs, taking a sip of his beer. "Nana hadn't said anything, but I can't say I wasn't having similar thoughts. Why do you think I didn't care that Jaxon wanted to tag along to Hawaii? I know you guys assume that I overlook shit, but I notice a lot more than you think."

Both Jaxon and Holden have already nodded, so we all turn to Declan. With all eyes on him, our big brother, the one who stares down Hollywood bigwigs without flinching, *squirms*.

"Look, I don't know. Jacinta still has her issues, and I'd hate for her to think we were abandoning her for something that Harlow might not even be interested in. We hardly know the girl."

"Okay, that's fair enough. I have my own reservations about all of this; you guys know my history. I don't think I could ever be the man that she needs even if I have the rest of you to pull up the slack. I'll spend time with her, help keep her safe, and God knows I can't deny that she's sexy as hell, but I'm not committing to any of this right now." Even though the words coming out of my mouth say I'm not all in, that pang in my chest tells a whole different story. For the first time in a while, I'm almost disgusted with myself. What happened to the decision I made in the stables? What happened to giving her… and myself a chance? I can see Kai looking at me, wanting to talk about the change of heart but I can't right now. I will keep her safe, and maybe when I stop being a fucking coward, I'll be able to see if this can turn into something more.

"Let's just take it how it comes but keep the idea in mind," Oliver insists. "It really could be the solution to our problems, and I don't know how we didn't see it before."

"Maybe because no one has ever been right for all of us," Holden says quietly before standing up. "With all of that to think about, I need to crash. Goodnight." I watch Oliver's face as Holden walks away, the sadness that he tries to hide. Maybe Harlow can help fix that too.

One by one, my brothers say goodnight and disappear inside, leaving me on my own. Pulling out my phone, I ring my handler at the FDCT and fill them in, hoping that they might be able to do a little digging too. Any help we can get to figure it out will be welcome.

Chapter Twenty-Six

Jacinta

Once the police had finally left and I went to bed, I spent hours tossing and turning, my mind not able to let go of the thought that someone wanted me dead. Have I really been *so* bad that someone has decided a permanent solution is in order? It's not like I ruined the girl's life… right? Do I really deserve to die for just messing with her a little? That memory of the mannequin dressed up as me, a bullet hole in the middle of its skull, just won't leave my mind.

First thing in the morning, bleary-eyed and feeling way too introspective for the early hour, I'm on the phone with my fucking therapist. I've been avoiding this moment up until now, but my insecurities are slowly eating away at me, and I need answers. So far, I've been removed from my job, pissed off my brothers, triggered Jaxon, and now someone wants me dead. It feels like the universe is continually piling shit on me, and that nasty voice in my head, the one that sounds like my bitch of a mother is saying, *"But you deserve all this and more, you useless girl. I knew you would cause nothing but trouble. Can't you see that's why I left you? Poor little abandoned girl, bringing nothing but shit to everyone's lives."*

In the most terrible case of ironic phrasing in my life, I decide to just bite the bullet for once. My life is literally at stake, and I need to figure out how the fuck I can fix all this before my time runs out. Before she finishes saying good morning, I'm already blurting out the whole story, telling her how I reacted to Harlow, my punishment, my conversations with my brothers… all of it. By the time I'm done, I'm nearly out of breath and she's completely silent. I hear a deep breath and take my own, knowing she's about to hit me with some kind of reality that I'm definitely not going to enjoy.

"Jacinta, we have been through all this before, each time a new woman has come into your father or your brothers' lives. You need to slow down and ask yourself the hard questions, force yourself to think about what you really feel instead of hiding behind that surface anger. When your anger leads, it always exacts a cost, and this time, it seems like that bill is higher than ever. What is it about Harlow that scares you the most? Is it the worry she might replace you in the hearts of the ones you love? Or is it that she might actually be someone *you* can learn to love?"

We talk back and forth about it, and by the time we finish, I have to own up to the truth. I'm scared to be hurt again, scared that I don't know how to choose the right people in my life. If I keep my family all to myself, I never have to branch out, never need to make space for another person in my life or in my heart. I made a mistake once, and the damage of that night can't be undone. I can't make whole again the family that's incomplete because I trusted the wrong person, and I guess that guilt is part of what drives me too. The idea that my own family might be damaged by an outsider, the victim of one poor decision to let a bad person in, is something I have nightmares about.

I need to accept that it's okay for me to feel these things; I'm not broken because I get scared or feel guilt or have insecurities. That's what my therapist has been telling me for years. I need to know my triggers and question my reactions, but then I need to not let them rule my life and my decisions. And that's where I epically fail, time after time. In the past, it's been all too easy to let my hurt lead the way. Aside from Holden's friendship with Hope, the women in my brothers' lives have always been unimportant in the grand scheme of things. Either their own choices or a little help from me have gone a long way in showing who they really were.

But Harlow is a different story. She arrived

already having an established and loving relationship with Nana and Poppy, and she means something to Dad. *She's not temporary.* That's the part that scares the fuck out of me, and I don't know how to deal with that yet. Now I don't really have any option but to admit that how I *have been* dealing with her is wrong and needs to change, but that doesn't give me any real clue as to how I move forward.

My therapist makes an excellent yet terrifying point. My choice all those years ago tore a family apart, and my choices now are threatening to tear *my* family apart. I can't bring someone back from the dead and make that right, but I can stop myself from hurting my own family. Now all I need to do is convince everyone that I'm genuine, earn my way out of Dad, Nana, and Poppy's bad graces, and find a way to make amends with Harlow. *Because that's going to be easy.*

After my phone call, I move to my design table which overlooks the back patio, feeling calmed by the rhythm of the trees moving in the breeze. The sunlight sparkles off the pool, and I can see horses kicking up their heels in the early morning. Taking a seat and picking up a pencil, I allow my hand to drift over a blank page as my mind drifts.

Although I was resentful to start with, the last few days have been nothing short of blissful. To not have to worry about the day to day running of Neighpalm Couture and to be able to concentrate on designing has been a break I hadn't realized I needed. Fashion is such a cutthroat, superficial industry that I sometimes wonder why I got into it, but it's times like these when the muse is active and my creativity can flow that remind me why I do it. All the rest of it, the meetings, the fake smiles, and all the drama, I put up with so I can do my one love. Make fashion that people look amazing in. All the textures, cuts, and colors are my idea of recreational drugs, and I get a thrill whenever I'm working on a new line. When I get to immerse myself in the fabric supplies and all the haberdashery. Gah, it's almost better than an orgasm. Though maybe I just haven't been getting the right kind.

Looking down at my pad, I realize I haven't been sketching clothing designs at all. Sitting in front of me is a wolf which has a very familiar looking human face. Alex stares back at me, his green eyes piercing me from the page. I drop my pencil in surprise. *What the fuck?*

Maybe the book I've been reading has been working its way too deeply into my head. When Harlow had told me about hers that day in the limo, I'd immediately gotten a copy for myself. During my time off, I've been devouring the series with a voracious appetite. My dreams have been full of three gorgeous wolf shifters, two with very familiar faces and bodies, the third strangely blank for some reason. *Well… what does it hurt to fantasize a little? Can't get myself into trouble if it's all in my head.* My mind drifts back to a very stimulating dream that's haunted me for days, asleep or awake, and a smile crosses my lips.

But a sudden slamming of a door and the revving of a car has me jumping up, my heart racing with panic as I take off in the direction of the noise. No one needs to know that I almost fall on my face as I try to shake off the all too pleasant stupor of my daydream.

Chapter Twenty-Seven

Harlow

It's late in the morning when I next open my eyes. After tidying the stables with the rest of the family, I practically fell into bed next to Princess. Not bothering with a shower, I'd just stripped off my clothes and climbed into bed naked, not caring if anyone was planning to barge into my room the following morning, too tired to give a crap. I slept deep and long, exhausted both physically and emotionally from all that had happened the previous day. God, it's hard to believe that it was only yesterday morning that I had that crappy non-interview. So much has happened since.

Lying in bed when I first wake, my mind flits from Holden to Thomas and then to Kai. All the flirty conversation, heated looks, and the memory of Holden's teeth on my neck make my toes curl inside my blankets, but Princess' plaintive meow has me sitting up and looking around for her. She's not on the bed next to me, and my heart starts to race when she meows louder. It sounds like it's coming from the side of my bed. Looking down, I find her lying in the clothes that I had stripped off last night. She looks up at me and meows again, the sound almost urgent. Throwing back the covers, I slowly make my way out of the bed so as not to startle her, and when I crouch down next to her, there's a little wet bundle lying next to her side.

Scrambling around, I get my phone off the bedside table and message Declan to come quickly before moving back to pet her, cooing words of encouragement to help relax her.

It's not long before my door bursts open, Declan rushing in with an enclosure in front of him. Putting it down, his eyes almost bug out of his head when he sees me. Why is he looking at me and not as his precious Princess? Frowning, I look down. Crap, I'm naked again. I'd forgotten that in my excitement of seeing her in labor.

Jumping to my feet, I hurry to my wardrobe to put something on, feeling his eyes following me all the way. I throw on a fresh t-shirt and a pair of yoga pants then hurry back out, caring more about Princess than the embarrassment I should be feeling right now. He's picked her up, clothes, wet bundle, and all, and put her inside the enclosure. He's sitting next to it, muttering words of encouragement to her. Princess is busy licking the wet bundle beside her, occasionally pausing to lick Declan's hand as he strokes her.

"Did you have an ultrasound done on her? Do you know how many kittens she's carrying?" I ask, sitting down on the bed so I don't disturb their moment. Right now, she doesn't seem to be in any distress.

He looks up from her, a broad grin on his face. "Four. They usually have less in their first litter than they do in following ones." He looks back down, so I don't have to hide my eye roll or the smile that crosses my face at the slightly lecturing tone in his voice. I cannot believe they still don't know I'm a vet. Honestly, with all of their money and connections, I'd expected them to dig into my personal life ages ago.

Standing up, I pat him on the shoulder. "Alright then, Grandpa, I'm off to get a coffee. You want me to bring you one too?" It's only now I'm noticing he's shirtless and looks like he too just rolled out of bed. Shame he sleeps in shorts... or maybe he just remembered to put some on before he left the room. Unlike other people who will remain nameless. Me. I'm nameless.

Leaving him and Princess to it since they seem to have it under control, I head to the living area. Each step is punctuated with a yawn and a stretch, my body and mind still not ready to be totally awake. Not watching where I'm going, I just about run straight into Cecelia.

"Oh hey, shit, sorry. I didn't see you there," I blurt out, and she grimaces as she rubs the foot I stepped on when we collided.

"Clearly," she says in a haughty voice.

I look around her for Dad, but he's nowhere to be seen. "Where did you come from?" I ask curiously. I hadn't seen her anywhere during the commotion last night; surely, she would have come out if she had been here when all the noise was going on.

"I got here a little while ago. Brad wasn't coming into work today, but he still needs to sign a few things, so I brought them out for him to read over." She steps around me and starts to head to my dad's bedroom, but I move in front of her.

"Is Dad not awake yet?" She tries to sidestep me, but I won't let her, earning an annoyed huff that gets nothing but an eyebrow raise from me.

"No, he's not, you little brat. Now get out of my way so I can go and wake him. He won't mind at all."

A throat clearing behind us has her paling slightly when she looks over my shoulder. "Oh, I beg to differ, Cecelia. Head on back to the living room and he will come out when he's ready. Better yet, I'm sure all of that stuff can be emailed. It *is* his day off after all, and if it had been important, he would have done it yesterday." Declan's voice brooks no argument, but I'm close enough to see the silent fury flashing in her eyes before she pastes on a smile and simpers at him.

"Of course, Declan, I'll just pour myself a coffee and wait."

"No, go back to the office. Unlike him, I'm sure you have plenty of work to do." He crosses his arms, and she ducks her head, that fury flashing briefly again.

"Ok, if you could just tell him I was here..." She turns and leaves, her heels silent on the carpeted hallway, but I notice she's limping quite drastically. Jesus, I hadn't realized I'd stepped on her quite so badly. I should feel a little guilty, but I don't. I follow quickly after her, my gut telling me I need to make sure she actually leaves and doesn't double back somehow. Declan stays behind, heading back into my room to check on Princess, most likely.

Leaving my wing, I reach her just as she pulls open the front door and storms out, slamming it shut behind her. The noise echoes through the house, and I quickly rush forward to watch as she gets into her car and floors the gas, sending rubber burning over the cobblestone until she hits the drive and gravel goes spewing out behind the car. She must be holding her hand on the horn too because it blasts out as she zooms down the driveway. I watch in amusement as the car fishtails slightly and she desperately tries to correct it before it can careen into one of the fences running along the driveway or one of the big trees. As she disappears, out of the other wing thunders the rest of the Summers siblings in various disarray, all looking like they have been rudely awakened.

"Fuck, what was that?" Kai groans, leaning against me to peer over my shoulder at the now empty driveway.

"Just Cecelia," I answer, watching Thomas hurriedly hide his gun behind his back. I wave a hand at him, unfazed. "You don't need to hide it. Guns only scare me in the hands of the wrong person, and I don't think that's you." He gives me a little nod of acknowledgment.

"God, that bitch woke me from a perfectly good daydream about me and three wolf shifters," Jacinta mutters, a little disoriented. *Huh, did she steal one of my books?* That has me raising my eyebrows, but it's Jaxon's reaction that breaks the ice and has all of us laughing.

"I don't want to think about you with one wolf shifter, let alone three." He shudders and returns the way he came, mumbling under his breath about flea treatments and needing giant pet doors.

Oliver and Holden try to leave at the same time, running into each other then doing this awkward back and forth dance before they manage to coordinate. Holden gets past first and hurries away. We all watch the interaction with interest, and I turn to Kai once they're out of earshot. "What was that about? They were funny last night too, after everything settled down."

Kai and Jacinta snort while Thomas just watches them, concern fogging his eyes. "*That* is them being idiots, and it's been going on for years," Kai explains, wrapping his arms around me all the way. "Harlow, it's too early. Come back to bed and snuggle. I'll sleep so much better if you're with me."

A shiver runs down my spine as he nuzzles into my neck, but I untangle myself and push him away reluctantly. "As much as that sounds good, I need coffee, and Declan is back to being a birthing coach in my bedroom. I promised I'd bring him coffee too."

"Kittens!" Jacinta squeals like a little girl, a look of pure joy crossing her face. As much as I hate to admit it even though a part of me is definitely less hostile than before, she's much prettier when she smiles. She runs off in the direction of my room without a backward glance, and Thomas rolls his eyes with a groan. "Declan is going to be useless all day now. Come on, let's put on a pot of coffee so at least he isn't a complete grizzly." Thomas heads off to the kitchen, tucking his gun in the back of his gym shorts, and Kai blows me a kiss before returning the way he came.

By the time I reach the kitchen, Thomas has already filled the coffee machine with water and is just dropping in the grounds. Mrs. Hayton doesn't seem to be anywhere around, so I'm guessing she's probably busy elsewhere at the moment. Heading to the cupboard, I'm grabbing some cups when I hear Dad's voice.

"Was that Cecelia I just saw drive off? What was she doing here, and why did she feel the need to use the damn horn?" Dad grumbles adorably as he takes a seat at the kitchen island.

"Apparently, she had things for you to read and sign." His eyes widen slightly, coming together in a slow blink like they're still blurry from sleep but he's still trying to focus.

"Was there a reason she couldn't just email them?" This time it's Thomas' turn to snort.

"What, Tom, spit it out! I'm still not firing on all cylinders," Dad snarls grumpily, which I still think is adorable. At least since it's not directed at me, anyway. He's like a baby bear who's just woken up. "And I call dibs on the first cup. Privilege of being the one who paid for the coffee maker." He eyes the coffee machine like it's the holy grail, so I'm guessing I come by my fondness for coffee legitimately.

Thomas, or I guess Tom, pulls out his gun and shoves it on the counter before crossing his arms and leaning against it, facing Dad. "Well, Dad," he parrots, "that woman has been trying to get into your pants for a while now, and you're too damn oblivious to notice. Anything she can do to get you to notice her is fair game as far as she's concerned."

Silence fills the kitchen as I watch Dad process

Tom's words. He seems to stumble over them before he takes a deep breath and gets his thoughts sorted. "I have *never* shown that woman anything but professional courtesy," he defends himself. "In fact, haven't I always taught you kids never to mix business and pleasure?" Tom flinches a little at this, and Dad stands up, going over to him. "Tom, no, I'm sorry. That's not how I meant it. What Clarissa did was *not* your fault." He pulls him into a hug, and I see Tom shudder before pushing Dad away and reaching for the mugs I'd laid out. Turning his back to us, he pours four mugs of coffee now that the machine has finished.

"Just be careful, Dad. That woman has a goal, and being dressed in white with you waiting at the end of the aisle features heavily." Tom passes us a mug each, his face devoid of all emotion again while Dad practically grasps at non-existent pearls.

"She's not much older than Harlow! That's just gross." It's Dad's turn to shudder before he blows on his coffee. With a sigh, he takes a sip and then grimaces. "Ugh, where's the milk and sugar, Tom?" He gets up and heads for the fridge, muttering about evil black coffee and how he doesn't know how his boys can drink it like that. I watch in amusement as he liberally doses his coffee with sugar and milk then offers them to me. I don't care how I have my coffee. I can drink it both ways, but today I'll be grateful for a little extra kick in the way of sugar.

I doctor mine and then pick up the other mug. "Does Declan take it black?"

"Yep, just like his soul," Tom jokes, shooting me a small wink and smile. My mouth drops open in surprise at his humor.

"You're taking him a cup?" Dad asks in surprise, a hopeful look on his face.

I shrug. "Yeah, Princess is in my bedroom, having her kittens, and he's supervising, so I offered to bring him a cup."

"He didn't ask for your help?" Dad questions, causing Thomas to frown.

"Why would he need her help? He's been through this a few times with previous Princesses."

Dad rolls his eyes and opens his mouth, likely going to spill about my career, but I quickly stop him. "I'm sure you're right, Tom. Declan and Princess don't need any help." I cross my fingers that it stays that way. It's become a bit of a game for me now. How long can the Summers siblings be totally oblivious, assuming I'm nothing more than a horse trainer? Though if she seems to be having problems, of course I'll step in. Animals first, always. No one-up on the Summers siblings is worth putting pretty Princess at any kind of risk.

I wave goodbye, but before I can get far, Dad pipes up. He seems to be a bit more together now that the coffee has hit his system. "Harlow, are we still on for that ride?"

"Yeah, that sounds good. I need to work the

horses once more before we take them tomorrow, so a ride across the estate will help loosen them and get some energy out before having to truck them tomorrow." Dad beams at me, all signs of grumpy bear gone.

"Let's have lunch and set out a little later this afternoon. That gives us all a chance to wake up after last night's late one, and it will be cooler too."

Tom's frowning as he pushes off where he's been leaning against the counter. "Are you sure that's a good idea after yesterday?" He looks between the two of us with a concerned crease in his brow.

"Well, why don't you come with us if you're so worried?" Dad suggests. "Maybe the rest of your brothers would like to too, maybe even Jacinta. It's been a while since we all went for a family ride. Everyone has been so busy, and I miss having you all around at the same time." Dad has a pout on his face, and I can tell by the way Tom's shoulders sag that he feels guilty. He misses the slight gleam in Dad's eye and the quick grin that crosses his face when Tom agrees, our devious dad quickly reining it in when he sees me watching. *Hmm, that didn't seem the least bit rehearsed.*

He slowly winks at me, and I hide my chuckle as I leave the kitchen. That man is the king of manipulation. He's got his kids figured out, and it looks like I've quickly joined those ranks. Dad's got my weakness completely right. So long as animals are involved, I won't argue about him meddling.

My mom's manipulations had always been a hit you over the head, in your face style that left at least one party, usually me, bruised in more than one way. I'm not used to this gentle, well-meaning manipulation that leads more often to laughter or family bonding than personal trauma, but I think I can live with this scenario. I much prefer everything about Dad's approach to parenting, even if it results in more time with the Summers siblings.

Chapter Twenty-Eight

Harlow

Princess had four adorable kittens by the time lunch was over, and Declan was as proud as punch as he animatedly told everyone who would listen all about the whole process. He also passed around his phone which was full of pictures of the four cute fluff butts. All were resting nicely in my room in their enclosure, so I guess I'll be seeing a bit more of him. I know enough about his relationship with his cat to know that he won't be content to just leave me in charge of them. He put a litter box and some food and water in it for Princess and left them be for the time being.

When I went back to my phone, I found messages from both Hope and Alex, scolding me for not calling and telling them about what happened last night. Jesus, how did they find out so quickly? I'm assuming Holden told Hope, but who told Alex? I send them both quick messages telling them I will call tonight before doing a little careful stretching to assess how my leg is feeling. The after-shocks that had bothered me after falling off Samson and getting pushed into the pool have calmed, and right now I'm feeling pretty good. So long as I don't have any rough landings today, I think I'll be in a nice recovery zone. I'm a little surprised it's not sore after all that dancing, but maybe Holden has some kind of magic touch. *That's definitely not something we can get into right now,* my brain lectures. Once my head's out of the gutter and stretches are taken care of, I get changed into my riding clothes and head out.

As I make my way to the stables, I'm waylaid by a braying sound, and with a smile, my eyes search for my two favorites. They're grazing in a paddock in the warm sun, and thankfully, Jenny and DS look no worse for wear after yesterday's ordeal. Pulling a carrot that I'd stolen from the fridge out of my pocket, I snap it in half, the sound making DS look up from her patch of grass. Happily, she trots over to where I am, Jenny not far behind. Holding the carrot in my flat hand, I feed one to each of them before giving them a pat and continuing on my way.

When I get there, the stable is a flurry of movement. Every one of my adopted brothers is there and so is Jacinta. Each person is in charge of tacking up a horse under the supervision of Luke and Josh.

"Morning, Harlow, looks like you've got a lot of volunteers today. Luke and I are going to be out of a job," Josh jokes, grabbing the saddle that Luke passes him and lifting it onto Delilah's back.

Luke's face looks a little strained. I guess he must be worried about what Chuck will say if he doesn't help me. "Don't worry, Luke, I'll let Chuck know that you got outvoted," I joke, and his eyes widen with concern before he brushes it off.

"No need for that, Harlow. I know he won't mind." He puts his head down and continues to help with the tacking up.

Everyone has a horse in front of them except Jacinta. She just seems to be helping, but then her palomino sticks her head out of the stall, and I remember. She can't ride her at the moment.

"Jacinta, would you like to exercise Delilah for me?" I ask, pointing at the white mare.

Jacinta jumps in surprise when I call her name, and she looks everywhere but me to start with until her gaze eventually meets mine.

"Are you sure you don't mind?"

I shrug. "She needs to be ridden, and you seem to be without a horse at the moment, so go for it."

A small smile crosses her face as she thanks me and takes the reins from Josh, heading out of the stables to mount.

Looking around, I can see that Dad has got Zeus, while Thomas has Hercules. I have no concerns about Dad. Chuck had already regaled me with tales of his horsemanship before I came out to the West Coast, but my eyes are watching the tall quiet brother. I need to assure myself he knows what he's doing before feeling happy that he's riding one of Chuck's horses.

It quickly becomes apparent to me that he's no amateur. It also becomes apparent that every single one of the guys are wearing breeches and long boots. Holy shit! My eyes drop to the asses lovingly encased in tight riding pants, and I thank the lord above for the invention. Everywhere I look, there are rock hard butts that I would like to sink my teeth into, much like DS had done to Oliver. Speaking of which, he must be feeling better because he's riding as well.

A clearing throat has me looking back up to discover Kai has once again caught me ogling every single one of his brothers, but instead of looking pissed off, he's just amused. "Ready, Harlow?" He smirks and nods his head at the door in question, but I know I'm caught, so I just wipe my mouth to make sure no drool escaped then salute him.

"Sure, ah, I just have to grab my helmet." I hurry away before he can say anything about my wandering eyes, almost colliding with Josh coming out of the tack room.

"Sampson is all ready for you, Harlow," he

tells me, taking a drink from a bottle of water in his hand. "I saw you eyeing Thomas," he says, but there's no snark or censure. I blush slightly, but he ignores it and continues. "Every one of them can ride a horse, don't worry about them, and if they accidentally give a command, it will be fun to see what they do." His grin is a little wicked as he says this. "Makes me almost wish I was coming with you," he adds, but then his grin drops. "Listen, I didn't get a chance to ask if you were okay last night. It must have really shaken you up to come home from a night out dancing and find that." His words have me backing up slightly, eyes narrowing.

"How did you know I was out dancing?" I ask, a little suspicious now. This thing has started to make me a little paranoid.

"Oh, I heard Holden telling the others about the band he saw last night, and he mentioned that you had been there with Hope." His eyes sparkle at the mention of Hope's name, and I breathe a sigh of relief. I see how it is. I give him a quick wink, and it's his turn to blush before he moves out of my way, clearing the path to my helmet.

When I come back out, the stable is empty of all people and horses except Luke holding Sampson. I take the reins from him, but he stands in my way, twisting his hands in agitation.

"Are you sure you don't want me riding one of the others, Harlow? I wouldn't want anything to happen to any of them just before they need to go to the set tomorrow."

"It will be fine, Luke. Why don't you see if Josh needs a hand mucking out the outside yards? Especially while they're empty," I suggest, and he moves out of the way so I can head over to where all the others are. When I get there, they're all mounted and talking quietly. Josh comes up to me and cups his hands, offering me a boost on to the tall stallion, and I smile my thanks.

He's tossing me up and over when the sound of a motorcycle comes faintly through the open air. "Where did Luke go?" Josh asks, watching the four-wheeler with a little trailer drive off into the distance.

"I suggested he muck the paddocks for you. He must have actually listened." Josh smiles widely, his expression easy going.

"Great, thank you, Harlow. That's going to make my knock off this afternoon nice and early." He whistles as he walks away from me, happy as can be.

"Glad I can help," I shout after him before gathering my reins and quickly following after everyone else.

The next hour flies by. The pace starts off slow and relaxing as we warm the horses up, but by the time we make our way to the start of the cross-country course, everyone is jeering at each other with excited chatter, talking over one another.

"Okay, Harlow, we'll let the others go first. You can watch them over the first couple of jumps, and then I'll follow you, bringing up the rear," Dad suggests.

"Sounds good," I tell him, and one by one, his adopted children prove Josh right. Each and every one of them looks like they're at home in the saddle, showing that they have been taught to jump correctly. Each of them makes their way over the first jump without hesitation. It's an easy brush fence which isn't too high. It actually looks like it gives you two height options, two foot or three foot, but all choose the higher one. Kicking Samson into a slow canter, I circle around in front of it before heading toward it. I can feel his muscles bunching under him as he lunges up and over, landing neatly on the other side. He throws in a little buck of excitement as we canter away from it which has me shouting with glee. After that, I trail along behind Holden as we wind our way through a nice rolling course designed with jumps that are challenging but not enough to make the ride stressful.

The sound of the wind in my ears and the thundering hooves blocks out all noise as the woody area we had been riding in opens up to a field with a water jump up ahead. Lined up on the other side are the others who've already been through it, all but Dad, Holden, and me. Holden goes first, and I watch the bay gelding he's riding go up and over the jump, splashing down into the water beyond, but as he lands, two things happen. I hear a loud, violent crack, and then the horse rears in the air and Holden tumbles backward into the muddy water below.

"No!" Dad shouts from behind me, and I kick Sampson into a gallop, racing toward the pond. Holden's horse has cantered out of the water to the other side to stand with the other horses. As I reach the pond, I pull back on the reins and Samson slides to a stop. Barely waiting for him to settle, I throw myself off of him and barrel into the waist high water where I saw Holden go down. *Why hasn't he gotten up yet? This isn't that deep.* Dropping to my knees, I search blindly through the water, not sure exactly where he fell in.

"I think he hit his head on the jump when he went backward," Declan shouts as the others run over. He's in the lead, immediately barreling into the water like I did and joining me in the search for Holden while the others wait anxiously and try to keep Jacinta from hyperventilating.. She's full on sobbing now, and my heart is in my throat as I wait for Declan to finish checking the other end of the pond, my own search still coming up empty..

Finally, he comes up out of the water like a mythical sea creature, dragging his unconscious brother with him. Thomas and Kai run over, helping drag him to the shore then begin administering CPR, the two seamlessly working together with much cooler heads than I'd be capable of right now.

By this point, Oliver's standing by my side, his hand squeezing mine, and he gasps in relief when Holden starts to cough, muddy water coming up and out of his mouth when he's rolled onto his side.

It's only then that I notice his chest.

Too busy watching the guys try to resuscitate him, we originally failed to see the cause of the fall, but the bright red blood seeping through his gray t-shirt soon tells the whole story.

"Holy shit. Someone call an ambulance! Holden's been shot."

The end for now …….. Bah bah bahhhhhhhh

Thank you for reading!
I hope you enjoyed the book. It would be super awesome if you could leave a review wherever you bought it, because I love to hear what you thought of the story.

Want more of Harlow and the gang?
Pre order Book Three here
Tormented Girl

Want to keep up to date with new books coming soon? Sign up to my newsletter here
Newsletter

Another way to do that is to join me Facebook group. I drop teasers and giveaways in there all the time. Here's the link
Lexie's Ladygarden

Visit my webpage and check out reading orders and what else I've written.
www.lexiewinston.com

Acknowledgments

Thank you to all the normal crew this book wouldn't be possible without you all.

Michelle for your invaluable editing.

Emma for all the late night and early morning chats.

Infinity Book Designs for the cover

My beta team for being super awesome as usual.

Grace and Hope for being my rocks

Thank you Brook Lowther, Jenny Her and Alicia Spalding for your name suggestions, Raquel, Jace and Rowena respectively.

Thanks to all the members of Lexie's Ladygarden you guys are the reason I continue to do this. Love you all.

Check out something else by me. This one is coming mid 2021. A Sci-Fi reverse harem romance.

Apprentice

Galaxy Circus 1

PLEASE BE AWARE THIS IS UNEDITED AND SUBJECT TO CHANGE. PLEASE DON'T COMPLAIN TO AMAZON IF YOU FIND ERRORS AS THEY WILL BE FIXED BEFORE BEING PUBLISHED.

Chapter One

"Miss Jenson, thank you for responding to our letter so quickly," Mr Ryding, the weaselly looking lawyer says to me from behind the large walnut desk. He's fidgeting with the papers in front of him; stacking them, picking them up, tapping them, and then placing them back on the table in front of himself. He's done it half a dozen times. While I sit there waiting for him to say more, he straightens the pens in the holder to the right of him on the desk. It seems like he's doing everything in his power to avoid making eye contact with my very confused self.

"I'm sorry I'm not sure I understand you. I received a letter from your office saying I have been bequeathed something and that I must present myself in person to sign some papers to receive it. Now, you are also telling me, it was from a grandfather I didn't even know existed, and obviously didn't want me, as I spent the first eighteen years of my life in foster homes"

He looked up, briefly pausing his fidgeting. "Yes that's correct. Though it's grandfather's plural."

Plural? I puzzle internally, never mind, I'll come back to that.

"John, William and Eric Adams are your paternal grandfathers and it wasn't that they didn't want you." His shifty eyes soften briefly, "They weren't able to find you. Your parents were estranged from them and they were not notified immediately when your parents had their accident. When you were placed in foster care, they weren't in the States at the time." He shuffles his papers again. "When they did eventually find out, John rushed back, but by then you'd been placed in the system and your name changed by request of your parents will. You'd disappeared and were well hidden. Due to the nature of their business, they decided that maybe you were better off. Their job was constantly traveling, never settling in one place for very long. No place to raise a child or so they thought. They believed you were safe and loved." I scoff out loud. "Otherwise they would have claimed you immediately." He assures me.

"So why am I finding out about this now? I'm assuming they're all dead? Why leave it until I have no chance of getting to know them or of finding out about where I'm from?" I struggle to understand. "Why did they leave it until it was too late?"

The shifty look in his eyes is back and the fidgeting obviously isn't cutting it as he gets up from his desk and starts to pace behind it. Marching back and forth in front of the big picture window which holds the view of the river, his office backs onto. He stops, takes a deep breath and turns to look at me.

"Well actually that's not quite true. The Mr Adams's have not passed on, they've decided to retire, and the family business must pass down to a family member only, and you're the one that was chosen. They contracted our firm to find you. It has taken quite a while, I can assure you."

"Excuse me?" I gasp, "Are you saying my grandfathers are alive and want to meet me?" As a little girl I would have dreams of a family member swooping in to rescue me from the never-ending cycle of foster homes. I finally gave up around the age of thirteen. I wasn't one of those kids who were beaten or abused in care, I just never seemed to fit in. Never really included or felt like I was one of the family. It would've been nice to know there was someone out there who wanted me. Of course my very sceptical nature decides this is too good to be true.

“Why the fuck am I dealing with a lawyer and not them directly?’ my surprise turns to anger. “Can they not even be bother or are they too fucking chicken to face me themselves.” I can practically feel the steam escaping from my ears. My Ryding swallows nervously and brings a finger up to try and loosen his collar slightly.

“Ah… but… They’re…” He stammers my anger taking him by surprise obviously.

Taking a deep breath I try and calm down. Don’t take it out on the lawyer Lila he’s just the messenger

“Why me? I’m assuming there are other family members they could turn too?” I rub my eyes, I can feel a headache brewing. They have been steadily getting more frequent and this meeting is not doing me any favors.

“Yes, well no. There are other family members but not directly. You are their only grandchild, and they’ve decided that it’s time you join the family legacy and that you get first option. All the details are in the package.” he sits back down at the desk and gestures to the stack of papers he’d been fidgeting with. “You’re required to spend twelve months with the business, learning all the ins and outs. If, at the end of the twelve-month period, you’re unwilling to continue, the business and the role of CEO and all it entails will pass on to the next eligible family member and you will carry on with life as if the previous twelve months had never really happened."

I stare at the package like it's a snake that's going to bite me. I just don't know what to think. Do I ignore it, sign it over now and wash my hands of the whole debacle? Or do I take a leap of faith and at least meet the men that could be the best or the worse thing to happen to me.

"Can I have some time to think about this" I ask, "It's quite a decision I need to make."

Mr Ryding shakes his head, "I'm sorry but this decision needs to be made now. Our firm has been looking for you for a while and I'm afraid we're out of time. You need to be on a plane to London in two days time. We're going to need an answer now."

It's my turn to start pacing. Jumping out of the chair I've been sitting in, I start stalking back and forth across the room, the pounding behind my eyes has intensified and I rub my temples in an attempt to alleviate it. What to do? It's not like I have anything keeping me here. I don't have many friends, mainly acquaintances. My best friend and roomie is head over heels in love with her partner, she'd be ok if I left. I have a dead-end job in a bar that pays crappy, but keeps me busy. I guess there is nothing specifically stopping me from going. I've always dreamed of adventures, sure that there must be something better in life than what I have been living.

"All right," I tell him, making the decision, "I'm in, show me where to sign."

He goes to the stack of papers on the table and pulls some out. "You need to sign here, here, and here. One of them is a non-disclosure form. No matter what happens, from here on, you are bound by a confidentiality clause. Even if at the end of twelve months you change your mind, everything you see and do will be confidential. A plane ticket is also in the pack, in your name with the details of your flight in two days' time. You'll be met at the airport and a driver will take you to where you need to be. For your peace of mind, you can tell people where you are going and why, but there is to be no sharing of any other details. It's actually a good thing that you don't have a huge circle of friends." I feel a bit insulted at this comment and surprised that he knows that.

"We've been looking for you for a while, we know everything about you" He replies to my look, a little defensively

"Yeah ok, because that's not creepy or rude" I reply sarcastically.

I busy myself signing papers, and by the time I'm finished my hand aches and my head throbs incessantly. Gathering them all together, I shove them in my hand bag; I'll read it all when I get home. "So what business have I just signed my life away too?" I ask Mr Ryding, thinking this is probably something I should have asked before signing. Fuck I'm an idiot, why didn't I ask that first? I mentally slap my impulsive self.

"Have you heard of the Galaxy Circus?" He asks, slightly distracted with gathering all his copies of the paperwork.

"Oh yes, isn't that, that spectacular circus that claims it has aliens as its performers. It pops up randomly throughout the globe and is always sold out." I nod enthusiastically, "People have been trying to debunk them for years. I remember reading that PETA were trying to gain access to prove that their animals are mistreated. They have some special dispensation that allows them to have circus animals, as they claim their animals are shifters, so therefore not really animals." I laugh loudly, "It really is a clever gimmick, and they're lucky that people are gullible enough to believe that rubbish."

He looks at me, a strange glint in his eye. "Are they gullible or just looking to be entertained?" He questions me. "Well whether they're gullible or not is besides the point, it still attracts huge crowds when it does tour. It is one of the most popular circuses' around, even out selling *Cirque du Soleil*, with less shows each year."

"Well what has that got to do with my grandfathers and the business I just signed on to learn the ropes to.

My Ryding looks at me and smiles an oily looking grin. I think it's the first time I've seen him smile since I walked in the door. "Well Miss Jenson with the papers you signed, you just joined the circus."

I flop back into my chair in shock. Guess I should have read all the paperwork first.

"Well Fuck"

PRE ORDER IT NOW

CPSIA information can be obtained
at www.ICGtesting.com
Printed in the USA
BVHW080121090221
599638BV00001B/113

9 780648 793359